THE BLUE DILEMMA

Cynthia,

My LONG TIME FRIEND. WE GO
BACK A LONG WAY. I COULDN'T HAVE
COMPLETE THIS BOOK WITHOUT YOUR
HELP. THANK YOU SO MUCH !!

Maurice A. Britz

10/27/19

THE BLUE DILEMMA

MAURICE A. BUTLER

Print information available on the last page.

Rev. date: 10/14/2019

To order additional copies of this book, contact:
Xlibris
1-888-795-4274
www.Xlibris.com
Orders@Xlibris.com
802557

CONTENTS

To my sons, Steven D. Johnson and Cardell M. Butler, who have brought me so much pleasure. I have watched you grow into fine young men, husbands, and fathers. You make me proud every day.

To the men and women of law enforcement that hold, in high regard, the principles of community policing and perform their job with honesty and integrity in the face of unimaginable circumstances.

ACKNOWLEDGMENTS

Though this is a fictional tale, this book would not have been possible without the support and contribution of numerous people.

Readers/Editors

ADRIENNE PRICE, my classmate from Cardozo High School and Bowdoin College. Your wisdom and sharp eye for detail helped me transform my ideas into reality.

CYNTHIA BELTON, my longtime friend. We have known each other since Powell Elementary School. I am eternally grateful for your expertise, as well as your friendship. Your knowledge of the English language, with all its nuances, kept me in line and helped me to stay focused. Your encouragement kept me going.

PATRICIA BUTLER, my wife and best friend. You have the uncanny ability to finish my thoughts even before I do. We are kindred spirits. Without you, there is no me.

Poet Extraordinaire

ASA THORN, your poetic genius always astounds me, and makes me hopeful that one day I can be as good as you.

First Responders

To the brave men and women of the DC Police Department, DC Metro Transit Police Department, DC Fire Department, Baltimore County Police Department, and Baltimore City Police Department, thank you so much for taking the time to share your experiences with me. To hear and see what you have to go through every day has given me a greater respect for you as individuals, and makes me appreciative that there are people like you willing to do the job. Thank you for your service.

Contributors

I would like to thank the other contributors who gave me insight on growing up in different sections of Washington, DC and Prairie Village, Kansas.

PREFACE

There are usually two sides to every story. I was driving up Georgia Avenue in northwest Washington, DC one day, when I pulled up to a red light and stopped. Suddenly, I heard the sound of sirens wailing in back of me. When I looked in my rear view mirror, I saw the flashing lights of a police car that had stopped directly behind me and a police officer slowly walking up on the driver's side of my car.

I had done nothing wrong, as far as I was concerned, so there shouldn't have been anything for me to fear; and yet there I was, scared to death. My heart was racing as though I had just seen a ghost, or better yet, as though I had just finished a two hundred-yard individual medley swimming race. I gripped the steering wheel as hard as I could, keeping my hands in plain view. When the officer got to my window, he had a huge smile on his face which caught me totally off guard. He warmly greeted me and didn't ask for my driver's license or anything. He just informed me that I should have stopped at a white line, which was about twenty feet from the entrance of the fire station that was across the street. Even though I wasn't blocking the fire station, nor had the light turned red before I got to the white line, I didn't argue. The officer told me to have a nice day and allowed me to drive away.

Thinking back on that incident made me wonder why I reacted the way I did. Could it have been the recent uproar concerning the killing of unarmed black men across the nation that unnerved me? Or could it have been that I didn't see an individual approach me, but a nameless, faceless uniform whose intentions were a mystery to me?

Months later, I was coming out of a basketball game at Dunbar Senior High School. It was dark, the streets were dimly lit, and I was by myself. As I walked down the street, I saw a group of young men standing on the corner. They weren't doing anything wrong, but my street senses started to tingle, indicating that danger could be lurking. I am a product of an era where street gangs controlled their neighborhoods with an iron fist, and anyone who didn't belong in that neighborhood was a candidate for a good ass-whopping. I also heard that youngsters had rejuvenated the "knock-out" game. That was the practice of young guys walking up on senior citizens and trying to knock them out with one punch. I thought about crossing the street, but that would have been considered a sign of weakness which could have stimulated an attack, so I held my head high and continued walking towards them. Suddenly, I saw a police car parked on the next corner, with a nameless, faceless uniform sitting in the front seat. I got an acute sense of relief upon seeing him as I walked calmly to my car.

The main characters in both stories were the same, but the emotional reactions were diametrically opposite. I found the love-hate relationship that citizens, especially in the black community, have with the police to be very interesting and worth further research, especially in today's politically charged atmosphere where police officers are viewed as demons. As a result, I sat down with numerous police officers who talked about topics like departmental sexism, racism, desensitization to violence, suicide, community relationships, corruption, marriage, fear, urban plight, the war on drugs, and the motivation for becoming a first responder. I wanted to know how they were able to run towards danger when everyone else was running away. I wanted to know how they were able to deal with the carnage they were exposed to every day. I wanted to know how they felt when fellow officers committed acts that could be deemed criminal. I wanted to know what made them tick. More importantly, I wanted to know what happens to an individual once they put on that blue uniform and to what extent putting on that uniform impacts their values and individuality. They shared their experiences with me, which I used to develop the fictional characters for this story.

The fictional story that I wrote, however, isn't just a story about the police. It is a story about four distinct individuals who happen to be police officers. This story could have taken place in any urban area in America, but I chose one of the toughest residential sections of the nation's capital as the backdrop mainly because it is the city in which I grew up. I chose to take a different view of the love-hate relationship with the police because there are usually two sides to every story.

BOOK I

CHAPTER 1

PROLOGUE

What the Hell Did You Say?

As Officer Brown strolled into roll call, she was a bit nervous because today was the day. She had been cut loose and no longer had to ride with her training officer. She would be by herself, in her own patrol car and on her own in the street. This was the day she had to prove that she was worthy of the badge, the gun, and all of the training she had received. Because of her petite size, and the fact that she was a rookie, she knew the veteran DC cops doubted her toughness and ability to back them up when things got dicey. But she felt she was more than ready and was anxious to prove that she deserved to be in the job.

Shanita Brown was an attractive, caramel-skinned, twenty-four-year-old black woman with a chest so large she could barely squeeze all of her boobs inside her bullet-proof vest. When she walked to the back of the briefing room, every head would turn her way. With her hazel eyes and flawlessly braided long auburn hair, she looked more like a fashion model than a police officer. Even other female officers would throw her a glance _ some in admiration, some with envy, and others with lust. Her rose-petal perfume preceded her entry and lingered long after she left the room. Her infectious smile was so contagious that on your worst day, you couldn't help but smile along with her. She knew, however, that her smile and good looks would carry her only so far. She knew that sooner or later someone would test her resolve and her willingness to mix it up. Little did she know that today, her first solo day, would be that day. Her excitement increased as she got into her police vehicle and slowly cruised down Branch Avenue SE.

"Sam 28 start for the 7A domestic," the dispatcher called out.

"Sam 28 responding to the scene … 10-78 … step it up!" Officer Brown replied.

"Perpetrator reportedly has a weapon. Wait for backup before engaging."

The call came in over the car radio. A violent domestic situation was in progress on Alabama Avenue SE, which was only two blocks away from her location. She responded that she would handle the call because she was in the vicinity.

As Officer Brown pulled up, she observed a man on the porch punching a woman in the face. Although she had been told to wait for backup, she knew she had to do something before this man seriously injured or killed the woman. Officer Brown jumped out of her cruiser and ran toward the porch. The woman who was being beaten looked to be in her twenties, and the man, who Officer Brown later found out was the woman's boyfriend, had bloodied and broken her nose. Apparently, this wasn't the first time he had hit her. Old bruises, now green and yellow, lay scattered across her light-skinned face. She tried to cower away from the blows but seemed helpless. Officer Brown drew her weapon as she rushed toward the porch.

"Sir, I need you to move away from the woman and lay down on the ground face-first!" Officer Brown commanded.

"She's all right! The bitch just needed to keep her mouth shut! Nothing to see here," the perpetrator shouted as if to no one in particular.

"Sir, I need you to move away from the woman right now!"

"Fuck you!"

As Officer Brown moved closer to the porch, the perpetrator leaned down as if he was going to get on the ground; but instead, he picked up a huge butcher knife that was on the ground and took a

2

couple of steps towards her. Officer Brown took up the slack on the trigger of her service weapon, tilted her head to the side, and closed her left eye.

"Sir, I'm not going to tell you again. You might enjoy hitting on women, but you got me mixed up. I'm not the one. You take one more step, and I am going to blow your black ass away. You just test me. Now drop the knife and get on the fucking ground!"

The man froze like a deer caught in the headlights. He took a long look at Officer Brown and realized that she was not bluffing. He heard sirens coming in from all directions and raised his hands high in the air.

"Put the knife down and put your fucking face on that pavement."

Beads of sweat popped on Officer Brown's forehead and under her armpits as her chest heaved faster and faster, making it difficult to breathe normally. She desperately wanted to tear her bullet-proof vest off so she could get more air in her lungs, but fortunately, her breathing returned to normal when her backup arrived. Officer Kelly walked up to her and calmly reassured her that everything was OK.

"You cool, Officer Brown?"

"Yeah, I'm good."

Officer Kelly gently touched Officer Brown's arm, slowly lowering it. Officer Brown hadn't realized that she still had her weapon aimed at the perpetrator's head, even though he was on the ground and other officers were handcuffing him. She took her finger off the trigger and returned her weapon to its holster. The perpetrator, now in handcuffs, was seated on the curb of the street staring up at Officer Brown with a look of disdain. As Officer Brown was walking to her vehicle, he yelled out at her,

"Hey, bitch, you think you're tough. If you didn't have that gun and that badge on, I'd beat your bitch-ass!"

"Whatever."

The other officers remained quiet, but their looks and silence spoke loud and clear. When you are in the streets, threats have to be answered swiftly and firmly. If not, you will be labeled weak and become a target for every punk or thug who thinks they can intimidate you. Even though Officer Brown was a rookie, she knew that much. She also knew that "Whatever" was not the appropriate response and that something more was needed. The officers picked the perpetrator up off the curb and just walked him to Officer Kelly's car. As he passed Officer Brown, he repeated his threat; and this time he spat on the windshield of her car.

"What the hell did you say to me?"

"I said you're a bitch, and if you didn't have that badge and that gun, I would fuck you up. Yeah, I know who you are. I know you've got a daughter, and I know where you live. I should go by there and fuck your daughter up too!"

Officer Brown was furious. It was one thing to swear at her, but her daughter was off-limits, and she knew that this chump had to be taught a lesson. She walked over to her cruiser, took off her gun belt, vest, and shirt. She then walked over to Officer Kelly and pleaded with him to "un-cuff this piece of shit." Officer Kelly hesitated for a few seconds. He looked at her and then looked at the perpetrator. He wasn't sure if she could handle this dude, but he proceeded to take off the cuffs.

"Look, dude, you think you're all of that, and I am tired of your mouth. You've got to learn to respect me and this uniform. You got me fucked up right now, and so ..."

"Oh, you don't know me, yo! You're just another bitch, and I'm gonna slap the shit out of your bitch-ass!"

"Oh, so you want to see the bitch in me. OK, this is what's up. This is how this is going down. I'm gonna whip your ass, and you're not going to give me any more shit for the rest of your life."

"You ain't gonna whip my ass. I'm gonna ..."

Before he could utter another word, Officer Brown summoned all of the strength she could muster and threw a right hook that landed on his jaw. The punch stunned him and knocked him off balance. Before he could regain his composure, Officer Brown was on him with a series of lefts and rights to his face and his gut that doubled him over. He was able to get off one punch. Even though she saw it coming, it grazed the side of her right cheek and hurt like hell. She then delivered a swift frontal kick to his groin, which sent him sprawling to the ground. Next, she delivered a decisive kick to the side of his head, which pretty much ended the confrontation. Officer Brown stood in the middle of the street with only her T-shirt, police trousers, and boots on, while the whole community watched her teach this guy a lesson. Nobody seemed upset. They all knew he had it coming. As she started putting her vest and shirt back on, she looked at the expression on the face of each of her fellow officers. She knew she was one of them.

My Air Jordan's

It was getting close to five o'clock, which meant that if he didn't leave the house, he would miss the 5:15 bus. Earlier in the day his sister had implored him not to leave the house looking like that, as she had done for most of his life. She knew that if he walked out of the house with that outfit on, he would be the subject of ridicule and would end up getting into another fight with one of the neighborhood boys. But he didn't care. He had on a yellow-and-gray paisley shirt, a pair of green high-water pants, and a brand-new pair of black-and-red Air Jordan sneakers. He knew the Jordan's didn't match his outfit, but everybody had a pair of Jordans, and he had worked hard for several weekends to save enough money to buy them. He was proud of them and wanted everybody to see.

Fifteen-year-old Leon Anderson was a big kid for his age. In fact, he was six feet-four, dark-skinned, with thick black braids, and a wicked scar over his left eyebrow - an ever-present reminder of one of the many fights he had been in. Even though he was a high school freshman, the guys on the football team called him Big Lee out of respect for his size and athletic prowess. His size made him an imposing figure, but in reality, he was as gentle as a lamb. He was a good student and wanted to be a biochemist one day. He loved watching police shows like Cops, New York Undercover and CSI Miami, and thought maybe one day he could become a crime scene investigator, or even a police officer.

Big Lee loved visiting his grandmother, who lived in a small house in an affluent neighborhood near the Watergate Hotel in northwest Washington, DC. It gave him an opportunity to get out of his own neighborhood. Plus, she had cable. As his routine weekend visit came to an end, he walked to the bus stop and sat down on the bench. Knowing that the bus would take a while, because it was on the weekend schedule, Big Lee decided to take out his chemistry book and work on his homework. He observed a police cruiser slowly driving by but thought nothing of it. Minutes later, that same cruiser drove by again, and it appeared that the officers were looking for something. Again, he was unconcerned, but thought this did seem a little odd. The cruiser drove by a third time and this time it stopped. Two officers, one black and the other white, got out and approached him.

"Son, what are you doing in this neighborhood?" the white cop asked.

"I just came from my grandmother's house and ..."

Before Big Lee could finish his sentence, the black cop pulled out his gun and put it against Big Lee's head.

"Put your hands up as high as you can get them, big boy, and slowly turn around," he barked.

Big Lee started to tremble, and his heart started racing because he had never stared down the barrel of a gun and had no idea what was going on. Both cops frisked him, handcuffed him, and shoved him into the back of the police cruiser. They drove him a couple of blocks and suddenly stopped and parked the cruiser. They forced him to get out and had him stand under the street light. After a few seconds, he heard a small female voice saying,

"That's him! He is the one who did it."

Big Lee was arrested and taken to the Second District police station, where he was booked for robbery. He allegedly robbed a nearby hotel. The hotel clerk said he had jumped over the counter, took the money, and ran from the hotel. She had seen that the robber, who was black, had on a worn-out pair of black-and-red Air Jordan tennis shoes.

How could this be happening to me? Big Lee thought as he sat in a holding cell with several other young black men. *I didn't do anything. Dad is going to kill me!* He was scared to death _ not only of the situation he found himself in, but more so of the thought of what his father was going to say and do to him when he got home. He knew his father would not come down to get him because his dad always said to him, "Whatever mess you get yourself into, you have to get yourself out of."

Because he was deep in thought, he had not realized that one of the inmates had come and stood over him, looking him up and down.

"You a bamma," the inmate said in a loud and accusatory voice as if he wanted everybody in the cell to hear. "Why don't you let me see those shoes?"

"I ain't no bamma, and you ain't gonna take my shoes."

Big Lee already knew what was going to happen next. He knew that if he let this guy take his stuff, he would be labeled a punk, and everybody else would try to punk him. So Big Lee got off the bench, stood toe to toe with this guy whom he towered over, and decided that he would get in the first punch. But before he could throw the punch, a police officer came to the holding cell and called his name. He was allowed one phone call. Of course, he called his mother.

He was transported to the juvenile detention facility over on Mount Olivet Road. Being incarcerated, even though it would only be for a couple of days, was an experience that he would never forget and never wanted to have again. The food was horrible. For dinner, he was given a bologna sandwich that seemed as though it had been left out for fifty days, a fake fruit cup, and some juice. He didn't get anything else to eat until six o'clock the next morning, and all he got then was some applesauce and two graham crackers. This was especially hard for him, because one thing he enjoyed in life was eating. The guards looked at him like he was an animal and treated him as such. Most of the inmates were misguided young souls. Some acted like they were tough, but they weren't so tough without a gun in their hands. And then there were the really tough ones who preyed on the others. Big Lee knew that jail was not the place for him. His father's words about hanging out in the streets and getting into trouble hit home, and he never wanted to be anywhere near a jail again. More importantly, he began to realize that jail was no place for anyone. He wondered how many of these young men were there for something they did not do, just like he was, or how many were victims of their environment and upbringing. The notion of becoming a police officer started to crystalize in him, and he knew what kind of officer he wanted to become.

Welcome to the Jungle

"Where you from, Stevie?"

"I was born in Topeka, Kansas, but raised in Prairie Village, Kansas."

"Prairie Village_ oh, so you a farm boy! Well, you're not in Kansas anymore! Welcome to the jungle. You are about to see every Coon, mop head, Spic, Jew and liberal hippy this side of God's creation. That's why we white boys got to stick together."

"How many inaugurations have you been through so far?"

"This will be my fourth. I did the Bush inauguration and the two Obama inaugurations. The last inauguration for the nigger president had wall-to-wall people on the National Mall. There were so many people you could barely move. There were people as far as the eye could see. It seemed as though every nigger in DC came out that day, but I really couldn't understand why so many God-fearing white folks were there to see that. It was revolting. But I guess you can get used to almost anything after working around these jungle bunnies for so long. I have to admit, though _ things were pretty peaceful. I understand we expect to have some trouble this year."

Steven Sullivan had recently gotten out of the police academy, had worked briefly in the Second District, but his first real assignment while stationed in the Seventh District was to cover the inauguration of President-Elect Donald Trump. Officer Craig Hoye was assigned as his training officer, and Steven found him to be a colorful individual. Officer Hoye was a ten-year veteran who was born and raised in West Virginia and had some very peculiar attitudes about people who were different from him. Steven did not understand that type of thinking and objected to the language Officer Hoye used. It seemed that he was bitter and angry all the time. But he heard that Officer Hoye was knowledgeable about policing and decided to ignore some of the offensive metaphors and learn as much as he could about police work before he had to go out on his own. Steven guessed Officer Hoye thought he was one of the good old boys, and so he could talk freely; but he wondered what Officer Hoye would think if he knew Steven had a black girlfriend.

Steven, or Stevie as his fellow officers liked to call him, was assigned to a foot patrol unit in the Seventh District of the Metropolitan Police Department in Washington, DC. During inaugurations and major events, which occur frequently in the District of Columbia, officers from each district are detailed to a Civil Disturbance Unit (CDU). Each district has four CDU platoons, which include one rapid response platoon. The rapid response platoon is armed with riot gear, which includes riot helmets, full pads, shields, gas masks, and weapons. The other platoons have just their regular uniforms with a riot helmet and a gas mask. The purpose of the CDU platoons is to maintain order while protesters exercise their First Amendment rights. When violence or disorderly conduct erupts, the rapid response unit is deployed to the area to support other units on the scene. The word was out that this year, there would be a series of organized protests of the incoming administration and the number of protesters was predicted to be large. Officer Hoye kept saying that the niggers from the Black Lives Matter movement were coming to make trouble, but other officers said the anarchists were coming.

The anarchists are a group of masked protesters who show up at various rallies dressed in all black. Their lawyers accompany them along with photographers and videographers, to make sure their rights are not violated. The lawyers typically wear lime green neon caps, so everyone knows who they are. Prior to this inauguration, the lawyers had gone to court to challenge police use of body-worn cameras to record anything during the inauguration, because it is a First Amendment assembly. They argued that the recordings could be used to identify people participating in the protest, which would be a violation of their civil rights. Even though the law states that if you are on public space you can be recorded, the court struck a compromise, stating that recordings would be taken and used *only* if people were engaging in unlawful acts.

Stevie and the other members of his unit were initially stationed at one of the entry checkpoints, where they were letting people into the National Mall. They were there for about an hour when they had to move to another checkpoint, where there were about 1,000 to 1,500 protesters. The protesters were at the point where they were ready to push their way past the checkpoint to get in, but decided not to when more police arrived. The unit had to redeploy when they got the call that 300 to 400 anarchists were marching and obstructing traffic at Seventh and D Streets, NW. Several units showed up, including a motorcycle and mountain bike unit, to put more police in the area for a potential showdown. The anarchists started marching, doubling back and running through the park with the police shadowing their every move.

When the anarchists got to Thirteenth and I Streets, someone took a pole and smashed out the window at a Starbuck's. After that, all hell broke loose. People began hurling trash cans and throwing newspaper containers into the street, and smashing anything they thought they could destroy. The protesters started heading to L Street when the order came to create a line with the foot patrol on one side and the motorcycle and mountain bike units on the other, enclosing the protesters. The protesters tried to rush the police line and fight their way out. At this point, the police employed pepper spray and explosive ordnances, which were grenades containing stink balls or small rubber pellets. The protesters knew that the gig was up, so they threw up their hands and surrendered. There were over two hundred thirty people arrested and charged with felony rioting. They had caused over one hundred dollars' worth of property damage, so this time, a slap on the wrist would not be the order of the day.

Steven was exhausted by the end of the day. When he had thought about being a policeman, he didn't envision a day like this. He wouldn't have much time to recuperate because there was a massive women's protest march scheduled for the next day.

"Hey, Hoye, you know all of those people we arrested today? I didn't see any black people, Hispanic people, or Asian people. I only saw white people!"

"Don't get smart, rookie! Just wait till you get your ass east of the river! Wait till you get your ass out there on the street. We'll see how smart you are, then. You're gonna have niggers coming out of your ass. You just wait!"

Going Home at Night

Gregory Harris, a twenty-five-year veteran of the police force, couldn't imagine doing anything else. He loved being a police officer and interacting with the community. His numerous roles in those twenty years included being assigned to a motorcycle unit and a mountain bike unit, working for a Tactical Anti-Crime (TAC) unit where he did jump-outs, working undercover, and working as a homicide detective. His most cherished role, however, was as a foot patrolman walking a beat in the city's infamous Seventh District. The Seventh District, which is located in the southeast section of town, has been characterized as one of the toughest parts of the city_ plagued with violent crime, extreme poverty, deteriorated public housing, and high unemployment. Some cops say that police officers who work in 7D do more police work in five years than officers in other districts do in an entire career.

"No matter what part of the city you are in, people are all the same," Officer Harris said in response to a question from a news reporter doing a story on the rising crime rate in 7D. "They have the same interests you have, and the same goals you have. Maybe they don't have the same means that you do, but they all want to be successful. Nobody wants to hang out and do nothing, but if they don't have anything to do, that is what they end up doing."

Officer Harris waved at several adult residents and stopped to talk to some of the kids playing in an apartment courtyard as he and the reporter strolled down Savannah Street, SE in Congress Park.

"What has been your absolute best day on the job?"

"Every day I am able to help someone in the community and get to go home at night is my best day! I have had a lot of best days. I get a lot of pleasure in helping people, and I have done that a lot. I get

11

satisfaction out of people being happy, if that makes any sense to you. So my best day is always ongoing. When I talk to somebody and the situation gets resolved and everybody is happy, that feels really good to me. Now, there have been times when I have had to put my hands on people, lock them up, and, in some cases, commit bodily harm; but that comes with the territory. For the most part, if you know how to talk to people and you know how to develop relationships with people, you don't have as many problems as people may think. I have a good relationship with the people on my beat. I know a lot of the families and their kids. Parents would call me, even when I was off duty, with information that we needed to know. They would call me if their kids were being disrespectful or if their kids were messing up in school. I would often come by their house to talk with the kids, give them money from time to time to buy a soda or snacks and help them with their sports teams."

"What has been your absolute worst day on the job?"

Officer Harris paused for a few seconds as if he was searching for the right thing to say before answering the reporter's question.

"Wow, my worst day. I would have to say the day when my partner and I responded to a call for a domestic dispute. A lady called and said she wanted to get her husband out of the house because he was trying to kill her. So we responded to the scene, and when we got there, we could not find anybody there except the woman. She told us to come in and said, 'He's in here!' We start to search the house when all of a sudden, we hear this eerie sound coming from behind us. This lady pulls out a machete from the closet and starts rushing toward us. We drew our weapons and told her to stop and drop the machete. She continued to come at us screaming and wielding the machete, so we shot her, several times. We found out later that she was an outpatient from St. Elizabeth Hospital_ the mental facility_ and was on medication. That information was already in the system, but nobody told us the lady was crazy. That lady, unfortunately, lost her life, and it may have been avoided if we knew all the information before we got there, and if more officers had been at the scene.

"That was the first time I ever had to kill anyone, but it wasn't the last. In my years on the force, I have seen a lot of death, and I have been forced to take lives. It is a part of the job, and unfortunately, you get used to it. Dealing with her death, however, was hard. I was brought up to always respect women and to never put your hands on a woman. I had never seen that type of behavior from a woman before, and so that bothered me for a while. I understood that I had to get over it in order to do my job. I had to process it real quick. I did a lot of praying and a lot of thinking to see if there was something else I could have done in that situation. Things happened so fast. At that point, I had to make a quick decision. Either I was going to get sliced by that machete, or I was going to go home! I decided that I wanted to go home that night!"

CHAPTER 2

SIMPLE CITY

Summertime and the living is easy. Kids sitting out on the porch eating popsicles, in the yard catching fire flies, or on the street playing double-Dutch, and *red light, green light*. The lazy sky turns fiery red as the sun starts to drop below the horizon and the street lights begin flickering on. The melodic sounds of children gleefully playing is broken by mothers chanting a familiar tune, calling for their loved ones to come into the house because there is nothing good that can happen in the streets after the sun goes down. This daily scenario can be replicated all over America from small towns to bustling urban centers, but for Shanita Brown, the scene plays out a bit differently. In her reality, those melodic sounds of summer are interrupted by the sounds of gunfire, police cars zooming down the street with sirens blaring, and the ominous blue and red lights illuminating the night sky while in hot pursuit of cars speeding away from violent scenes. For Brown, it's scenes of mothers wailing as another child lies face-first on the ground with blood and brains pouring out, or her father yelling, "Get on the floor," as stray bullets crash through the windows.

Down the street from where Shanita lives is a public housing project_ 274 low-rise apartments and townhouses officially named Benning Terrace, but often referred to as Baby Vietnam or Simple City. It earned these nicknames as a result of the rash of murders and violent gang activity that plagued the community during the 1990s. On an average summer day, Shanita would be confronted with guys shooting craps on the corner, selling drugs, robbing kids of their Air Jordan tennis shoes or North Face jackets; young people getting jumped by large groups of other youths; friends getting locked up and sent away; and all the other entrapments that come along with poverty and despair. And then there was the ubiquitous presence of death and grief. But this became Shanita's playground. This was the way it was, and so she learned to deal with living under these circumstances just like everybody else. Somehow, she felt that people shouldn't have to live like this, and maybe one day she could change things in her community.

Shanita was raised in a modest three-story house on Forty-Fourth Place in southeast Washington DC. The house was the largest on the block. It had a huge backyard dotted with cherry and peach trees, and served as the central location for many neighborhood barbecues and cookouts. At one point, there were fourteen siblings living in the house along with Shanita's parents, Olivia and John. Olivia, after eight years of being a stay-at-home mom, found a job working the midnight shift at St. Elizabeth Hospital. John worked for the fire department, which took him out of the house for long periods. This left a pecking order where the older Brown children were left in charge, and everyone had to chip in to keep things operating smoothly. By the time Shanita was old enough to share in the household duties, there were only eight children in the house. Her older brother was tragically killed in a car accident, and five others had grown up, moved on, and had families of their own. That left six girls and two boys, all two years apart in age.

The Browns were one of the few families in the neighborhood that had a mother and father living in the house_ a fact that envious neighborhood kids never let Shanita forget. Having a mother and a father in the house to help provide for, guide, and mold them, however, did not stop them from going through tough times. Mr. Brown, an ex-marine, always worked and brought his money home; but it never seemed to be enough. Before Olivia got her job, trying to make ends meet with only one salary coming in made survival difficult. There were times when the electricity or gas got turned off; and other times, it was the water. There were times when water had to be heated up in the microwave in order to take a bath, and times when they ate cereal with water instead of milk for breakfast or mayonnaise sandwiches for dinner. Shanita hated mayonnaise, so she would have a mustard sandwich instead. There were many nights when they went to bed hungry. During the winter, her parents sealed the windows with plastic to keep the cold air from coming in. Life was sometimes hard, but the tough times forced them to be a close-knit family.

Olivia was a stay-at-home mom for the first seven years of Shanita's life. She had always wanted to become a doctor but had to drop out of college when she became pregnant. The babies kept coming, so she wasn't able to return and fulfill that dream. When she was younger, she was attractive and had men constantly seeking her attention. She clearly understood what men wanted from women and what they would do to get what they wanted. As a result, she was very strict with her daughters. When they were young, she tried to keep them sheltered, not letting them go too far from the house to play, but instead allowed them to invite their friends to play in the house or in the backyard. When the girls got a little older and could take care of themselves, she decided to go back to school to get a license as a registered nurse. At this point in her life, being a nurse was some fulfillment of her original dream, which helped to stem the growing resentment and frustration she felt. Her foray into the world of work came when she got the opportunity to work in the hospital, but this also took her away from her kids. With working at night and sleeping during the day, she had little time or energy to spend doing things with her kids.

It was Shanita's godmother, Jessica Jackson, who stepped in to help raise Shanita when her mom went back to work. Jessica was a middle school teacher and a vocal community activist who lived down the street in Simple City and was always trying to make things better for the residents there. Jessica knew that children and idle time was a bad combination, so she made sure that Shanita and her sisters always had something positive to do. She taught them how to jump double-Dutch, and even started a community double-Dutch team that competed with other teams. She taught Shanita how to ride a bike, took her roller skating, and enrolled her in organized activities like summer camps, track and field, cheerleading, and a debutant program called Petals of Primrose, where she got involved in modeling, dance, and drama. Shanita found herself hanging out with Jessica more and more, especially during the summer.

John was a hardworking, jovial guy who was always telling funny stories and making people laugh. When life got really rough, he was known to take a drink or two. When he started drinking, he would get loud, display a quick temper, and people knew to steer clear of him. He loved his children, though he was a stern disciplinarian when he was around. Olivia, for the most part, handed out discipline in the form of spankings; but it did very little to improve the behavior of the kids. But when John gave out the whippings, nobody wanted any part of that. One day, Shanita's teacher called to say that Shanita had been disruptive in school. John happened to be home and answered the phone. When Shanita got home, he gave her the whipping of her life. He told her, "The next time I find out this is happening, it's gonna be worse!" He did not tolerate any of his kids being disrespectful to authority. After that beating, Shanita became a model student and made the honor roll every semester. Shanita's mom was shocked at her turnaround. She commented, "Oh, so when I hit you, you didn't change anything, but when he does …." Shanita's response was, "Nope. I don't ever want that man to hit me again!"

John was a big, muscular man; and the kids in the neighborhood called him Big John. Whenever something was getting ready to go down in the neighborhood, the kids would walk Shanita up the street to her house and make her go inside. They would often say, "Oh no, your dad is Big John, and he will come and get us if we let you get mixed up in this!" As a result, she was able to avoid getting directly involved in a lot of the drama that took place.

Big John would take his kids out to the backyard and show them how to defend themselves by using jujitsu, a skill he learned while serving in the marines. Teaching his kids how to fight was important, especially because of where they lived; and he made sure that if someone wanted to fight one of his kids, that person would have to fight all his kids. He would say, "When you are getting ready to get in a fight, you have to get in the first punch and hit as hard as you can, because you may not get another opportunity." Big John got his kids to form a circle and got one of them to step into the circle with him so that he could demonstrate.

"The first thing they will expect is for you to attack the face, and so that is the area they will look to protect. If you kick them in the shin, the private area, or stomp on their toes, that will bring their hands and attention away from their face. Then you go in for the kill. You have to close the distance immediately and use your hands, your knees, your elbows, your feet, and every part of your body in the attack. You have to be relentless and merciless. Either they are going to get you, or you are going to get them. You may not win every encounter, but if you are vicious enough, people will think twice about wanting to engage you in the future. Even a loss can be a win. You can't let people push you around and think they can get away with it."

Shanita did not get into many fights, but her dad's advice and training came in handy one day when she was in Fletcher-Johnson Middle School. As she walked to her locker, she could see kids hanging around and looking at her for no apparent reason. She also heard them whisper about something. The buzz around school was there was going to be a fight at three o'clock, and a small crowd began gathering outside of the school in anticipation of the show.

"Girl, you'd better go out the back door and run your ass home," implored Cynthia, who was Shanita's best friend.

"Why?" Shanita asked with a startled look on her face.

"I heard that Erica was telling everybody she was going to get you today, and she has her crew with her."

"Why?"

"She said that you thought you were cute, and she was gonna mess up your face. Girl, you'd better run!"

Shanita's heart dropped to her feet. She couldn't understand this. She hadn't done anything to Erica. She knew Erica was the leader of the Simple City Crew, who would often jump other girls. Anyone who dissed her had to be crazy.

"But I didn't do anything to her!"

"Girl, you'd better run!"

The fear began to grip Shanita, paralyzing her hands and feet. As she pondered her fate and what she should do, her mother's voice rang loud and clear in her head: *Girls don't fight. Girls run.* Shanita put her books and her book bag in her locker, snuck out through the side door, and took off running as fast as her feet could take her.

"There she goes," shouted one of the onlookers, who did not want to be deprived of a good spectacle. Erica and her crew took off running after Shanita with the ravenous, swelling crowd following closely behind. Shanita reached her house just in the nick of time, ran inside, and slammed the door behind her. Feeling safe, she peered out of the door window, hoping that the crowd had simply gone away; but much to her dismay, they were standing on her stoop, shouting for her to come out.

"You might as well come on out and get it now," Erica shouted. "You got to come out sooner or later!"

As Shanita peered through the window, a ray of hope blasted through the clouds of doom when she saw her two brothers and her sisters hastily approaching the house. Her oldest brother, Alfred, briefly stopped to talk to somebody in the crowd before approaching the house. He opened the door and confronted his baby sister.

"You've got to go out and fight that bitch," Alfred commanded.

"What! I'm not going out there. They're gonna jump me."

"Ain't nobody gonna jump you. But I will tell you this_ if you don't go out there, I'm gonna beat you myself. You can't let people intimidate you. Now, get your ass out there! Now!"

The room suddenly became hot. Sweat started pouring from Shanita's forehead. Her heart felt as though it was trying to force itself out of her throat. She felt trapped and doomed at the same time. She either had to fight Erica or get beat up by her brother. Her fate was sealed, and she seemed to be out of options. Where was her father when she needed him? She frantically tried to remember his self-defense instructions. She quickly put on a pair of tennis shoes, gathered her hair under a skull cap, wiped the sweat from her forehead, and opened the door.

The crowd formed the familiar semi-circle until the combatants entered the human arena. The crowd turned the semi-circle into a complete circle, closing off all avenues of escape.

Hit first and close down the distance, Shanita thought, remembering her father's instructions.

Erica moved toward Shanita, boasting about what she was going to do. While in mid-sentence, Shanita swiftly and forcefully delivered a devastating kick that strategically landed on Erica's right shin. Erica instinctively reached down and grabbed her shin as the searing pain traveled up her leg. When she dropped her hands to grab her shin, Shanita threw a powerful right-left punch combination to Erica's exposed face. The crowd screamed, "DAMN!" in unison. Though stunned, Erica's reaction was to try to grab Shanita's hair, which, unfortunately for her, was neatly tucked under the skull cap Shanita had put on. This anticipated move gave Shanita the opportunity to grab Erica by the collar; drop low, thus pulling Erica forward; and throw her over toward the ground in a perfect jujitsu move that would have made her dad proud. Shanita jumped on top of a prone Erica and began delivering a series of rapid, vicious punches to her face. The crowd looked on in stunned amazement. Alfred and his siblings had informed the crowd that this was going to be a one-on-one fight, and if anybody jumped in, there was going to be hell to pay. Alfred had street credibility because he was one of the biggest drug dealers in Simple City, and no one wanted to cross him. The viciousness of Shanita's attack stunned Alfred who had never seen his baby sister fight before.

"OK, baby girl, that's enough," Alfred ordered. A cryptic smile emerged on his face as he watched her continuously pummel her opponent.

"Oh, hell no! I want this bitch to feel every bit of this," Shanita shouted so everybody could hear.

Alfred grabbed his little sister, pulling her off of Erica's motionless body. As Shanita regained her composure, she turned to the crowd and eye-balled each girl in the Simple City Crew as if to say, *If you fuck with me, you are going to get the same thing!* As she turned to go back in the house, she gave Erica one last kick in the stomach and spat in her face.

Alfred wondered where all this hostility was coming from. After all, she had always been the quiet and smart one in the family who stayed away from the street life and who never got into trouble. When they got into the house, he asked her what had gotten into her. She didn't reply, but only looked at him as if she didn't know what he was talking about. She went upstairs, washed her face and hands, went into her room, and opened a book as if nothing had happened.

Alfred just shook his head and chuckled. It seemed that his little sister was tougher than he ever imagined. Needless to say, Shanita never had to worry about being bothered again. Word got around quickly. Erica and Shanita became steadfast friends until the night Erica was killed in a knife fight in Simple City.

*   *   *

As Shanita got older, her inquisitive nature caused her to explore the world outside of Simple City. When she turned fifteen, she received two gifts that enabled her to become free of her physical and emotional surroundings. One was a 15-speed bicycle that her dad gave her, and the other was a diary that her mom gave her. The bicycle was almost like her first car and her first taste of freedom. She would get up early each Saturday morning and explore different parts of the city, each time heading in a different direction. One Saturday, she rode over to Anacostia, where she saw the Large Duncan Phyfe Chair and the Frederick Douglass House. On another Saturday, she rode past the Shrimp Boat and the Langston Golf Course on Benning Road in Northeast. On one occasion, she ventured through LeDroit Park, Howard University, past Ben's Chili Bowl and the Chinatown Friendship Archway in Northwest. She really enjoyed the Fisherman's Wharf and the sight of the boats docked on the Washington Channel in Southwest. People would see her riding and would later say to her mom, "Oh, I saw your daughter the other day near …" Her mom would reply, "Oh, no, you didn't …." When her mom would ask Shanita about it, she would always deny it, saying, "Nope, they sure didn't see me!" She would be out all day long but made sure she was home before the street-lights came on.

It was during these Saturday excursions that Shanita began people-watching. She acutely discerned how people in each section of the city looked different. The difference was not just racial or ethnic in nature. She saw how people's economic status impacted the way they looked and carried themselves. She noticed that the people on Minnesota Avenue in Northeast looked hard and worn down compared to the people in upper Northwest. She realized that the way things were in Simple City was not the way things were everywhere. She used to visit her dad at the fire station where he worked and observe everything that went on. She was fascinated by the fact that when other people ran out of a burning building and away from danger, firefighters were running into the building. She would ask her dad what made him do that. His initial response would be, "Because that's my job!" When asked to explain further, he would say that he felt it was important to do something to help people and to help his community. He would often say, "You just can't sit on the fence and watch life go by. You have to get involved! If you don't stand for something, you will fall for anything." When asked about how to conquer the fear that danger presents, his response would be, "Training. You could always train your mind and body to do anything, even conquer fear. When you face danger, your mind might stop working, but that is when your training takes over."

The bicycle was indeed a wonderful gift, but the diary brought Shanita pleasure beyond her wildest imagination. She found that through writing, she could be who she wanted to be, have conversations with herself, and have the freedom to express herself without judgment. All the things she felt, all the things she observed, all the things she wanted to do could be kept in her diary; and nobody could come into that world unless she wanted them to. Even though she lived in a house full of people, there were times when she felt totally alone. It was during these times that she would curl up in her bed or sit by the window in her room and write in her diary.

She loved her older sister Gwen, who was really her stepsister; but her dad would not allow anyone in the house to use the word *step*. "We are all in the same family," he would often say. Of all her siblings, Shanita liked Gwen the best. They were only three years apart, and Shanita would follow in her big sister's footsteps. Gwen was a senior at H.D. Woodson High School, but when it was time for Shanita to go to high school, she desired to do something different and go to a school outside of her neighborhood. One day Gwen came into Shanita's room and told Shanita to put her cute clothes on because they were going to a go-go dance at Woodson. Shanita had never been to a go-go dance before and never really had a desire to go, but Gwen felt it was time for her little sister to grow up and stop being a tomboy. Gwen felt that her little sister was gorgeous with her pretty eyes, budding breasts, and long flowing hair. It was high time for Shanita to start becoming interested in boys.

Gwen didn't care much for go-go dances, or go-go music for that matter. She preferred the old-school house parties where the atmosphere was much more intimate. At the house parties, there were usually fewer people, primarily just your friends, and the soft music allowed you to get close with whomever you were dancing with. The go-go dances were loud, and anybody could come in. Often, some kind of violence would erupt because guys would always try to show how tough they were, or rival crews from different neighborhoods were *beefing*. Times were changing, so it was off to the go-go dance. Shanita didn't really want to go, but she adored her big sister and enjoyed hanging out with her. This dance, however, would change her life forever.

As students entered the school, a loud voice bellowed out, "Take off your shoes and put them on the table!"

"Damn, they think we are at the Black Hole Club or something," said an anonymous voice from the sea of faces eagerly waiting to get into the high school dance. The reply was tinged with mock sincerity, as each person dutifully took off their shoes, lined up, passed through the metal detector, and was searched by fierce-looking security guards _ a scene that had become all too familiar at inner-city school functions and provided a small sense of security.

It was Valentine's Day. Throughout the city, balloons, flowers, candy, and words of love and romance were being shared. Photographers began setting up their backdrops for photo sessions, with loving couples posing in embraces. It was the perfect time for a romantic evening, with dim lights, soft music, and dancing with the person you adored, or that person you wanted to get to know better. This, however, was not the time or the place for that to occur. As patrons migrated to the cafeteria where the dance was to be held, they were greeted with ceiling-sized speakers that seemed suited for an outdoor concert rather than a closed-in high school cafeteria. When the band started playing, the thunderous vibration from the music caused the fabric in the clothes of the patrons to oscillate. Many of the adults who were supervising the dance immediately moved to the far end of the cafeteria and placed their fingers in their ears in an attempt to shield the assault on their eardrums. The kids, however, moved closer to the stage and the monstrous speakers like moths to a flame.

The crowd started jumping and shouting as the band belted out a familiar EU tune or Backyard hit that was characteristic of the rhythmic beats of DC's own go-go music. Shanita was shocked that the lead singer/rapper was one of her neighborhood friends. By nature, he was a shy, quiet person who kept to himself and never caused any trouble. She was stunned when she saw this normally low-key kid morph into a screaming, sweat-dripping entertainer who controlled the crowd with his voice and gyrations. It seemed that the louder he rapped, the wilder the crowd became. When the crowd got too raucous or too close to the stage, he would lower his voice and the music, and the crowd responded with a calmness of their own. When the crowd became too passive, the beat got heavier and the music got louder. The go-go, hip-hop beat seemed to whip the crowd into a frenzy that could have exploded into an ugly scene, but the experience of the band members kept things under control. Shanita couldn't help thinking, *Now that's power!*

Shanita began to wonder when the boys were going to ask the girls to dance, like they do in the movies. After all, this was supposed to be a Valentine's Day dance. Instead, everyone seemed to dance by themselves, or in small groups, gripped by the syncopations of the beats, causing them to lose themselves in the moment. The scene reminded her of a poem entitled "Drums" written by one of her favorite poets, Jacintha Wadlington:

When the beautiful beat
Of Africa
Invades my veins
I twirl around
In a whirlwind of joy
The rhythm
Making me lose
The inhibitions I had
Before I started spinning
The rhythm of Africa
My heart
My heritage
Making me faint
With joy that flows through my veins
The
Beat
Of
The
DRUMS

Several large, powerful security guards, along with members of the faculty, surveyed the dance floor, searching for signs of potential trouble. They wanted to make sure that everyone would have a safe and secure evening. Everyone was having a good time until one guy took offense because someone from a rival gang stared at him a little longer than he thought appropriate. A fight broke out; security shut down the dance, and made everyone leave the school. On the way home, Gwen asked Shanita if she enjoyed her first dance. Shanita replied that she had a really good time, but she left the juicy stuff for her diary:

February 14, 2006

Dear Diary,

    I went to my first go-go dance tonight and had a really good time. I didn't dance at all, but something amazing happened. I was standing near a wall, and all of these little boys kept coming up to me trying to talk and get my phone number. I politely turned them down, telling them that I already had a boyfriend. It was a small lie, but I didn't want to hurt their feelings. Then I saw this gorgeous dude standing in the middle of the dance floor, and he was looking at me. He was a tall, dark-skinned hunk with hazel eyes, a budding mustache, and Lord, have mercy, the bulge in his pants made me sweat. He smiled at me and then started walking in my direction. My heart started racing, and I thought I was going to pee on myself.

He walked over to me and asked me for a piece of gum. I pulled out my pack of Doublemint, and there was only one stick left. He said he didn't want to take my last piece, but I quickly blurted out that I had another pack. I gave him the stick of gum, and he asked me my name. We started talking. It seemed that the music and all the people in the room just vanished into thin air, as if we were the only ones there. I don't even remember everything we talked about, but it seemed that we talked for hours. He said his name is Curtis Johnson. He is a sophomore and is on the basketball team at H. D. Woodson. He asked me what school I went to. When I told him I went to a charter school in Northwest, he said, "Oh, so you're an uptown girl." I told him, "Not really. I grew up around here, but my mom didn't want me to go to school with all of my neighborhood friends, so she sent me to that school."

I didn't want the evening to end, but as usual, people started trippin', and Gwen came up, snatched me by my arm, and said, "Let's go!" Before I left, he got my address and phone number and said that he would call me. I really hope so!

*   *   *

Curtis Johnson lived in Simple City with his grandmother. His mother and his father were killed in a car accident when he was eight years old, and he had been living with his grandmother ever since. His grandmother was a tough woman who had been the victim of sexual and domestic abuse growing up. She grew up in Barry Farm, a housing project in southeast Washington, DC, and lived a hard life. Once, two guys were stabbing her nephew right in front of her home. She ran outside, took the knife from them, and beat up both of the guys. As a result, she did not allow Curtis to hang out in the streets or hang with the boys in the neighborhood. With the exception of playing sports at the local recreation center, he stayed in the house watching television and playing video games. Once, Curtis snuck out of the house to go to a dance with his teammates. When he got home, she was waiting in the living room with all the lights out. When he shut the door, she turned on the lights and wore his butt out with a switch from a tree. He never did that again. As he got older, he began to resent the tight control his grandmother had on him, but he loved and respected her so he tried following all her rules.

Curtis was a gifted athlete, with a body that some girls described as looking like that of a Greek god. His sheltered life, however, made him shy and awkward around girls. His good looks and athletic prowess made the girls flock around him in an attempt to curry favor from him. He would often find notes in his locker from girls who said they wanted to have his baby. Others would leave their name and phone number. Once, he found a pair of panties in his locker with a note that said, "I'm yours, if you want me." He would listen to guys in the locker room talk about the girls they had sex with, accompanied by all the sordid details. He would laugh along with the crowd but would not reveal the fact that he was a virgin, for fear of the ridicule he knew he would be subjected to. People around him assumed that he had plenty of action with the ladies because girls were always throwing themselves at him, but little did they know.

Shanita assumed the same thing, which made her even more surprised when he came up to her at the dance. He summoned the courage to call her on the phone one evening and ask if he could come over. He really liked her because not only was she extremely attractive, she was easy to talk to. He didn't have to talk much because she carried most of the conversation. He began coming by her house as often as he could. When he finally asked if she would be his girl, she ecstatically said yes.

April 1, 2006

Dear Diary,

Curtis asked me to be his girl, and I thought my heart was going to jump out of my chest. When I said yes, he kissed me softly on my lips, which kind of surprised me. It was so nice, but I don't know … I expected him to be more aggressive. He is the nicest, gentlest guy I have ever met. When he comes by my house, he always brings me stuff like candy, flowers, or chewing gum. We go out to the movies, or to eat at IHOP on the weekends. He treats me like a queen. He even took me over to his house to meet his grandmother. She was very nice to me, but I can tell she is not one to be messed with. The thing that surprises me is that he could probably have any girl he wants and he chose me! I can feel myself falling head over heels for him.

I guess this is what falling in love must be like. I feel like I am losing myself in him. It feels like a high that I can't come down from. All I want to do is be around him, hear his voice, and be in his presence. He is the center of my world. Everything I do is beginning to revolve around him. When I start to make plans to do certain things, they include him. When I want to go here or there, he is the first person I think about sharing those types of memories and experiences with. He would make me laugh when I needed to laugh and made me smile when I was sad. I would go to his basketball games and watch him run up and down that floor with a sense of pride that I didn't know existed. I would smile when I saw all the other girls melt in his presence or try to get him to pay them some attention. I don't get upset because I know he is mine, but I am aware of all the things they are willing to do to get him. We haven't had sex yet, but I know sooner or later, it is going to happen. I think it might have to be sooner, rather than later, before one of these fast girls tries to use what they got to get what they want.

One of the things that I do regret ... well, maybe regret is not the right word . . . is the fact that I am beginning to lose myself and not in a good way. I am beginning to lose myself, to the point where I have started to change who I am to fit what I think he wants in a woman. I have stopped riding my bike and exploring the city in order to spend more time with him and do the things he likes. I have started to dress a certain way, speak a certain way, and unfortunately, I have had to dumb myself down because intellectually, we are not on the same level. For example, we went to a play at the Arena Stage. Afterwards, the actors came out on stage and talked to the audience about the play. One actor used a word and asked if anybody knew what that word meant. I guess it was a big word to most of the people there, but I knew what it meant. Instead of raising my hand and explaining what it meant, I just sat there because I was afraid to make him feel a certain way. That is the way it is when I am with him. I have always been an outspoken person when it comes to my beliefs or the things I care about. I don't talk about politics and social issues when I am around him because I know those aren't his interests. So I have become somebody else for him and am losing myself in the process.

Curtis had been spending more time at the Brown household hanging out with Shanita, much to the delight of the Brown family. Everybody liked Curtis. Big John was fond of the idea that his baby girl had hooked a nice guy who was also a popular athlete. Curtis was respectful and seemed to have a good head on his shoulders. Big John couldn't hide his disappointment that his sons had become street thugs. More importantly, he felt guilty that he wasn't around the house more to guide them. Shanita's sisters were happy that Shanita had grown out of her tomboy ways and had finally gotten a boy of her own, especially such a good-looking boy who was very popular. Olivia had always cast a doubtful eye on this boy hanging around her daughter, but the more Curtis was around, the more she began to trust and like him.

It was Alfred, however, who seemed to have his eye on Curtis the most and went out of his way to make him feel comfortable. "If there is anything you need, Curtis, just ask," Alfred would constantly say. "I got your back." When Curtis needed anything like a new pair of tennis shoes, a new jacket, or new school clothes, it was Alfred who gave him the money. Alfred knew that Curtis didn't have a lot of money and wasn't about that street life. He also knew that Curtis's grandmother kept him on a tight leash, so he made sure Curtis had a little money in his pocket so that he could take Shanita out once in a while. He didn't want Curtis taking his sister out looking like a gump, so he would hook Curtis up with fine jewelry and the latest fashion wear. Curtis was appreciative, and he and Alfred became close friends.

Two weeks before the city basketball championship, Curtis injured his ankle working out in practice. He was determined to play and not let this injury interfere with an opportunity of a lifetime. The pain, however, was relentless. As he sat on Shanita's front porch waiting for her to come out, Alfred came out on the porch and sat down.

"How you holding up?" Alfred asked.

"I'm hanging," Curtis said, "but this ankle has me trippin'. There is no way I'm gonna miss this game, though. The trainer said there's no real damage. He said if I can deal with the pain, I can play without damaging it further. I'm good."

"Well, I've got something for that pain. Just take this little pill an hour before the game, and you won't feel a thing. In fact, it might even help you elevate your game!"

"Man, you know I don't do drugs."

"Hey, I'm looking out for you! Pro athletes use this stuff all of the time. How do you think they get through those injuries? Where do you think I got them from anyway? Listen, use it just this once, and after that … after all, this is the championship!"

"OK, man. I'll give it a try, just this once. Good looking out!"

"Look, I need you to do this one thing for me, though. I need you to take this package up to the school and give it to Mr. Chaney_ you know, the guy who teaches history. Wait for my money. Tell him if he doesn't give me my money, I'm gonna fuck him up!" As Shanita came out onto the porch, Curtis and Alfred stopped talking. Curtis stealthily put the package in his gym bag. Alfred gave Curtis a wink and said, "See you lovebirds later," and took off with a huge grin on his face. As he walked away, Alfred whispered to himself, "Got him."

Curtis became one of Alfred's best sellers. In one month's time, he had amassed a total of $150,000. Hustling was something Curtis had done all of his young life, but up until now, the hustles had been totally legitimate. It started out with shoveling snow during the winter months to make money and cutting lawns during the spring and summer months. He would hang out at the grocery store and help elderly people load their cars or help them carry their groceries home. He also had a scheme where he would go to the corner store, buy a bag full of candy, wait for the stores to close, and then sell the candy to kids in the neighborhood for twice the price. He was always likable and people felt comfortable around him. When he started hustling for Alfred, it started with selling pills to his teammates and other athletes, and then to other students in the school. Next, he graduated to selling cocaine, which brought in a lot of money. When the crack epidemic took Washington, DC by storm, he began selling crack on the streets. He was making so much money part-time, that he decided to drop out of school and sell full-time.

Shanita was distraught that Curtis had become a drug dealer, but at this point, she was totally in love with him and could not see herself leaving him because of this. She kind of felt guilty because she thought she was the one who got him started. She always believed that what she did at the roller-skating ring was the catalyst for his foray into the street life.

Jessica had decided to throw a skating party at the Crystal Skate Rink. Curtis's grandmother would not allow him to go because he was on punishment. She was trying her best to get control of him. While at the skating party, Shanita took a picture with another boy, and when Curtis found out, he was livid. Even though Shanita said nothing was going on, he was suspicious. Curtis was so hurt that he broke his grandmother's good vase. He felt that it was his grandmother who prevented him from going to the party. He was a man now. He had just turned eighteen years old and felt that he was getting a little too old to be getting punished by her. He started to flex his independence and told her that she couldn't keep him in the house anymore. He began disregarding her rules altogether until she had finally had enough and put him out of her house. Initially, he spent the night with a close friend until that got old and his friend's mother asked him to leave. He then turned to staying in hotel rooms with his drug money until he was able to convince one of his relatives to rent an apartment for him. He would have gotten the place himself, but didn't know where to start or how to go about getting his own place. Shanita always believed that he got into the drug game to make money to pay for his apartment. It was all her fault. *If only I hadn't taken that picture.*

The relationship between Curtis and Shanita advanced to a new level once he got his own place. They had been dating for almost three years now, and he had been getting ridiculed by his boys because he never talked about his sexual exploits with her. They all assumed that he wasn't hitting it, and they were correct. He was more than ready to go all the way, but he respected the fact that she wasn't ready. The sexual tension between the two of them, however, had always been high. They had done a lot of kissing and plenty of foreplay, but never actual intercourse. Not having a place where they could have privacy was always the issue. Once, they were on the couch in the living room in her parents' house, and he had gotten as far as getting her pants off and had his exposed, rock-hard penis rubbing against her thin panties. It was about to happen when suddenly her brother came downstairs to get something out of the refrigerator. Everything stopped at that point. That killed the mood, but only increased the tension.

She became increasingly curious about sex and wanted to feel what it was like to have him inside of her. Most of her girlfriends were not virgins, and all they talked about was having sex. They talked about who had a big penis and who didn't. They talked about how many orgasms they could get and how wonderful they felt. They also talked about the best way to get a man and to keep a man_ which was good food and good sex. During these conversations, she had to remain quiet because she had nothing to offer. Also, she loved him very much and wanted to give herself to him. She was happy that he was patient and never pressured her or tried to force her to have sex. She also knew that once he had gotten into the drug game, he would be exposed to all sorts of women, any of whom would do almost anything to get what they wanted. After he got the apartment, she decided it was time to go all the way and give it up.

On her eighteenth birthday, Shanita decided that this day would be the day. She was going to become a woman in more ways than just her age. She decided to skip school. It was near the end of the school year anyway, and her teachers were reviewing old work in preparation for final exams. Curtis had given her a key to his apartment, so she decided to hang out there. She was looking for something good on television but could find little that interested her during the day, so she turned on the VCR. Much to her surprise, there was the raunchiest tape of pornography that she had ever seen. She had seen what they called soft porn before, but this tape showed everything! The women in the video were doing things that she couldn't imagine doing. As much as she was stunned by what she was looking at, she couldn't turn her eyes away. Her sister once told her that all men have porn somewhere in the house. They try to hide it, but they always leave it in the easiest place to find _ the VCR! She watched the entire video as if she was doing research for a project. The only thing she really knew about the sex act itself was what she heard from her girlfriends and what she had seen on television.

When Curtis came home, he was happy to see her there. She had a look on her face that made him utter, "What's up?" She walked up to him and gave him a passionate kiss and then led him into the bedroom. She seductively took off her clothes and then began to disrobe him. As his ravenous eyes raked over her naked body, his mind began to explode with the thought, *Oh shit, it's about to really happen!* When she embraced him and gave him another passionate kiss this time, he experienced two physical reactions: his knees buckled, causing him to be off balance and stumble, and his penis became as hard as a rock. He cut his usual habit of petting and fondling short. He was finally going to do "the nasty," and he wanted to get right to it. As he rubbed his penis between her vagina's lips, gently stroking her clitoris, she thought she was in heaven. It felt so good that her body began to pitch and heave uncontrollably. *So this is what they have been talking about. Finally!*

Her feelings of blissful passion ended abruptly when he inserted himself into her. For Shanita, everything stopped at that moment. The passion, the excitement, the curiosity, the love, and all those feelings dissipated and were replaced by the pain that emanated between her legs. Her girlfriends didn't tell her about this part. At this moment, all she wanted him to do was stop! She let out a shriek, which Curtis mistakenly thought indicated pleasure, so he increased the intensity of his strokes. The pain slowly subsided, but she was extremely relieved when he began to grunt and groan and then climaxed. As they lay in each other's arms, Curtis was basking in the glow of the affirmation of his manhood while Shanita was thinking, *Thank God, it's over!*

June 13, 2009

Dear Diary,

I am a woman now. We had sex last week, but I really didn't enjoy it. It hurt like hell. In fact, it hurt the first couple of times we did it. I talked to Gwen about it and she said not to worry_ it will get so much better the more I did it. She said that as a woman, I had to learn about my body and how to pleasure it and how to pleasure him. Maybe I was doing something wrong. This produced some insecurity in me because I began to think that if I didn't know what I was doing, he might go to somebody else. I didn't want to ask Mom about it because I already know what she would say. She used to constantly tell us about those "no-count boys" who go sniffing around every woman they see, and all they want is to "get inside your pants." So I bought some more of those porn tapes and started doing some research on my own.

Gwen was right! It did get better. Now I like it so much that I want to do it all the time. I hope I am not becoming a sex addict like the girls portrayed in those books. The thing is that I love it when he is in me.

The street life is beginning to change Curtis. He is becoming cold and heartless . . . I guess you have to be when you are *in the game.* But when he is with me and especially when he is in me, I feel the softness and tenderness that has always been in him. When he empties his seed in me, he seems totally helpless and at my mercy. It's like while we are in bed, I can control him and make him do what I want.

Nobody knows I am having sex, with the exception of Gwen, of course. I wouldn't dare tell Mom. She's not around that much anyway . . . And if Dad ever found out! I did confess to my godmother the other day, though. She said there was something different about me. I was like, how could she tell? I guess she knows me better than anyone else. Anyway, when I told her that I wasn't a virgin anymore, the first thing she asked me was what type of birth control I was using. If looks could kill, I'd be dead right now. She gave me a look that seemed to say, *Are you stupid or something,* when I told her I wasn't using anything. She said I needed to get my mom to take me to the doctor so I could get on birth control pills. She also said that I needed to make him use a rubber. I told her that I would ask my mom to take me, but I knew that was a lie. There was no way I was going to tell Mom that I was doing it with one of those "no-count boys." Now I wished I had listened!

Trust was something that was critical to Shanita, and she was loyal to a fault. She trusted Curtis, and in turn, he trusted her. He demonstrated his trust when he started giving her the money he earned from hustling so she could put it in a safe place. His plan was to put aside enough money so he could buy a Jeep. She put the money in a small, portable safe her brother used to use to keep his money and hid it in her closet. At one point, she counted up twenty thousand dollars that he had saved. He told her that she could buy whatever she wanted, but just let him know how much she needed. She refused to spend any of the money.

Curtis called one Saturday and told her he was coming to get the money so he could pay for the Jeep, and he wanted her to go with him. She told him that she was glad he called because she had something very important to tell him. She had gone to the drug store the previous week and gotten one of those pregnancy test kits. She took the test and showed the results to Gwen. There were two lines visible on the indicator.

"This line is faded. That means I'm not pregnant, right?" Shanita pleaded.

Gwen picked up the package and re-read the directions.

"No, you're pregnant," Gwen reluctantly replied. She pointed to the indicator. "It says a line could be faded, but you can definitely see two lines."

"Oh my God, I'm pregnant!"

"What are you gonna tell Ma?"

"I'm not gonna tell her!"

Shanita didn't know how she was going to tell Curtis that he was going to be a daddy, but she had to think of something quick because he was on his way over. She wasn't even sure how she felt about it herself. They had been together for a year, and she loved and trusted him. She was really nervous, so she put on one of the cute outfits that he liked so much and went to the closet to get the money out of the safe. When she opened the safe, however, it was empty! She stood there stunned as she gazed into the empty safe. She could not believe what she was seeing. Then panic set in.

Oh my God! Oh my God! What the fuck! Where is the money? This man trusted me with everything and now it's gone! What am I going to do?

The only thing Shanita could think of was to run.

CHAPTER 3

GETTING ALONG

All eyes followed them as they sat down in the Hartsfield-Jackson Atlanta International Airport restaurant. What a pair! She was stunningly beautiful with her long, brunette hair, olive skin, and green eyes. Her low-cut, V-neck blouse revealed the top of the word *Rebel,* which was tattooed on her left breast. He looked like he could have been a professional football player with his six-foot-four, 240-pound sculptured physique that dwarfed her shapely body, his jet-black skin, and his huge hands that looked like they could crush the back of the chair that he pulled out so she could take her seat. As ominous as he may have looked to others, she knew that he was as gentle as a lamb, even though she had only known him for a few months. He was attracted to her because of her enticing smile, warm personality, keen intelligence, and willingness to engage in conversation about almost any subject, be it politics, religion, or sports. Her good looks were just a bonus.

Leon Anderson first met Roya Korrapatti while he was driving a bus for DC Metro. He remembered the first time she got on his bus. She gave him the friendliest smile he had ever seen and simply said, "Hi." That caught his attention because no one usually said anything to him, unless they were asking for directions. She would get on the bus the same time every day and would speak to him. After a while, she began sitting in the seat directly behind him, and they would chat while he drove. He finally asked her out, and before he knew it, they were involved in a relationship. It wasn't long before he took her to meet his mother and father, which was a first for him.

Roya had an interesting background, which provided them with much to talk about. She was born in Dodoma, Tanzania, which is one of the poorest countries not only in Africa but in the world. Her father was born in Bombay, India, and her mother was from Tehran, Iran. Her father was working in Iran as an architect before the 1979 revolution when he met and fell in love with her mother, who was an interior designer. Her father went to Tanzania because he was one of the architects who helped design the tall Bank of Tanzania, while her mother did missionary work in the villages to help the people who were suffering from devastating hunger and malnutrition. Once the building was completed, her father moved the family to the United States, where they became naturalized citizens.

Roya couldn't help but notice how people in the restaurant kept staring at them as if they had committed a crime or something.

"Leon, doesn't it bother you at all that these people keep staring at us," she whispered.

"Nah, don't even trip on that," he replied. "They just mad because they're not as beautiful as you, or as handsome as me! Anyway, I'm used to it. So don't worry your pretty little head about it."

"Yeah, but it is getting creepy."

"It is what it is. You can ignore it, or if it bothers you that much, just stare back at them. They will eventually turn away. Now, what do you feel like eating?"

After having a quick bite, Leon and Roya boarded the plane heading to the Caribbean island of Grenada, which was his mother's home. When he was small, his mom used to tell him stories about living on Spice Island, the name her beloved Grenada had been given because it was the second-largest producer of nutmeg, cinnamon, and mace in the world. It had been said that when you toured the island, you were surrounded by the scent of nutmeg wafting through the air. His mother would often talk about the dazzling white sand beaches, the clear blue ocean water, the warm ocean breezes, and the breathtaking waterfalls located in the mountain rain forest. She fondly reminisced about the absence of major crime on the island, the fact that it was impolite to pass someone on the street without saying hello_ an offense for which your parents would give you a good thrashing_ and that the use of bad language in public was punishable by a heavy fine, or even imprisonment. She had always promised to take the family to visit her cherished home, but things kept getting in the way, and they never made the trip. Leon decided to make the trip on his own and was elated that Roya consented to go with him. What he found, however, caught him a little off guard and stunned him.

As the plane started its descent, Leon could already see the beauty that his mother had described: the sandy beaches, palm trees, and magnificent sunset. As he rode in the taxi to their hotel, he realized that she hadn't told him everything. She never mentioned the scantily- clad women with big breasts, ample behinds, and warm smiles, which added to the island's allure.

Hmmm, maybe I shouldn't have brought Roya on this trip, he thought.

The next day, he and Roya hopped in a van and took one of the guided island tours. He sat in the back of the van looking at the sites when his heart began to sink. The tour guide gushed about the rain forest, the exotic flowers, and the monuments to liberation; but what Leon saw was the conditions that the people outside of the main city had to live in. Instead of looking at the flowers, he saw the immense poverty and hopelessness in the eyes of the men sitting by the side of the road, or lying on a table in the numerous open bars that outlined the small roads. He was shocked at the condition of the homes, the majority of which were rickety and dilapidated, with their broken boards and holes in the roof. They reminded him of the homes of slaves and sharecroppers in the South that he had seen in his history books. Virtually every six inches was a billboard sign that outlined the devastating effects of HIV-AIDS. He saw children dressed in tattered clothing, sliding down the hills on cardboard boxes. They would curiously look at a tourist and ask, "Are you from away?" These conditions made him sad. He expected something different based on his mom's nostalgic reflections. All of a sudden, the ocean water didn't seem as blue, the sun wasn't as brilliant, and the breeze no longer had a cooling effect. His mom didn't tell him about this part.

His perceptions began to change the longer he stayed and as he began talking to the islanders. The people were extremely friendly and talked about their island with great pride. They seemed genuinely concerned that he and his date enjoy themselves. Neither the color of his skin, the style of his clothes, nor the language he spoke seemed to matter. He was measured by how he acted and how he treated the people around him, and that was refreshing. There was an old guard who greeted him outside the hotel every day. The old man would always have some friendly words of wisdom that he would share with the hotel guest:

"Slow down, mon," he would say to Leon. "No problem, every ting OK! You Americans are always rushing, tryin' to catch a glimpse of life, but you are losing the race. You need to slow down, relax, and enjoy life!"

Leon learned that time was not an enemy, and there was no hidden message in the word *hello* . . . it really meant hello. After a week on the island, Leon became cognizant of an incident that showed how much the island culture had begun to influence him. He and Roya went to the Island Wharf Restaurant for dinner and waited for what seemed like hours to get served, waited for almost half an hour for the bill to come after informing the waitress that they were ready to go. Instead of getting upset, they sat enjoying each other's company, listening to the sounds of the waves crashing against the shore, and embracing time. If he had been back in the States, he probably would have been furious.

"We've been together for a few months now, but I really don't know much about you in terms of where you grew up, how you grew up, and what helped turn you into this wonderful man that you are today," Roya exclaimed. "You know a little about my background and history, and now I want to know about yours! I am especially interested in hearing how you deal with racism and the people like the ones who kept staring at us in the airport. It didn't seem to bother you at all."

"Well, there is not that much to tell," Leon replied.

Roya settled back in her seat, flashed that beautiful smile, and said, "Well, just start from the beginning."

"OK! My mom was pregnant with me when she, my dad, and three older sisters moved to the United States from Grenada. I grew up in the Adams-Morgan neighborhood in northwest DC. It got the name during the 1960s by combining the names of two formerly segregated elementary schools_ the all-white John Quincy Adams Elementary School and the all-black Thomas P. Morgan Elementary School. When we first got there, it was a predominantly black middleclass neighborhood. At one time, DC was referred to as Chocolate City because the majority of the city's residents were black. But now that has changed significantly. The community is now very ethnically and culturally diverse. This community, which is close to the Mount Pleasant and Columbia Heights communities, has made the area a gateway for immigrants, especially Latino immigrants, and young white professionals.

"My childhood was fantastic. I grew up right off Sixteenth and Kalorama Road NW, near the old Kalorama Skating rink. My mom never let us go there, though, because she said crazy people hung out there. Our playground was Malcolm X Park. At first, it was called Meridian Hill Park, then the name was changed to Malcolm X Park, and now the name has switched back to Meridian Hill Park. These name changes mirrored the changing demographics of the neighborhood, and the city for that matter. The park was always filled with people, and it was our playground. I remember going over to the park with my mom, brother, and sisters. We would rip and run around the park. There was always a group playing live music, and the atmosphere was always festive. There was a cascading waterfall that emptied into a pool on the lower deck near V Street. We weren't supposed to, but we swam in that pool all the time. You could stand at the top of the park and see the entire city. We used to watch the Fourth of July fireworks display from there. We had some good times."

"What did your parents do for a living?"

"My mom worked as a maid, and my dad drove a cab. Most of my friends' mothers and fathers worked as janitors or cleaned offices downtown. We may have been poor, but I never knew it because we always had enough to eat and clothes on our backs. We lived in a three-bedroom apartment. When my younger brother was born, we shared a room, my sisters shared a room, and my mom and dad shared a room. We all had chores to do. My oldest sister was in charge of making sure everything was done, but as I got older and started to get bigger, I began taking control of the house, and even telling my big sister what to do.

"I had to learn how to cook and clean because my mom didn't want me to grow up dependent and without any skills. She would always say, 'Look, when you get to the age where you are going to have a woman, get married, or whatever, you want to be able to do everything. If both of you are able to do things around the house, you can do things together. You shouldn't sit around the house and do nothing. And if you don't get married, then you need to know how to do things for yourself.' I think she felt this way because when my dad got home from work, he wouldn't do anything around the house. This was always an issue with her because she worked just as hard as he did. He was an only child growing up, so a lot of things were done for him, and so even after he married my mom, he didn't know how, or refused, to do anything for himself. He got drafted right after high school and was sent to Vietnam. My mom says something happened to him during the war. He doesn't talk much about it, but he still has nightmares.

"My mom was very strict. She pretty much ran our family. When she came home from work, the house had to be clean and the dinner prepared. On the weekends, we had to scrub the windows and vacuum the floors before we could go out and play. She was always telling us that people will treat you the way you treat them, and that you always should aspire to be a good person. A good person in her view was one who didn't do anything wrong and who looked out for people who couldn't look out for themselves. It was instilled in us to not only protect each other, but to protect our friends and neighbors as well.

"Believe it or not, my first encounter with racism, or I will use the word *bigotry*, came from my own people. It all started with being teased because of the way I spoke and the accent I had. We spoke English, but in the house my mom and sisters would speak a Grenadian dialect called Grenadian Creole. It was like broken English. My grandmother, who worked in the cafeteria at George Washington University, always demanded that we speak proper English when we were out in public. She would often say we couldn't get ahead in America speaking broken English. So I got mocked a lot by the other kids because I spoke too proper or 'white' as they used to say, and I had a heavy accent.

"Then I started getting teased because of my dark skin. We had a thing called joning, or playing the dozens, where kids would make fun of you because of something you would do or the way you looked. I would always get ostracized by my peers because I was dark. They would say things like, 'Man, you are darker than that car over there,' or 'Somebody turn on the lights so we can see Leon!' They would call me ugly and call me names like midnight, black cat, or tar-baby. Everybody would laugh. I would laugh along with them, but on the inside I was really crushed. The thing about it was that the other kids who were just as dark as I was would tease me the loudest. I guess they didn't want anyone to tease them so they would strike first and hardest."

"Oh, that is so cruel," Roya interjected. "How did that make you feel?"

"I would go home and cry sometimes. I began to think that I was ugly. All the cool guys had wavy hair, or very fair skin. I had neither. I would try to get my hair to become wavy by putting a lot of grease on it at night and wearing a stocking cap, but as much as I tried, my hair just wouldn't act right. I couldn't get any play from the girls because I was skinny, my hair was nappy, and I was dark skinned. The clothes I wore didn't help much either. We didn't have a lot of money, so we couldn't buy the latest shoes or outfits. Whatever we had on was clean, but it wasn't what everybody else had."

"How were you able to deal with all of that?" Roya asked. "Do you still feel that way about your appearance?"

"Please!" Leon laughingly replied. "My mom wasn't having that. She would always pull me aside and tell me how beautiful I was. She would tell me that I looked like her favorite movie star who was Sidney Poitier. She even bought me a poster of him and put it on my bedroom wall. Then when people like Mohammed Ali started proclaiming how beautiful he was and black people are, and James Brown started singing, 'Say it loud … I'm black and I'm proud,' attitudes about my skin tone began to change. Black was in, and soon I started being admired instead of ridiculed. I started making a little money when I got a job delivering the newspaper, and so I was able to buy some clothes, and even a pair of Air Jordan's, which was the popular tennis shoe that was out when I was in junior high school. Also, as I got bigger and my body started to develop, people stopped teasing me because they knew I would beat the shit out of them!

"My first encounter with white folks occurred when I went to high school. I was originally supposed to go to Cardozo High School, but they changed the boundary lines, and so I had to go to Wilson High School, which was located in upper northwest. That school was very diverse in terms of racial and social makeup. There were upper class black kids, who lived in upper northwest in an area we referred to as the Gold Coast; white kids, who lived on the other side of Rock Creek Park; and foreign kids who lived on Massachusetts Avenue and whose parents were diplomats. I had a really good white friend named Arnold Blake, who actually lived in Bethesda, Maryland, and whose parents were doctors. One day, he invited me to hang out at his house, but that didn't go too well. He tried to introduce me to his mom, who was standing in the kitchen with her back turned. When she turned around and saw me, the smile on her face turned into a frown. When I extended my hand to greet her, she gave me a look that let me know I was not welcome, turned, and just walked away. It was like my hand had shit or something on it and she didn't want to touch it. I was like, *Wow*! Arnold was a little embarrassed and just said, 'Well, that's my mom.' We hung out in his room for a while, but needless to say, I was never invited over there again. I didn't have too many problems at Wilson because most of the people were cool, and I was a popular football player. When I got to college, however, that was another story.

"I got an athletic scholarship to attend Prairie Village College in Kansas. It was a small predominantly white college with only a handful of minority students. My parents paid for my airplane ticket, gave me a little spending money and a goodbye kiss, and sent me out into the world. When I got there, all I had was fifty dollars in my pocket, and a footlocker and a suitcase that held everything I owned. I was on my own for the first time in my life, and I was very excited. I had to catch a cab to get from the airport to the college, which cost me thirty dollars! When I arrived, I went up to the information desk at the student center, introduced myself, told the man sitting at the desk that I was a freshman, and asked where I could get the key to my dorm room. The old white guy sitting behind the desk took one look at me and dryly said that I couldn't get my dorm key until the next day when freshmen were supposed to arrive. I told him I was on the football team and I didn't have anywhere to stay for the night. He looked at me and said, 'That sounds like a personal problem to me. Sorry, buddy, I can't help you.'

"I was stunned. Here I was, an eighteen-year-old kid, out on my own for the first time. My first thought was, *Welcome to college!* Then panic began to set in. I didn't know what I was going to do. I had twenty dollars in my pocket, which was supposed to be for the personal items I needed to get, like toothpaste, deodorant, soap, a blanket, and other stuff. More importantly, I didn't have my mom or my dad to tell me what to do or to comfort me. So I put my suitcase and my footlocker in front of my dorm room door and just started walking around the vacant campus. I was trying to figure out where I was going to sleep for the night when I saw a bench and thought maybe I could sleep there. I walked back to the student center and found that the cafeteria was open, so I decided to try to get a bite to eat. As I sat there trying to figure out my next move, a group of guys stormed into the cafeteria to get lunch. It turned out that the upper-class football players were on campus because they were supposed to report a day early. I guess I looked at the wrong date on the letter I received.

"I will never forget that voice that sang out, 'Hey man, why don't you come over and join us?' The guy who called out was named Charles Gray. Everybody called him Chuck. He had a boisterous laugh, a charming demeanor, and was one of the friendliest persons you would ever want to meet. He was one of only three black guys on the team. Now I'm thinking, *Oh great, maybe he will let me sleep on his floor until I can get my room key!* I took my tray over to their table, introduced myself, and thanked them for their hospitality. When Chuck asked me which dorm I was staying in, I said to myself, *Great, now I can explain my dilemma.* When I told him what the man at the information desk told me, Chuck started laughing. 'Aw, man, don't worry about that. That guy has done that before, and it is usually the black guys he does it to. I will take you over to Buildings and Grounds after lunch and get you your room key.' I slept in my dorm room that night. There was no linen or a pillow on the bed, so I slept under my coat on the mattress. It was the best sleep I ever had.

"Being one of a few blacks on the team wasn't so bad. There were awkward times when we would go on road trips throughout the Mid-West, however. Whenever the team would go to a restaurant to eat, the black players would get stared at like we were monkeys or something. Every time I would open my mouth to put food in it, someone was looking down my throat. One time, a waitress even said, 'We never get your kind around here.' I responded, 'What, you mean other football teams never eat at this restaurant?' After a while, I learned to ignore things like that. Something happened, though, that I couldn't ignore.

"During my sophomore year, our head coach, Jim Calhoun, made the statement that all positions were open. He said that if you wanted to start, all you had to do was work hard and beat the man in front of you. Chuck was extremely delighted because he was a quarterback and desperately wanted to play more. He was a star in high school and touted as having a 'million dollar arm,' as one sports reporter wrote. His only problem was that he was black, and at that time, blacks weren't supposed to be intelligent enough to play the quarterback position in college or the pros. That didn't faze Chuck, who resisted the coach's attempts to get him to switch his position to wide receiver. Our starting quarterback was a white guy named Michael Carpetti. He was very popular with the team and fans because he took the team to the small college playoffs the previous year, but he didn't have a strong arm. We had a strong running game, but when we got into the playoffs, teams shut that down. Coach Calhoun was concerned because Carpetti couldn't make the deep throws. When we started practice the following year, Chuck demonstrated that he was much better throwing the ball than Mike. He threw touchdown after touchdown during our scrimmages and demonstrated that he could handle being the quarterback in spite of his skin tone. The week before our first game, Coach Calhoun announced that Chuck would be our starting quarterback, and that is when all hell broke loose. That announcement was met with an eerie silence, strange, angry looks amongst many of the white players, and even some of the coaches.

"When we got to the locker room, I remember sitting in front of my locker and hearing some of the linemen, who were sitting on the bench a few lockers away from me, loudly stating that they weren't going to block for 'that nigger!' I was shocked. Those guys sounded really angry. I couldn't understand that anger because Chuck was better than Mike and proved it in practice. Up until that point, I had never seen any racial animosity on the team, and I thought we were a really close team. I guess I was wrong. The rest of the week went off without a hitch, so I thought things had settled down and returned to normal.

"Our first game was an away game. We stayed in a hotel, and Chuck was my roommate. What I didn't know was that over the summer, Chuck had decided to change his religion, and now he was a Muslim. He would take out his prayer rug and pray several times a day. That night, he prayed for strength and to have success in the game. Before going to sleep, he told me that he was going to light up the score board during the game and make the coach and the team proud of him. He said he knew that Coach Calhoun's decision wasn't popular with the team and that he was going to do everything in his power to prove that the coach made the right decision. The next day, he only stayed in the game for six plays. Every time he went back to pass, two or three defenders swarmed in, untouched, and tried their best to not only take his head off, but to destroy his spirit. Every time he touched the ball, the offense lost yards; and the last time he got gang-tackled, he fumbled the ball. The ineptitude of the offense forced Coach Calhoun to replace Chuck with Mike, and the offense began clicking on all cylinders. Chuck sat on the bench the remainder of the game with his helmet on and his glossy eyes staring into space. When we got back to school, Chuck quit the team. The two other black players quit in protest, leaving me all alone on the team. I was devastated."

"You know, that just makes me so angry," Roya softly said. "I just don't get that! Why do people act like that? Why did you decide to stay on the team?"

Leon hesitated for a few seconds before responding to Roya's question. The roar of the ocean waves seemed to get louder as they angrily crashed against the helpless shore, snatching every morsel of sand they could and returning them to the depths of the dark blue water.

"I don't know how to quit," Leon finally said, shaking his head and throwing up his hands as if to imply that, that was something she should already know, but why should she?

"Quitting is not in my DNA. Football was my life, and I loved the game. If I wasn't playing the game, I was preparing to play the game. And besides, I was on scholarship. If I wanted to stay in school, I had to play. Furthermore, I wasn't going to give them the satisfaction of running me off. Oh, but I was very angry, though. I didn't know how to react, so I just shut down and played ball."

"What do you mean you shut down?"

"I stopped talking to all of my teammates. I didn't know what to say to them, so I didn't say anything. I felt isolated and totally alone. I felt that no one cared and everyone was against me. I had always been taught, especially by my mother and my grandmother, to not judge people by what they look like but by how they act and what they do. But now, all I saw was white people, and I began to put them all in the same boat. Being in practice was awkward, and the coaches and my teammates didn't know what to make of my silence. Soon, I began to hear that I was being called a black militant! I'm pretty sure that wasn't the only name I was called, but I didn't understand how they came up with *militant* simply because I stopped talking."

"Did you do that for the rest of the season?"

"No, and it was interesting how that played out. When we went on overnight road trips, the coach had to assign me a roommate. I roomed with a guy named Steven Sullivan, and we became best friends. I found out later that he volunteered to be my roommate on road trips. Steven was cool, and he was not shy about asking me anything. He was the one who broke the ice when we were on one of our road trips. He asked me why I stopped talking and how I felt about things. We talked about race, and he told me that he was totally blind when it came to the color of a person. I thought, *Yeah, right!* But he was true to his word and treated me like nothing ever happened. He just wanted to play ball and have fun. After a while, I started calling him Stevie Wonder. When he asked me why I called him that, I replied, 'Because Stevie Wonder is blind too.' No one else understood what we meant, but the name caught on. Stevie reinforced my grandmother's teaching concerning judging people by their character and not the color of their skin."

The waitress finally came back with Leon's change. After leaving a hefty tip, Leon and Roya decided to take a leisurely stroll on the beach. They walked in silence, listening to the waves and gazing at the sunset. Leon stopped and turned toward Roya. He took her hand and looked into her eyes.

"Can I ask you a personal question?" he asked.

"Sure, you can ask me anything."

"You were born in Tanzania, which makes you African. Your mom was born in Iran, your dad was born in India, and now you live in America. What do you consider yourself?"

"I'm mixed, but I consider myself Persian American."

"Why did you choose Persian American?"

"I guess that is because my father adopted my mother's religion and culture after he met her in Iran. He was a non-practicing Hindu until he met her and then converted to the Bahai faith. The Bahai is a religion that teaches the essential worth of all religions and the unity of all people. It has faced persecution since its birth in Iran. My parents left Iran before the Islamic Revolution because Bahai marriages weren't recognized there, so they got married in India. My dad, however, was very passive, and even though the Indian culture was rich, my mother's Persian culture was dominant in our family. I guess it is just like some black people in America. They might be the product of a mixed marriage, but they consider themselves African American."

"You are so right about that! My father considers himself African American even though he has relatives who are Native American from the Nottoway tribe and has white relatives as well."

"Now, can I ask you a personal question?" Roya asked.

"Sure, what's up?"

"You went to college and served in the military, so what made you decide to become a bus driver?"

"After coming back from Iraq, I was looking for a job and wasn't sure what I wanted to do. An army buddy told me about an opening at Metro, so I took it until I could find something better. But I won't be there much longer."

"Why is that?"

"Before we left to come here, I found out that my application has been accepted. I am going to be a Metro Transit cop."

"Why in the world would you want to do that?"

CHAPTER 4

We Gonna Dance

"Isn't that Eugenia's youngest son out there on the street?"

"Yeah, that's him! Girl, I know Eugenia would be turning over in her grave if she knew her youngest son was out there buying drugs."

"Well, she is turning right now because that's him. That's a damn shame too. He was such a nice young man … so respectful."

"Girl, drugs don't care who you are, or how nice you are. Once you get hooked on that mess, you're done. Look at him out there. I guess that stuff done turned him into one of those crackheads."

Every evening, Mrs. Selby and Mrs. Thomas, both long-time residents, would sit on the porch of their small two-story house located in Sursum Corda and observe everything that went on. Nothing escaped their gaze, or their judgment for that matter; and they were sure to let everybody know what they saw. If a child was doing something that they shouldn't have been doing, the watchful old ladies would let the parents know, and would even suggest the type of punishment they thought appropriate. If an outlandish crime had been committed, the police could always depend on them for information and support. When the neighborhood kids wanted to get into some mischief, they made sure it was out of the sight of the old women who sat on the porch, and who sometimes sold candy to the neighborhood kids. Life in the neighborhood had never been all peaches and cream, but there was a time when decent, hard-working people came home, raised their kids in peace, and neighbors looked out for one another.

The crack epidemic of the 1980s and 1990s changed all of that. The epidemic had turned hard working neighbors, and many of the neighborhood children into either crackheads, whose only goal in life was to get their next fix, or crack dealers, who would do anything to claim and maintain authority over the open-air drug market. The dealers operated in the open, without fear of punishment, for if anyone snitched to the police, there would be hell to pay. And now the "game" seemed to have claimed Eugenia Harris's son. Little did the old ladies know, however, that Gregory Harris was not really a crack head but an undercover police officer trying to set up a drug sting. Little did they know that he was still one of the good guys trying to clean up the neighborhood that he loved so dearly.

Sursum Corda is a small neighborhood located in northwest Washington, DC, within sight of the US Capitol. The area draws its name from the Sursum Corda Cooperative Apartments, a 199-unit low-income housing project constructed in 1968. The original plans were developed by alumni of Georgetown University and called for a unique 155 resident-owned and 44 renter-occupied townhouses on four acres, arranged on courtyards and alleys around a horseshoe-shaped street which closed off the neighborhood in an attempt to promote a sense of community. It was named Sursum Corda, a Latin expression meaning "lift up your hearts," which is intoned at the start of the Eucharistic Prayer during Mass. A group of nuns from the religious institute of the Religious of the Sacred Heart were among the first residents. The community rapidly grew into an African American community, initially with working families of moderate to low income, followed by an influx of families on public assistance.

Gregory Harris's parents, Robert and Eugenia Harris, were both members of the military and moved into the neighborhood after they retired. Robert, who was originally from Rocky Mount, North Carolina, had been a sergeant in the army, while Eugenia, a native Washingtonian, had been in the navy. They met when Robert walked into the Garfinckel's Department Store in downtown Washington, DC, where Eugenia worked; fell in love at first sight; and decided to get married after a whirl-wind romance. Robert got a job at the waste-water treatment plant, where he had to work twelve-hour days to make ends meet. He would come home for dinner, get some rest and then go back out to a second job working security at a nightclub. They purchased a small, two-bedroom house in Sursum Corda. The house became even smaller when the children started arriving. Renee was the first child to arrive, followed by Gregory, and then Geoff, which made sleeping arrangements quite difficult. Robert and Eugenia shared a room, Gregory and his brother shared a room, which meant that Renee, who had to give up her room when the boys arrived, had to sleep on a pull-out sofa in the living room. This, of course, didn't make her happy, but she loved her brothers to death, and they her.

Prior to the crack epidemic, violence and mischief was prevalent in the neighborhood, but no more than in any other neighborhood. The public housing apartment complex brought in numerous low-income families, and as a result, the area was saturated with numerous young boys and girls who lived in close proximity to one another. Everything in the neighborhood was community based. You knew your neighbors, and your neighbors knew you. If your weren't home before the street lights came on, your parents would call out of the window or come out on the porch and yell your name. You would either hear them calling you, or someone else would echo that your parents wanted you to come home. The axiom, "It takes a village to raise a child" was prevalent in the neighborhood because each parent took on the responsibility of chastising any child if they were caught doing something wrong, or reporting it. Parents were feared and revered.

When violence would occur, it was usually when one neighborhood would challenge another neighborhood, either as a result of a neighborhood football game or someone messing with a girl from another neighborhood. That was the situation one Saturday afternoon when Gregory and his brother Geoff were coming home from a basketball game at the Randall Playground. They were walking under the bridge where I-95 ends, leading into the city near Dunbar High School, when a group of guys, who claimed that Geoff had been messing with one of the member's sister, started chasing them. When Geoff saw the guys coming, he took off running. The guys were able to circle Gregory like a pack of wolves, preventing him from escaping. Gregory knew he was in trouble but was happy that his brother was able to get away. He put his back against the wall and waited for them to launch their attack. The first punch came from the biggest guy in the group followed by a rain of punches and kicks from the pack. Searching for the weakest link in a feeble attempt to escape, Gregory started swinging wildly but was caught with a punch that sent him sprawling to the ground. At this point, the only thing he could do was to ball up into a fetal position and try to protect his head. People in passing cars blew their horns in an attempt to stop the savage beating, but to no avail. The light started getting dim as unconsciousness began to overtake his senses, and then suddenly, he heard Geoff screaming his name. Gregory thought he was dreaming, but soon realized that Geoff had returned with a group of boys from the neighborhood. Geoff had returned to the scene with the cavalry to save the day, just like in the movies. The boys took off running when they saw Geoff and the Sursum Corda boys coming. Though beaten and battered, Gregory felt a sense of pride that he took on those boys and got in a few good licks of his own.

In Sursum Corda, the older guys would teach the younger guys how to defend themselves. The older guys would have boxing gloves and headgear and would often force the younger guys into a makeshift boxing ring to see who they could depend on if a neighborhood fight would break out, and who needed to learn how to fight. This makeshift arena is where Gregory Harris earned his street reputation. He was a quick learner, and though small in physical stature, he was very athletic. His quick hands, cat-like reflexes, and fearless nature earned him the admiration of even the older guys. They knew he could be depended on if a fight broke out.

Gregory had to use his boxing skills quite often when he was young because he always had to defend his older sister Renee. He and Renee had a special bond. When Gregory was small, Renee was given the task of taking care of him while their parents were at work. She hated the fact that he had to tag along when she went to the movies or wanted to hang out at the playground with her friends, but she had no choice. Renee's mouth would always get her into trouble. She liked to fight and would fight anybody, male or female. When she would come home bruised from a violent encounter, it was Gregory who would sit with her, dry her tears, and nurse her back to health. When she would get into fights at school, it was Gregory who would have to either defend her or make sure her fights were fair and no one would jump her. When she got pregnant and had a son, it was Gregory she would call on to be her babysitter. When a guy tried to rape Renee, it was Gregory who got his hands on a gun and went out looking for the guy. The guy had grabbed her and tried to take her behind some bushes near the playground. She struggled to get her gloves off, and when she did, she tried to scratch his eyes out, kicked him in the balls as hard as she could, and punched him harder than he anticipated. She didn't even scream for help. She got pleasure out of beating the shit out of him before he took off running. When she heard that her little brother went looking for him, she caught up with him, took the gun, and told him not to worry, because she doubted that "piece of trash would ever try to rape anybody again." It broke Gregory's heart when Renee got caught up and became one of the many neighborhood crackheads.

Gregory's father was a strict disciplinarian, and even though he was not able to be around his kids as much as he would have liked to, he made sure they knew the difference between right and wrong and respected authority. If one of his kids got into trouble, he had a saying that nobody wanted to hear. He would say, "We gonna dance tonight!" That meant a severe butt -whipping was in store for whoever got into trouble. Before the butt -whipping was administered, he would always give a speech: "You are not going to disrespect these teachers because I didn't raise you that way." Or, "You are going to do exactly what you are supposed to do. In school and in the community, you are going to be a role model, and I am not going to have it any other way!" He had another saying that he would repeat over and over until it was ingrained in everyone's brain. He would say, "Do the right thing, not the popular thing!"

Gregory didn't get into trouble very often, but there were times when he had to "dance" with his father. There was the time when he and a few of his classmates were joning on each other, and he started to laugh. The teacher saw him laughing and asked what was so funny. Gregory's response was, "You don't need to know what we were laughing about." Her retort was, "Oh, so I don't need to know about it? OK, I'm going to call your father and see what he has to say about that." "Please, Ms. Quick, don't call my father. He's probably not home anyway. You can call my mom, though." The teacher called Gregory's father and put Gregory on the phone.

"I'm not going to say anything right now," Mr. Harris quietly but sternly said, "but when you get home, you can bet we're gonna dance!"

Gregory knew what that meant. He counted each minute for the rest of the school day, dreading when three o'clock came because he didn't want to go home. When he got home, Gregory thought his dad would be at work but got the surprise of his life when he opened the door and his dad was waiting for him with the "black belt." Mr. Harris administered a butt-whipping so severe that Gregory knew he would never disrespect his teacher again, or any authority figure for that matter!

Then there was the time when Gregory and his friends were in the alley throwing rocks. A police car came through and stopped to see what was going on. The officers surrounded the boys and asked what they were doing.

"We were just throwing rocks, and we weren't bothering anybody, Officer," one of the boys said.

"Well, we got a call that you kids were breaking people's windows!"

"We didn't mean to, Officer. We didn't realize we were breaking anybody's windows."

"Well, you are, so let's go."

The police officers put the boys in the squad car and took them home. They told the boys' parents what they had done and that each child had to show up at the Police Boys and Girls Club the following day, or they would press charges. The officers had already spoken to the people whose windows had been broken, and they agreed that making the boys join the Boys and Girls Club was a good punishment and, as a result, would not press charges. Gregory and his father "danced" that night, and the next morning, Gregory's mother took him down to the club. Joining the Police Boys and Girls Club turned out to be one of the best things to happen in Gregory's young life.

The relationship between the police and the community prior to the crack epidemic had been cordial and supportive, thanks to the Officer Friendly program. Back in the day, Gregory and his friends did not fear the police. In fact, the police were the people you would call when you needed help. If you got lost, you would look for a police officer. If you needed a ride home, the police would give you a ride, and there was no stigma attached to getting out of a police car. This cordial relationship between the community and the police department was stimulated by numerous community-policing initiatives that included the Officer Friendly program. The Officer Friendly program started in Chicago in 1966 and spread throughout the country when, in 1974, the Sears and Roebuck Company partnered with the Virginia Police Department to fund programs nationwide. It was designed to humanize children's perceptions of police officers and their work, and to improve rapport between children and police. Classroom kits for school children were developed and spread out in elementary schools across the nation. These kits included coloring books, videos, board game, and teaching guides with activities. Kids were taught how to protect themselves from strangers, how to protect their families, and not to fear the police.

Other community-based police programs included bands that played popular music in schools and parks, summer camps and Police Boys and Girls Clubs. In Washington, D.C., the Side-by-Side Band, which was composed of all police officers, would come to schools and the kids would rock to their go-go music. The police officers who played in the band were looked at as being cool, and kids wanted to be just like them. Gregory got the opportunity to go to Camp Brown, which was a summer camp sponsored by the DC Metropolitan Police Department. There was a lottery, and the kids selected got to go to this co-ed camp out in the wilderness for two weeks, free of charge. Gregory got the opportunity to participate in activities like canoeing, hiking, swimming, building camp fires, and making arts and crafts.

Kids from all around the city would attend, and this was where Gregory met his first girlfriend. He fell in love with Erica, but was heart-broken when at the end of the two weeks, they had to leave the camp, and he never heard from her again.

Officer Friendly became a phrase that was associated with all the community-police initiatives and even became the adopted name of the many police officers who walked the beat in the community_ the good ones, that is. There were some officers whom everyone respected. These were the officers, like Officer Lee, who patrolled the neighborhood in Sursum Corda and developed positive relationships with the members of the community. He was so respected that even the drug dealers refused to sell or congregate on the corners when he walked the beat. This type of respect was not shown to all police officers. Everyone knew Officer Lee cared about them and the community, but when other officers showed up who did not know how to talk to the residents, or who always tried to move people off of the corners when all they were doing was talking, they were usually greeted with cold stares and angry responses like "Fuck you!"

When Gregory and his friends arrived at the Police Boys and Girls Club, they were introduced to organized sports like football, basketball, and boxing. Police officers volunteered to serve as the coaches for the teams, which further developed positive relationships with the young boys and girls in the community. At that point, the officers knew everything about the kids, their parents, how they were doing in school, and whether or not they were getting into trouble. The officers who served as coaches became surrogate parents and positive role models, which also further helped to develop positive relations within the community. Gregory joined the Boys and Girls Club recreation football team and enjoyed it a great deal. He later went on to play football at Dunbar High School. Boxing, however, turned out to be his best sport, and he caught the eye of several of his coaches. They felt that if he concentrated on the sport, he could be really good, maybe even turn pro. As a result, he had very little time to get into mischief because he was under the watchful eye of his coaches and was forever fearful of "dancing" with his father.

The positive relationship between the police department and the community came to an abrupt end during the late 1980s and early 1990s in Washington, DC when crack cocaine was introduced and swept through the city by storm, leaving numerous communities devastated in its wake. There had always been a presence of drugs in the community, but this was something different. Marijuana was readily available and pervasive in schools, and especially in the night clubs. Heroin, though inexpensive, was more prevalent before the 1970s, but had taken a backseat to the new crack. Powder cocaine was usually limited to the people who hung out in the upscale nightclubs and higher-income people who could afford it. Crack, on the other hand, was cheap, simple to produce, ready to use, and highly profitable for dealers to develop and sell.

Crack is merely a different form of cocaine. To produce it, powder cocaine is dissolved in a solution of water and baking soda or ammonia. The solution is boiled to separate out the solid, and then the solid is cooled and allowed to dry. It is then cut up into small nuggets, or "rocks." The resulting crystal substance_crack, is purer than the powdered cocaine because the process for producing a rock of crack eliminates the need for dealers to dilute it, as they do in stretching powder cocaine in order to gain more profit. Crack rocks contain between 75 percent and 90 percent pure cocaine. In addition, because crack is consumed by melting the rock, then smoking and inhaling, it is transmitted into the bloodstream and to the brain much faster as opposed to powder cocaine, which is snorted through the nose. This creates an intense, euphoric, but short-lived high, lasting as much as five minutes, but far more intense. Whereas powder cocaine could cost up to two hundred dollars an ounce, crack was sold in single quantities for as cheap as five, ten, or twenty-dollar chunks, thus making it easily affordable, even for the poorest customers. Once introduced, it spread like wildfire, impacting communities all over the nation. The speed by which it exploded in Washington, DC took everybody by surprise.

The immediate impacts of this scourge on the communities in Sursum Corda were numerous and long-lasting. One of the major impacts of this devastation was the change in the relationship between adults and children in the community. The availability and addictiveness of the drug turned large numbers of people into drug addicts_ often referred to as crackheads, crack addicts, or crack zombies who would do anything to get high. Respectable mothers, who at one time helped to raise their neighbor's children, were now having sex with sixteen- and seventeen-year- old guys for drugs. One afternoon, some dealers made the mother of one of Gregory's best friends suck the penis of an old homeless crackhead named Jimmy in front of everybody. Gregory's friend became the target of many joning sessions, and he would fight any and everyone who brought up his shame.

Young drug dealers now became the bread-winner in many of their households, which caused a role reversal. The term hustling took on a new meaning. During the 1960s and 1970s, children used to hustle to make money by working a paper route, cutting grass, shoveling snow, or helping old ladies take their groceries home. Now *hustling* referred to young boys standing on a street corner selling drugs. Dealers would often employ young teenagers as runners and lookouts, since the Rockefeller drug laws mandated harsh penalties for anyone over eighteen in possession of illegal drugs. The kids now earned enough money to pay the rent and buy the groceries. This created a situation where the parents could no longer tell the child what to do. If the child didn't feel like going to school, he didn't. In some cases, the child was encouraged not to go to school so that he could get his rest before going back on the streets to make the money. Some parents even became one of their child's most reliable customers.

Neighborhoods became killing zones as kids jockeyed to control the best corners to sell their drugs. Dealers were forced to arm themselves and their crew with arsenals of weapons in order to protect their turf from rival dealers and neighborhood crews. According to law enforcement sources, the fact that Washington, DC did not have organized street gangs and established territories like in Los Angles was one of the reasons that selling crack caused so much bloodshed. All territory was virgin land to enterprising entrepreneurs, like Rafael Edmonds III, who used extreme violence to establish a hold on the crack market in Washington, DC.

The meaning of life itself became an unintended victim of the crack epidemic. The proliferation of so many weapons caused so many young guys in the neighborhood to rely less and less on their ability to fight and more and more on the use of those weapons. Almost every night, you could hear the sounds of gunfire followed by police sirens, with mothers whaling and dead bodies lying in the middle of the street surrounded by chalk and police tape, all playing out a morbid symphony. Soon this symphony started playing out during the daylight hours, and there seemed to be no escape from the carnage. The carnage itself became a way of life. Growing up in an environment where the vicious addiction and aggressive paranoid behavior that crack produced, resulted in a generation of desensitized children who had the means, the capacity, and willingness to kill another person for the slightest transgression, be it a small debt owed, a stare that lasted too long, or even an inadvertent slip of the tongue, which could be perceived as disrespect. Homicide rates got so out of hand that Washington, DC was given the infamous nickname "the Murder Capital," and every night, a television show was broadcast called *City Under Siege.*

As the police waged a war on drugs, one unintended casualty was the police-community relationship. The police became a militarized force using military tactics, uniforms, and equipment in order to compete with the potent, heavily armed drug dealers and their crews. Tension would sometimes flare up between frustrated citizens who were trapped in their communities by drug dealers who had taken control of the streets and the police department who seemed to be unable to do anything about it. Police officers, in turn, became frustrated with members of the community who refused to tell who was selling drugs or who was responsible for the rising murder rate.

The Metropolitan Police Department shifted directions from the defunded Officer Friendly program to the D.A.R.E. (Drug Abuse Resistance Education) program in an attempt to wage this war on illegal drug use. The primary goal of the D.A.R.E. program was to teach elementary school children effective resistance and refusal skills so they could say no to drugs and to build social skills that would enhance their self-esteem so they would not even think about selling or using drugs. Though the intentions were honorable, studies showed that this program had absolutely no impact on its intended goals. Instead of the program attempting to develop police-community relationships, it became more about getting kids to tell who was selling drugs, which created a wedge between the police and the youth.

The proliferation of drugs in Sursum Corda had a personal effect on Gregory Harris. It saddened him to see that people he grew up with were strung out on that stuff and to watch his community devastated by the effects of crack. The fact that he was a gifted athlete under the watchful eye of his coaches, who were police officers, coupled with his desire not to "dance" with his father, enabled Gregory to escape the grasp of the drug world. The drug dealers usually gave athletes a pass and didn't bother them because they wanted to see them do well. His sister Renee, however, was not so lucky. Renee was extremely intelligent and articulate and loved to read. Gregory would always see her with a book in her hand, and she would often thrill him with the stories of Greek mythology that she loved to read out loud. She had a very vivid imagination and would often try to take on the characteristics of the characters she would read about. She would read a novel about a doctor one week and the next week would volunteer at a hospital as if she were playing out a role. She would read a crime novel and soon thereafter join the police cadet program at her school. Her vivid imagination, unfortunately, caused her to experiment with crack, and she fell into the pitfall of the world of drugs and could not escape. Gregory tried everything he could to help her, but she fell deeper and deeper into the abyss, which soon led her into a world of prostitution, and, ultimately, death. At her funeral, Gregory pledged that he would do whatever he could to stop this from happening to anyone else so that no one else would feel the grief that he was feeling at that moment.

CHAPTER 5

INTO THE STORM

"Honey, what's wrong?" Michelle asked with a very concerned look on her face. "You are turning a little blue in the face, and your leg seems to be twitching a little bit."

"Babe, if you only knew," Steven responded with a far-away look in his eyes. "You see those clouds? You feel that air? You see the leaves on those trees bending in the breeze? I've seen this before, and I don't care to see it again! This reminds me so much of that tornado that hit Topeka back in 1984, or maybe it was 1986. I don't remember the exact date, but I will never forget that day!"

Steven and Michelle had been dating for three years, and even though she thought she knew him pretty well, new tidbits of information came out every so often that surprised her. He didn't talk about himself a lot, and it was difficult to get him to talk about his inner feelings; but today he seemed to be in some kind of deep, reflective mood, so she tried to pry as much as she could out of him. She poured him a glass of wine, sat down close to him and snuggled.

"You were in a tornado," she inquired. "Tell me about it."

"Well, we were living in a trailer park in Topeka, Kansas at the time," he said.

Huh_ a trailer park, she thought. *I thought you grew up on a farm!*

"We lived in a double-wide trailer that was like four hundred square feet. It was really small. It had a living room, two bedrooms, a bathroom and a little kitchen thing. The trailer initially belonged to my aunt on my ma's side. When my ma got pregnant with me, her dad put her out and didn't want to have anything to do with her. So my ma went to live with her aunt. When her aunt died, she left the trailer to my ma. The trailer was so tiny that as soon as you opened the door, you were in the kitchen. It had two small bedrooms and a small area that I guess you could call a living/dining area.

It was me, my ma and dad, and my little brother, who was seven years younger than me living in that tiny little trailer. The news came over the radio that the tornado was quickly approaching, and if you didn't have a basement or a storm shelter, you needed to go to the nearest school. That warning siren kept blasting, and to this day, it sends chills up my spine whenever I hear one go off. I had never seen my dad scared of anything, but on that day, I saw real fear in his eyes, so I knew this was bad, and I started to get scared too. He drove us to the local high school, and we got there just in the nick of time. The thing I remember about the school was that it had so many windows. I remember that because I remember the awful sound of those windows breaking and hitting the floor when the tornado came through.

"We were frantically hustled into the basement. It was so crowded you couldn't even sit down. We were standing shoulder to shoulder. It is funny how you remember very small details when you are scared, but I remember it smelling really funky_ a combination of armpits, body odor, sweat, and bad breath. The noise from the wind sounded like a freight train rumbling right near your ear, and you could hear things crashing into the ground and into each other, sounding like bombs going off. At that moment, I thought we were going to die! Everybody stood there eerily quiet with a frightened look on their faces until this one lady started whimpering and then began screaming, 'We're going to die!' This made everybody a little bit more nervous. Her screams kept getting louder and louder, and soon people started getting really annoyed. I heard someone whisper, 'Would you please just shut the fuck up!' There was this guy holding her and trying to calm her down. I think he was her boyfriend or husband or something. After a while, he just punched her in the face knocking her out cold. She slumped over in his arms, and he just held her tight. I didn't want him to hurt her like that, but I was glad she was not screaming anymore. So was everybody else. When I think back on it, however, I think her silence heightened the fear, because now, instead of listening to her screams, we were listening to the destruction outside that seemed to be getting closer. My stomach was churning a mile a minute, and I remember desperately needing to go to the bathroom, but because there were so many people crammed in there, I couldn't move. I told my dad that I had to go. He just looked at me as though I had done something wrong and told me to hold it. I tried as hard as I could, but before I knew it, I let out this long, loud, smelly fart. I kind of chuckled when I heard this lady, who was standing directly behind me exclaim, 'Oh, my God!' Maybe she was reacting to the sounds of destruction going on outside, but I thought she caught a whiff of my smelly fart.

"When it was over and we got outside, it was crazy. Everything was flat! Entire rows of houses had been swept away, cars had been flung in the air like toys and landed upside down. One car had even been thrown on top of a building. I heard on the news that the tornado ripped through downtown Topeka, damaging many of the buildings, including the Kansas State capitol building. It also tore through the airport, overturning airplanes and emergency trucks. When we got back to our trailer park, our trailer was gone! It was nowhere to be found. My ma started crying, and my dad just stood there looking at the empty spot where our home used to be. Everything we owned, which wasn't much, was in that trailer and now we had nothing. I was eight years old at the time, but I remember it like it was yesterday. We were able to get a few things from the Red Cross and were able to stay in the school's gym for a couple of nights. Then we drove to my granddaddy's farm in Iowa, where we stayed for a while until my dad was able to get on his feet and find a job.

"I actually liked living on my granddaddy's farm. My granddaddy was my hero. He let you know ahead of time what he wanted you to do and then left you on your own to do it. He would always say, 'You know how this is supposed to go. Don't make me have to do it!' There is a lot of stuff to do on a farm, and you don't fart around_ you just do it. I had to get up early in the morning, do my chores, and then go to school. The farmhouse was pretty big, and I shared a room with my brother. It was so much nicer than that little trailer we used to live in.

"We lived on the farm for about three years until we were able find a three-bedroom house with a yard and a basement in Prairie Village, Kansas. My dad had gotten a job driving one of those emergency tow-trucks and saved enough money to purchase his own truck. With some investment money from his father and relatives, he was able to start a small truck-towing business in Prairie Village. My ma got a job teaching in the local elementary school. The neighborhood was great, and there were a lot of kids. When I was young, we used to ride our bikes everywhere. We had a creek at the bottom of the hill. The neighborhood kids would go down there, and everybody would play in the creek. There was a five and dime store up and around the corner, probably a half mile away, so we would ride our bikes up there and get our nickel candy and all that good stuff. We had a hill near the school, and the kids would slide down the hill just on their shoes. I remember one kid wiping out. He fell on his head, knocking himself out. We were always doing cool stuff like playing with model rockets that used to shoot up in the air. During Halloween, we would create a haunted house in somebody's garage. If nothing was going on, we would just hang out together and have a good time. Life outside of our house was pretty cool, but there was a storm raging inside of our house.

"My dad worked very hard to keep his business afloat. His hours were long, and when he came home, he was usually tired and hungry. My ma worked hard as well, and when she came home, she was just as tired. My brother and I had a lot of chores around the house that we had to complete before they got home and before we had to do our homework. When my dad had some free time, we did a lot of great things together, like hunting, fishing, and camping. Those were the good times. More often than not, however, things were bad around the house and it usually happened when he would start drinking. He was a very nice man most of the time, but when he got that liquor in him, he was argumentative and unpleasant to be around. I could always tell when he had been drinking because he would always pick a fight with my ma. It was usually never a physical thing. He would just pick at her about stupid stuff. One night, she got tired of it, and things got a little physical.

"I must have been around eleven years old when it happened. I was lying in bed that night when I heard them arguing. I hated it when they did that. I would lie in bed, cover my ears, and try to drown it out. Even though I loved my dad, I hated him when he would get drunk and start those arguments. This night, he seemed a little more agitated. I heard him shout:

'Where the hell you been, and why ain't my dinner ready?'

'Your dinner is in the oven like it always is. I told Steven to warm it up when you got home,' she replied.

'Well, it wasn't ready! Where the hell have you been?'

'Ernest, I'm tired, and I don't feel like doing this tonight!'

'Doing what? I asked you a simple question.'

'I told you this morning that we had a faculty meeting after school.'

'No damn faculty meeting lasts that long!'

'After the meeting, a few of us went over to Mulligan's for a few drinks to unwind. It was a long day at work. We just wanted to unwind a little.'

'Uh-huh, unwind, I bet. Was Jerry there?'

'Here we go again. Yes, he was there. So where ten other teachers! Why are you so hung up about Jerry? He doesn't mean anything to me. He is just a colleague.'

"The argument went on and on and got louder and louder. I tried to drown it out, but this seemed a little different from all the other shouting matches. I don't know why, but I got out of the bed and walked to the door of their bedroom. Just as I got to the doorway, I heard her say,

'Well, if you paid me a little more attention and we didn't have to go through all of this bickering, maybe I wouldn't have to go out to unwind!'

"Much to my amazement, I saw his hand go up and slap her right in the face. He hit her so hard that blood spurted out of her mouth. She seemed stunned for a brief second and then went into the buzz saw, hitting him as hard as she could with that rapid swinging motion. I was shocked. I had never seen my dad hit my ma, and neither had I seen her so angry. He pushed through her blows, grabbed her around the throat, and started choking the shit out of her. She struggled to free herself without success, so she reached behind her and picked up a clock that was on the dresser. She hit him in the forehead with that clock. Blood went everywhere. It was one of those old-fashioned clocks with the metal knobs on the back. You know, those knobs you used to use to wind the clock up, set the time, and set the alarm? Well those knobs must have stabbed him in the head. When he released her to grab his head, she took off running. He was like a madman! He screamed, 'You bitch,' and started chasing her. As she ran past me, she screamed, 'Call the police!' I went to pick up the phone, and my dad screamed, 'Put that motherfucking phone down and take your little narrow ass to bed!'

"I didn't know what to do, so I ran back to my room. I don't know how she did it, but she ran out of the house and didn't come back for a couple of days. She finally came back, and they tried to make things work, but things where never the same after that night. They eventually got a divorce, and my dad moved out of the house. The one thing that bothered me about that night, and still haunts me today, was that I didn't do anything. I should have called the police like my ma asked me to do, or at least tried to stop him from hitting her. I did nothing. I remember lying in bed that night traumatized by what just happened and vowing, through my tears, to never sit by and do nothing again when someone was in need.

"I kind of miss having my dad around. Even though I didn't like it when he would argue with my ma, he taught me right from wrong, to respect authority, and to always do my best. I guess I loved him. He was an old farm boy and didn't take any foolishness. He used to always get on me about not doing well in school. I wasn't a very good student in school. In fact, I kind of hated school. I couldn't sit still for long periods of time. I guess I had ADHD. I was more of a visual learner. When I had to deal with stuff like algebra, I just couldn't get it. I was able to get geometry, physical education, and art, however, because I could see it. My grades were average, C's and D's, until I got interested in playing football in the ninth grade.

"I have always liked physical activity. A lot of my friends were on the team, so I decided to go out. That first week really crushed me. I was getting hammered every day. I think it was because I didn't know what I was doing. I wasn't a big kid, but I enjoyed the contact. Two or three weeks into it, I started to get the hang of it. One of the starters broke his leg, and the coach put me in at offensive guard. I was only 150 pounds, and I was going against guys who were 260 pounds, which made for some interesting days. Believe it or not, the things I was learning in school, like angles and leverage, started to make more sense to me, and it helped me to be a better football player. I was small, but I was quick, I knew how to stay low, and I paid attention to the details, like technique and footwork. Two weeks later, the coach put me in at defensive tackle, and now I was going both ways. We played a six-man line. At the snap of the ball, we would slant and shoot the gaps. We were so small that when the ball was snapped, we were in the backfield before the offensive linemen had come out of their stance. We were literally taking the handoffs from the quarterbacks or tripping them up as they backed away from the center. I loved it. By the time I graduated, I had earned an athletic scholarship to Prairie Village College in Prairie Village, Kansas."

"Hon, you want some more wine?" Michelle asked as she snuggled even closer to him.

"Sure," he replied.

"I'm curious. What made you decide to become a cop? Where there any police officers in your family? Somehow, you just don't seem like the type."

"Well, that is an interesting story. Believe it or not, I always wanted to go into business for myself. I wanted to own a McDonald's franchise."

"Stop playing! You wanted to sell hamburgers?"

"Yep! In fact, I started working at McDonald's when I was fifteen years old. I worked there in the summer and when football season was over. In high school, I started taking the training program and realized that McDonald's was the gateway to whatever you wanted to be in life. I wanted to be an owner and live the Ray Kroc dream_ the American Dream. I became a manager when I was seventeen and found that I liked it. I liked the business side of it and the people side of it. I bought in to all of that. After I got out of Prairie Village College, where I got a degree in business management, I got into a McDonald's management program. Once I completed that program and the advanced management program, I went to Chicago so I could go to Hamburger University, where I finished my training and got my official degree in hamburger ideology.

"I worked ten years for the company and came this close to getting my own store. After working five years in one location, a new owner bought a store that was in a great location but was losing money, and he asked me to come in and run it. He used to own a bunch of 7-Eleven stores in Overland Park and decided he wanted to give up his 7-Eleven stores and join McDonald's. I don't know how he got my name, but he told me that he didn't know anything about the McDonald's concept and wanted me to help him run it. During my first week, I went into the store and didn't tell anyone who I was. I pretended I was a customer, sat in the store, and watched how the operation was running for an entire week. Stuff was going out the front and back door. Everybody was stealing, and that was one of the reasons the store was losing money. In addition, I didn't like the way they were treating customers. I learned early that you treat people the way you want to be treated. I felt customers were taking their money elsewhere because they were being treated like crap. Who wants to spend their money someplace where they are treated like that? The McDonald's concept is that people come in for the experience. The food is good, but it is not that healthy. When people see those golden arches they know that when they come in, it feels like home regardless of where they are. I told him what I saw and gave him my recommendations for improving the store. He gave me the go ahead to do what was needed to do to turn things around.

"The first thing I did was to fire *everybody*. I told them why they were being fired, and if they wanted to reapply, they could, but they had to tell me why they wanted to work. We put out ads stating that we were hiring and gave people the opportunity to work, but only if they were willing to put the customer first. We made it all about the customers. We started hiring older workers, installed a camera system to observe everything that went on and even started playing soft music in the store. Within a year, that store went from losing $100,000 a month to being the number 1 store in the region. At the point when I left, it was making $1.5 million a year."

"Why did you decide to leave?"

"I was working fourteen- and fifteen-hour days and making only forty-two thousand per year. That was OK at that time because I was young and unmarried. I was going into my tenth year with the company, when things began to change. The owner decided to become more involved in the day-to-day operations of the store and started cutting cost so he could keep more of the profits. He began to hire younger workers, paying them less, and as a result, a lot of them didn't want to work hard. The most important thing, however, was that I realized that working in the private sector provided very little security. I learned that in all things, when you are in the private sector, you are at the whim of the boss. If he came in one day and said, 'You know what, it was great, but I don't need you anymore,' then that was it. You pack up and move on. You could have given the company twenty or thirty years, but at the end of the day, it meant nothing. There was no retirement plan, and no one you could turn to, to say you were being treated unfairly. I knew one day I was going to get married and have kids, and I needed more security than that. I decided that I needed employment that would provide a retirement plan, have a union where I could have some protection and still be able to give back to the community, which was very important to me."

"But why the police? Why would you go from having a safe job where you were assured to come home every night to a job that was dangerous and you could get killed at any moment?"

"There was this police officer that I hired to watch over my store. His name was Jessie Owens. Jessie was a cool guy. He would come in, get something to eat, and read the newspaper. My store was located in a shopping center, and there was a Popeyes store across the street. Jessie would park his car at the Popeyes parking lot and sit in my store. I said to him one day, 'You mean to tell me that you have a full-time job with a pension and a union, and I am paying you twenty-five dollars per hour to sit in my store, and they are also paying you to park your cruiser over there?' He smiled at me and said, 'Yep.' That planted a seed in my brain right then. In addition, I felt that by being a police officer, I could serve and give back to the community that I grew up in.

"Then there was the day we got robbed, and that changed everything!"

CHAPTER 6

TO PROTECT AND SERVE

Curtis Johnson put on a fresh shirt, a pair of baggy jeans, and his new Tims. He was not used to being up this early in the morning, but he was unusually excited. With the money he made last night, added to the money he had given Shanita to keep in a safe place, he finally had enough to get that Jeep he had his eye on. He was on his own. Making his own money and getting his first car added to the list of things he felt made him a man even though he was only sixteen. Driving around in a brand-new Jeep Cherokee would also make him even more visible. Now, people in the hood would see that he was moving up in the world.

As he walked down the street, he saw a jet-black Escalade with gold trimmings, matching gold rims, and tinted windows coming down the street. It was a sweet-looking ride, but it was moving too slow. This caused Curtis to become suspicious. He put his hand in the small of his back where he kept his gun just in case. The car came to a stop directly next to him. When the window rolled down, a huge smile broke out across Curtis's face when he saw his old friend and teammate Patrick Jenkins in the car with two guys he didn't know.

"What up, Curtis," Patrick said.

"Nuttin'," Curtis replied, still smiling.

"Where you headin'?"

"Going to see my lady. I'm fixin' to get me a ride today."

"You still messin' with Alfred's sister? What's her name?"

"Shanita."

"That's right, Shanita Brown. She's a cute one. I bet you ain't fucked her yet!"

"Stop playing. What you been up to? You still ballin'?"

"Nah, I let that shit go just like you did. Hop in. We'll give you a ride."

"That's OK. She just lives a few blocks from here. I'm good."

Before Curtis knew what was happening, two of the guys jumped out of the car with their guns drawn and aimed at his head.

"Get your punk ass in the car," one of them barked.

They grabbed Curtis, took his gun, the wad of money in his pocket and his wallet, and then pushed him in the back seat next to his good friend Patrick.

"What the fuck, Patrick! What's this about?"

"You know what this is, nigga. We gonna ransom yo ass. I hope you got someone who is willing to give up the cash. If not, then, oh well."

"Man, don't do this shit to me. I thought you was my boy! Count the money your boys just took from me. You just got eleven grand. Let me go!"

"Fuck that! I know you can get more. You working for that nigga Alfred, right? I know you got way more than this."

"Let me make a call."

"Call whoever the fuck you got to call, but we want one hundred thousand dollars, and if you don't get the money, you're one dead motherfucker."

As the car sped off down Suitland Parkway into Maryland, Curtis could not hear anything except the pounding of his heart that was trying to break out of his chest. He hadn't been in the game that long, but he had seen his share of violence. Images of dead bodies lying in the middle of the street were all he could think about. He could not believe this was happening to him. He had a gun, but it was for protection. He had not killed anybody. It took all the strength he could muster to keep from pissing or shitting on himself. His only hope now was to get Shanita to bring him the money he was going to use for his new ride and hope that would be enough.

They hustled him into an apartment, flung him down on the couch, and told him to make his call. He dialed Shanita's number and prayed she would pick up quickly. The phone rang and rang. While it was ringing, he had a disastrous thought.

What if Shanita brings over the money and they kill us both?

While the phone was ringing, one of the guys went into the bedroom and came back with a pillow. Curtis looked the guy in the eye and knew something bad was about to happen. Pee started trickling down his leg. Finally, Shanita's younger sister picked up.

"Hello, who dis," she asked.

"This is Curtis. Put Shanita on the phone."

"She ain't here."

"What do you mean she ain't there? Where she at?"

"She took off on her bike a few minutes ago like she was in a hurry."

"Where the hell did she go?"

"Man, I don't know. When she gets on that bike, who knows where she goes. She usually don't come back for hours. I'll tell her you called."

Curtis looked as though all of the blood had drained from his face as he hung up the phone. He desperately tried to think of someone else he could call to get the money. Before he could say a word, one of the guys hit him in the head with the butt of the gun, knocking him to the floor. Then the guy reached down, put the pillow over Curtis's face and shot him in the head several times.

"Damn, man. Why the hell you do that," Patrick shouted. "He could've got the money from somebody else."

"Who you think he was going to call next? He was going to call that nigga Alfred. I'm not tryin' to mess with that muthafucka right now. He got too much muscle. This way, he won't know who did his boy. We got eleven large from this bamma. We can snatch somebody else. Now, clean this shit up, and let's get the fuck outta here."

*   *   *

Shanita was scared to death. She didn't know who took the money out of the safe. More importantly, she didn't know how to tell Curtis the money was gone. He had trusted her with everything. She had not touched a penny of that money even though Curtis had told her she could use whatever she needed. She wasn't sure how he would react, or what he would do now that all of the money was gone. She also didn't know what he would do when she told him she was carrying his baby. To make matters worse, if that was possible, she just got the news that she had received a full scholarship to North Carolina Central University and now was wondering if she had to give that up because she was pregnant. And what was her mom and dad going to say when they found out she was pregnant? She knew her dad would be extremely disappointed, but her mom would be furious. All of these thoughts rushed through her head. She knew Curtis was on his way and would be here soon. Fear quickly turned into panic. She needed time to think. She instinctively kept riding.

She pedaled as fast as she could, not going anywhere in particular. She rode for what seemed like hours, but it did little to clear her head or ease her confusion. As she rode down Alabama Avenue and crossed over Suitland Parkway, the voices in her head kept getting louder and louder:

Curtis: *I'm on my way over to get the money so I can finally get that Jeep. I want you to go with me. I want us to do this together.*

Gwen: *No, you're pregnant! The directions say a line could be faded, but you can see two lines. What you gonna tell Ma?*

Ma: *These boys want only one thing. Don't bring no babies up in this house!*

As she continued to ride, the tears in her eyes began to swell up to the point that it became difficult to see where she was going. She stopped in front of Turner Elementary School, got off her bike, and sat on the school steps. What was a small trickle of tears soon became an avalanche, releasing all of her emotional turmoil. She put her head in her hands and wept. A police car slowly pulled up to the school and stopped. Officer Gregory Harris got out of his cruiser and slowly approached Shanita. She looked very familiar to him, but he couldn't put his finger on where he had seen her before.

"Young lady, are you OK? What seems to be the problem?"

*   *   *

When he was young, Gregory Harris and his father would sit in the living room and watch police television shows like *Adam-12*, *Starsky & Hutch*, and his favorite show, *SWAT*; but never in his imagination did he think he would become a police officer. No one in his neighborhood ever thought about becoming a cop. He had always believed that he would either play in the NFL or become a professional boxer. His small stature and lack of speed minimized his chances of becoming a professional football player, while boxing, though he was good at it, became an arduous task with all the time needed for training. He decided to go to college and major in business management and accounting. When he returned home, he found that it seemed like everybody had the same idea and the same degree, and as a result, he had difficulty finding a job in accounting or marketing. Needing a source of income, he applied for jobs at the US Post Office, the DC public school system, and the Metropolitan Police Department. He took the test for each and decided that whichever called him first would be the job he would accept. The police department was the first to respond, and so he joined the force.

Much to his surprise, Gregory got a great deal of satisfaction from becoming a police officer. He had always had a protective nature while growing up in his neighborhood. He was the type of guy who would go out into the street to stop traffic so the old folks could get across. He also felt guilty that he was not able to protect his sister from the evils of drugs. His sense of duty to his community initially came from his mother, who used to tell him all the time, "Baby, you just can't sit on a fence and watch life go by! You have to get involved. You've got to help people." In addition, when he was in college, he would attend the meetings of the Black Student Union, and it was drummed into his head that he had to go back to his community and pull other brothers and sisters out of the depths of "degradation and despair." He had thought that his way of giving back to the community was to set up his own businesses and give people in his neighborhood job opportunities, but that idea never came to fruition. Now he was a cop. He fondly remembered the Officer Friendly program and the officers who kept him out of trouble when he was young. But he also remembered the cops who harassed him and his friends just for hanging out on the corner. He decided that he would be one of the good cops who would help people rather than harass them for no reason.

Getting through the physical endurance training in the police academy was a breeze for him. The limit of push-ups, sit-ups, and crunches were a joke as far as he was concerned. All he had to do was twenty-five sit-ups, twenty-five push-ups, thirty-five jumping jacks, and run a mile. His workouts in football and boxing were much more rigorous than what the academy required. The classroom training was a little more challenging because he was unfamiliar with the law. He didn't know much about the justification for stop and frisk, search and seizure, or due process. He knew the police used to stop him and his friends all the time, but he never understood why. He thought that the police was just messing with them. He was intrigued by these subjects, and having just come out of college, he knew how to study and how to prepare for exams. The subjects covering human relations and community policing seemed to resonate with him, especially the part about protecting and serving the community. He quickly became one of the stars of the academy and graduated with honors. Everything he learned in the academy was put to the test on his very first day on the job.

On his first day on the street, Officer Harris was riding in a patrol car with his training partner, a police sergeant who ultimately was killed while on duty a few years later. They were cruising down Savannah Street, SE, in the Seventh District. Officer Harris had heard stories about how hard it was living in Southeast, or "across the bridge," as people in Northwest used to say about that part of town, but he had never been anywhere near there before. Suddenly, a guy jumps out of a car and starts running. Sergeant Jones had heard stories about how this Officer Harris was supposedly some young academy superstar who was going to be the next super cop, and so the sergeant yelled, "Go get him, rookie!"

Officer Harris jumped out of the cruiser and started chasing the young suspect who was in a full sprint, running through people's yards, and jumping over hedge bushes. After a short pursuit, Officer Harris caught up to the suspect, tackled him to the ground, cuffed him, and tells him not to move. Reality suddenly hit Officer Harris because not only didn't he know how to properly work the radio, he didn't even know where he was so he could tell his backup where to come. Soon a large crowd of people began to gather around him and started asking him why he had stopped the young boy. As he began frantically looking around for a street sign or some landmark he could use to identify where he was, Officer Harris began thinking, *What in the world have I gotten myself into?* He observed the street signs and realized the nearest intersection was Eleventh Place and Congress Street, SE. As the inquiring crowd got closer, Officer Harris picked the suspect off of the ground, picked out who he thought was the toughest person in the crowd, and loudly responded,

"This young brother stole a car and was driving recklessly in your neighborhood. He almost hit a young child before jumping out of the car in order to escape. It might have even been your car he stole. Who knows? I got to get him off the street before he hurts someone. I really don't want to put another young brother in jail, but when you do the crime, you got to do the time. Now, please give me some room so I can do my thing."

Satisfied with Officer Harris's response, the crowd slowly began to dissipate as they saw a police car quickly approaching. Sergeant Jones had parked his car in a nearby alley and was watching the whole incident. When Jones finally decided to approach, he walked over to Officer Harris and said, "Not bad, rookie," before helping him get the suspect in the back of the police car.

Officer Harris was later given a foot-patrol beat in Congress Park, the same area where he stopped the car theft. He made it his mission to do everything he could to establish positive relationships with the people in the community who look at the police with a bit of suspicion. He believed that if you treated people with respect and you were consistent with the way you did things and with the message you were giving them, they would understand why you were there. There were times, however, when he had to put his hands on people.

One incident occurred while Officer Harris was walking his beat on Fourteenth Place SE. One of the street activities that the guys participated in was called "wreck-yard." The guys would form a huge circle in the middle of the street, two combatants would put on a pair of boxing gloves, enter the makeshift ring, and slug it out. Juju, the boisterous neighborhood bully, was the reigning champion, who reveled in knocking people out. Juju saw Officer Harris and challenged him to enter the ring.

"Hey, Officer Harris," Juju shouted. "The police don't know how to fight. All they know how to do is shoot people or jump people. Why don't you take off that gun and put these gloves on so I can whip your ass?"

"Dude, I grew up just like you," Officer Harris replied. "You really don't want to see me."

"Yeah, whatever! I hear you talking, but I don't think you want to put on these gloves."

The crowd of young men began laughing. Every eye turned to Officer Harris to see what he was going to do. Officer Harris knew this was a challenge he could not pass up, especially if he expected to get any respect in the neighborhood. He knew that street credibility was just as important as his weapon; and without it, his job would be almost impossible. He also knew that sometimes he had to hurt some people in order to protect others. All the crowd saw was a five-foot-eight young guy trying to "play" cop. What the crowd didn't know was that Officer Harris was the reigning police academy boxing champ and had won the junior amateur Golden Gloves Boxing Championship when he was young.

A large crowd began to gather around in anticipation of the spectacle. Officer Harris called his partner on the radio. He told his partner to come and get his gun, badge, and equipment and then come back in fifteen minutes. Officer Harris took off his shirt, put on the gloves, and entered the makeshift ring with the loud-mouth challenger. The combatants cautiously circled each other when, suddenly, Juju launched an attack, swinging wildly. Officer Harris saw the amateurish attack long before it happened, easily sidestepped it, and delivered two sharp punches to the Juju's face. The crowd roared in approval with each devastating blow. Officer Harris then delivered a series of well-placed punches that Juju did not see coming, nor could he defend against them. Juju was knocked to the ground face-first and landed awkwardly with his butt sticking straight up in the air. The crowd erupted in laughter. Several of Juju's friends picked him up off the ground and pushed him back into the makeshift ring. Juju didn't seem to be in too much of a hurry to continue the contest. Officer Harris decided to end this exhibition by delivering one precisely placed, lightning-fast, three-punch combination that sent Juju to the ground again with snot and a trickle of blood coming out of his nose. The beaten challenger lay there flat on his back for a couple of seconds before regaining his senses. The confrontation was over. Everybody continued laughing at Juju and started patting Officer Harris on the back. Officer Harris took off his gloves, helped Juju up, and gave him some dap, a familiar form of respect.

After the fifteen minutes agreed upon, Officer Harris's partner pulled his cruiser up to the crowd and returned Officer Harris's gun and equipment to him. Officer Harris put on his gun belt and police stick, buttoned up his shirt, and, with a sinister smile on his face, continued walking his beat. He never had a problem from anyone in the neighborhood again.

*   *   *

Shanita tried pulling herself together so she could respond to Officer Harris, but it took her a few minutes. She didn't want to tell him the real reason she was crying so she just told him that she just found out she was pregnant and didn't know how to tell her mother or her boyfriend.

She didn't like nor did she trust the police.

"Sweetheart, are you going to be OK," Officer Harris asked again.

"Yes, I'll be all right," Shanita responded. "I'm just a little upset right now."

"Would you like me to give you a lift home?"

"No disrespect, Officer, but I just want to be left alone. In fact, I'm just about to leave. Thank you for your concern, but please get out of my face and leave me the fuck alone."

"Young lady, I'm just trying to help you out. Why are you being so nasty?"

"Because I don't like the police."

Officer Harris kept having this feeling that he had seen this girl somewhere before, and he couldn't shake that feeling.

"What did I ever do to you?"

Shanita thought about how she would respond for a couple of seconds and then started to explain her feelings about the police. Her disdain for the police resulted from their relentless pursuit of her brother Alfred, as well as an incident that took place a couple of months ago. She knew her brother was dealing drugs and knew one day either the police or the "game" would catch up to him, but what the police did was not only illegal, but just plain wrong. One day a young guy in the neighborhood had gotten killed, and everybody was outside to see what was going on. When the police started investigating the scene, they saw Alfred and immediately grabbed him, threw him up against the car, and started rummaging through his pockets. When the police didn't find anything, they released him and said, "You see that body over there? Well, we are going to do the same thing to you if somebody doesn't beat us to it!" They didn't seem to care who heard them either. Her mom and sisters were out there and heard the threat. Her mom screamed, "That's my son! You're going to get him for what?" One of the officers responded, "We didn't know you were out here, but that's OK because we are going to get him another day. And you know exactly why."

A couple of weeks later, Shanita's parents were working late. Alfred had left the house, so that only left Shanita, her sisters, and her younger brother. She heard a loud knock at the front door, so she and her sister rushed downstairs to see what was going on. Suddenly, there was a big boom, and the door came crashing down. The commotion scared the life out of everyone, and they started running back upstairs. As she started running, one of the intruders grabbed Shanita by the foot and tried to restrain her. Not knowing who the intruders were, she kicked the person who grabbed her foot, enabling her to briefly get away and continue running up the stairs.

That is when she heard the man shout, "Police, stop, or I will blow your ass away!"

She stopped dead in her tracks and threw her hands up in the air. Suddenly, she realized that the police were in their jump-out gear. They had on helmets, bullet-proof vests with POLICE inscribed across the chest in big bold letters, masks, and had the largest guns Shanita had ever seen. All Shanita and her sisters had on were panties and a T-shirt because they were just getting ready to go to bed. Not only would the officers not let them get dressed, they started taking pictures of the girls while still in their panties and T-shirts.

Shanita didn't quite understand why they did that, and she and her sisters started complaining. One of the officers actually went through Shanita's photo album and took pictures of her in her swimsuit. When one officer tried to take a picture of Shanita's younger sister, Shanita ran over and knocked the camera out of his hands. Another officer came up from behind Shanita and grabbed her around her breasts, pushing her to the floor, threatening to arrest her if she didn't shut up. While he was "restraining" her, he seemed to spend extra time fondling her butt and breasts as if he was searching for a weapon, but Shanita knew exactly what he was really doing. The girls stood in their bedroom half-naked while the officers ransacked the house searching for drugs, weapons, and anything that might be illegal. They didn't even present a scarch warrant. She found out much later that the pictures of her and her sisters were being passed around the police station like it was a big joke, and that even some of them were posted on the walls for all to see.

Oh, so that is where I had seen her, Officer Harris thought. *I knew I had seen that pretty face and body someplace before!*

"I understand why you feel the way you do," Officer Harris said, "but not all cops are like that. Just because I put on this uniform doesn't mean that I act like everybody else who wears the uniform. You have some good cops and bad cops, but the majority of us aren't like that. I just hope you go home and have an honest conversation with your parents about your situation and hope things work out for you. If you need help with anything, here is my card. You can give me a call anytime."

Officer Harris gave Shanita his card, got back in his cruiser, and took off. Shanita realized that the conversation with Officer Harris did help her to calm down and come to grips with her situation. Maybe it was the anger that was swelling up in her chest when she thought about the police coming into her home and disrespecting her and her sisters, or maybe it was just the conversation alone that made her think about something else. At any rate, she knew she had to go back home and face the music. She still didn't know what she was going to say to Curtis. The first thing she had to find out was who took the money. She got on her bike and started her journey home.

Officer Harris decided go see one of his old friends. He drove to the Sixth District Police Station and went to the second floor_ and there it was. A semi-nude picture of the girl he just finished talking to surrounded by pictures of her in her swimsuit were plastered all over the wall of his friend's office.

"What up Rick?" Officer Harris asked.

"Nuttin'," Rick replied. "What you doing around here?"

"Who's that chick you got up on the wall?"

"You know Alfred Brown, right?"

"You mean the drug dealer?"

"Yep, that's his little sister. She's fine, ain't she? We're gonna get that motherfucker, and then I'm gonna fuck his little sister!"

"Boy, you crazy!"

"I might be crazy, but I'm gonna get them both. Why you want to know?"

"No reason. I was just admiring the view."

* * *

Shanita finally got home and gingerly walked her bike up to the house, expecting Curtis to be there waiting for her. She knew he was going to be pissed because she wasn't there when he got there, and she also knew he was going to hit the ceiling when he found out she didn't have his money. She wasn't sure what he would do, however. He had never raised his voice at her, much less gotten violent with her, but she just didn't know what to expect. Her mind was racing trying to figure out who could have taken the money. The money was in the safe that her brother gave her. The only ones who knew the combination were her, her mother, and Alfred. Alfred was currently in jail, so he couldn't have done it. In addition, he had so much of his own money that the money in the safe was like pennies to him. That left her mom.

When Shanita got into the house she was shocked to find that Curtis wasn't there waiting for her. She asked everyone in the house if they had seen or heard from him. Her younger sister said that he had called a couple of hours ago, but no one had seen him. Shanita called his cell and home number several times. No answer. *He probably went on to the dealership to get his new ride,* Shanita thought. She was kind of relieved that he wasn't there. This would give her time to find out what happened to the money. She spent the rest of the day in her room trying to figure out her next move. She heard the door slam and knew her mom had just gotten home from work. Shanita immediately ran downstairs and confronted her about the stolen money.

"Ma, did you take that money out of my safe?"

"Well, good afternoon to you too," her mom replied. "Now, is that any way to greet your mother? I been working all day, and I don't need you or anybody else barking at me when I first get through the door!"

"But Ma, this is really important. Do you know what happened to the money in the safe?"

"Yes, I know, and yes, I took it."

"That money didn't belong to me, and I need to get it back ...today!"

"Who do you think you are talking to, young lady? Any money that comes into this house belongs to this house, and I can use it as I see fit. I needed that money to post bail for your brother so he can get out of jail. I also need to start paying for his lawyer. You know those cops planted those drugs on him. I'm not having my baby stay in that place another night! Who did the money belong to anyway, and why was it being kept here?"

"That was Curtis's money. He is on his way over right now to get it!"

"What was Curtis doing with that kind of money anyway, and why in the world was he keeping it over here?"

Shanita didn't respond to her mom's last question. Her head was spinning. Regardless of who took it, the money was gone. Now she had to figure out what to tell Curtis. She turned and started walking away.

"Shanita, I asked you a question! Don't you walk away from me!"

Shanita stopped dead in her tracks and took a deep breath before responding. She turned toward her mom but couldn't look her in the face. With her head tilted downward, Shanita whispered,

"He had been saving it up because he needed the money to help raise our baby."

Shanita knew that was a lie, but she didn't want to tell her mother that he was a drug dealer on top of everything else.

"*Baby*, what do you mean baby ... Lord Jesus!"

"Ma, I'm pregnant."

The look on Shanita's mom's face turned from indignation to one of rage. Before she knew what she was doing, she smacked Shanita in the face. The smack was so loud it sounded like fireworks going off on the Fourth of July, which caused Shanita's sister to come running to see what was going on.

"Get out! What do you mean you are pregnant? What are you going to do? What did I tell you about bringing babies up in this house? Get the fuck out of my house!"

Shanita walked out of the house not knowing what she was going to do or where she was going to go. She thought she had cried out all the tears she had in her earlier that day; but when she got outside, the tears began to flow uncontrollably again. Gwen came out to comfort her and suggested that she spend the night at her god-mother's house. Gwen told her that when she got pregnant, Ma threw her out of the house too, but later let her return after she calmed down. Gwen walked her sister down to Jessica's house and told Jessica what happened. Jessica was a little disappointed in the fact that Shanita had gotten herself into this mess, mainly because Shanita was the smart one and everybody expected her to go to college and make something of herself. She didn't burden Shanita with her thoughts.

She just gave her a big bear hug and told her to try and lie down, and that they would talk about it in the morning. Shanita walked to the guest room and tried to get some sleep. It had been a very trying day. Before she got in bed, however, she tried calling Curtis again, but to no avail. She wondered why he would not return her call. She desperately needed to talk with him.

The next morning, Shanita got a phone call from her father. He asked her to come down to the fire house so they could talk. When she got to the firehouse, she could see the disappointment in her fathers' eyes.

"Hey, baby girl, how you doin'?"

"I'm OK. Daddy, before you say anything, I know you are disappointed in me, and I am so sorry. Please don't be mad at me! I don't think I can take it if you were mad at me too. Not right now."

"I would be lying if I said I wasn't disappointed right now, but you are still my baby girl, and I will always love you. I assume Curtis is the father. Are y'all getting married? What about college? Where are you going to live? I just want to know what your plans are."

"I really haven't had the time to give it much thought. Ma is mad at me right now, and Curtis hasn't returned my phone calls. He and I were supposed to be going together to buy a car yesterday, but he never showed up. He doesn't even know that he is going to be a daddy. I guess I will have to put college off until after I have my baby. Everybody is excited about me having a baby and said they will help me so I wouldn't have to do this by myself … everybody except Ma, of course. I hope you are happy for me too."

"Baby girl, you just don't get it. Let me give it to you straight. Everybody who said they were going to help you out, a year or two down the road, they are going to be nowhere to be found. And don't expect any help from Curtis either. You are going to be raising this child all by yourself. You can just forget about college! Now you've got to find a job, work forty hours a week, come home tired to a crying baby, find a babysitter, and you won't be able to go out or do the things you like anymore. You are going to have to worry about getting life insurance, health insurance, taking her to doctor's appointments, and picking out schools. You are literally going to be raising another life. Your life will no longer be yours! If you have this baby, you have got to have the mind-set of a single parent."

If, Shanita thought. She had not even considered getting an abortion. She was scared when she first found out she was pregnant, but the thought of having Curtis's baby and sharing the love with him grew on her to the point that she became excited about her pregnancy. After listening to her dad, however, the idea of getting an abortion began creeping into her thoughts. No one had broken it down to her like that. Her father's words gave her a different perspective. Deep down, she didn't want to get an abortion. She didn't believe in it, but her dad had scared her, so she began seriously thinking about it.

"Daddy, do you think I should get an abortion?"

There was a long pause. Her dad moved closer to her; the expression in his eyes had softened, and his voice had grown quiet, almost inaudible.

"Baby girl, I can't tell you what to do. On the one hand, the child doesn't need to suffer because of the circumstances of the parents. Even though circumstances right now aren't good, circumstances change. Ultimately, the right thing to do is not always the best thing to do. You just have to make the best decision and do what's in your heart. Whatever your heart tells you to do, just do it."

Shanita's dad gave her a long, warm hug. She needed that more than anything at that moment. The ringing of her cell phone interrupted the moment. It was her godmother, Jessica.

"Shanita, your mother just called. She wants you to come home right now."

That message surprised Shanita a little. Her mom had just thrown her out of the house, and now she wanted her to come home. She had hoped that her mom would come around and welcome her back in the house, just like Gwen said she would, but she never thought it would be this quick. She asked her dad if he had anything to do with her mom's change of heart. He said no. Shanita gave her dad a kiss good-bye, thanked him for his brutally honest advice, and started home. On the way, her thoughts were running wild. Would getting an abortion be the best move for her at this moment in her life? What would Curtis have to say about that? Would Curtis even want to marry her or drop out of sight like her dad suggested? What would Curtis say when he found out the money was gone? Would he leave her? What about college? When she walked in the door, she felt something was wrong.

Everyone seemed to be in a somber mood, but nobody said why. They were all huddled around the television watching the news. She meekly said hi to her mom and asked if they could talk. Her mom did not respond. Everyone's eyes were fixed on the television screen. Gwen walked over, took Shanita by the arm, sat her down on the couch, and turned up the sound. A reporter was standing near the Fourteenth Street Bridge, giving his report.

"This is the spot where the body was fished out of the Potomac River yesterday. The body was so bloated and the face riddled with bullets holes that it was hard to make a positive identification. Authorities have since identified the body as that of local high school basketball star Curtis Johnson."

*　　*　　*

Officer Harris got home and put his TV-dinner in the microwave. He got a cold beer out of the refrigerator, sat down, and turned on the TV. He had gotten used to coming home to an empty house, and every day after work he followed the same routine. His wife, whom he loved dearly, had left him two years ago, saying that he loved the job more than he loved her, and she couldn't take it anymore. She was tired of him being gone most of the time, him not being able to talk about anything else except who got shot or who got arrested, his quick temper, and his excessive drinking. The last thing she said to him before she walked out of the door was that she couldn't compete with his job. He wanted to beg her not to leave, but instead he simply said, "It is what it is."

CHAPTER 7

THE REUNION

When Steven Sullivan got to work, his early-shift employees were standing at the door giving him the evil eye. In unison, they all shouted, "If you are five minutes early, you are already late," which was the saying he would preach to them almost every day. He really liked the group he was working with. He had fired all the workers he thought were lazy and finally got the group of people he could mold into a workforce he thought could turn the McDonald's franchise into a profitable one. He had hoped that one day he would own his own franchise, but for the time being, he was content with being the store manager. It was customary for him to get to work long before everyone else so he would have time to open up, get the place ready for his workers and still have enough time to sit down, have a cup of coffee, read his newspaper, and get himself ready for another hectic, but profitable day. Today, however, he was a little late. With sleep caked on the side of one eye and his breath still smelling like Wild Irish Rose, he responded to his workers with a cynical, "Yeah, yeah, yeah."

He had spent the previous day with Emily Laskey, which had ended with a long session of sex that kept him up until the wee hours of the morning. Emily was a nice girl who he liked being around, but he wasn't feeling her the way she obviously felt about him. They had been good friends since high school, so it didn't faze him when she invited him up to her apartment for a night cap. They had just gone to the movies and had a bite to eat at a local restaurant_ not a real date, just two friends hanging out. She put on a pot of coffee and then slid into her bedroom to change into a revealing one-piece dress that accentuated her small, but firm rear end. After serving him a cup of coffee, she sat down close to him as she engaged in small talk and a light review of the movie they had just seen. The closeness of her body, along with her enticing fragrance, began to cause his manhood to rise and his thoughts to drift from the mundane conversation. He clearly understood what was going on, and even though they were "just friends," he decided that there was no harm if they enjoyed each other physically. He would find out much later that, in fact, it caused irreparable harm to their friendship. Their eyes met, the conversation stopped, and the next thing he knew, their lips were locked, and they were passionately fondling each other. She abruptly got up, grabbed his hand, and led him into the bedroom, which was engulfed in scented candle light. When he entered her, she gasped loudly, and her body shuttered uncontrollably in reaction to the rhythmic ebb and flow of their intimate dance. He was quite surprised at quiet little Emily. He had never thought of her sexually, so her unbridled passion was a little unexpected. When it was over, he was ready to leave so he could get a little bit of sleep before he had to go to work. She desperately wanted to cuddle, and it was apparent when she grabbed his manhood that she was not through with him yet. He thought, *What the heck.* So when she began to aggressively fondle him again, he decided to stay for another round.

Before sleep finally grabbed him, his thoughts drifted to his college days and ultimately to the girl he thought had gotten away_ Michelle Johnson. Earlier that day, he started opening the pile of mail that had been sitting on his desk for days. He reluctantly opened a letter from his college, which he assumed was another request for money. Contrary to his thoughts, it was a letter requesting his presence at the alumni reunion. His initial reaction was hesitancy. He did not want to go back and face his college buddies, who were probably successful doctors, lawyers, educators, professional athletes, or business owners while he was a hamburger salesman. He had second thoughts when he saw another letter, which was from Michelle asking him if he was going to be on campus for the reunion. Even though she was two years behind him, it appeared that she was going to be on campus to participate in a panel discussion on racial diversity and was eager to see him. He wondered how she got his address.

That letter came as a pleasant surprise. As he read it, he couldn't help smiling from ear to ear. It stimulated his journey down memory lane about his college experiences. He reminisced about his professors; the pressure of hour-exams and writing papers; the constant workload, the long, hungry nights; the football games; the wild parties; and the environment where having uncommitted sex was the rule rather than the exception. He fondly remembered his many conversations with Michelle and how he desperately wanted the relationship to go farther than it had. He vividly remembered his last conversation with her. She had just broken up with her boyfriend, and in his attempt to get closer, he invited her up to his room. She gave him an enticing smile as she declined his offer, stating that because of his reputation with the ladies, she knew that if she had gone up to his room, it would end up with them having sex, and she wasn't into casual sex. He laughed, grabbed her hand, looked into her eyes, and told her that no matter how long it took, even if they were old and gray, one day they were going to get together and make love. She smiled, turned around, and simply walked away.

Michelle Johnson was a tall, dark-skinned black girl with breasts that jutted out like a mountain range, a very ample behind, piercing eyes that seemed as though she was looking right through you when she spoke, and an ever-present infectious smile that made you want to be around her all the time. She always wore her hair in a short, neatly cropped afro and walked around campus like she was the queen of the Nile.

Michelle was an enigma to Steven. She was intelligent and independent, a serious, outspoken, and passionate feminist, fiercely proud of her African American heritage on the one hand, but free spirited and goofy on the other. She would often find humor in the smallest, wondrous, unsuspecting, and mundane things. Michelle was also an outstanding artist who could take one look at a person and then draw a flawless portrait hours later, as well as an outstanding soccer player who didn't mind getting dirty and sweaty while mixing it up with her opponents. She was very sexy and feminine on the one hand, but had a tough grittiness that made you think twice about making her angry. She was born and raised in a section of north Philadelphia known as Glenwood, a residential area that is considered part of the infamous Philadelphia Badlands. The neighborhood, which has one of the highest crime rates in the city, has a lot of row houses, which have been neglected, with windows boarded up, porches that had caved in, and surrounding grounds covered with trash. It is very much a wasteland, over run by drug dealers and stray cats.

Michelle had gotten numerous scholarship offers to attend prestigious schools in Philadelphia, as well as historically black schools in the South, and yet here she was, attending a small, predominantly white school in the rural Midwest. Her rationale for attending Prairie Village was she wanted to experience something different. She wanted to get as far away from Philadelphia as she could.

Steven happened to meet Michelle when he stopped by her room to visit a girl he was pursuing. The school used to put the pictures of all of the incoming freshmen in a book that the football players used to refer to as the "fresh meat book." The players, who were on campus early for football practice, would get a hold of the fresh meat book, sit around and point out which freshman girl they were going to "get." Once a girl was claimed, that player had two uninterrupted weeks to pursue her. If he was unsuccessful in that amount of time, she was fair game for anyone to pursue. There was always an argument over who would get first crack at the really pretty girls and even though, according to the "code," the person who selected one was supposed to have uninterrupted time to pursue her, other guys would sneak around and make attempts to talk to the same girl. Steven wasn't as experienced at chasing girls when he first got to Prairie Village. In fact, he was a virgin until the summer of his freshman year. While others argued over the hot girls, he would select the girl who was the least likely to be wanted by anyone else. The plain girls were usually shy, lonely, and less likely to resist his advances. When scanning the book, he claimed Becky Crawford, and, of course, no one opposed his choice.

When the freshmen arrived on campus, it was like a herd of wildebeests trying to safely cross an alligator-infested river. In an unwitting game of the birds and the bees, the freshman girls had no idea that they had already been inspected and parceled out to the one with the strongest rap or the smoothest approach. The football players stood eyeing their prey, ready to pounce at a moment's notice. Steven found Becky and offered her and her parents his assistance in getting her luggage up to her room. He told her if there was anything she needed, she could always depend on him. He also told her that he would be more than willing to take her around so she could see the campus. Little did she know, he had a huge sign placed over the bed in his room that read, "DA CAMPUS."

A week later, Becky invited Steven to come over to her room so they could talk after she got out of class. When Steven knocked on her door, however, it was Michelle who answered. Becky had not returned from class, so Michelle told Steven he could come in and wait for her. After sitting down, Steven and Michelle started a long, friendly conversation that seemed to last forever. He had never talked to any black girls before. In fact, he didn't know very many black people at all. There was only one black kid in his high school, and there were only three black players on the football team. Michelle was easy to talk to, wasn't bad to look at, and had a refreshing laugh that forced him to laugh along. When Becky finally arrived, he couldn't help feeling disappointed that his and Michelle's conversation had come to an end. He wanted to know more about her.

Steven did not get the opportunity to sit down and talk to Michelle again until the second semester when he saw her studying in the library. He had seen her in passing, but all they shared was a friendly smile and a cordial hello. Going to the library wasn't his favorite thing to do, but he had a paper to write for his sociology class, so he had no choice. He grabbed a seat at the table where Michelle was working. She flashed that beautiful, contagious smile, gave him a warm hello, and continued doing her work. He felt a warm, tingling sensation as he sat down and started his work. After a few minutes of "hard" research, he struck up a conversation. He asked her how she had been doing, and she asked why he hadn't been around to see Becky anymore.

"Becky and I are friends, but she really isn't my type," he responded.

"Oh yeah, what is your type?"

"I like strong girls who have a sense of humor and who like sports."

"Oh, really! I bet you like any girl who will drop her panties at your beckon call."

"Why would you say something like that?"

"I know how all you football players are."

"Now my sociology professor would call that a stereotype. Not all football players are the same. You should know better than that."

"Well, that's not what I heard, but I feel you."

The librarian stealthily walked past them and told them they had to lower their voices. Michelle started gathering up her books and prepared to leave.

"Why are you leaving?" Steven asked.

"I'm about done here for today. I'm gonna get some lunch before I have to go to soccer practice."

"You mind if we have lunch together?"

"Wait a minute. Are you tryin' to holla at me?"

"Would that be such a bad thing?"

"I've never hung out with a white boy before."

"Well, maybe you should give it a try. You just might like it."

"I might, but I've already been around the campus, and I have no intention of seeing "DA CAMPUS," if you know what I mean."

"Ha, ha, ha! So, I guess you heard about that?"

"Oh yeah, Becky told me all about it."

"I really would like to get to know you a little better. You think we could go out sometime?"

"Well, I don't know if you know this or not, but I have a boyfriend. The Black Student Union is sponsoring a play at the campus theater, however, and I would love for you to come."

"I just might take you up on that. You like football?"

"I like all kinds of sports, but I haven't gone to one of our games yet."

"Let's make a deal. I'll come to one of your soccer games, and you come check me out at one of my football games. Deal?"

"I can do that. It's a date."

"A date?"

"Boy, you know what I mean!"

Steven never showed up at the play, but he showed up at the library every day for the rest of the semester, around the time he thought Michelle would be there.

On the last day of school, Steven walked to his dorm room and found a note attached to his door.

> Dear Steven,
>
> Just dropped by to congratulate you on your graduation and to say good luck in whatever you wish to accomplish in life. I wanted you to know that I have enjoyed our many conversations. Maybe one day, when we are old and gray, we can meet again and talk some more.
>
> Love, Michelle

He thought to himself, *Ah, damn!*

* * *

Steven was a little groggy from sleep deprivation when he opened up the McDonald's. He was normally very observant of his surroundings, but his dull senses probably caused him to miss the strange figure lurking in the shadows near the trash bin in the parking lot. As soon as he opened the door, that strange figure leaped out of the shadows with the quickness of a leopard pouncing on an unsuspecting meal. Before anyone knew what was happening, the dark figure materialized holding a Glock-9 handgun and demanded that everyone "get inside, put your hands up, and shut the fuck up!"

As the adrenaline started rushing through Steven's body, he could feel the hairs on the back of his neck stand out, and his senses came into sharp focus. He immediately got between his employees and the gunman, allowing them to enter the store first. As he stood facing the faceless man with the hazel eyes, he began going through a range of thoughts and emotions.

Please don't shoot me!

Why is this happening to me?

Is this how it's going to end? Is this the end of the road?

Why don't he just take the money and get the hell out?

There is something familiar about this guy, but I can't put my finger on it.

Time began to slow down to a snail's pace as the man pointed the gun in his direction while making a litany of demands.

"Go get that money in the safe you've got hidden in the back room!"

Seconds seemed like hours, and hours seemed like days. Suddenly, Steve's mind began racing a mile a minute.

Wait a minute. Something ain't right here. How did he know about that safe?

Usually, we only keep enough cash in the safe to start the day, but that doesn't amount to much. I didn't go to the bank to deposit the money we made yesterday and left it in the safe. But how could he have known that?

If I hadn't been late today, I probably would have been here by myself. Maybe he knew that too.

This smells like an inside job to me.

The masked man forced Steven and his employees to go into the back room. From time to time, he would turn his head as if he were looking for someone to appear. He seemed really agitated and told Steven to hurry up and get the money. Maybe he knew that Deputy Owens usually drove by from time to time while he was on duty, to make sure everything was OK. He waved the gun close to Steven's face, telling him to move faster. That was when Steven noticed the masked man's fingernails. His nails were filthy and looked like he had been biting them instead of clipping them, which made them look raggedy. One of the first guys Steven fired when he first became store manager was a guy everybody called Grumpy. Steven had to tell Grumpy almost every day to wash his hands and clean his nails because he was working around people's food and his hands would turn the customers off. He also told Grumpy that he should clip his nails instead of biting them, but Grumpy didn't listen and was often seen biting his nails and spitting the ends on the floor. After several warnings, Steven finally had to let Grumpy go. Grumpy was very upset when he got fired.

Steven knew he had to do something soon. If this guy was Grumpy, Steven knew he was kind of weird and was probably looking for some payback. Steven also felt more responsible for the safety of his employees than for himself. This guy seemed very agitated and would probably do something stupid. A car passed by the store, and when the masked man jerked his head to look at the car, Steven saw his opportunity. Steven lowered his head and drove the crown of his forehead into the man's jaw, grabbed the man, pinning his arms to his side, and drove him into the wall with a perfect tackle that would have made his football coach proud. The man was stunned as the gun fell harmlessly to the floor. Both Steven and the man fell to floor. One of the employees rushed over and kicked the man in the head, knocking him unconscious. Another employee pulled out a cell phone and dialed 911. Steven pulled the man's mask off, and lo and behold! It was Grumpy. Steven got in one good punch to the unconscious man, a payment for putting him through all of this drama.

The police arrived shortly, and Deputy Owens, who had been cruising around the area, was one of the first officers on the scene. When he asked what happened, all the employees told of how Steven foiled the man's attempt by tackling him and wrestling the gun away from him. They exclaimed that Steven probably saved their lives and that he was a real hero. Deputy Owens congratulated Steven but told him the next time that something like this happened, he should just give up the money. Steven told Deputy Owens that there wasn't going to be a next time. This was it for him. Ever since his conversation with Deputy Owens about the job security police officers have and their opportunities to make a lot of extra money, Steven had given serious consideration to changing careers. More importantly, the adrenaline rush that he experienced during this episode, along with the fact that he saved the lives of his employees, made Steven even more convinced that becoming a police officer was something that he wanted to do. He even found that he appreciated the admiration they had shown. Steven made up his mind. No more pushing hamburgers. He was going to become a cop. The only problem was the Sheriff's Office in Prairie Village had only seven deputies, and all of those positions had been filled. In addition, one of the requirements to become a sheriff's deputy was that you had to have five years of police experience. That meant that if he wanted to do police work in Prairie Village, he had to go somewhere else to get the experience_ but where?

*   *   *

The phone rang five times before Big Lee picked it up.

"Is this Leon Anderson," the voice bellowed.

"Yes, who is this?"

"This is Officer Taylor from Metro Transit Police. We received your application and took a look at your test scores. We would love for you to come down to our office and do an interview. Can you come down on Thursday at 10:00 a.m.?"

"Sure. Thanks a lot, Officer Taylor. I'll be there at ten."

Big Lee was excited. He was really tired of driving the bus every day and having to put up with all the antics that went on. Plus, he wanted to do so much more for the people in his community than drive a bus. There were a couple of times he had to put his hands on people because they were either being disruptive, had threatened him, or were threatening other people. It seemed that when people got on the bus, they brought the problems of the world with them. But when he would pull the bus over and pull his six-foot-four frame out of his seat, people got the message. Instead of having to tangle with him, they would usually sit down and get very quiet.

One time, there was this guy who was harassing an elderly lady. She was seated in the front of the bus, which is usually reserved for seniors or people with disabilities. This guy got on the bus and loudly told this elderly lady to get out of her seat so he could sit down because he was tired. She was obviously scared and got up so the belligerent man could sit down. Big Lee pulled the bus over, went over to where the man was sitting, grabbed him by the collar, and threw him off the bus, shouting, "Get your punk ass off this bus and don't come back until you learn to respect your elders!" The riders on the bus roared their approval. After a while, word got out "not to start any shit on Big Lee's bus, or he would get you."

The middle and high school kids were a little harder to handle, though. They usually boarded his bus in large groups and were usually very loud and boisterous. He would never hesitate to tell them to settle down, or lower their voices, or check their behavior. He went out of his way, however, to try to help the young kids whenever possible. His desire to do whatever he could to help the young kids develop along the right path and navigate their way through the troubles and pitfalls he knew they would encounter stemmed from his experiences as a young black man, as well as the experiences he encountered while stationed in Iraq.

One day, while driving the bus, he saw a young man sitting at the bus stop reading a book. It reminded him of the day he got arrested and sent through the juvenile justice system for doing nothing but being young, black, and in the wrong place at the wrong time. He was also sitting at a bus stop with his book opened when the police approached him, put a gun to his head, and accused him of robbing a hotel. They put the handcuffs on him, drove him to a corner, and stood him under the street-light. There was another police car present with someone sitting in the back seat. One of the officers asked the hidden figure leading questions like, "Was he wearing shoes similar to the ones he has on now? Was he dark like this guy?" When his case went to court, the defense attorney pointed out that those were leading questions. The witness happened to be an elderly white lady who, according to the defense attorney, had only seen him for a brief moment and would naturally say yes to those types of leading questions. The attorney was able to get the case thrown out of court when the shoes, which were introduced as evidence against him, were not only the wrong size, but one shoe had gum embedded in the sole and left an impression on the counter, whereas his shoe had nothing.

The judge threw the case out of court, and his records were expunged. The experience, however, lasted forever.

When his army unit was stationed in Iraq, Big Lee was saddened by the poverty, ever-present hunger, devastation, and conditions that the children had to deal with every day while growing up in a war-torn environment. In spite of the depressing conditions, Big Lee marveled at how the children were able to smile, play among the ruins, and act like this kind of existence was normal. When they would come up to him, he would often offer them parts of his rations and candy. He felt sorry for them. No one should have to live like that, he thought.

His unit was deployed to the city of Fallujah, where they were engaged by insurgents and got into an intense firefight that would make your hair stand on edge. His squad came under fire emanating from a house, killing one of his best friends. The sergeant instructed Big Lee and two of his buddies to clear the house where the shots were coming from. The house was a two-story building, and each room on the first floor had to be cleared before the squad could reach the second floor where the insurgents had been spotted. As the three men cautiously entered the building, Big Lee heard a noise coming from one of the rooms. The room appeared empty, so the men started to go up the stairs.

Suddenly, they heard a faint sound, and Big Lee quickly turned his attention to the room they had just left. As he turned his head, a small figure darted from under the bed and tried to run out of the door. Big Lee whipped his weapon in the direction of the running figure and pulled the trigger, firing a burst into the back of the head of the fleeing figure. He then turned and continued cautiously followed his teammates up the stairs. When they got to the top, the insurgents had somehow disappeared. After a thorough sweep, the men declared the building safe and returned to join their unit.

As they exited the building, Big Lee saw the figure he had wasted. The figure turned out to be a small boy who couldn't be any more than eight or nine years old. At the time Big Lee fired his weapon, he didn't think about or care about who he was shooting. In the heat of the moment, it was kill or be killed, and his mindset was to kill anything that moved. Now that the adrenaline had subsided and he had time to reflect, he was disheartened that he had killed the young boy, who probably wasn't doing anything except trying to get out of the way. Even though the boy's face was no longer there, the image of that dead boy stuck with Big Lee and would haunt him long after he left Iraq.

Big Lee knew that driving the bus helped to pay the bills, but he had to do something more significant and meaningful. He sent in applications to the Metropolitan Police Department (MPD) in Washington, DC, the US Park Police, and the police departments in Montgomery County, Arlington County and the Metro Transit System. Public Law 94306 gave Metro the right to create a police department with police jurisdiction in Maryland, Virginia, and the District of Columbia. Of all the applications he put in, Metro was the first to respond, so Metro it was. He was looking forward to his interview.

Officer Taylor told him he had aced the written test, and based on his experience playing football and being in the army, he wasn't worried about the physical test. So as far as he was concerned, he was in. After hanging up the phone, the mailman dropped off his mail. There was a letter from Prairie Village College requesting his presence at his ten-year reunion celebration. He was intrigued by the thought, and even though returning to Kansas wasn't high on his priority list, he felt that seeing his old football buddies would be nice before he started his new job. Maybe Roya would go with him and he could show her off to his buddies. That would be nice.

*   *   *

The college administration had invited several of the former student leaders of the Black Student Union to the school to participate in a panel discussion on racial diversity. The participants were put up in a motel about a mile from the school, and a fifteen-passenger van was rented to transport them back and forth. Dean Chase, the administrator who organized the event, asked for a volunteer to be responsible for driving the van so the participants could come and go as they pleased. Michelle Johnson jumped at the opportunity. She told Dean Chase that her father owned a van and would let her drive from time to time. In reality, Michelle's parents didn't even own a car. Michelle was always looking for new experiences and treasured the idea of the freedom that the vehicle would provide. The van was parked in the parking lot. She jumped in to give it a test run while everyone was getting settled in their motel rooms. She knew how to drive and figured it wouldn't be too difficult to adjust to the size of the van. It was a bit awkward at first, but she was able to master it after a few minutes of practice.

When it was time for the panel discussion, the participants began filing out of the motel. Michelle drove up to the front and unlocked the doors so they could begin boarding. When everyone was in, one of the participants joked, "Michelle, you know how to drive this thing, don't you?" Michelle turned around with the biggest smile on her face and replied, "Now, Adam, don't you start no stuff! Sure, I know how to drive this thing, but it might be a good idea for you to fasten your seat belt!" She let out a hearty laugh and took off down Route 1 toward the campus.

*   *   *

Big Lee and Roya arrived at the Charles B. Wheeler Downtown Airport in enough time to catch the shuttle heading to the college. When Big Lee stepped off the plane and into the airport terminal, a flood of memories began rushing back. He remembered the very first time he boarded the shuttle to get to school as a freshman. He remembered having fifty dollars in his pocket that had to last him until his parents could send him more, and the ride cost him thirty dollars. Now here he was, a grown man taking that same ride. He placed his luggage on the ground next to everyone else's luggage as the driver began loading them on board. When the driver finished packing the luggage, there was one piece left sitting conspicuously on the ground, with the door still open. It was Big Lee's suitcase. Big Lee picked up his bag and threw it up in the back of the van and slammed the door. *Welcome back to Kansas,* he thought. *It doesn't look like much has changed.* Roya was furious.

"Don't trip," Big Lee said. "He just lost a big tip."

"I don't see why that doesn't piss you off," Roya rebuked him.

"It's not worth my time or energy."

"I'm going to start calling you the gentle giant from now on … my gentle giant."

"I can live with that."

*   *   *

Steven arrived on campus long before the festivities were scheduled to start. He had enough time to leisurely stroll around the small campus, and he started his journey down memory lane. He was eager to see his old dorm room, just to see if it looked the same and if "DA CAMPUS" sign was still hanging up. He stopped at the campus police station and inquired about openings and finally stopped by the football field before attending the opening reunion ceremony. He was happy when he saw his football coach and some of his former teammates, but the activities were mundane, he couldn't have cared less if he had participated or not. His eyes lit up when he strolled into the on-campus cafeteria, a place he remembered for the horrible food and the cafeteria ladies who always gave him a hard time because he complained about the food so much. But there was his good friend Leon Anderson, sitting next to this gorgeous woman.

"Big Lee, how's it hanging, old dude," Steven hollered.

"My man, Stevie Wonder, how you been, old friend," Big Lee responded with a huge smile on his face.

"Forget that. Who is that lovely lady you're sitting next to?"

"There you go. Now you know I'm not going to let my lady anywhere near your punk ass. Roya, this is my good friend and former teammate Steven Sullivan, but I call him Stevie Wonder."

"Hi, Stevie, it's good to meet you. If your last name is Sullivan, why does he call you Stevie Wonder?"

"Well, to be honest, I don't really remember. Maybe he can tell you."

"I remember my sophomore year when I was very angry about the way I was being treated because I was black. My parents raised me to believe that you should always judge a person by their character and not by the way they looked. I always believed that until I came to this school. When I got here, people did some strange things that made me feel like I had done something wrong. For example, when I would get on the elevator, white people would get off. I always got stared at when I went into a restaurant, followed around in a store like I was going to steal something, and even told by a few professors that they thought black people were lazy ... imagine a professor saying something like that. I couldn't understand why people who didn't know me would hate me just because of the way I looked. That tripped me out.

"After an incident on the football team, I became what you would call the angry black man. I stopped talking to my white teammates, and I actually began hating white people. I began acting toward them the same way they acted toward me. When the football team went on road trips, Stevie asked to be my roommate. He was the only white boy who wasn't afraid to talk to me at that time, and we became good friends. We talked about everything. We even argued a lot, but he was always honest with me, or at least that is what I thought. I started calling him Stevie Wonder because he acted like he was blind to all of that racial stuff, but he was able to see the real me and see into my soul. He helped me to see that not all white people were the same and reminded me that I should follow the training of my parents and not judge people just because they were white."

"Well, Stevie, I am really happy to meet you! That kind of answers some of the questions I had about him and how he is able to put up with a lot of things that have recently happened."

"So, Big Lee, what have you been doing these days?"

"Well, after college, I joined the army and did a stint in Iraq. After getting out of the army, I went from job to job until I landed a gig driving a bus in DC. I just applied to be a police officer for the Metro transit system in the DMV and I have an interview next week."

"The DMV, what is that?"

"That is what we call the area that includes the District of Columbia, Maryland, and Virginia."

"That's interesting because I have decided to become a police officer myself, but I'm looking for a job because there are no job openings around here. Plus, they are telling me that I need experience before I can get a job. How in the world can you get experience if you can't get on the force?"

"Hey man, why don't you move to DC? They are always looking for good people. You white boys shouldn't have any problems. In fact, there are so many police districts in the area. You can't miss. I can hook you up with some very inexpensive apartments and if you can't find anything, you can stay with me until you can get on your feet."

"That sounds interesting. Let me think about it. Wait a minute, y'all. I'll be right back. I see someone that I just have to talk to."

Steven heard that familiar laugh that had captured his imagination so many years ago. He wouldn't admit it to himself, but it had captured his heart as well. Steven saw Michelle Johnson sitting at the "black table" talking to one of the professors. That section of the cafeteria was referred to as the Black Hole when Stevie and Michelle were in school. The cafeteria was voluntarily segregated into sections during those days. Most of the black students sat together, as did the Hispanic students (Little Havana), the Asian student (Chinatown), the jocks (the Locker Room), the science brains (the Lab), the young Republicans (Geek City), and the farm boys (Animal Farm). The frat boys and girls ate together in their frat houses.

Steven gingerly began moving toward her table as if he didn't know what to say or do. He felt like that awkward kid he was when he was younger, before he became this popular football star. Before he got to her table, she suddenly turned around as if she knew he was coming. She flashed that brilliant smile, stood up, gave him a warm hug, and started talking as though they had been friends forever. One of the things he liked about her was that she carried the conversation most of the time. He asked if they could go somewhere to talk. She excused herself from the professor, and off they went.

They walked and talked as though they had been the best of friends for decades. She had moved to Washington, DC, got a job as an art teacher in a local high school, and was the head soccer coach. She talked about how her engagement to her boyfriend fell through, and he talked about his dreams and aspirations. She suggested that maybe he should think about moving to DC if he wanted to get a job in law enforcement. They got on the elevator in the library and went to the top floor, where you could look out and see miles and miles of flat land in every direction, and they talked some more. Before they realized it, it was one o'clock in the morning. Michelle looked at her watch and stood up in a panic. She had forgotten that she was the driver of the van that transported the panelists to and from the motel.

"Oh shit, I've got to go! I've got the keys to the van and they are going to be furious with me. There was supposed to be a party at the Black Student Union tonight, and I know everyone wanted to go back to the motel to change. Oh, they gonna be mad!"

"Don't worry. All you got to do is flash that gorgeous smile at them, and they will forget all about being angry."

When they got on the elevator and the elevator doors closed, she leaned up against him and gave him a passionate kiss on the lips. That caught him totally off guard. They looked into each other's eyes and passionately kissed again. He couldn't believe he was there kissing her like that, especially when they had never even held hands or anything before. Her body was so soft and her gaze so sensual it gave him feelings he had never felt before. At that very moment, he knew he was moving to DC.

CHAPTER 8

SECOND CHANCES

Engine Company #19 got the call concerning the smell of gas at a house on Benning Road. Truck #3 was dispatched to the scene, and when they arrived, they found an elderly couple engaged in a battle that to some seemed funny but to most was a sad commentary on how things had deteriorated in the community. The old man, who was bleeding profusely from the forehead, had his hands wrapped around the old woman's throat and was trying to choke the life out of her. They had gotten into an argument over what she had cooked for dinner, according to the statement she gave after everything calmed down, and he supposedly slapped her. She had had enough of his verbal assault, and when he hit her, she went crazy. She grabbed the nearest object she could find, which happened to be an iron frying pan and smashed it into his forehead.

After they had been separated, Shanita Brown, the emergency medical technician (EMT) in charge on the fire department rescue truck that had been dispatched along with the fire engine, forcefully told the old man to have a seat in the next room while the other firefighters swept the house searching for gas leaks. This wasn't the first time they had been called to this house for some type of disturbance. Shanita just couldn't understand why they stayed together because they always got on each other's nerves and were always fighting. Shanita was able to move the old man into another room in order to defuse the situation, and began treating his wound. Before she could finish dressing his wound, she could tell he was getting riled up again as he attempted to go after the old woman.

"I'm gonna fuck you up, Bertha! You just wait," the old man screamed.

"Shut the fuck up, you old fart," the old woman hollered back.

"You'd better sit your old ass down and be quiet," Shanita asserted. "I don't know why y'all can't get along. But I tell you what, somebody is going to jail today!"

When the police arrived on the scene, Officer Andy Wallace chuckled as he spoke to Shanita.

"Well, it seems like you've got everything completely under control. I don't need to be here."

"Stop playing, Andy, and do some work," Shanita replied.

"No, really, Shanita. You should consider joining the police department. You have the temperament for it, and you'd make a great cop!"

Shanita helped the old woman into the ambulance as the old man was placed in handcuffs and placed in the police cruiser. The old man looked like he got the worse of the encounter, but after the old woman calmed down, she began complaining about chest pains. On the way to the hospital, Shanita shook her head and wondered what was wrong in the world that people had to act like that. She wanted to shake some sense into the old woman, but she knew the old woman would return to the same situation after treatment and get abused again. Shanita wanted to do more to help, but there was very little she could do about it. She thought about Andy's suggestion that she should consider being a police officer. Most of the people she knew and hung out with now were either firemen or cops anyway.

When she did her training at the fire and EMS training academy, she had met many police officers because the fire academy and the police academy were right next to each other. In fact, they actually did some of their training together, and there were competitions between firefighter recruits and police recruits. As an EMT, all she could do was fix people after they got hurt. Maybe as a police officer, she could do something more meaningful to stop people from getting hurt, or at least help bring people to justice for doing the hurting; plus, with the availability of overtime, she could make significantly more money being a cop. Ten years ago, for her to even think about becoming a police officer was unimaginable, but now, she was really thinking about it. Now she had to think about someone other than herself. She had to think about her daughter, Princess.

* * *

Ten years ago, Shanita sat on her mother's couch stunned when she heard the news that Curtis, the love of her life and the father of her unborn child, was dead. *This can't be happening, not now,* she thought. A feeling of helplessness and despair tugged at her heart, but she had cried so much the last couple of days that there were no more tears left in her to shed, so she just sat there in a state of shock. The news reporter's mouth was moving, but no sound was coming out. Her mother gave her a hug to console her, but Shanita couldn't feel her touch. She couldn't tell if it was day or night. Her world had come crashing down all around her, and there was absolutely nothing she could do about it.

This can't be happening! Not now!

Deep down, however, another feeling began to emerge, which caused her to feel ashamed and conflicted. She couldn't believe it, but she began to feel a sense of relief. She always knew that someday this would happen. She knew that most people in the drug game ended up either in jail or dead. She had tried to stop Curtis from selling drugs several times, telling him that it was wrong and dangerous, but he wouldn't listen. Curtis was her first, and she loved him so much, so she stayed with him. Somehow, she knew this day would come.

Then there was the issue of the missing money! She had no idea how she was going to resolve that situation, and she knew whatever was going to happen wasn't going to be pretty. She knew that Curtis was going to think she stole the money and wasn't quite sure how he would react. She couldn't tell him that her mother took the money, and she definitely didn't want her brother to get involved. Now, none of that seemed to matter.

The next day, she went back to the apartment to get some things and found police tape on the door, preventing her from getting in. Two days later, she got a call from a Detective Saunders, who asked her to come down to the station to answer some questions. Detective Saunders wanted to know all about her whereabouts the day Curtis got killed. Detective Saunders was very professional, but the way he looked at her made her feel uncomfortable. She didn't trust the police anyway, especially when she knew they tried to plant drugs on her brother in order to lock him up, and she couldn't help but feel that Saunders suspected her of being involved in Curtis's death somehow. She told him that on the day in question, she was riding her bike and remembered talking to an Officer Harris. She remembered him because he was cute and was so nice to her. He had given her his business card, which she put in the back of her wallet. She pulled it out and gave it to Saunders.

Detective Saunders checked out her story, but would remain suspicious until the murder got solved. He knew, however, that unless he could find a witness who was willing to talk, which was unlikely, this investigation would end up being another cold case_ another useless thug who was destroying the community, gone.

"Ms. Brown, are you planning to leave the area anytime soon?"

"Yes, I have been accepted to North Carolina Central University in Durham, North Carolina. I will be attending their summer enrichment program in a couple of weeks."

"Can you give me your cell phone number and e-mail address in case I need to get in touch with you with any further questions?"

"Sure, but why do you need my e-mail address?"

"I have to cover all my bases and be able to get in touch with you if something comes up."

After the death of her boyfriend, the murder investigation, and with a baby on the way, Shanita began sinking into a state of depression and knew that she needed to get away from everything. She decided that even though she was pregnant, she was going to accept the scholarship and go to school until it was time to have her baby. She loved being in school and was a very good student. Her best subjects were math and science. She wanted to become an obstetrician. She worked in the National Institute of Health's Stay in School program, which gave high school students the opportunity to work in the science labs during the summer and after school. This program encouraged students to go to college, and even offered financial support. She also loved writing and was considering journalism as a potential career. She had a strong desire to change the way minorities were portrayed in the media.

When she got accepted into the Dorothy Gilliam Journalism Summer Program at NCCU, she went down for three weeks and fell in love with the campus, the people, and college life. Being in North Carolina was different from the city life she was used to. The pace was much slower, the people more hospitable, and there was less drama. More than that, the freedom she felt was exhilarating. She could walk around campus at any hour and feel safe. She was able to escape the rules of her mother, father, and her godmother, the rules of the streets, and more importantly, she was finally able to breathe. The new environment, meeting new people, and learning new things took her mind off of her troubles_ at least for a little while. The journalism program was rigorous. She soon realized that journalism was not for her. She loved to write but found journalistic writing too restrictive. She was more of a free-form writer. She loved expressing herself through poetry and essays, so when she returned in the fall, she decided to try the pre-med program.

Her first full month at NCCU was fulfilling and therapeutic. Going to classes and being able to sit down and have intellectual discussions and debates enabled her to exercise her mental fortitude and express her ideas, which was refreshing. Then there were the parties. During the summer program, there were ten girls she hung out with, and they were inseparable. Six of them returned to the fall semester, and they became even closer. They went everywhere together. They went to all the fraternity and sorority parties together and knew all the frat boys and upper-class boys. Soon the boys on campus started calling them the "sexy-six."

Guys were all over her, trying their hardest to get her to go to bed with them, but she wasn't having it. The more she turned them down, the harder they pursued her. She was able to politely turn them away without hurting their feelings or acting like she was above them in anyway. One by one, the members of the sexy-six fell victim to the onslaught, but she remained steadfast. One guy got closer to her than all the others. His name was Rick Adams. He reminded her of the young and innocent Curtis she had fallen in love with. Rick was a senior. He was a smooth talker and was so cute that he had girls chasing after him. Shanita initially tried to fend him off by stating she had a boyfriend back home and wasn't interested in a physical relationship. This ploy did not seem to deter him. She had to admit to herself she liked the attention he was showing her, as well as the fact that he could have had any girl he wanted and yet he was pursuing her. She became enamored by his persistence and soon allowed herself to start to like him. She debated whether or not to tell him about the child growing inside of her. She also debated whether or not to give him some.

After the party one night, he walked her to her dorm room, and she did not resist when he leaned in close and gave her a long, passionate kiss. It had been a while since anybody had kissed her like that. She was taken aback by his smell, his hard body, his soft lips and his powerful grip when he drew her close. She was also startled by the hardness and size of his rising manhood as he drew her even closer. She was ready to cave in right then and there, but instead gave him a small push, stopping his advance. He did not seem upset by her resistance. He simply said good night and walked away, leaving her yearning for his touch.

She tried going to bed, but it was almost impossible for her to go to sleep. She got up; put on a short, revealing outfit; and doused herself with an alluring perfume that she borrowed from her roommate. *Tonight was going to be the night,* she thought. Her body had been turned on, and she knew there was only one way for it to be turned off. She headed over to the senior center where Rick lived. When she got to the third floor, she saw Rick standing in front of his dorm room passionately kissing Amanda, one of her closest girlfriends in her sexy-six crew. *You dirty dog!*

She was furious when she got back to her room. She couldn't decide, however, who she was angrier with. Was she mad at Rick because she really thought he liked her when, apparently, all he wanted was some booty? Was she angry at Amanda because Amanda knew she liked Rick and friends don't do that to each other? Or was she mad at herself for allowing this boy to get that close to her heart? As she began to reflect on what just happened, she began to get a horrible feeling in her gut and didn't know whether she should cry or stay angry. She felt as though she had been stabbed in her heart and in the back at the same time. That was a helpless feeling. She decided that it would be a cold day in hell before she would let anybody get that close to her again. She was so glad that she hadn't revealed her secret to Rick, or anybody else for that matter, but she knew she couldn't hide it for long. Shanita never told Rick that she saw him that night with Amanda when he came sniffing around. *You dirty dog!* He seemed puzzled by her sudden coldness and stand-off-ish attitude. After a while of being kept at a distance, he ended his pursuit of her and started spreading rumors that she must be a dyke.

Shanita didn't care what Rick was saying about her, or what he thought about her. In her mind, he had been dismissed, and she began concentrating on her academics. She wasn't going to let any boy define who she was or force her to do anything she didn't want to do. She was doing extremely well in her classes the first semester.

Right before the Thanksgiving break, one of her girlfriends commented that she shouldn't eat too much turkey over the break and that she needed to join a dance class or do something physical, because she was beginning to develop a little tummy. Then, one day, Shanita's anatomy and physiology instructor asked her to come by her office during her office hours.

"Shanita, you have been doing an excellent job in my class. I usually don't have many freshmen in my class."

"Thanks, Ms. Winston. I really enjoy your class. I had an anatomy class in high school and found it very interesting. It was one of my favorite classes."

"Are you feeling OK?"

"Sure. Why do you ask?"

"Shanita, how many months are you?"

"Why, whatever do you mean, Ms. Winston?"

"Come on, Shanita, I might have been born yesterday, but I was up all night! I have seen so many young ladies come through here, and I know the signs. Your clothes have been getting tighter and tighter, you're starting to wear clothes that aren't yours and are two sizes too big for you as if you are trying to hide something, your breasts are beginning to get fuller and have started to sag, your cheeks are getting fatter, and your constant trips to the bathroom are so revealing. So I ask you again, how many months are you?"

Shanita hung her head. Her look of amazement suddenly turned to resignation. A tear began to trickle down her cheek.

"Four months. Are you going to take my scholarship away?"

"No, honey. The school would never think of doing something like that. We do want you to be safe, however, and we wouldn't want you to do anything to hurt the baby. When you start getting close to having your baby, you will probably have to take a leave of absence. But I'm sure you will be able to keep your scholarship and return when it is safe. First, you need to go to health services and let them know what is happening so they can check up on you from time to time. Then you need to have a conversation with your academic advisor and let her know."

Shanita returned from the Thanksgiving break and completed the first semester. She decided to leave campus after the first semester because her body had started going through changes that frightened her a little bit. She had seen how her sisters reacted to being pregnant, and she always thought they were being melodramatic, but now it was her turn. Her morning sickness increased in frequency and intensity, and her weight gain caused her back to start hurting. More importantly, her anxiety level, about the life growing inside of her, began to make her feel the need to be near her mother and sisters who could help her with this new experience. Her friends at school thought she was leaving because she had been put on academic probation. Too much partying, they thought.

Let them think what they want, Shanita thought. *They don't need to know my business.*

Being back home and away from the freedom and independence that college offered added to her anxiety. The hustle and bustle of street life, the nagging of her mother about when and where she could go, the snoopiness of her sisters, and the memories of Curtis's death began to haunt her, making her wonder if coming home was such a good thing after all. She withdrew from everything and everyone, spending countless hours in her room, not answering any phone calls, and coming out only to eat and bathe.

It was an old friend that helped to get her out of this state of depression and return to the world. The friend was her journal that she found under the bed one day while cleaning up. She picked it up and started reading older entries, laughing at some and crying at others. Writing had always helped her to calm down and deal with the issues in her life. One day she picked up her pen and began chronicling her pregnancy.

January 22, 2007

Dear Diary,

I'm home now, but just for a little while. I hope to go back to school after I have my baby and get back on my feet. I got to get out of DC, or at least get my own place. Ma is bugging out. At first, she says she doesn't want any more babies in this house, and yet she keeps showering me with so much love and attention that it is becoming overbearing. She means well, but sometimes she goes overboard.

This pregnancy thing is a real trip. It is so weird having something growing inside of me, feeling it kick, going to the doctor's office and hearing the heartbeat, and watching my stomach get bigger and bigger. It is unbelievable how my body is changing. I'm a lot heavier than I used to be, and it has destroyed my beautiful shape. Being this big produces many struggles ... struggles like getting out of bed, a chair, or getting out of a car, and even sometimes rolling over is a lot more difficult than it used to be. Sometimes I even need help, and that is difficult for me. I don't usually depend on anybody for anything, especially now that Curtis is gone. And I am out of breath a lot now. Before, I could run up a flight of stairs and be OK, but now, after three or four steps, I am tired and need to take a break.

I am a little concerned because I have never been this big in my life. I have gone from 115 pounds to 180. That is a big transition for me. I'm like, oh my God! Am I ever going to lose this weight? Is it going to come off? Am I supposed to gain this much? I've been reading a lot of medical books and talking with my sisters, which helped me to realize that this is what to expect. I am looking forward to delivering and see where I will be after that.

Another thing is this stiffness. I get stiff a lot. I started going to a yoga class to deal with the stiffness and the joint pain, especially around my pelvic area. My doctor told me that the baby is actually stretching my hips open. That's wild! Then I started doing aerobics in the swimming pool, and that was much better. Being in the water is less stress on my body and is very soothing.

The worst thing is that it seems like I have to pee every five minutes. And then there is the diarrhea! My God! I have been sitting on that stool so much I think I have developed hemorrhoids! I'll be glad when this baby finally comes.

I also have a lot of anxiety because now that there is a life growing inside of me, I feel vulnerable. Sometimes I feel that I can't protect it. I worry about people bumping into me too hard, or what I eat and drink. I also appraise situations differently now. If I am driving, I am not going to speed through a yellow light because I could run the chance of getting hit or hitting somebody else with a child. Before, I was more likely to go through that yellow light. I am more careful as a result of being pregnant. I think through things more now, and I realize that I am not just living for myself.

I started thinking about all the things my dad told me when he first found out I was pregnant. Now his words are coming back to haunt me. How am I going to raise this child? How am I going to be able to pay for things? Will I have to do this all by myself?

*   *   *

Shanita got in touch with Mrs. Flag, her supervisor, when she was in the NIH Stay in School program. She told Mrs. Flag about her dilemma and asked if there was a temporary job she could get until it was time for her to have her baby. Mrs. Flag always liked Shanita and was very disappointed that Shanita had gotten herself in this situation. She was able to get Shanita a temporary job working in the medical records department of a rheumatologist's office. This was great for Shanita because she wanted to be around doctors so that after she completed college (which she had every intention of doing) and it was time to go to medical school, she would have somebody to write letters of recommendation for her. Shanita also wanted to soak up whatever information there was that would help her in the field of medicine and she figured that working in a doctor's office would help her do that. The doctors in the office loved her attitude and work ethic. They were constantly encouraging her to go back to college and get her degree and then go on to medical school.

The job gave Shanita a little bit of money, and she saved every penny. Her daily routine included going to work and then coming home to watch television. She didn't get out much and yearned for the freedom and activities she had for the brief time she was in college. From time to time, she would go down to the firehouse to visit her dad. She hadn't been around him that much when she was growing up because he was always working. He would work one twenty-four-hour shift from 7:00 a.m. to 7:00 a.m. the next day and then have three days off. On his off days, he would work a part-time job. But now it seemed important to Shanita to be close to him. She asked him if there was anything she could do at the fire house in order to pick up a little extra change. Her dad offered to pay her, out of his pocket, to come down and cook when it was his turn to cook. Shanita jumped at the opportunity.

When she was young, she would always see firefighters in the grocery store buying food and often wondered how they got their meals. Now she knew. Firefighters had to take turns cooking the meals for the entire station. A group would buy the groceries and come back to the firehouse to cook breakfast. Then they would all sit down and eat together. After they cleaned up the kitchen, they would participate in daily drills to keep their skills sharp, wash the fire trucks, clean the firehouse, and then sit around and wait for the next run. They would prepare lunch, clean up after lunch, prepare dinner, clean up after dinner and then sit around and wait. After cooking the meals when it was her dad's time to cook, the firefighters fell in love with Shanita's cooking and chipped in together to pay her to cook all the meals when she was available. She ended up cooking dinner during the week and all the meals on Saturdays and Sundays.

She enjoyed hanging around the firehouse and found life there to be quite interesting. There was a combination of guys who were full-time paid employees and some who volunteered. Shanita didn't get the opportunity to pledge when she was in college, but she went to as many frat and sorority parties that she possibly could in such a short period of time. Hanging around the firehouse was like being in a frat house. Hanging out with the guys was fun. With the guys having so much free time, there was a lot of joking, card playing, and fooling around as a distraction from the boredom. She also felt very safe in this environment. The guys treated her more like a sister than a conquest and tried to be on their best behavior when she was around. She started spending most of her free time there. She enjoyed the camaraderie, the time to contemplate and be quiet, as well as being in the company of her dad. There was a back patio where she would sit, watch the sun set, think about the future and write in her journal.

February 15, 2007

Dear Diary,

    I love it here. Being at the firehouse is very pleasant, and there are some real characters that hang out here. Most of the guys are white, but there are a few brothers and two black girls. One white guy is a real trip, but I kind of like him. He is real friendly, always got something funny to say, and is in everybody's business. One of the black girls, Frieda, drives the ambulance at night. She doesn't talk much, but she is cool. The other girl, Ashley, is a paid firefighter, and she is tough. She is cute, but I can tell she is not one to be messed with. She is kind of hard. You can tell by just talking to her that she has had a hard life. She is really smart, though.

Then there is that Mike Holiday! He is really cute. We seemed to hit it off immediately. We are about the same age. He seems really shy. He came to the department as a result of being in the firefighter cadet program at Theodore Roosevelt High School. I was first attracted to him as a result of our conversations. The depths of our conversations are amazing. We would talk about everything under the sun. He would even call me sometimes when I wasn't at the firehouse, and we would talk and talk and talk. His pretty eyes helps a lot too. He seems to look right through me with those eyes. And the fact that I am carrying someone else's baby doesn't seem to bother him. I wonder what he is really after.

*　　*　　*

The longer Shanita hung around the firehouse, the more she began thinking about her future and how she was going to handle being a mother and going to college. She began having doubts about returning to North Carolina on her own with a child to take care of. She sat down with Ashley one evening and engaged in a heart to heart conversation.

"Say, girl, can I holla at you for a minute?"

"Sure, what up?"

"You got a child at home, right?"

"Yeah, his name is Brian, and he is my heart."

"How did you do it?"

"Do what?"

"Raise a child and work here at the same time."

"Girl, that was the hardest thing I ever had to do in my life! I got pregnant during the summer between my ninth and tenth grade year in high school. I got summer jobs and worked little odd jobs. All the money I earned basically went to my child. His dad went to jail, so his friends helped me out with a little money so I wouldn't have to go on welfare. I joined the fire department right out of high school. I joined because I had a child and knew that to have the lifestyle I wanted to have, or at least a better one than the one I grew up with, I needed a career and not just a job, and I needed it right away. I graduated number 10 in my class, so college was always something my counselors and the people in my life wanted me to do, but I didn't feel like that was what I needed to do. With me having a child, I was like, 'Who is going to watch my child while I go away to school?' And if he was with me, that was going to be even harder trying to go to class every day. So I applied and got accepted to the fire fighters academy."

"Who watched Brian while you were in the academy and when you had to do those twenty-four-hour shifts?"

"My grandmother would watch him. When my grandmother couldn't do it, I had a really close friend of my mother who took me in when things got rough, and she would help me take care of him. Are you thinking about joining the fire department after you have your child?"

"Well, not at first, but now that I have been hanging around here, I am giving it some thought."

"My advice to you is to think about it real hard and weigh your options. Really make sure this is something you really want to do! A lot of people get into it thinking that the money is good and the schedule is great, but they are not thinking about what we have to do. Think about it. There are men who are afraid to do what we do. You have to be a crazy person to be a firefighter. People are running away from danger, and we have to literally run into it. And there is a lot of shit we see too.

"Everyone who works here has to be trained as an emergency medical technician, an EMT, so we have to fight fires and help people who have been hurt. Usually a fire truck gets to the scene of an accident first, and so we have to handle medical emergencies before an ambulance gets there. I had to personally deal with a lot of injuries, like shootings, people who got shot in the head but were still talking, car accidents, children and older people committing suicide, overdoses, rapes, and on and on.

"One day last month, we got a report of a car accident. When we got there, guys in the neighborhood had already pulled the truck driver out and beat his ass. When we got to the truck, there was a little girl. I think she might have been about seven or eight. Not only did the truck driver hit her, but a piece of her head got caught under the truck. The truck had actually dragged her. Once we got to her, she was kind of bent up under the wheels of the truck, and there was blood everywhere. So just seeing that was horrible. I don't think I did too well with that. But that is what we do in addition to running into burning buildings filled with smoke so hot it will burn the eye-lashes from your eyes. I did get some satisfaction months later when the little girl's mother actually brought her ... she made it ... to the firehouse to talk to me. The little girl said she wanted to talk with the person who helped her. That was kind of touching and is something that will always stick with me. It is days like those that make this job fulfilling.

"Yeah the money is good ... I went from being a poor eighteen-year-old with a baby to making thirty-six thousand dollars, and that was back then. Now I make around sixty-three thousand dollars, and that is only working seven days a month. But this has got to be something you really want to do and not something somebody else wants you to do! So think real hard about it."

"Thanks, Ashley. You have given me a lot to think about."

"No problem, girl. And that dinner you made tonight was slammin'."

March 4, 2007

Dear Diary,

I decided that I am going to put off going back to school for a while. I think I am going to stay close to home where I can get some support with my baby. I think I am going to join the fire department. I can get some practical experience in the medical field working as an EMT and make some money at the same time. That way, when I return to North Carolina, I will have enough money to pay for my own apartment and day care or afterschool care for my child.

Ouch! Damn, that hurt. This baby is kicking the heck out of me. My mom said that when the baby kicks really hard, that means it is going to be a boy. We went to the doctor the other day to see the sonogram and found out it is going to be a girl. I was really excited. I started thinking about names. Curtis used to call me his princess all the time, so I'm gonna name my baby Princess.

*   *   *

The call came over the radio to check out a domestic situation involving a man with a gun. Officers Gregory Harris and Daryl Garner where the closest to the area and did not hesitate to respond. As the police cruiser approached the address, Officer Harris saw a familiar figure standing on the porch of the house. Anytime there is a call that includes "man with a gun," the anxiety level is always high; but this case somehow seemed different. When Officer Harris came closer to the steps of the house, he realized the figure standing on the porch was his father. This couldn't have been happening because his father had died earlier from pancreatic cancer. The figure looked at Officer Harris and eerily whispered, "Don't go into this house!" Officer Harris turned to his partner and said, "Did you hear that?" "Hear what?" Officer Garner replied. When Officer Harris turned back around, the figure was gone. *What the fuck,* Officer Harris thought before pulling out his gun and knocking on the door.

No one answered the door, but the door mysteriously opened, seemingly all by itself. Hesitantly, Officers Harris and Garner entered the house with guns drawn. When they got in the house, the door violently slammed behind them. It was so dark they could barely see two feet in front of them. As they slowly walked down a long dark hallway, Officer Harris suddenly realized that his partner had vanished, and he was all alone. As his eyes adjusted to the darkness, he realized there was a figure standing in the middle of the hallway motioning him to come closer. As he slowly ventured down the hallway, he realized it was an attractive woman dressed in a revealing negligee.

Officer Harris hesitated before getting too close, but forged ahead with extreme caution. When he got close enough to touch the woman, she suddenly turned into a hideous creature with large, sharp teeth dripping with saliva and emitted a horrible loud scream. Before he could react, the horrible creature pulled out a machete and chopped off the hand holding the gun. She then knocked him to the floor, and with both hands gripped around the machete, tried to chop off his head. As she raised the machete above her head, Officer Harris reached into his boot and pulled out an old-fashioned switch-blade that he kept for added protection. With a touch of a button, he opened the knife and repeatedly thrust it into the chest of the creature in an attempt to stop her attack. The creature let out a long, loud laugh before bringing the machete down on his throat chopping off his head.

Officer Harris suddenly woke up from this nightmare drenched in a pool of his own sweat. He then realized that he was sitting on his easy chair in the living room of his empty house. He had begun to drink more and more, especially after his wife left him and told him she wanted a divorce. She said that she was tired of the foolishness and couldn't take it anymore. His wife's departure, along with the death of his father and the suicide of his partner, took place within a three-month period and added to his depression. After his heart calmed down, he took another long swig of the bourbon he had just poured and began to try to make sense of the nightmare. Everybody in the dream was actually dead except for him. Maybe they were trying to tell him something. Maybe he was next.

He took the death of his father really hard. His father was his hero and taught him everything he knew about life and responsibility. His partner, Officer Garner, had taken Officer Harris under his wing and taught him how to be a true policeman. They had become very good friends in the process. It was Big Daryl, or Big D, as everybody affectionately called him, who taught Officer Harris how to unwind from the job by downing a few brews after work. Two weeks after Officer Harris buried his father, Big D went home, put a gun in his mouth, and pulled the trigger. Officer Harris felt betrayed that Big D didn't confide in him and tell him what was troubling him. They had talked about everything, and Officer Harris felt that maybe he could have helped Big D work through his problems. The creature in the dream was actually a real woman whom he and Big D had to kill when she attempted to hack them with a machete when Officer Harris was a rookie. Even though he had since killed other criminals, this had been his first killing, and he couldn't seem to let go. That incident has haunted him ever since.

Officer Harris took one last swig of his drink, and in a drunken stupor, looked down at the gun sitting in his lap. Maybe it was his turn to go, he thought. He checked to make sure the gun was loaded, put a bullet in the chamber, clicked off the safety, and looked down the barrel. Suddenly, the phone rang, waking him from the trance he was in.

"Hello, is this Officer Harris?"

"Yes, who is this?"

"This is Jackie Smith. I live on Fourteenth Place in Congress Park. You patrol my neighborhood. You gave me your card and told me that if I ever needed anything, to give you a call."

"Oh yeah, I could never forget you, Ms. Smith? How you doing?"

"Not so good, Officer Harris. I got a little problem, and I need to ask you a question."

"Go ahead … shoot."

"Well, you know my son Daquan? Well, he is only eleven years old, and he is beginning to smell himself. He thinks he's grown and can do and say what he wants. Well, he is in for a rude awakening because I'm not having that in my house. I'm getting ready to kick his little ass, and if he bucks, there is going to be some furniture moving around here. I want to know if I am within my rights as a parent to discipline his ass without going to jail."

"That's a hard one. Let me answer that this way: DC law 2-22 says corporal punishment is considered child abuse and is against the law. Corporal punishment includes spanking with the hand or any object to inflict pain or discomfort. Now if I or most black police officers were to show up and your son was acting out, we would say whip his ass. I would even lend you my belt! I have always believed that if you spare the rod, you spoil the child. It is rough out there, and if we don't get control of our kids when they're young and instill some discipline, they will probably end up getting in trouble later on.

"Now, if a white officer who was raised differently shows up, he would probably read you the law and maybe arrest you for child abuse. If it was my child and he was acting out and talking back, I would tear that butt up!"

"Well, I'm letting you know right now_ I'm getting ready to catch a case because I am not having it! Not in my house! Thank you so much, Officer Harris. I'll see you around the way."

Officer Harris hung up with a smile on his face. He sat there for a few seconds thinking about Ms. Smith and the conversation he just had with her. She was kind of cute. He had never thought of her in that way, but now that his wife was gone, maybe he would give her another look. He took the bullet out of the chamber and put his gun away.

*　　*　　*

Shanita woke up in a pool of blood, or so she thought. There was a searing pain in her pelvic area, and she thought she was about to die. Thinking that there was something terribly wrong, she screamed out in a panic. Her mother and sisters came rushing into the room, calmed her down, and told her that her water broke and there was nothing to be afraid of. They took her to the hospital and called her dad.

Once in the hospital, she was given medication to reduce the pain of the contractions. Then, she was hooked up to a heart monitor to keep track of her and the baby's heart. There seemed to be some minor concern because she was able to dilate only seven centimeters.

She was given an epidural to help her deal with the pain. Shanita was able to take her mind off of the pain by watching television, but began wondering why the nurses kept running into the room looking at the monitors. After some prodding, the nurses told her mother that every time she had a contraction, the baby's heart rate would drop. When the contractions stopped, the heart rate would go back to normal.

The doctor finally told Shanita that it was too risky to have a vaginal birth because she wasn't sure if Shanita would be able to safely push the baby out because she had dilated only seven centimeters. Then the doctor recommended that Shanita have a C-section, which was like a slap in the face. The last thing she wanted was to have the doctor slice her open like a tuna. Shanita wasn't trying to hear the doctor's recommendation and started crying. But through her sobs, she could hear it on the machine every time her baby's heart rate dropped and finally decided to suck it up and have the C-section. She wanted to do whatever it took to get the baby out of there the quickest way possible so that the baby would be OK.

She was taken into the delivery room, where she gave birth to a healthy girl. Then they took her back to the recovery room, where she passed out for a couple of minutes. After she regained consciousness, everything seemed normal, and the nurses thought her passing out was because of a slight drop in her blood pressure. Suddenly, however, Shanita started bleeding a little bit more than usual. She was whisked away to another recovery room, where she started hemorrhaging and then went into cardiac arrest. The alarms on the heart monitors started screaming as the nurses and doctors rushed to her room.

When Shanita's dad walked into her room, he had to wipe away the tears welling up in his eyes. He looked down at his daughter who was strapped to the bed, swollen to twice her normal size. She was almost unrecognizable.

"How you feeling, baby girl?"

"I'm a little sore, but I'm OK. I can't move my arms or my legs. Why am I strapped to the bed like this?"

"Some complications developed with the birth. The doctor said that during the delivery, some of the amniotic fluid from the baby went into your blood-stream, causing your blood to thin out. You went into cardiac arrest and started bleeding uncontrollably. They had to give you several blood transfusions. You needed so much blood that you emptied the blood bank. They said that you had an amniotic embolism. They also said that you are very lucky because 61 percent who have that usually don't make it, and those who survive usually have neurological damage. So by all rights, you should be dead right now. We almost lost you, but you are fine now. It looks like you've got a second chance at life! How much do you remember?"

"I remember them giving me the epidural. In the beginning it just took over my lower body, like from my abdomen on down. Then they gave me a stronger shot and I had absolutely no control over anything. I couldn't even swallow. I couldn't control my muscles to swallow, so they had to stick a tube down my throat to suck the saliva out. I kept telling them I couldn't breathe. I was very nervous, but I was numb. However, I felt everything! I felt when the doctor made the incision and when she cracked me open. I felt when she was stitching me back up. I could feel it, but I was numb, so I just felt the pressure. Even when they took the baby out, the doctor had to use her elbows to push down and take her out. I was lying down on my back, and they had a pad on my chest so I couldn't see everything they were doing down there. But when they took her out and raised her up, I could see her. Then they took her over to the table. Ma was the first one to hold her. I heard my baby cry, and I was able to reach out and touch her while Ma was holding her. I was really sad that I couldn't do the skin-to-skin, or I couldn't be the first one to hold her.

"When they took me to the recovery room, I must have passed out. I don't really remember too much after that. I do remember a nurse asking me a lot of questions, but I couldn't understand what she was saying. I tried to talk but couldn't, which was really strange. They brought in a little dry-erase board and asked me to write something. When I tried to write, I couldn't make my letters out. I had lost my ability to write. My handwriting was all over the place, and they were trying to make out what I was saying. It was really weird. How is my baby? How is Princess?"

"She is doing fine. Your mom took her home."

"How long have I been here?"

"It's been about a week. They say you should be able to go home in a couple of days. The guys at the firehouse have been asking about you, especially Mike. He has been up here a couple of times to see you, but because he wasn't family, they wouldn't let him in the room. What's up between you and him anyway?"

BOOK 2

CHAPTER 9

THE ACADEMY

It had been almost twenty years since Gregory Harris had hung around the courtyard enclosed by the horseshoe-shaped streets in his old neighborhood in Sursum Corda. Most of his friends and neighbors had long since gone. They had either died off, were in jail, or had simply gotten lucky and moved away to a better neighborhood. After he went to college, his parents were able to escape the once proud community that was devastated by the open-air drug trade and never looked back. The neighbors who remained were trapped in an environment by a new breed of ruthless young drug dealers who did not seem to care about the community, who they killed or robbed, or even life itself. Life in the old days was hard, but at least you cared about the people in your community. If there was a beef, you usually settled things with your fist and most of the violence was against people from other neighborhoods or rival gangs. Now it seemed like these young kids preyed on the people in the community and on each other.

When Gregory was asked to go undercover to make drug buys in the community so the police could identify the leaders of the new drug gangs, he accepted without hesitation. He was always chasing money and accepting assignments that required a whole lot of time away from home and his young wife, which in retrospect, was probably the reason she left him. Not only did doing undercover work increase his pay, but it gave him the opportunity to do something for the community that raised him. Whoever was left in the community who might have known him probably didn't know he had become a police officer so he was fairly confident that his cover would be safe. When he showed up in a postal carrier's uniform with his shirt tail hanging out and dirt splotches covering his pants, no one was the wiser. People probably thought he had just succumbed to the temptations of drugs, like his sister and so many others.

As he did his slow-bop walk across First Place, he started looking for a guy called the Candy Man, in order to make his purchase. Even though he had never seen the Candy Man, it was easy to recognize him because he weighed over three hundred pounds and always had a lollipop in his mouth. Gregory began asking some of the young guys on the street if they had seen the Candy Man, or if there was someone else he could score from. A kid who, couldn't have been more than eight years old, pointed to one of the alleys where the Candy Man usually hung out and sold his goods and told Greg he could probably find him there. Gregory quickly peered at a window in one of the apartments where the rest of his police team where perched at the window, capturing everything on video, and nodded in the direction of the alley. As he slowly turned, headed toward the alley, two young guys rapidly walked up behind him. One of the guys quickly walked in front of Gregory while the other one lagged behind. Gregory's instincts began to kick in, realizing there was something wrong with this scenario. The guy in front slowed down, turned, and asked Gregory if he had a match for his cigarette. Before he could respond, the guy in the rear quickly approached and hit Gregory in the back of the head with the butt of a gun, knocking him to the ground.

Gregory lay on the pavement in a semi-conscious state, not being able to move and unable to feel anything. Somehow, however, he could hear everything that was going on. The two young men began riffling through his pants, taking his wallet, money, and anything they could find of worth. Fortunately, Gregory kept his service weapon in his waistband in the front of his pants under his shirt. He had a pair of spandex pants under his trousers which kept the gun in place even if he was running. As Gregory's senses began to return, he opened his eyes and could see the robbers going through his wallet. To Gregory, it seemed that the robbers were moving in slow motion. After taking his money out of his wallet and discarding it on the ground, one of the robbers walked over, stood over Gregory, and aimed his gun at Gregory's head. Something startled the shooter, who turned his head to see what the commotion was. That slight turn of the head enabled Gregory to reach for his gun, and he got off four rounds. Two shots hit the robber in the chest and one in the arm. The other robber took off running into the alley and out of sight. The commotion that interrupted the shooter was Gregory's backup, the police officers who had hidden in the apartment as they videoed the entire scene.

"Greg, you cool, man?" one of the arriving officers asked. Gregory sat on the curb with blood dripping down the back of his head, his gun pointed at the robber who was lying on the ground and bleeding profusely. The robber was rolling over and over, clutching his chest and screaming. Smoke was still piping out of the wounds from where the hot bullets entered his flesh, burning the skin.

"Shut your punk ass up, you dumb bastard," Gregory shouted at the robber. "Yeah, I'm good. I have a hell of a headache, though. Did you catch the other one?"

"Nah, he got away, but we've got him on tape, so he won't get too far before we catch his ass."

After the shooting, Officer Harris was taken off street duty for six weeks and was instructed to see the police psychiatrist for consultation. It was police procedure for officers involved in shootings to see the psychiatrist for six sessions to talk about the incident and ensure the officer is emotionally fit to return to work. Officer Harris knew the drill, but since this was not his first shooting, he did not want any time off. He wanted to return to duty as soon as possible. His sergeant, however, would not allow him to go back to work until he took the required time off.

Instead of taking a trip somewhere, which a lot of officers do to relax, relieve the stress, and rejuvenate, Officer Harris used his time working out in the gym at the police academy located on Blue Plains Drive in southwest Washington, DC. He spent one afternoon lifting weights, and he couldn't help noticing a new class of recruits working out and trying to get in shape. He was amazed at the condition, or lack of condition, most of the recruits seemed to be in. He was also struck by the racial make-up of the class. Out of the twenty-six members of the class, there were two black male recruits, two black female recruits, one white girl, and the rest white boys. He thought that one of the black female recruits looked very familiar. As he sat on the weight bench and observed the recruits working out, he began thinking,

> *Oh my God, look at all of these college-educated white kids trying to get a job working these black neighborhoods. They look like they are scared to death, and this is supposed to be my backup coming? Lord, have mercy! Look at this shit. These guys are little nerds with guns. I bet none of them can fight. Well, there looks like a few may have been former athletes, or ex-military who have been around blacks and can handle themselves, but the rest of them look like little nerds with law degrees. These nerds probably couldn't get a job wherever they are from and want to see what policing is like before they move back to wherever they came from. They are going to get into the hood, and the first thing they are going to do when a brother approaches them is pull out their gun and start shooting. Sheesh!*

Officer Harris returned to lifting weights and then suddenly had a thought. He increased the weights he was lifting up to 240 pounds, and before getting under the weight bar, he asked for someone to spot him. No one moved. He asked again, a little louder this time. The first recruit to respond to his request was Steven Sullivan. Before Officer Harris started lifting, he asked Steven where he was from.

"I'm from Prairie Village, Kansas," Steven responded.

Uh-huh. "What brings you to DC?"

*   *   *

Steven Sullivan arrived in Washington, DC on a Greyhound bus that pulled into an enclosed parking area in Union Station. His trip was long and arduous, taking over seventeen hours, but he enjoyed every minute of it. Other than Prairie Village and Topeka, Kansas, and a brief stay on his grandfather's farm in Iowa when he was young, he hadn't really been anywhere, so this bus trip was very eye opening. He had never seen mountains before, except on television, and was in awe when he saw the Capitol, the White House, and the towering Washington Monument. He was fascinated when the assortment of faces of what seemed like thousands of people of all races and ethnicities rushed through Union Station like they were in a hurry to get to wherever they were going, never stopping to say hello or even smile. Everyone seemed to be in such a hurry. Union Station seemed like a museum itself, with its decorative ceilings and statues of ancient soldiers with swords and shields perched on top of doorways. He asked a security guard how he could navigate this maze and get to the front door. As soon as he stepped into the frigid February air, he saw Big Lee and his beautiful girl, Roya, waiting for him in their car. Big Lee motioned to him to hurry up so they could leave before he got a traffic ticket.

"How was your trip, Stevie," Big Lee inquired.

"It was great. A little long, though."

"Why didn't you just fly? You could have gotten a flight for about the same price the bus trip cost."

"Yeah, I know, but I would have had to find a way to Kansas City to catch the flight. Plus, I wanted to see America."

Big Lee decided to give Stevie a scenic tour of DC before taking him to the Woodner Apartments where he had a studio apartment. He drove around the Capitol, around the National Mall, past the Kennedy Center, through Rock Creek Park, up Sixteenth Street to the Gold Coast, and back down Fourteenth Street and across Arkansas Avenue back to Sixteenth Street, until he reached the parking lot of the Woodner.

"What's that building over there?"

"What building?"

"Right over there!"

"That's not a building. Those are row houses. People live behind each one of those doors. Come on, Stevie. You've got to do a little better than that! You mean you've never seen a row house before?"

"Never. You mean to tell me people live on top of each other like that? What if I want to play my music loud? Wouldn't my next-door neighbor hear it?

"He'd tell you to turn it down, or he'd learn to love your music. You adjust and keep it moving. Man, you've got a lot to learn about city living. Have you put in your application to the academy yet?"

"I submitted an entrance card on-line. They sent me an e-mail to schedule a date for the police exam and started the background check. I take the exam the day after tomorrow. Was the exam hard?"

"Please! It was a little generic entrance exam, which was nothing police-related. It was just general life questions, more or less judgment questions. I can't imagine anyone not passing it. I guess they want to know if you are intelligent enough to get through the courses you have to take at the police academy. Then they give you a psychological exam to determine what type of personality you have. They told me I had a type-A personality. I didn't know what that meant, but they said most police officers are classified as type-A personalities.

"Then you have to take a physical and the physical agility test which they call the PAT. The PAT is a timed obstacle course you have to go through. There are six different stations. You start off at a police car and then run through the gym, up the steps, down the steps, then back to the gym. Then you have to pull a 180-pound dummy for about forty or fifty feet across a line, then run under a table, go through some cones, and climb over a fence. You have to make it in a certain time. At the beginning of the course, you are told that a suspect was wearing such and such color shirt. At the end of the test you have to remember the description of the suspect. Finally, you have to do the physical test, which is a piece of cake. You have to do something like fifty push-ups, twenty-five sit-ups, ten pull-ups on the monkey bars, and, finally, run a mile and a half in something like thirteen to twenty minutes. The times are age-based and gender-based. You should have no problem passing any of that stuff. We did way more than that during football practice."

Big Lee took Stevie up to his studio apartment and showed him around the facility, where he could go to get something to eat, and how to get around the city using public transportation. Big Lee was currently staying at Roya's place on Connecticut Avenue, so he told Stevie that he could stay at his apartment as long as he needed, just as long as he didn't mess up the place too bad. Big Lee also gave Stevie the phone number of a friend he worked with at the M. Loeb warehouse corporation, a wholesale food store that catered to the small corner stores in the area, in case Stevie needed a part-time job to bring in a little cash while waiting to start at the academy, or just in case the academy thing didn't work out. Stevie thanked him and offered to pay a little something for letting him stay there. Big Lee graciously declined, stating he was always willing to help a friend in need.

After Big Lee and Roya left, Stevie stood in the middle of the small studio apartment and began to wonder how this new adventure was going to turn out. He gazed out of the window, which revealed a huge wooded area; he thought Big Lee referred to it as Rock Creek Park, which separated this section of the city. He also saw that the roadway was jammed with cars emptying out onto the city street, which seemed to be even more jammed with cars. He realized that he had a lot to learn about this city, especially if he was going to be responsible for fighting crime and making people safe. He decided to use the public transportation to venture out, explore, and observe the people. He began to feel a little bit overwhelmed and wondered if he had made the right decision. A little bit of loneliness and homesickness began tugging at his heart. Before unpacking his things, he got on the phone and dialed Michelle's number.

*   *   *

Big Lee was crouched in the standard shooting stance at the Northern Virginia Criminal Justice Training Academy gun range, getting in some practice so he could qualify for his shooting certification. He had been accepted by the Metro Transit Police Division, which is a tri-jurisdictional police agency that has jurisdiction in Maryland, Virginia, and the District of Columbia. The Metro Transit Police Department is responsible for the safety and security of both Metrorail and Metrobus systems, serving a population of 4 million within a 1,500-square- mile area. This meant that if a transit police officer witnessed a crime in DC and the person jumped on the subway train and crossed into Maryland, the officer had the authority to arrest the suspect in Maryland. Then there would be an extradition hearing in Maryland, and the suspect would be extradited back to DC to face whatever charges were pending there.

The Northern Virginia Criminal Justice Training Academy, which lasts six months, is a combined academy that includes seventeen participating law enforcement agencies throughout northern Virginia, as well as several in the District of Columbia and Maryland. Staff from Maryland would come to the Virginia Academy and teach the laws and procedures used in Maryland and recruits would spend time in the DC police academy to learn DC law. The basic academy training got recruits a Virginia certification. Maryland's academy standards are parallel with Virginia's, and there was a reciprocal agreement where Maryland would accept the Virginia certification. Recruits, however, had to spend time at the DC academy in order to be certified in the District. Qualifying for shooting was a different matter. Recruits had to take three different shooting tests, one from each district, in order to successfully complete the academy training.

Before he got to the academy, Big Lee thought the academy would be a cakewalk because he had been in the military and had gone through a tough basic training. The academy is a paramilitary organization, so they try to base the academy off of military basic training standards, incorporating its structure and discipline. It is about teaching people how to take orders and do what you are told. The main difference, however, was that in the military, they trained you not to think for yourself but just follow orders. To be a police officer, you have to know how to think for yourself. There are times when you are by yourself and you have to know when to use your discretion and when not to use your discretion.

The toughest part of academy training for Big Lee was the marathon runs he had to do. Running long distances wasn't his thing.

He could run and jump with the best of them but couldn't understand why he had to run four miles. He would always complain to the officers, "What do we have to run four miles for? I'm not chasing anybody for four miles. If I had to chase someone that far, I would just have to bust a cap in his ass and be done with it." Shooting, on the other hand, was something that he was very good at; after all, he had done his fair share of training, shooting and killing when he was in the army.

Big Lee felt that the weapons training he was receiving in the academy was inadequate and was ill-preparing recruits for what they could possibly face out on the street. When on the shooting range, he could tell that many of the recruits were actually afraid of handling the very tools they were given to use. Some would barely pass the shooting test, but more importantly, he could tell that some would use extremely poor judgment when forced to pull their weapon. In a war zone, it was very simple: shoot to kill anyone not wearing the same uniform you have. But on the street, you have to assess the situation and use your judgment. At the first sign of trouble, some of these newbies would pull their weapon and start shooting, endangering the lives of everyone in the area.

The history of the police department's use of weapons mandates was a bit confusing, which further exasperated the training. At first, officers were told not to draw their weapons until they saw a weapon. Then it went to, "You could draw your gun, but you have to hold it at your side until you see a gun." Then it evolved to, "You could draw your gun and hold it at the ready position until needed." Big Lee knew that there were things that you had to be able to glean from experienced police officers that would put you in the position to succeed. Those things were not being taught at the academy.

Big Lee rolled in the paper target he had been shooting. He scored twelve shots center mass and five head shots. *Bring on those shooting tests,* he confidently thought.

*   *   *

Steven Sullivan arrived at the MPD Police Academy every morning, forty-five minutes before the 6:30 a.m. formation. This gave him the opportunity to put on his uniform, making sure everything was in place, spotless, and that he had all of his gear. He had to memorize the code of ethics, so he would review the part that his recruitment class was currently on so that if he was called to recite it, he would not mess it up and get the class in trouble. He would then proceed to the cafeteria, where he wrote down the daily broadcasts, which included who the watch commander was, the roll-call sergeant, the weather for the day, and the code word for the day.

Promptly at 6:30 a.m., formation was called, and the class would march into the commons area or inside the gym, depending on the weather; raise the flag; recite the pledge of allegiance; and sing out accountability information. The class sergeant or one of the class officers would come to test the class. They would go through the line inspecting uniforms and would ask questions like, "What is the definition of probable cause? Give me a probable cause misdemeanor." Or basically any question about a lesson pertaining to the DC code. If you didn't know, or if anything was missing on your uniform, the whole class would be disciplined with push-ups or short runs. Once inspection was completed, you would form up, march back inside, and get your day started.

The rest of the day was split up between physical fitness training (PT) and class work. There would be two hours of PT each day, which included running, push-ups, weight lifting, and self-defense training. They would also work with the fire department cadets. The fire department academy was right next to the police academy, separated by a wood line. The fire academy cadets would cross over the line, running, and loudly singing their cadences, and the police academy cadets would do the same. As part of the PT training, the police academy cadets would have to run up and down the fire academy burn tower with a heavy water hose over and over again. There was a great deal of respect given to the training that the fire department cadets for being able to do that type of conditioning, endurance, and strength training.

After physical fitness training, the rest of the day was geared to classroom training. Just like Big Lee had said, it was just like being in college. The subjects taught included laws of arrest, search and seizure, criminal law, traffic regulations, community policing and ethics, and human relations or cultural training. The majority of the cadets in Steven's class were white and not from the DC area. Many were not from urban areas at all. There was a lot of cultural sensitivity training because Washington DC and the communities they were being prepared to serve were so culturally and racially diverse. Trips were planned to go to the National Museum of African American History and Culture and the US Holocaust Museum for those people who were unfamiliar with the plight of African Americans and Jews.

During his off-hours, Steven would spend time touring the city using public transportation in order to familiarize himself with the communities he could possibly be working in. From time to time, he would take the Metrorail and just watch the different types of people who would get on, their behavior, and interactions. Most of the time, however, he would take the bus so he could actually see the communities in the different sections and neighborhoods. He noticed a stark difference between the communities northeast and southeast across the Anacostia River. In those communities, there was a scattering of commercial ribbons; but for the most part, they were void of a central business district. The residential areas were poorly lit and the people he could see on the street seemed worn by a harsh life.

On the weekends, Steven worked the part-time job Big Lee got him working as a cashier at the M. Loeb warehouse. The job was easy and a distraction from his lonely weekends. One Saturday, he had just gotten off from work and threw himself across the bed when, much to his delight, he got a phone call from Michelle.

"Hey, Steven, what 'cha doing tonight?"

"Not one single thing! What you got in mind?"

"A few friends and I were going to the Bohemian Caverns down on U Street for a bite to eat and to listen to some good jazz music. You up for it?"

"Sure, I'd love to. What time?"

"Meet me at my house at about 8:00 p.m. and we will walk down to the spot. I live at 1226 Euclid Street NW Do you know where that is?"

"I'll find it. See you at eight. And, Michelle … thanks."

Steven showed up promptly at 8:00 p.m. When Michelle opened the door, he was floored by her beauty and warm smile. In the back of his mind, he couldn't help thinking about the last time he was with her and the passionate kiss she placed on his lips. He could vividly remember her smile, the curves of her body, the firmness of her breasts, and the passion in their embrace. Just the thought of it got him aroused. She asked if he had any problems finding her place, to which he replied, "Not one bit." He had gotten comfortable traveling on the bus and her house was a short walk from the bus stop on Fourteenth and Euclid. He was amazed at the size of her house, which had three stories and a basement. In fact, most of the houses on that block were enormous, which was different from the small, compact row houses he had seen throughout the city. She grabbed a light jacket to fend off the cool night air, and they started walking down to Eleventh Street. As they passed a school sitting on the top of a large hill, he asked,

"What school is that?"

"Oh, that's Cardozo High School."

"Is that where you teach?"

"Heavens, no. I wish it were, though. That would mean I could walk to work and could sleep much later. I probably would be late to work every day! I teach way across town at Anacostia High School."

"Why don't you just teach at this school since it is one block from your house?"

"I don't get to make those decisions. Once you get accepted in the school system, they send you were there is a need or opening."

"What do you teach?"

"I teach art. I also am the girls' soccer coach."

Steven and Michelle arrived at the Bohemian Caverns, and Steven understood why it got that name. When they entered the building, he saw the ceilings were low, giving you a claustrophobic feeling. There were also what looked like stalactites hanging from the ceiling, and so it looked like you were in a cave. He had never seen anything like that before. When they got to the table where her friends were sitting, he couldn't help noticing that they seemed surprised when she introduced him.

"Hey, y'all. This is my good friend Steven Sullivan. He's from out of town. We went to school together."

"Hey, Steven," they replied in unison. "Welcome to Washington."

"Hi, everyone."

"What brings you to DC?"

"I was trying to join the police force in Prairie Village, where I am from, but they didn't have any openings. One of my good friends suggested that I try here, so here I am."

"Where is Prairie Village?"

"That's a small town in Kansas."

"How long you been in DC?"

"Just a couple of months. I started at the police academy two weeks ago. Where is the restroom?"

When Steven left the table, Michelle's girlfriend, Toni, turned to her with a sinister look on her face and said, "Girl, I didn't know you liked playing in the snow. What you doing with a white boy?"

"Girl, don't start that shit. We're just friends."

"Just friends … yeah, right! Have you fucked him yet?"

"You're such a slut. And no, I haven't fucked him yet, but I might give him a little sumptin', sumptin' if he acts right. Now be nice!"

When Steven returned, they all engaged in friendly conversation, ate some good Caribbean food, and listened to the soulful sounds of a jazz band called Collaboration. Steven and Michelle walked arm-in-arm all the way back to her house. They made small talk, and before he knew it, they were at her door. He desperately wanted to come in so they could have a "complete" evening, but she stopped him at the doorstep and thanked him for a wonderful evening. He asked when he could see her again, and she replied, "Maybe next Friday evening." She gave him a quick kiss on the cheek before turning away and closing the door.

The next week, Steven called her to set up a date for the upcoming Friday evening. She told him that they would have to do it on another day because she had been given the opportunity to work the concession stand at Anacostia's basketball game. The money she received from the concession stand would go to paying for new uniforms and equipment for her soccer team. Even though she wanted to go out, she couldn't pass up on the opportunity. Though he was a little disappointed, he understood. He still wanted to see her, so he decided to go to the game at Anacostia. His desire to be around her was growing every day. When he wasn't doing push-ups at the academy, or studying criminal law in DC, he was thinking about her.

The game at Anacostia started at 8:00 p.m., so after leaving the academy for the day and freshening up a bit, he hopped on the subway and took the green line to Anacostia station. He had to take two buses in order to get to Sixteenth Street in Southeast. As he got off the second bus, he began to feel a little uneasy. The sun had gone down, the streets got very narrow, and the small lamp post gave very little light. The darkness seemed to envelope him, and the walls of the subway train and bus were no longer protecting him. He was out there all by himself and was walking the ominous streets that everybody kept talking about at the academy. He began wondering if he had made a mistake by coming there.

Suddenly, he heard a commotion and turned to see what was happening. A small loud crowd began gathering up a side street, and he strained to see what was happening. A young black male suddenly took off running, followed by a group of four other young men. Before the young male got far, the other men captured him and started punching him in the face, back, stomach, and wherever they could find an opening. The punches were so loud and vicious it shocked Steven to the point that he was sad and afraid. The unfortunate victim fell to the ground and balled himself into a fetal position, trying desperately to fend off the blows. The attackers began kicking and stomping on the young man's head and body. The loud screaming of the victim slowly faded as he lost consciousness. The attack reminded Steven of a pack of lions or wolves chasing down their prey. He felt sorry for the young victim. Steven thought about trying to help the young man, but the thought quickly faded as a large crowd gathered to watch the savage beating. The crowd of on-lookers included several adults, and he wondered why they didn't do anything to stop it.

Steven continued his trek toward the school when he saw a group of black males standing on the corner engaged in jovial conversation. He became extremely nervous, especially after observing the attack, wondering if the same thing could happen to him. The men stopped their conversation when they saw him cross the street. They started laughing as one of them screamed out, "White boy, we ain't gonna do nothin' to you." They continued their conversation. When Steven got to Sixteenth Street, he saw a police cruiser parked on the corner with its red and blue lights flashing. Steven blew a sigh of relief. The cruiser was a beautiful sight to see. He walked over to the cruiser and asked one of the officers if the school on this street was Anacostia High School. The officer said yes, it was. "Whew, thanks officer," Steven replied.

When Michelle saw Steven standing in the hot dog line at the concession stand, she was shocked.

"What in the world are you doing here?"

"I just wanted to see you. In fact, wherever you are, I want to be there too. Whatever you are doing, I want to do it too. I just want to be near you."

"How did you get here?"

"I took the train and two buses."

"Boy, you are crazy. That wasn't the safest thing to do, but I guess if you are going to be patrolling these streets, you've got to learn them for yourself. When the game is over, I'll give you a ride home."

"I would much prefer to go to your home!"

*   *   *

"Class 16-6 ... ATTEN-HUT! FACE FRONT! TAKE YOUR SEATS! Today we have a special guest. He is a decorated officer who has arrested his fair share of bad guys, has been shot at, has been praised for his work on the streets developing positive community relationships, and has just finished another stint of undercover work where he was responsible for bringing down a notorious drug ring.

He is here today to share his expertise and some knowledge that will probably save some of your lives. Put your hands together for Officer Gregory Harris. Give him your undivided attention. There will be a test at formation tomorrow, so listen carefully!"

Officer Harris stepped to the podium in the classroom and looked out at a sea of white faces, with a few black faces scattered among the crowd. Sitting in the audience were Cadets Steven Sullivan, Shanita Brown, and Leon Anderson, who with his fellow cadets from the Northern Virginia Criminal Justice Training Academy were there to learn about DC law. After giving birth, Shanita joined the fire department and served with distinction. She completed the firefighters' training academy, got her EMT certificate, and quickly rose to the position of officer in charge. She developed a romantic relationship and briefly moved in with fellow firefighter, Michael Holiday, who seemed like a nice guy; but then she realized that he was too controlling. She was determined not to be controlled by anybody. She enjoyed the thrill of a being a first responder, but having to work twenty-four-hour shifts and stay in the firehouse was an obstacle to raising her child. She decided that becoming a police officer was a good career move.

"Good morning class 16-6. As Officer Taylor said, my name is Gregory Harris. I was born and raised right here in DC and have been on the force for twelve years. In my capacity as a police officer, I have walked a beat in one of the roughest neighborhoods in DC, have been in numerous fist fights, shootings, drug investigations, and arrests. But more importantly, if something happens in the neighborhood, I have developed such a rapport with the people in the community that people will call me or pull me to the side on the QT and let me know what's going on or who's involved. Somebody at the academy felt I had something of value to your development, so they asked me to come in and give you the heads-up on what it is really like out there on the street.

"I don't know why you are here, but there are some serious questions you need to ask yourself and be able to answer if being a police officer is really what you want to do. If you are squeamish, then this ain't the place you want to be because you are going to see some things that will turn your stomach. If you are afraid to fight, then this ain't the place you want to be because you will definitely be involved in street fights. Are you willing to kill someone? Do you have the ability to kill someone? I mean, you never really know the answer until you have done it, but if you say to yourself, 'No, I don't think I can kill someone,' then this is not the occupation for you. The odds are high that you will encounter a situation where you will have to make the decision to kill someone, or be killed. Give those things some serious thought.

"Now, before I get started, I'd like to know a little about you and what makes you want to be a police officer. Young lady, what's your name and why are you here?"

Officer Harris pointed to a young female cadet who looked like she was about five foot two tall and couldn't have weighed more than 120 pounds.

"My name is Melody Cash. I have always admired the police. At one point I thought I wanted to be a lawyer. When I was seven years old, however, this movie came on called *SWAT*. My dad was really big on law enforcement. He always wanted to be a cop. When the movie came out, I would watch it over and over with him. So me and my dad really connected over that. I would always tell him that I wanted to be on a SWAT, or that I wanted to be a police officer. So this has always been a dream of mine."

"Oh, so you got daddy issues!"

The class erupted in laughter.

"This ain't *SWAT* and this ain't TV. The majority of you will not get a cushy assignment working in the Second District, or 2D. You will not be working in Georgetown or downtown. Most of you will be sent to 7D or 6D, where life is hard and things are rough. What makes you think you can be a good cop?"

"Sir, I was born and raised in DC. I probably have more experience than most of the people in this room regarding that rough life. I don't shy away from drama. I just own it and do what I have to do!"

"OK, I can respect that." Officer Harris pointed to a young-looking white cadet. "You, what's your name, and why are you here?"

"My name is David Kinkel. I want to protect and serve the community."

"Bullshit! Where are you from?"

"I'm from Harpers Ferry, West Virginia."

"Harpers Ferry … isn't that where John Brown got killed? Why are you in DC?"

"Well, I tried getting on the force there, but Harpers Ferry is a small town, and the police force isn't very large. There were no job openings there. Plus, everybody said that if you could make it in DC or New York City, you could make it anywhere, so here I am."

"Uh-huh." Officer Harris pointed to a black cadet. "Tell me your story."

"My name is Barry Brinkley. I'm from North Carolina, but I live in DC. To be honest with you, I was working in the school system, got turned off, and started looking for an out. Even when I was in college, I thought about retirement. I always felt that when I got to be seventy years old, I did not want to have to be working. It kind of made me sad when I saw elderly people out there working because they couldn't make ends meet. Looking at the school system, you had to have thirty years and be fifty-five before you could retire. I started working in DC public schools when I was twenty-four, which meant I would have to work thirty-one more years before I could retire. I felt like thirty years was too long to have to be able to deal with other people's kids with all of the restrictions the school system puts on you. I have an aunt and an uncle who work for MPD, and I talked with them about it. They said all you have to do is work for twenty-five years on the force, and there is no age restriction. To me, it was a no-brainer!"

"Trust me, if you hated kids and parents then, you'll probably hate some of them even more now. And hate is never a good way to start a relationship. What about you, sir?"

"My name is Tony Tripaldi. I'm from New York. I needed a job and saw an on-line ad that said MPD was hiring."

Officer Harris decided to call on one more cadet before he started his presentation. When he looked over the room, he saw a face that he recognized.

"And you young lady, what's your story?"

Shanita Brown thought for a second. *Should I tell these people my business? I don't want to be too preachy. Oh, what the hell!*

"My name is Shanita Brown, and I am from DC. When I was young, I hated the police. I had a brother who went to jail. He did sell drugs, but on the day they arrested him, the cops planted the drugs on him. When they got him into custody, they beat him up pretty good. To me, that was wrong. I felt like the police didn't relate to the people in my neighborhood and were always talking down to us or harassing us for no reason. I felt that if you break the law, you should go to jail, but cops didn't have to belittle you, frame you, or treat you as less than a human being just because of the way you look or where you live. When I became a firefighter, I got to know some cops who were pretty decent people and who cared about the people they served. I looked up one day and realized that most of the people I knew where cops. I would listen to them talk cop talk all day, every day, so I decided to become one of them. Also, those twenty-four-hour shifts as a firefighter made it difficult for me and my daughter."

That's where I remember her from, Officer Harris thought. *Her brother was that big time drug dealer everybody was after. She was the one with the big tits whose picture was on the wall at the precinct. How did she get to be a police officer?*

"Cadet Brown, let me ask you a question which will lead directly into part of my presentation today. When you were a firefighter, what made you run into a fire and face possible death, when everyone else would be running away? What did you think about? Were you ever afraid?"

"You really don't think about the danger. You just do what you were trained to do. We used to say, 'We put the wet stuff on the red stuff_ that's what we do.' It was crawling into a building to see which room was on fire. When you found it, you'd start hitting it with every pattern we were trained to use until the fire was out. I never feared for my life. I think the only time I was fearful was the first time I learned to wear the face mask and had to crawl around. When I was training, I would say a little prayer until I could control my breathing. After that episode, I just focused on the task at hand and followed my training."

"Thank you, Cadet Brown. Does anyone know why first responders are able to run toward danger when everyone else is running away?

Has anyone ever heard of the fight or flight syndrome? Let me try and explain it this way. When you perceive danger is lurking, your survival skills take over and your body produces a substance called adrenaline. Once adrenaline starts to flow into your body, the part of your brain that deals with fine motor skills shuts off. Only the big motor skills are available to you. When that happens, you are either going to panic and run away, or you are going to go all in, stand your ground, and address the source of danger. So if you are one that normally panics, then you will find that law enforcement is probably not the field for you. But if you decide that you can go all in, you are like that firefighter when the house is on fire_ you run into it while everyone else is running out, without thinking. If you cannot run into that building, this is probably not the profession for you. You cannot hesitate, because that moment of hesitation could cost you your life or your partner's life.

"A lot of what we teach you here is how to stay in control, how to remain calm in the face of danger, and how to function when certain parts of your brain shut down. You won't be able to tie your shoe-laces when that adrenaline starts pumping because that requires fine motor skills. We train you to build muscle memory so that you can function in times of high stress.

"Let me give you an example. A lot of research that the department has done showed that officers during the 1960s were being killed with shell casings in their hands. What the researchers found was that during training, officers were required to pick up their own shell casings and put them in their pockets so that their trainers didn't have to clean up after them. Well, that behavior was being exhibited on the streets, and officers were being killed because instead of quickly reloading their guns, they were taking time to pick up their shell casings, which was a direct result of muscle memory in a ramped-up situation where the brain ceases to function properly. They were actually in a gun-fight and normally, they wouldn't spend time picking up shell casings, but that was what they were doing because that was the way they were trained. When you are in a fight, you don't think about what you are doing_ you just do it. As a result of this research, the police department changed the way officers were trained."

"Officer Harris, I got a question."

"Yes, what is it, Cadet Banks?"

"I've seen on the news that a suspect was shot by the police over forty times. Why is it that after a suspect is shot and falls to the ground, they keep shooting him? Once the shooting starts, is the intent to kill him?"

"We are not trained to shoot to kill. We are trained to shoot to stop. We used to be trained to shoot center mass, but after that situation in California where two bank robbers wore body armor and killed a lot of police officers during a gun battle, our training shifted to shoot two to the body and one to the head. In that California case, nobody thought about shooting them in the head because the part of the brain that tells you to do that had shut down. So now, you are taught to shoot to stop the person. As long as the threat is coming toward you, you continue to shoot that person. Once the threat is stopped, then you are supposed to stop shooting. The problem police officers encounter today is that too many times, the suspect is wearing a bullet-proof vest, or they may be so high on drugs that they seem to have superhuman strength, and they will keep coming at you. As a result, some officers will use a hollow point bullet as the first bullet in the magazine followed by regular police-issued rounds. The hollow-point, which by the way is illegal, will immediately put a suspect down. I'm not saying you should do that because, it will get you in a world of trouble, but that is what some officers do.

"No one can say, however, whether you fired one time or fifty times because counting is a fine motor skill, and again, during a fight, that part of your brain has shut down. Usually, at the range, you fire until your magazine is empty. Someone could ask you how many times you fired, and you may say that you fired seven times, when in reality, you have emptied your magazine. You may only remember seven shots because the total number is something the body doesn't register when you are in a fight.

"I have been in a number of fights where I have had to use my weapon. I feel that my training has prepared me well for what happens on the street because I am still here. So it is very important that you listen to your instructors here and take your training seriously. It could possibly save your life or the life of your fellow officers. Are there any more questions?"

*   *   *

It was getting close to graduation, and Shanita Brown could finally see the light at the end of the tunnel. She had taken all of the physical stuff they threw at her, including the endless number of push-ups, the nine-mile runs, four-mile runs, and the countless number of times she had to run up and down the tower steps. She was even able to handle what the drill instructors called the zoo. That was when the instructors took her class to a football field and made her class walk from one end to the other mimicking, whatever animal the instructors called out. They would say, "Oh, you are an alligator." The class would then have to get down on all fours and walk to the other end of the field like an alligator, or a duck, or a kangaroo. The classwork and memorization of statutes, though tedious, gave her no concern with regards to her passing the exams because she had a really good memory. Learning how to shoot was fun, while learning when to shoot made her stay focused. Lurking in the shadows, however, was something that stayed on her mind and gave her cause for great concern. She knew ultimately that before she could complete all the academy requirements, she would have to face the Animal.

The segment of training called defensive tactics was the one aspect of academy training that she didn't look forward to. She had heard horror stories from other people before she got to the academy, about how the instructors were going to try to break you down mentally and physically. One of her girlfriends told her, "Eventually, you are gonna have to fight this dude they call the Animal. I got my ass whopped by the Animal. When I came home, I was black and blue all over. You can punch and punch, but he's got on five inches of foam padding, so he can't feel it. This training is meant to push you and demand that you push yourself further because you are literally fighting for your life. And those people who get into the ring with the Animal and tap out before the designated time is up are considered a police officer liability. You are given another chance, and if you tap out early again, you are recycled to another class and have to start all over."

D-Day arrived, and everyone seemed to be very tense. The cadets used the expression D-Day because it was the day when cadets were introduced to defensive tactics training. There were various phases to this training designed to reproduce scenarios that police officers could face when out on the street. During one scenario, two cadets were selected and were surrounded by their classmates who were holding bags that prevented them from getting out of the circle. The cadets in the circle were forced to fight each other with the batons.

Another scenario was called Stand your ground, where they were taught defensive tactics to prevent attackers from getting their baton or weapon. There was also a scenario that involved one cadet and two instructors. This was meant to teach awareness, but also to drive home the point that you can put yourself in a dire situation where you are drawn in with a potential altercation with one individual, develop tunnel vision, and never see the second assailant who walks by you. And then there was the fight with the Animal.

Knowing how to fight and defend yourself is a very important skill. Many academy instructors felt that if you didn't know how to fight before you came to the academy, there wasn't really much they could do to prepare you for what you ultimately would face on the street. Police policy prevented officers from using deadly force when the suspect didn't have a weapon, which meant you had to know how to defend yourself. Instructors were very hard on the female cadets, especially the ones they felt were too meek and mild to handle confrontation. Some female cadets, in preparation for this fight, would stuff towels down their uniform to try and pad their bodies, thinking they wouldn't feel the blows. This only infuriated the instructors, making them hit harder or be rougher than usual.

The Animal looked around the circle of cadets until his eyes stopped on Shanita. "OK, sugar britches, it's your turn," he said. "Bring your sweet ass in this ring!"

The Animal weighed about 230 pounds and was six foot three inches tall. The padding he wore made it seem like he was 300 pounds. He stood like a giant with his gloves on and an ominous glare in his eyes, which spewed disdain. "I'm gonna smash that pretty little face of yours and make you quit," he snarled. Many of the instructors felt that Shanita was too good-looking and dainty to be a cop. For whatever reason, even though she took everything they threw at her physically, they thought she should be working in an office instead of working on the streets. Shanita's heart began racing as she took a long, hard swallow, put her headgear on, and entered the ring.

Shanita told the Animal to get on the ground and to put his hands behind his back. She kept her distance from him with her baton as her only protection. He started to turn around like he was complying with her request as she inched closer to him. Suddenly, he whipped around like a cat and threw a punch that caught her on the side of the head. She didn't see the punch coming because the boxing headgear she had on blocked her peripheral vision. Everything went blurry. That was when she realized that this was no longer training and that she was in a real fight. She became enraged.

I know this motherfucker didn't just hit me like I was a man, she thought. She dropped her baton, rushed him, drove her forehead into his chest, and started throwing rapid punches as hard as she could. The force of her flailing body caused both of them to tumble to the ground in what seemed like a life-and-death struggle. One of her punches caught him in the jaw, surprising him as he began badgering her arms and legs with his punches. The action was fast and furious and didn't stop until another instructor called time.

When it was over, Shanita couldn't remember much about the confrontation, but she heard the lieutenant who was monitoring the instruction tell everyone to put their bags down and give her a round of applause. "I didn't think you had it in you," he told her, "but you were handling your business. Good job." The Animal came over and gave her a pat on the back. "You're alright, sugar britches," he said. As she turned to get out of the ring, he gave her a pat on the ass. *Man. I'd like to hit that,* he thought. He then turned to another cadet and hollered, "All right playboy, it's your turn. Get your punk-ass in this ring."

When Shanita got back to her spot in the circle, her senses began to return. Her heart began racing again, and the pain in her arms and legs began to throb. But there was another feeling that began to rise in her chest. It was a feeling of pride and accomplishment that seemed to dull her physical pain. She lowered her head, wiped the sweat off her brow, and, with an enormous smile etched across her face thought, *I did it! Dad would have been so proud.*

* * *

Graduation day had finally arrived. After twenty-eight weeks of hard work, relentless running, training, learning, and discipline the cadets were now sworn in as new members of the police force, given their badges, and told to report to work on Monday morning so they could receive their assignments. They would have to continue their training on the street under the supervision of a field training officer (FTO) for another twelve weeks before they were cut loose and could work on their own or with a partner.

During the ceremony, Officer Shanita Brown looked out into the audience and could see her mother and her father proudly smiling at her. With them was her daughter Princess, who didn't seem to understand or care about what was going on. The admiration that seemed to emanate from the sea of family and friends in attendance was astonishing. Shanita embraced that good feeling because somehow, she knew that this feeling wouldn't last long. On this day, she felt that there was a lot of respect and honor for the uniform and the task at hand. After all, she would be risking her life in order to help the people in the community. She also knew that on the street, there was a great deal of disrespect for the people who put on the uniform and wasn't quite sure how she would handle people calling her names or hating her simply because she wore the uniform. Only time would tell.

Officer Steven Sullivan felt like jumping for joy when he saw his mother and his father sitting in the audience. Even though they were no longer married, they sat together giving the appearance that they were one happy family. After the ceremony ended, the newly sworn-in officers began taking pictures with family members and friends and congratulating each other. Steven had forged life-long bonds with several of his classmates, Shanita Brown being one of them. He began searching over the sea of faces looking desperately for one face in particular. He felt a tap on his back, and when he turned around he began smiling like a Cheshire cat. Michelle had promised him she would attend his graduation, and there she was. After they shared a warm embrace, he grabbed her hand and led her to where his mother and his father stood.

"Mom, Dad, I'd like you to meet my girlfriend. Her name is Michelle Johnson."

CHAPTER 10

RIDING THE RAILS

Officer Leon Anderson stood silently as he glared at his image in the full-length mirror. He had been accustomed to uniforms all his life_ from his football uniforms, to his army uniform, and his bus driver uniform, but this one somehow seemed different. When he was in his football uniform, he got glory, adulation, and all the women he wanted because people adored him. He even got a letter once from some football fan he didn't even know, asking him if she could have his baby. When he wore his army uniform, strangers would come up to him and thank him for his service. That gave him a warm feeling inside. His police uniform, on the other hand, was a different story_ some good, but most negative.

When he went back to his old high school wearing his police uniform, his principal was pleasantly surprised and proud, as were some of his former teachers. The adulation he received then and during graduation from the police academy quickly dissipated and was replaced by condemnation, accusations, and disparaging remarks from friends, some family members, and people in the community. His mother and his grandmother actually freaked out when they found out he was joining the police force. They thought it was a death sentence. Some of his friends from the old neighborhood couldn't understand why he would want to become a cop. They made comments like, "You should be ashamed of yourself. What were you thinking? How could you be a cop, and how can you be a part of a gang of people who are taking lives?"

He understood why people were angry, especially with the killing of unarmed black men across the country, which was being publicized on social media every minute of every day, as well as the attention being received from protesting professional athletes. But he wasn't killing anybody. Most of the people who were making those statements didn't know anything about him or what kinds of difficulties were involved in police work.

Just last week, there was an altercation at the Rhode Island Avenue Metro stop. The officer on duty told a young teenager that she could not eat in or around the subway station and asked her to put away her food. The young girl got belligerent and told the officer she was not putting away her food. According to the arresting officer's report, he asked the young girl three times to put away her food, and when she did not comply, he started writing her a citation. The young girl started cursing at him and knocked the citation out of his hand. The officer then attempted to arrest the young girl, and a large crowd began to form. The officer, who was white, called for backup. When Officer Lee arrived, he heard people in the crowd shouting, "Fuck the police!" Then the crowd turned their anger on him, stating, "You're no good. You don't have a mind of your own, because if you did, you wouldn't be wearing that uniform right now!"

Big Lee felt it wasn't fair to paint every police officer with the same broad brush simply because they were wearing a uniform. He had been on the job for only three weeks, and people were attacking his character without knowing anything about him. At the end of the day, this was a job like any other, like being a fireman, a lawyer, a doctor, a cashier, or a janitor. The difference was that this was a job that was very stressful. The veteran officers_ Big Lee referred to them as the old heads_ would always tell him that his number one job was to go home at the end of the shift. They would often say, "There is a possibility that when you put on that uniform, you might not get the chance to go home at night." The ironic thing was that officers were out there risking their lives to secure and protect a group of people who were the same people who were saying, "Fuck the police."

Roya walked up behind Big Lee, wrapped her arms around him, and gave him a warm embrace. "You all right, babe?"

"Yeah, I'm cool. I just had a long day today."

"It's late. Why don't you get out of that uniform, take a quick shower, and come to bed so we can talk about your day."

It had been a trying day. This was his first week working the night shift after doing two weeks on the mid-day shift. For the next two weeks, he would be on foot patrol, which meant he had to ride on the subway car from station to station on his beat, basically to present a police presence. He would be responsible for maintaining order, observing any crimes that may be committed, and writing citations for what Metro considered nuisance violations_ eating, smoking, drinking, or spitting on the trains.

During his first two weeks, he had been on vehicle patrol, which, to him, was a piece of cake. All he did was ride around with his field training officer, writing citations for people who ran the stop signs at the train stations on his beat, listening to the dispatcher for calls, or transporting people who were arrested to the appropriate district police station. His only problem was a disagreement with his field training officer. There were times when crimes were being committed that had nothing to do with Metro or the transit system. When something went down, like a fight on the street or a robbery, Big Lee felt he had an obligation to do something because he was a duly sworn officer of the law. His FTO said they had no jurisdiction over city crimes, and their responsibility was to report it to MPD and let them handle it. This did not sit well with Big Lee. During one occasion, he jumped out of the car to stop a group of females who were jumping another girl. Big Lee's FTO was furious and wrote him up for insubordination.

"OK, babe, something seems to be bothering you. Tell me what happened."

"Well, I was on foot patrol at the Gallery Place station and got a call saying there was a disturbance on the train and the train was headed my way. Now, disturbance is such a broad term. You never know what you are getting into. I go down to the platform, and as the train pulls in, I could see this man and a woman arguing. When the doors opened, I asked them to step off the train. They stepped off the train, and I am trying to figure out what they were arguing about. As they were explaining, another guy gets off the train, comes toward me, and punches me on the side of the head. I don't know why people always want to fight me, as big as I am, but I have been in my fair share, so I can take a punch. Now, the other guy, the guy who was arguing with the lady, jumps in it, and now I am fighting both of them. We are tussling, and everybody just stands there looking and shouting for them to kick my ass. Imagine that!

"I threw a punch, catching one of them in the temple, and he was out like a light. He dropped like a sack of potatoes. The other guy becomes more enraged and rushes me. I caught him with a punch and opened up a huge gap over his eye. The sight of his blood spattering everywhere seemed to calm him down. I pulled out my gun and said, 'All right now, is everybody good?' I then called for backup, put the handcuffs on the bloody guy, and checked to make sure the guy I knocked out was still breathing. I still didn't know what he and that lady were arguing about or why they decided to jump me. It turns out that the guy who sucker-punched me was a friend of the guy who was arguing with the lady. The sad thing about the whole situation was that the people in the crowd were looking at me like I did something wrong or I was the bad guy."

Roya drew Big Lee close to her and gave him a big hug. When she attempted to give him a passionate kiss, he turned away. That kind of shocked her because he had never done that before. She figured that he must still be upset.

"Babe, you're an enigma."

"An enigma … what do you mean by that?"

"You're like a big teddy bear one minute … all soft and cuddly, and the next minute, you are fighting like a caged animal. You were just in a fight two weeks ago, and now you are in another one today. What's up with that?"

"It's not my fault! I didn't start any of these fights. People come at me. Last week, that guy was acting crazy. I was trying to calm him down when he took a swing at me. I ducked and had to drop him. He didn't wake up until we got to the police station. When he woke up, he asked me who hit him. I told him, 'I hit you because you took a swing at me.' He said, 'I guess that was the wrong thing to do.' I said, 'Ya think?'

"Anyway, I would rather fight these people rather than pull out my gun and shoot someone. A lot of these cops today, especially the young, white ones, can't fight, so the first thing they do is to pull out their gun and start shooting."

"You got a point there. Come here baby. Let me relax your mind and give you something more pleasant to think about."

As Roya tried pulling Big Lee closer, he pulled away again and tried changing the conversation.

What the hell is going on, Roya thought. *Why is he pushing me away?*

"I've been meaning to ask you for a long time why you had the word *rebel* tattooed on your breast. I mean, don't get me wrong, I like it and think it's cute, but I have always wondered why that word. Did you use to be wild or something?"

"I guess I was a little wild when I was younger. My parents were very restrictive. They wanted me to be what they thought I should be, and that was not the lifestyle I wanted to lead. My father had this attitude that a woman's place should be three steps behind a man, and women should only speak when they are asked to speak. I never understood that kind of thinking. I have always been a free spirit and spoke my mind. Well, to be perfectly honest with you, there was a period in my life when I was buck-wild.

"When I went to college, I kind of got into drugs a little bit, and that changed me a lot. In fact, it wasn't a little bit_ I stayed high a lot. I think I stayed high because during my sophomore year, I got raped. I was hanging with my girls at a bar, and I met this cute guy. He seemed sweet. We went out a couple of times, and he was the perfect gentleman. I invited him to my dorm room one night, and he forced himself on me. I said no, but he wouldn't stop. He ...."

Roya began quietly sobbing. She expected Big Lee to grab her to comfort her, but all he did was grab her hand, holding it tight.

"Did you report it to the police or campus security?"

"No, I didn't know what to do. Because of my cultural upbringing, I thought I would have to be with this dude forever because we had sex. I was young and stupid. So I stayed with this horrendous person for almost two horrible years. He was racist, sexist, a liar, a cheat, and a drug dealer. That's how I got introduced to drugs. I didn't hang out with my friends for like two years because they couldn't stand him and couldn't stand him being with me. We started hanging out with his friends, who were kind of wild and carefree. I started doing some wild things, but it is hard to tell because I stayed high all of the time. It was a wonder I was able to keep my grades up.

"He was a gross human being, but he was my first. I finally decided to leave him after he beat me up. We got into it over something really silly, but when he put his hands on me, it was like I woke up from a drunken stupor. I got a restraining order, and he was not allowed on campus anymore. I threw myself into my studies, started hanging out with my true friends again, and was able to graduate on time.

"This tattoo is a reminder of that dark time in my life. But in a way, I think I have had a rebellious spirit all my life. In fact, I was thinking about getting my breasts enlarged so the tat would stand out even larger. What do you think? Would you like me even more with larger breasts?"

"Baby, I didn't fall in love with you because of your breasts, or even that beautiful smile, or that gorgeous body. I love your spirit, your good heart, and your stuff!"

They both started laughing, but when Roya jumped into Big Lee's arms, he extended his arm, keeping her at a distance.

"What's wrong with you tonight? You keep pushing me away. Did I do something wrong?"

"No, baby doll. This is hard for me to say, but remember I told you I busted this guy's eye open today and the blood splattered everywhere? Well, he told the paramedic who was treating him that he had AIDS. I was like, 'I'll be damned!' I took a battery of blood tests and the preliminary report came out negative. I have to come back in six months and do it all again. I'm sure I have nothing to worry about, but all of this shit just makes you wonder."

Roya sat on the bed in disbelief. She didn't know what to think or how to feel. She had just revealed a part of her life from which she hadn't totally healed, and now this. This was also the first time he said that he loved her. A small tear trickled down her cheek as she let out a loud sigh:

"Lord, have mercy!"

CHAPTER 11

TRAINING DAY

January 3, 2017

Dear Diary,

I haven't written in quite a while, but I've got to capture this feeling. Tonight was an amazing night. The shit got real! I went out on my very first patrol as a police officer with my FTO, Officer Anthony Fleming. Officer Fleming is cute, but he is crazy as hell. He knows his stuff, and I know I am going to learn a lot from him, but there is something about him that makes me feel a little uncomfortable. For one, he is a little too ghetto for me. He curses too much, has a quick temper, and treats people like they are beneath him. He calls me his *little rookie,* and that's OK, but from time to time, I would catch him looking at my butt, or staring at my breasts. He doesn't even try to hide it. I don't even like him like that. I don't know what his intentions are, but he can forget that.

Things started off slow. He showed me how I am supposed to write burglary reports, his way, of course, and how to organize my binder. Then we drove around the beat I was responsible for patrolling. He showed me all the hot spots and pointed out people of interest_ dealers, snitches, thugs, etc. He told me to remember this person and remember that person. He told me about the job and what to expect, laying the ground rules for the next twelve weeks. It was an interesting experience.

He and a few of his buddies have this thing called hunting. They ride around looking for someone to lock up. It's like a game with them. They seem to have a competition to see who can lock up the most people or who can get a more serious offense. Somehow, that doesn't sit well with me. I know we are trying to get offenders off the streets, but it seems like they look forward to arresting people for insignificant things. And even though he is black, he seems to treat black people so much harsher than he treats the whites. I wonder what that's all about.

We got a call for a traffic accident. When we got to the scene, there were two white women who had rear-ended two black guys. The white women admitted that they were at fault. The black guys were standing next to their car while the white women stood next to their car, and no one was arguing. Officer Fleming went over to the white women and asked if they were OK, but never asked the black guys, who got rear-ended, if they were OK. There was a beer bottle on the ground. Officer Fleming went over to the black guys, and in a very harsh tone, asked them if they had been drinking and if that was their beer bottle on the ground. Their response was, "We didn't hit them_ they hit us! Why are you asking us if that was our beer bottle?" Officer Fleming put his hand on his gun and said, "Did I ask you that? I asked you if that was your fucking beer bottle on the ground!" Later on that night, I questioned him about that incident, and we kind of got into it. I sat quietly for a while and then finally asked him why he was so mean and nasty toward the black guys but so pleasant to the white girls. His response was, "Rookie, just mind your business and do what I tell you to do." I wanted to curse his ass out, but I kept my cool.

Then he let me handle a traffic stop. I was surprised that he did that. I thought I would just back him up for a few days until I got the hang of it. His approach was different. He said, "You got to jump right in there and get your cherry busted. The best way to learn is to get out and do it."

We pulled over a car with a broken tail-light. There were five black males inside, which wasn't unusual because people were still out celebrating the New Year. The cool night air was a blessing, because I was so nervous. It felt like it was one hundred degrees outside. Officer Fleming told me to get the information from the driver and to write him a citation for failure to have rear illumination or something like that. When I approached the vehicle, the first thing I did was touch the car like I was instructed to do when I was in the academy. That is referred to as *the fatal finger print.* That is done so if you are killed and the perpetrator drives off, your finger print connects you to the car. When I was in the academy, they told me to touch the car with two fingers, but I would usually touch the car with all five fingers and my palm. I took my time so it wouldn't smudge.

As I approached the driver's side of the car, I could feel the hairs on my body stand up straight. I could feel the sweat gushing out of my pores like a waterfall and my underwear sticking to my butt. I was so nervous. When the driver rolled down the window, the overwhelming odor of marijuana hit me like a ton of bricks. That meant somebody was going to jail that night, and I would get my very first arrest. The driver looked at me and said, "What's the problem, Officer?" I couldn't see his hands and immediately got tense.

Before I could say anything, Officer Fleming, who had approached the car on the front passenger's side, screamed, "EVERYBODY PUT YOUR FUCKING HANDS ON THE CEILING!" The tone of his voice startled me. Not understanding what was going on, I instinctively reached for my gun and got myself into position to shoot into the car. Everybody in the car reached for the ceiling. Then I saw what looked like a gun lying on the lap of the driver. We got everybody out of the car and had them sit on the curb with their hands behind their heads. I then called for backup. My voice was quivering and I gave the dispatcher the wrong location. Officer Fleming, who still had his gun trained on the suspects, hollered with a tone of disgust in his voice, that it wasn't the correct location and gave the dispatcher the correct one.

When backup arrived, Officer Fleming walked over to me and said, "Rookie, you've got a lot to learn. If you don't learn how to do things quick, you are not going to survive out here. Just stick with me and you'll get it." I felt really bad because I should have had my gun out, or at least had my hand on it. That stuck with me the rest of the night. I got to do better.

It turned out that the gun the driver had was actually a Taser. There had been a string of something like twenty robberies recently, where the robbers used a Taser. In some cases the robber Tased the victims, and in other cases only threatened to do so. So I got a major bust as a result of a simple traffic stop.

We got back into the squad car and started hunting again. Oh, what a night.

*   *   *

Following graduation, Officer Shanita Brown got the call over the weekend that she had to report to the Seventh District police station on Monday. Roll call was scheduled for 11:00 p.m., and her first assignment was the mid-night shift, which went from 11:00 p.m. until 6:00 a.m. She, like the majority of her academy classmates, was assigned to 7D, where there was a growing need for police officers to patrol. That section of the city was plagued by poverty, high crime, and an abnormally high percentage of the city's homicides.

She was a bit nervous because she knew that even though her academy experience was informative in an incubated way, being on the street was a different animal. In the academy, she knew that nothing was really going to do serious harm to her. She was safe and secure. If something got out of hand, there was always someone there to say, "That's enough." In the academy, she was given scenarios of what could happen, basic information that she needed to know, what you could and could not do in domestic situations, vehicle law_ she couldn't possibly remember every code in the District of Columbia, and what avenues she could take to address these issues. But all the academy safeguards were stripped away once she got out on the streets, and she was naked to the realities of the real world. The thought of facing the dangers of the streets was very intimidating.

When she was a firefighter, people silently applauded when she and her fellow firefighters arrived on the scene because everyone knew that they were there to help. As a police officer, however, the mission was similar_ protect and serve_ but the perception of the community concerning police officers was very different, and often hostile. It was the police who often had to protect people in the community from themselves. That meant holding them accountable when they did wrong.

She knew that her real training would come during the field training officer process_ the FTO program. During this twelve-week process, she was paired with a veteran police officer who was responsible for introducing her to the beat she would be responsible for and showing her the ropes. She would start off with four weeks on the midnight shift, then four weeks on the evening shift, and, finally, four weeks on the day shift. At the end of the process, she would either be cut loose, which meant she would be allowed to patrol by herself or with another partner, or remediated, which meant she needed four more weeks of training. Many of her cop friends had given her the heads-up about the FTO process. If she was lucky, she would get a good training officer who would guide and support her. If she got a bad one, then life would be a living hell. A bad FTO was considered one of those guys who liked to sit around and do nothing, or maybe a cop who had no rapport with the community, or one who was simply an asshole. She had heard so many horror stories about bad FTOs. Some of them went on a power trip and acted like they were the be-all and end-all. One of her friends was actually put out of the police car by her FTO. Her friend said that the FTO stopped the car, told her to get out, and put her on the corner of a dark street all by herself in the middle of the night.

Shanita's number 1 concern, however, was being a single mom. She had to figure out how she was going to handle working the mid-night shift while raising her young daughter, Princess. Finding a babysitter who was willing to work nights or weekends was an arduous task. Her mother and her sisters were willing to pitch in when they could, but Shanita couldn't always rely on them. She had moved out of her mother's house and found an apartment in the northwest section of DC. So Shanita worked out a temporary arrangement with her mom where Shanita would pick up her mom and bring her over to the apartment so she could babysit. Then when Shanita got off work at six in the morning, she would have to pick up her mom and daughter, drive to her mom's home, and then go back to the apartment with her daughter, get her ready for school, take her to school, and then go back to the apartment to get some sleep. There would be times, however, when she would have to stay at work until she completed writing the reports from an arrest. That created a major problem with her plans. Soon, her mom decided that the arrangement was not working and that Shanita would have to come up with another plan.

Raising a child, while being a first responder, was a true dilemma. Both the fire and police departments took the position that the problem of raising a child was not their concern. When she asked the police department if she could avoid the mid-night shift because she was a single mom, she was told, "You chose to be a mother and a police officer, so handle it or find another occupation."

When Shanita was working with the fire department and Princess was an infant, she would come home tired and sleepy. One day, she put Princess on the bed and held on to her leg while she played. She would think she was awake until she heard a *thump* followed by a scream. Waking up in a panic, Shanita realized that Princess had fallen off the bed and hit the floor. This happened about three times, so she bought a play pen and would sleep in the play pen while Princess played. Shanita would put toys in the play pen, turn on the television, and would ball up in the play pen in order to get some peaceful sleep. The play pen was not very big, which created some physically difficult sleeping arrangements, but it provided Shanita some emotional rest and was her way of "handling" her dilemma.

In her search for another solution, Shanita was able to find a babysitter who would keep Princess overnight and on some weekends. One day, however, Princess came home and started asking questions about a movie she had seen on television while at the sitter's house. Princess was only seven years old at the time and was watching *The Players Club,* which was about women who danced in a strip club. After viewing the movie, Princess asked, "Mommy, what did those girls mean when they said, 'You got to use what you got until you can get what you want?'" That is when Shanita found out that the babysitter would allow the kids to watch whatever they wanted to watch on television without supervision. Princess never went back to that babysitter.

It was Shanita's god-mother, Jessica Jackson, who became a lifesaver and practically took Princess in as her own. Jessica had practically raised Shanita when Shanita was small, and so Shanita was so thrilled when Jessica offered a lending hand. Shanita knew she could never repay the debt she owed to Jessica. Having someone else raising her child, however, was something that bothered her. She was aware that she would miss some of the most important experiences in her child's life, but there was nothing she could do about it. Their financial well-being was dependent on this job. She also hoped that somehow, when Princess got a little older, they could have a normal mother-daughter relationship.

*   *   *

Shanita's four weeks on the mid-night shift were exhilarating, eye opening, and, in some cases, extremely disheartening. Working with Officer Fleming in 7D gave her an intense look into what she would face as a police officer once she got cut loose. There were some nights when they would accept fifteen calls because something was always happening. In contrast, officers who worked in 1D or 2D might get fifteen calls in a month.

Shanita's attitude and approach to dealing with the public began to change, especially after the Taser incident. She tried to maintain her calm demeanor and friendly disposition, but some people took her kindness for weakness. Because of her small stature and attractive, feminine appearance, several people she encountered on the street assumed that she was a pushover and therefore couldn't do her job. One suspect she encountered looked condescendingly at her when she approached him about an open beer can he had and told him he needed to put the beer can away. He responded, "Get the fuck out of here. What you gonna do? That gun belt weighs more than you do!" Her response was, "Boyfriend, you need to take that bass out your voice and put that beer can away, or you're gonna find out what I can do. This can go either real smooth, or it can go real hard. I guarantee you that if it goes real hard, you're gonna regret it!" He put the beer can in a paper bag and moved on.

One aspect of the job caused Shanita concern as well as consternation. The poverty and hopelessness that she encountered on the job was a little more than she expected. Though she grew up near poverty and got a glimpse of it when she was a firefighter, she had never seen it up close_ not like this. She had two loving parents who worked for a living and cared for her and her siblings and provided them with a safe home. But now, she was forced to see things that left her heartbroken and sad.

There was the time she walked into a one-bedroom apartment, and there were eight kids sleeping on a mattress on the floor, while the mother lay in the bed in a drug-laden stupor. It was dark because the electricity had been shut off, and the mother had run an extension cord from another apartment so she could boil water. When Shanita shined her flashlight on the floor because she thought she saw the carpet moving, she realized it wasn't a carpet but actually thousands of roaches. A little piece of her would die each time she saw little kids going to school with bite marks that they received from the roaches and mice, or when she would pull what they called a pack (package of heroin) out of a diaper bag and even out of the diapers on a child. For a mother to put her child in such jeopardy was unconscionable to Shanita. How could a mother do that?

To see so many people in her community strung out on drugs, suffering from mental health issues and homelessness gave her a sense of helplessness. She became a police officer because she thought she could make a difference and help people, but she quickly realized that she was powerless to help people unless they were ready to be helped. She had been used to people overdosing on drugs, but the difference now was that her efforts to stop them from using the drugs in many cases fell on deaf ears. The only thing she could do was to do her job. That meant locking people up and calling in Child Protective Services to take the children. There were many days when Shanita would go home and hold Princess as tight as she could, promising she would do everything in her power to keep her daughter safe and shield her from these horrors.

Shanita learned quickly that being a female on the force was an uphill struggle. When she was in the fire department, she went through a little hazing. They would play little pranks like hide the cards she used to study with, mess up her bed, or refuse to talk directly to her. But all of that stopped once she put out her first fire. Being on the police force was quite different. Many women had to act like bulldogs in order to get respect from people on the streets as well as people on the force. Sometimes that meant they had to act overly aggressive in order to make a statement. It seemed that female officers had to be ten times meaner than a male officer in order to get half the respect. Being an African American meant that her search for respect was twice as hard. She had to learn when to turn that bravado on and when to turn it off. Officer Fleming called that the light switch syndrome. It seemed that his light switch was always turned on. Shanita tried her best to keep the light switch off and stay as soft spoken and jovial as possible, but when it was necessary, she did not hesitate to switch it on.

Another situation that made being a female police officer hard was the fact that there was a lot of fraternization in the department between male and female officers. You had a few female officers who would sleep with other officers in order to get a cushy assignment or a promotion. That made it difficult for other female officers because there was an element in the department who felt that all female police officers were the same way. You had some officers who would sleep with a female officer then tell his partners that she was easy as long as you said this or did that. Another tactic was to refuse to back a female officer up if she did not comply with sexual demands, or claim that the female officer was not a part of the team and thus label her as an outcast. That was almost like a death sentence because the strength of the police was the ability to deal with a problem with overwhelming numbers.

Shanita understood that it was difficult trying to communicate with civilians_ especially when dating men_ about what police officers have to go through on a daily basis; and as a result, she found herself spending time and communicating with other officers. Some officers took her friendliness and willingness to engage in conversation as a signal that she was just like some of the easy officers. As far as she was concerned, however, she was not going to date anyone she didn't want to date, do anything she didn't want to do, or bow down to pressure from any man. She found out that she had to use her light switch with her fellow police officers the same way she did with the people on the street. Her training with Officer Fleming had been going well until the day everything changed.

*   *   *

When Shanita got into the squad car, she could sense that something was up. Officer Fleming had a strange look on his face and was unusually quiet. They drove their normal beat looking for action. After an hour of cursing in silence, Shanita confronted Officer Fleming about his unusual behavior.

"OK, Flem, what's up?"

"What you mean? Ain't nothin' wrong with me. What's wrong with you?"

"We've been riding around for almost an hour, and you haven't said much. You haven't even cussed anybody out. What's up with that?"

"I'm good. I just have a few things on my mind. By the way, what you doing after work?"

Oh Lord, here we go, Shanita thought. *I knew this would happen sooner or later.*

"A few of us are going to check out that new restaurant down by the wharf. It is called Tiki TNT. It is a Tiki bar and rum distillery. I hear that it is nice. Why don't you come along and go with us?"

"You know I got to go pick up my daughter after I get off work. I really don't have the time right now to hang out."

"Well, you got to eat sometime. You are coming to the end of the training process, and I thought maybe you and I could get away sometime, get a bite to eat, and talk."

"Flem, don't take this the wrong way. You're a nice person and everything, a little crazy sometimes, and we are cool, but I'm not looking for a relationship right now. All I have time for right now is this job and my daughter."

"Oh, I get it. You're too good to hang out with your cop friends!"

"Come on, Flem, don't go there. It ain't like that. I just don't have the time to fit in a social life right now. I ...."

"Uh-huh! And by the way, my name is Officer Fleming, rookie!"

They spent the rest of the evening driving around in silence. It was hard to tell if Officer Fleming was really agitated by their conversation and her rejection of him because he was usually salty with the people they came into contact with. But the silence was deafening. There were no usual quips about how people who lived in Section 8 housing were lazy, or how teens who wore sagging pants were just advertising for a homosexual score. After that evening, Officer Fleming made things real rough for Shanita. He told her supervisor that she was lazy and didn't want to do real police work. Pretty soon, even her coworkers began looking at her strangely and would whisper things to each other as she walked by. Soon, she began feeling like an outcast. When they got back to the station house one evening, the last thing she heard Officer

Fleming say to her was, "I'm cutting you loose, rookie. You're on your own now."

When Officer Fleming said that Shanita was on her own, she didn't think he meant that in the literal sense. She just assumed that she had gotten through the FTO process, and now she was a full-fledged police officer. But she later found out the ominous meaning of those words. One night, she had an accident on the South Capitol Street Bridge and called for assistance. She wanted someone to come and sit behind her car with the lights on because she didn't want another car to come around the curve and run into her. The dispatcher made a call for assistance, and lo and behold, nobody answered the call. She waited by herself for over an hour, until finally a police cruiser showed up with a white officer in it. It was Officer Steven Sullivan.

"Shanita, you OK?"

"Hey, Steven, yeah, I'm OK. I just had a little fender bender, but I'm good. I was just sitting here wondering where my backup was."

"Shanita, you and I are cool, and I will always have your back, but there is something you need to know. Nobody responded to the call because the word is out that you are not a team player and nobody likes you. They say you don't hang out with other cops or socialize with other cops."

"You got to be fuckin' kidding me right now! Not a team player? Just because I don't participate in 'going to church,' and don't sleep around, that makes me not a team player. Well, fuck it, then. If that is the way they want to carry this, I'll just do this shit by myself. You can leave if that is the way you feel!"

"Slow your roll. Don't get your panties all in a bunch. You know I'm not with all of that. We're from the same class at the academy. I will always have your back. Going to church, what does that mean?"

"Every morning after the midnight shift, officers would go somewhere, sit around, and drink. They call it going to church. First of all, I don't drink. More importantly, I've got a daughter that I have to look after, and nobody is more important than her. When I get off, I've got to see about her and make sure she gets to and from school. So I guess that means I am not one of the boys because I don't sit around drinking and talking about how many people I locked up. That's petty, but if that's the way they want to play it, fine!

"And that's just half of it. I've never seen this, but I hear they have this thing called baptizing, where they would take a person, who has been making trouble, creating problems on their beat, or just getting on people's nerves, and drop them off somewhere by the Anacostia River late at night. They hadn't committed any crimes other than the crime of being an asshole or an annoyance. Now that person would have to figure out how to get back home. When I would hear officers laughing and making fun of it, I would get on them saying that was so wrong and would refuse to be a part of that shit. I guess I wasn't being a team player then either.

"You know what, now this all makes sense. I was in a situation the other night and called for backup and wondered why nobody immediately responded."

"What happened?"

"A male and a female were on the street arguing. Come to find out, they were brother and sister. The female was pushing a stroller, and her brother was telling her that she didn't need to have the baby out in the cold. He tried to snatch the stroller from her, and she was screaming for somebody to call the police. When I arrived on the scene, he started yelling at me like I was his sister.

"First, I called for backup, but nobody came, so I handled it myself. I tried talking low to calm the situation down because when I do talk low, it forces people to tone themselves down so they can hear. This didn't work for him, and he got louder. Then I got loud with him, letting him know that he was getting ready to get his ass busted and then go to jail to boot if he didn't calm the fuck down. When he saw my demeanor change, he backed up and settled down. He broke down crying and said he was only trying to get his niece out of the cold. I told him that I understood that, but that was his sister's baby, and if she wanted her baby out in the cold that was her right. The main thing was they couldn't be out here creating a disturbance. They stopped arguing and left together."

"That's messed up. I tell you what_ here is my cell number. If you ever get in a jam and there is nobody to back you up, just give me a call. I got you! You should also find someone in this sector who will back you up. I know you think you can handle things by yourself, but you really can't. It is too dangerous out here for that. Remember what they told us in the academy_ strength in numbers. I get off in a few, but I'll wait here with you until the tow truck gets here."

"Thanks, Steven."

Shanita took Steven's advice and started what she called her posse. She realized that most of her problems and lack of support came when she was on the midnight shift. She got all the support she needed during the day and evening shifts. She assumed that this was probably a result of her being bad-mouthed by Officer Fleming. She found other officers who worked the midnight shift that she could depend on to support her and back her up.

Besides Steven, Shanita recruited Melody Cash, who was another member of her academy class. Melody had wanted to be a police officer all her life and seemed to enjoy every minute of her time on the job. She heard the rumors about Shanita and could tell that Shanita was lonely and hurting. She and Shanita became good friends and started looking out for each other. They both had the same philosophy of doing whatever they could to help the people in the community, but also felt that "if you do the crime, you got to do the time." They requested to become partners so they could ride together, but of course, that was denied. Once they got out of roll call, they would follow each other to calls and would back each other up. Shanita noticed that most of the men rode with a partner, but many of the women rode by themselves. There were a few cases where women were allowed to ride together, but that was unusual.

They also began to communicate with each other using their cell phones, especially if they had something to say that they didn't want everybody else to know. For example, nobody on the job knew that Melody was pregnant except Shanita. Melody's body was going through changes, like her breasts getting larger and more sensitive, causing irritation from wearing the bullet-proof vest. In addition, she would get extremely sleepy and from time to time would drive her cruiser to a secluded place and doze off. Shanita would listen on the radio for calls and would call Melody on the cell phone to wake her up and make sure she responded to the dispatcher's call.

The midnight shift was usually quiet during the week. There would be an occasional domestic call where people were fighting each other in the house, but for the most part, the action you got was usually traffic stops, accidents, or whatever you went hunting for. Friday and Saturday nights were a different story. Those were the nights when people went to the clubs and bars. As a result, there were plenty of fights, drunk-driving issues, and, unfortunately, homicides.

Shanita also found two unlikely sources who volunteered to be unofficial members of her posse. One was Officer Andy Wallace, who was the officer who suggested that Shanita become a police officer when she was working for the fire department. The other member, surprisingly, was Officer Gregory Harris.

*   *   *

March 25, 2017

Dear Diary,

Man, oh man. Oh, what a night! I got a call on the radio: code one, black man with dreads, wearing a red shirt, black leather jacket, and jeans; suspect is armed with a gun; suspect seen near the corner of Stevens Road and Wade Road SE. That was the location of the Barry Farms Housing Projects that were being redeveloped. Many of the low-income houses were being torn down, but most of the ones that remained standing were vacant and boarded up. That was a bad area and somewhere I didn't need to go by myself. I responded 10-99, which meant I was by myself and I acknowledged the dispatchers call. I called Melody on her cell and told her to respond 10-99 because I knew she was taking a quick nap, and I knew I was going to need backup on this one.

I then proceeded to the area where he had been spotted and saw who I thought was him standing on the corner.

When I saw him, I said, "Oh shit. That's a big dude." He reminded me of the Animal from my academy days. I have to admit that when I first responded to the call and headed there, I wasn't nervous. I really didn't have time to be nervous, but when I got there, I felt like shitting bricks. I pulled up and hesitated for a brief moment before getting out of the cruiser. I guess I was waiting for backup, but given what has been happening in that regard, I wasn't sure if anybody would come. The suspect and I locked eyes, and in that brief moment it seemed like he could read my thoughts; he knew I was scared.

I took a deep breath and finally got out of my cruiser. As I unsnapped the strap on my gun, I suddenly heard the sound of police sirens quickly approaching the area. That was like music to my ears! The dude also heard the sirens; gave me a disrespectful glare, as if he was disappointed that he didn't have the opportunity to confront me; and took off running into the housing project complex. Instinctively, I pulled out my weapon and yelled at him to stop. When he didn't stop, I took off running after him. I was terrified because I knew that if he had gotten into one of those vacant buildings, it would be difficult to find him; but more importantly, I would have to go in there to get him, and that was going to be very dangerous.

The Barry Farms Projects has a series of pathways and sidewalks that weave between the uniform-looking houses, which almost look like one of those old World War II prison barracks complex I used to see on television. The suspect was running at full speed, dodging and weaving in and out of the buildings. I pulled out my flashlight when suddenly I hear a gun-shot. The bullet hit a building behind me. That is when I realized that this motherfucker was shooting at me. I immediately ducked for cover. I think I took the deepest breath I ever took in my life when I heard footsteps coming in my direction. The footsteps were accompanied by flashlights, which made me think they had to be other police officers. When I saw Officer Harris and his partner, I wanted to kiss them. I had been calling out the addresses of the houses when I was chasing the suspect, and now it seemed like the cavalry had come to my rescue.

We got word over the radio that other officers on the scene had caught the suspect in another section of the complex trying to get into one of the vacants, but he couldn't get the board off the door. He had been swarmed by a dozen officers, and he gave up without a fight.

Even though I didn't physically catch the guy, I felt a sense of accomplishment because I went after him and didn't lose him. The whole situation was terrifying because the guy had a gun and he was shooting at me. But when he took off running, it was like my pride kicked in, and I had to catch him, or at least try. My heart didn't stop racing until well after I got back to my cruiser. When I got to my cruiser, I realized that I never secured the car. In fact, it was still running, and I didn't even put it in park. I'll probably get jumped on for leaving my car like that, but I didn't care. I'll just have to deal with that tomorrow.

CHAPTER 12

GEORGETOWN

"Man, you've got to be the luckiest son-of-a-bitch alive," exclaimed Jonathan Blake, who was one of Steven Sullivan's classmates at the academy. "How in the hell did you manage to get an assignment in 2D?"

"Luck of the Irish, I guess," Steven jokingly responded. "Only I'm not Irish! To tell you the truth, I don't know how I got that assignment. I hear there's not much action over in that part of town, but we shall see. Where did you get assigned?"

"Take a guess. I got 7D, of course. In fact, most of us got assigned to 7D. They say it's rough over there, and they need a larger police presence. I've heard some real horror stories. I just hope it's not too rough. I don't plan to be here too long. I just needed to get the training and a couple of years of experience so I can go back home and get a police job there."

"Where is home?"

"I'm from Durbin, West Virginia, population 293."

"Why in the world would you want to go back there?"

"I don't know, I guess I'm just a small-town guy. Don't get me wrong_ even though it's a small town, they have their problems too. They need law enforcement just like everybody else. People steal, cheat, and break the law, even in small towns."

"Well, I'm pretty sure you're going to get all the police experience you need where you're going. Good luck with that."

Steven Sullivan was told to report to the evening shift at the Second District police station following his stay at the police academy. This was the district that covered the Georgetown area, one of the more affluent parts of the District of Columbia and the area west of Rock Creek Park. He was eager to start his new job. After months of training, he wanted to get on the street, lock people up, and do what police officers do. He knew that people would still be out celebrating the New Year, and there would be plenty of action that required a police presence. He was supposed to spend several weeks with the field training officer training process, but his designated field training officer called in sick, so he was partnered with another officer until his FTO returned. Officer Paul Glass was a veteran officer who was a couple of months away from retirement. Steven and Officer Glass were introduced to each other during roll call. Steven felt that Office Glass seemed a little distant and reserved, like he didn't want to be bothered with anybody. *Maybe he just wanted to serve the rest of his time quietly,* he thought.

When they entered the squad car, the first thing Officer Glass said was, "Don't touch the radio!" That seemed a little odd because during his introduction and preliminary discussion, Officer Glass had explained a typical day on the job.

"We chase the radio," Officer Glass stated. "The dispatcher sends us on calls. It could be a domestic situation, drunk and disorderly people on the street, a traffic accident, a report of a 'porch pirate', or stuff like that. In between that, when the radio is quiet, we are on routine patrol, where we ride around so we can be visible. We show our presence, interact with people, and help them when we can."

"Porch pirate_ what's that?"

"That's when products ordered online are delivered to people's homes and thieves steal them off the porch."

"Oh, OK. I'm eager to learn everything you have to teach me, so let's get started."

"Slow your roll, rookie. You've got plenty of time to learn. When you rush into things, people usually get hurt."

As Steven and Officer Glass began driving around the area so that Steven could become familiar with the neighborhood and businesses, a call came over the radio about a traffic accident with no injuries. Steven did not touch the radio as instructed and waited for Office Glass to respond to the dispatcher. Officer Glass just kept driving without acknowledging the dispatcher.

"That's a few blocks away," Steven said. "Shouldn't we respond?"

"Nah, nobody was hurt, so let somebody else check that out. I don't want to spend the rest of the evening listening to complaining motorists and doing a lot of boring paperwork. Besides, it's almost time for a meal break."

Officer Glass stopped by a local restaurant, got a cup of coffee, a chicken salad sandwich, and a newspaper. He then parked his cruiser on the street under the Whitehurst Freeway Bridge and started reading his newspaper. Steven wasn't hungry, so he just sat in the cruiser while Officer Glass ate his sandwich. Soon, another call came over the radio, and Officer Glass didn't budge; then another, and still no response. Steven was sure that they would respond to the next call that came over the radio, but lo and behold, Officer Glass just sat there. The rest of the day, Steven and Officer Glass spent their time riding around the neighborhood and not responding to any calls.

This pattern of inactivity went on for the next two days. Steven was getting frustrated and unsure of what to do. At the end of the shift, he went straight to the sergeant on duty to get some advice.

"Sir, I don't mean to be disrespectful and I'm not trying to get anybody in trouble, but I have a real problem. My partner told me not to touch the radio, and he doesn't want to do any work. We just sit in the cruiser all day, and he won't respond to any calls. We get calls that are really close, but he does nothing."

"You know he is just another officer, just like you, right?"

"Yeah, but y'all put me with him, and he's supposed to be training me."

"True, but he's just another officer, and you are an officer too. He is not your FTO. He is not an official, and he is not a sergeant. It would be nice if he showed you some stuff, but he is just an officer that you are riding with. If you want to do some work, when the dispatcher calls your number, pick up the radio and respond. If he doesn't want you to touch the car radio, then use your own radio."

"Are you sure?"

"Yeah, rookie, he has no more power than you do. Do what you think is the right thing to do."

The next day, Steven was a little unsure of his newfound power and allowed two calls from the dispatcher to go unanswered. When the third call came across, Steven picked up the radio and said that they were responding to the call. Officer Glass was livid.

"What the fuck do you think you are doing? I told you not to touch the radio!"

"Look, man, this call is real close, so we are going to take it. If you don't like it, that's too bad. If you don't like me, that's too bad too, but if you think I'm going to sit in this car with you all day and do nothing, then you are truly mistaken. Now let's go, old man!"

"That's what's wrong with you young punks today. You don't listen. You think you own the world. You think you can just get in my car and do what you want. I hate you motherfuckers."

"Yeah, yeah, yeah. We are both police officers. If you don't want to ride with me, that's fine. But if they put us together, I'm going to answer the radio. If you don't like it, then you're just going to have to deal with it. Now, we've already told the dispatcher we were responding to the call, so it's on record. I think you need to put this car in gear and get going."

"I hate you motherfuckers!"

The next day, the sergeant on duty realized that pairing Steven and Officer Glass was not a good idea. Fortunately, Officer Tim Bailey reported to work off sick leave and was ready to work. Officer Bailey was a well-respected officer who had received numerous commendations for service. Officer Bailey had been assigned as Steven's original FTO and was eager to meet the new recruit.

"Hi, Steven, I'm Officer Tim Bailey. I will be working with you for the next several weeks."

"Hi, Officer Bailey, I am very happy to meet you. I've heard a lot about you, and I am eager to learn everything you can teach me."

"That's good to know. Let's get started."

As Steven and Officer Bailey headed to the parking lot to get their cruiser, Officer Bailey suddenly stopped in the hallway, turned to Steven, and stuck his finger in Steven's chest.

"Lesson number 1: I heard about your spat with Officer Glass. Officer Glass is an old cop who is not very good and has one leg out the door already. But there is one thing you've got to learn, and if you don't, you are going to have problems. Cops never snitch on other cops! We've got to depend on each other. It can get very dangerous out there on those streets. I've got to know that you have my back at all times, and you have to know that I have yours. You won't last very long in this business if you don't get that. If you have a problem with me or another cop, you handle it personally, but you never snitch! We clear?"

"Yes, sir!"

"OK, let's go to work."

On Friday, Steven got home exhausted after only two days of work with Officer Bailey. On their first day out, Officer Bailey promptly parked his cruiser on a side street off of M Street in Georgetown. Steven's initial thoughts were, *Oh, here we go again*, thinking that Officer Bailey was going to be just like Officer Glass and they would spend another day of inactivity. But, before he could say a word, Officer Bailey said, "OK, rookie, let's get out and learn the ropes."

When they left the police cruiser, Officer Bailey began patrolling the area on foot. He stopped in several of the trendy shops, bars, quaint restaurants, and an enclosed shopping mall along the M Street and Wisconsin Avenue corridor to talk to store owners and patrons. They strolled along the promenade in Washington Harbor, which was an area that contained a healthy mix of tourists and residents. It seemed that he knew everybody on the crowded streets, and they all seemed to respect him. He was talkative, gregarious, and genuinely seemed to care for people. Steven was very impressed.

Officer Bailey's knowledge of the history of the Georgetown area was impressive as well. As he and Steven patrolled the area, Officer Bailey talked about how Georgetown used to be a part of Maryland before the District of Columbia was created, and how the entire Georgetown neighborhood, with its historic eighteenth and nineteenth century homes, cobblestone sidewalks, and the peaceful C&O Canal, was designated a National Historic Landmark. The area, which overlooked the Potomac River, attracted many foreign dignitaries, movie executives (the film, *The Exorcist* was shot here), and federal workers, making obtaining housing more competitive and expensive. Outdoor and waterfront enthusiasts also flocked to the Georgetown Waterfront Park for some of the most picturesque kayaking, jogging, and cycling backdrops the city had to offer. Every day Steven had to listen to Officer Bailey rave about the area as if he owned property or stock in some of the luxurious hotels or bars and restaurants.

One day, Steven did some research on the Georgetown area so that he could hold a decent conversation and impress Officer Bailey.

"Hey, Officer Bailey, did you know that Georgetown was once a predominantly African American neighborhood?"

"Get the fuck outta here!"

"Yep, I read that a large number of slaves as well as free blacks lived in the area. Slave labor was used to construct many of the federal buildings in DC and provided labor on the tobacco plantations in Maryland and Virginia during the eighteenth and nineteenth century. When slavery ended, a lot of those families remained in the area."

"No shit. You mean *jigs* used to own these homes? I'll be damned."

What's a jig? Steven thought.

Two weeks of working with Officer Bailey was very exhausting and informative. There wasn't much police activity except for a few traffic violations, disorderly conduct, and what Officer Bailey referred to as quality-of-life crimes. Quality-of- life crimes included things like drinking or the use of drugs in public, gambling, public intoxication, and unlawful gathering. Steven did notice, however, that there was a disparaging difference in the way minorities were treated as opposed to whites.

For example, several times they got a call from the Georgetown University campus security force to recover drugs that were seized. Usually, the police department wouldn't seize the drugs for destruction but would keep them for investigation. The usual procedure is to obtain a warrant for an arrest. In two cases, where the students were white, the school decided that they wanted to handle the case internally because they did not want to risk the student being arrested and ruining the student's potential career or life. Officer Bailey would allow the school to handle it internally, and the seized drugs would be destroyed. However, when a black student was caught with drugs on campus, there were no concerns for the student's future. Officer Bailey would seize the drugs and arrest the student.

On another occasion, one busy Saturday evening, there were several jay-walking incidents where people crossed in the middle of a busy street or crossed against the light. However, when one black couple dashed across the empty street against the light, Officer Bailey stopped them and wrote a jay-walking citation. When Steven asked why he wrote them up, Officer Bailey simply said, "They broke the law."

*   *   *

When Steven got home after another long day, he settled down, got himself a drink, and turned on the answering machine. There were several messages, but the one that excited him the most was a message from Michelle. She called inviting him to attend a "white party" with her the next weekend. It was late, but just the sound of her voice got him excited as he hurriedly dialed her number.

"Hey, Michelle, I hope it's not too late to call, but I just got your message."

"Oh, hi, Steve. I'm glad you called. No, it's not too late. I was catching up on a little paperwork. You know a teacher's job is never done. I haven't heard from you in a minute. How ya doin'?"

"Wow, this past week has been incredible! My new training officer has been great! He is teaching me a lot about community policing, as well as the history of the area. The hours are long, and the work is kind of boring, but it has been rewarding. I was calling to respond to your invite. By the way, what the hell is a white party?"

"That's a party where everyone shows up dressed in all white," Michelle responded with a hearty laugh.

"Well, I don't have any all-white clothes. How about I show up butt naked? Would that work?"

"Oh, you got jokes. Boy, don't play with me! I wouldn't mind seeing you like that, but I don't think my friends would appreciate it!"

Hmmm, she wouldn't mind seeing me like that, Steven thought. "What day and what time does it start?"

"It's next Saturday at the Camelot Club and it starts at 10:00 p.m."

"Oh, wow! I'm sorry. I don't get off until 11:00 p.m. next Saturday and I will probably be real tired. By the time I clean up and get out there, it'll probably be over."

"That's too bad. I think you would have enjoyed it."

"Maybe we can hook up after the dance and just talk for a while."

"I think I like that. I can make you some hot chocolate to keep you warm."

"I can think of other ways to keep warm, but hot chocolate will be just fine."

"Boy, stop! I'll call you when I get home from the party."

It seemed like forever for Saturday to roll around. While on patrol, Steven could actually see his breath as he exhaled into the frigid evening air, and his fingers were so cold they actually felt like they were about to fall off. The weatherman had predicted a significant amount of snowfall that day, but not a drop had fallen. Neither the threat of snow nor the dropping temperature deterred the usual Saturday crowd of party-goers from descending on the Georgetown area. As tired as he felt, Steven got a burst of energy when he started thinking about his date with Michelle. He couldn't stop thinking about the passionate kiss they shared when they were at the reunion. Even though it was brief, he couldn't help thinking about how he wanted to do it again and much more. He had never spent this much time with a girl without making an attempt to get the panties, but somehow she was different. He enjoyed being around her and actually cared about how she felt about him. He had to be careful. He didn't want to move too fast or do anything to mess things up with her.

When she opened the door, Steven's mouth fell open. She was dressed in an elegant, tight, all-white pantsuit that accentuated her ample butt and girlish figure. Her smile sent a warm streak down his chest and into his stomach.

"Wow, you look fabulous!"

"Why, thank you, Steven. I really wish you could have come. We had such a good time."

"How were you able to keep the guys off of you looking like that?"

"What makes you think I kept them off of me? No, I'm just playing. I don't let anybody touch me unless I want them to. I'm a big girl. Take your coat off and let's talk a while."

"I've got a better idea. Let's go for a walk. I pass by that park over by Sixteenth Street every day and have never been inside. Let's go over there."

"You mean Meridian Hill Park? Boy, you must be crazy. It's almost two o'clock in the morning, and it's kind of dangerous over there. Plus it is freezing outside."

"Oh, come on. It'll be different. Don't forget, I'm a police officer. Ain't nobody gonna mess with us."

"OK, let me put on some warmer clothes and we'll give it a try. But if I get too cold, I'm not staying out there."

As Steven and Michelle walked arm-in-arm around the park, huge flakes of snow began to fall. The park was empty, and the only sound they heard was the sound of their feet crunching against the falling snow that rapidly began to accumulate. As they walked, they talked for what seemed like hours about their lives, their experiences, and their heartaches. They talked as if they had been friends for decades. He found out that she had been engaged before, but she called it off because she realized that her fiancé seemed more interested in his material things as opposed to beginning a life together. The few park lights gave off very little illumination, which added to the beauty, especially when they got to the end of the upper portion of the park that sat on a hill overlooking the city. This gave them an awesome view of the Capitol and the buildings that made up the federal portion of Washington DC.

"Steven, I've got to ask you a question. When we were at your graduation from the academy, you introduced me to your parents as your girlfriend. Why did you do that?"

"To tell you the truth, I kind of felt that way about you since the first day we met back in college. Remember when I came by your room looking for your roommate? We talked for quite a while. Talking to you was so easy and pleasant I wanted to continue, but it never happened. At the time, I thought it just wasn't to be, but I couldn't help thinking about you. We kept seeing each other from a distance, but we never hooked up. Every time I saw you, you had this smile that made me feel warm inside. Then when we met again during the reunion, and after that kiss, I knew we were meant to be together."

"I'm a little tired, and I'm getting cold. I think it's time for us to go now."

"Me too. I didn't want to say anything because we were having such a good conversation, but my balls are freezing!"

"You know what? This snow is coming down pretty hard. Maybe you should consider staying over the night. I wouldn't want you to get into an accident or anything."

When they got back to Michelle's home, they took off their coats and sat down on the sofa to continue their conversation. Not a word was spoken, however, as they gazed into each other's eyes. Before he knew what was happening, Michelle covered the space that separated them and planted a passionate kiss on his lips. She then grabbed him by the hand and led him upstairs to her bedroom. They separated from their passionate embrace long enough to take their clothes off.

Finally, he thought. *I can't believe this is about to happen.*

His eyes devoured her luscious body as though he hadn't eaten in a thousand years. His natural instincts began to take over as he picked her up and softly laid her across the bed. He kissed her on her breasts, her neck, her navel, her legs, and, finally, the sweet crevasse in between her legs. She let out a loud sound that startled him a bit. When he entered her, the sounds she emitted became louder and more primeval. Her body began to violently shudder as if she had no control over it. His thrusts became so aggressive that he feared he would knock her through the bed and drive a hole in her soul. Then she did something that startled him even more. She matched his aggressiveness with her own. The inner walls of her vagina clutched his manhood so tight he almost let out a scream of his own. No woman had ever done that to him. This turned him on even more. Before he knew what was happening, that feeling began rising in his loins, and he knew an eruption was imminent. Panic began to set in.

Oh, no, he thought. *This can't be happening. Not the kid! This has never happened to me before. I just got in! I can't be finishing this quick! She's gonna think I'm a gump.*

When it happened, he was transported into a world that he had never been before. It was a world where there was no sound, where different colors flashed in front of his eyes, where every muscle in his body started convulsing, and he actually thought he saw God. When he regained his senses, he started apologizing profusely, trying to explain that this had never happened to him before. She let out a sinister smile and told him not to worry because she was far from finished with him. She strategically placed her mouth over his manhood and began an oral massage that made him start speaking in tongues. Before she finished with him, the sun was streaking through the blinds, and the bed was drenched in sweat. He was totally spent and more content than he had ever been in his life. As he lay on the bed, he thought that there was no way he was going to let this girl out of his life.

I guess this is what love feels like, he thought.

* * *

Officer Bailey had developed a fondness for Steven. He took Steven under his wing and tried to teach him everything he could. This relationship was short-lived, however. One day while on patrol in Georgetown, Officer Bailey walked into a crowd of black couples who were outside of the Blues Alley Jazz and Supper Club. They had just come out of the club and were standing around talking when he told them they were creating a disturbance and had to move on. Steven was a bit surprised because they didn't seem to be doing anything wrong.

Later that evening, a group of white college kids from Georgetown University were loitering around a few shops on M Street talking loudly and creating a public nuisance. When Steven approached them and asked them to move along, one of the girls in the group, who was clearly drunk, cursed him out and told him to get lost. Steven asked her to lower her voice and move along, or he would arrest her. Her friends started to move on and tried to calm her down. As they started to pull her away, she turned and spat on Steven's shirt. Steven immediately grabbed the girl, forced her hands behind her back, pulled out his handcuffs, and placed her under arrest.

Officer Bailey, who had been engaged in a conversation with a local tavern owner, came over to see what the commotion was all about. When Officer Bailey saw the girl in handcuffs, he recognized her as the daughter of a Southern senator. He went to Steven and asked if he could let her go with a warning. Steven was adamant about her being arrested, stating that she could not spit on him and get away with it.

A week later, when Steven reported to work, Officer Bailey told him that he was being transferred to 7D effective immediately. When Steven asked why, Officer Bailey said that there had been a rash of murders over in that part of town and several officers had been reassigned to help address the problem. Steven's attitude was mixed. He was glad to be transferred to a place where some real police work could be done. On the other hand, he was little bit sad that he couldn't keep learning all the things that Officer Bailey could possibly teach him. Officer Bailey told Steven that he would do everything he could to see that his new FTO would be someone who would take him under his wing and continue to teach him about good police work.

*　　*　　*

"Hey, Craig, this is Tim Bailey. I'm sending you a potential new recruit for our group. He's a rookie and full of enthusiasm, but he needs a little attitude adjustment. Introduce him to the brothers of the Order and break him in gently. His name is Steven Sullivan."

"I got you, Tim! Give me a few weeks, and I'll have him hating these jungle bunnies! Heil Hitler."

"Heil Hitler!"

CHAPTER 13

OH, WHAT A DAY

Officer Gregory Harris was sitting in roll call at the Seventh District police station seething. The watch commander was rambling on about a gang that was going around kidnapping drug dealers and trying to ransom them off for large sums of money. Their MO was when they didn't get the money they were looking for, they would put a pillow case over the victim's head and shoot him in the face. The watch commander's fear was that if these crimes continued to escalate, there was going to be retaliation, or even worse, a full-scale war; and that was not good for anybody. None of this information seemed to faze Officer Harris, who didn't even seem to be listening.

Officer Harris had received numerous commendations and awards for his exemplary work on the police force. In addition to working on the street as a beat officer, he served in several different units including serving in a TAC unit where he was in plain clothes and did what they called "jump-outs"; a vice unit where he did narcotics and murder-for-hire investigations; an undercover unit where he purchased illegal drugs and guns; an FBI task force; a DEA task force; and he teamed with ATF units. Most of those assignments were given to him by his superiors, but he decided that he wanted to work with a SWAT unit and applied for a position. Working with SWAT was something he always wanted to do since joining the force.

He remembered watching the television show with his father when he was small and thought it would be cool to join.

There were only eight positions available when he applied, and there were thirty-five applicants. The application process included a physical test and a, shooting test, and he also had to submit a writing sample. He was the top applicant in the physical test, breaking all the records that existed. He scored in the top 10 on the shooting test, and in the top 5 on his writing sample. Guys already on the SWAT team were congratulating him and telling him they couldn't wait until he joined them on the team. They made comments like, "You really knocked that out of the park," and "We haven't seen anything like that before." He was told that he would be contacted if he made the team.

Three weeks passed, and he hadn't heard anything from the administration about his application. One day, while he was downtown, he happened to see several of the guys who took the test the same time he did, in full SWAT team uniforms. They were all white guys. Two of them couldn't even finish the run during the physical test, and one of them didn't even turn in the writing sample! He was stunned! When he passed the guys, they couldn't even look him in the face. When he approached the administration about his application, he was told that he didn't make it. When he asked why no one contacted him about the results of his application, the administrator just turned and walked away. He was the only black applicant, so as far as he was concerned he didn't make the team because of his skin tone. This wasn't the first time he had to deal with racism in the department, but this was a slap in the face, and it stung him pretty hard. They didn't even have the decency to call him to tell him he didn't make it.

One of the sergeants on the SWAT unit contacted Officer Harris and asked him to reapply. The sergeant said that the decision to reject him came from above. Officer Harris's reply was, "No, thank you! How in the world could I come over there and work with you guys and y'all got people who aren't even qualified. Suppose we had to go into a house, or through a door, or something. I know these guys aren't capable of doing what they are supposed to do. Why would I want to be a part of a unit like that? I would rather be on the street by myself.

Good luck to y'all." Officer Harris decided to return to working on the street in 7D, but he couldn't escape the disappointment.

Officer Shanita Brown sat in the same room as Officer Harris, but she was listening intently. The references to the kidnapping and killings of drug dealers forced a bad memory to resurface from the depths of her subconscious. Her boyfriend Curtis was murdered in the same way, under similar circumstances, so many years ago. Could this be a coincidence? Even though Curtis's murder was a cold case and never got solved, she got the eerie feeling that somehow there may be a connection. She was eager to learn as much as she could and to get out on the street so she could hunt these guys down and get revenge. Curtis was the love of her life, as well as the father of her child. He wasn't perfect, but he was hers. The irony of him being a drug dealer and her being a cop didn't escape her, though. Maybe if she had tried a little harder, she could have gotten him to stop doing what he was doing, and he would be alive today. She couldn't help but feel a sense of guilt.

Officer Steven Sullivan sat in the back of the room with his new FTO, Craig Hoye. *Now this is more like it,* Steven thought. *No more political rallies, no more rousing bratty, drunk college kids. This is real police work!* Steven was anxious to get out on the street and put to use all the things he learned in the academy. He couldn't help wishing, however, that he was still working with Officer Bailey because Officer Hoye was loud and colorful_ a real piece of work. But Steven knew that if he was going to be successful on the street, he would need Officer Hoye's knowledge and support. He was more than ready to get started.

"Are there any questions?" the watch commander bellowed. "Then let's get out there and get the bad guys! Remember, be safe out there."

*   *   *

When Officer Harris looked around the room, he noticed a similar pattern that had existed when he was working with the vice unit. Vice had maybe fourteen or fifteen officers, half white and half black. They would all leave the room together but would not go out together. All the white officers would ride together, and the black officers would ride together. They came from the same roll call, were in the same unit, were going to the same neighborhoods with the same instructions, but were self-segregated. Officer Harris began to feel that there was something wrong with that picture. It wasn't the 1950s or '60s anymore, but people were still acting like it was. When he saw the same thing happening in 7D, he decided to do something about it. So when roll call was dismissed and everyone headed to their police cruisers, Officer Harris jumped in a car with two white officers (Officers Charles White and James Canty).

"What the hell are you doing?" Officer White asked.

"We're going out," Harris responded. "We're going to the same place, so I'm riding with y'all today. We have been getting a lot of complaints from the community recently, and most of those complaints are about you white guys. I just need to see what the problem is so we can attempt to fix it. So let's go!"

Police radio dispatcher: "Charlie 2, 507, Corner of Fifth and MLK Avenue SE. Unlawful gathering, group of unarmed black men."

Charlie 2: "Ten-four"

With sirens blowing and lights flashing, Officer Harris and his newfound partners sped to the designated location. Officers White and Canty got out of the cruiser and approached nine black men sitting on the wall. There were open beer cans scattered all around the men, but nobody had a beer in their hand. Officer Canty unhooked the strap on his gun and put his hand on it as he approached the men, which did not go unnoticed.

"What's the problem, Officers?" one of the black men asked.

"We got a call of a disturbance," Officer White responded. "Everybody off the wall and put your fucking hands where I can see them."

"For what? We ain't done shit. We just sittin' here."

"This is an unlawful gathering. There are open alcohol containers, and by law, we have every right to tell you to move along. Now if you don't disperse, I'm going to lock your broke-ass up and your baby mamas can come visit you on the weekends!"

"Fuck you!"

At this point, Officer Harris got out of the car, walked over to the crowd, picked up the open beer cans, and poured the beer on the ground.

"Gentlemen, drinking in public is against the law. Since nobody was holding a beer can, technically, you were not drinking. We got a complaint, however, so we would appreciate it if you break this up and leave the area."

"We don't gotta leave! Fuck you, you bitch-ass nigga! If you take off that gun and badge, I'd beat your little bitch-ass."

Officer Harris walked very quickly up to the person who made that remark and got very close to his face. In a low and quiet voice, he responded, "Dude, I'm not here to go back and forth with you. At this point, no one is locked up because nobody had a beer in their hand. Everybody is leaving, so you need to go on about your business. Now if you don't, I'm not gonna lock you up. What's gonna happen is you and I are gonna go to that alley over there where nobody can see us, and we are gonna see who the real bitch-ass is. Now, I suggest you go along with your boys so you don't get embarrassed out here."

The crowd quietly dispersed. Officer Harris and his partners returned to their cruiser and continued patrolling the area.

"Man, you know why you guys are getting so many complaints?" Officer Harris said. "You can't talk to people like that! You can't just grab them and throw them around like they are a piece of shit. That is not why you are in this neighborhood. You are here to work for them. And there was no need to put your hand on your gun, Officer Canty. Were you scared?"

"But they keep doing the same shit all the time even though they know it's wrong," Officer White responded.

"Well, what else is around for them to do? This is their neighborhood. They will probably never leave this neighborhood. Then you guys come in from Pennsylvania or West Virginia or wherever you're from and try to force your power on them because you are police. None of you guys are that tough by yourself. So don't come into the neighborhood acting like you're a bad-ass when you are not. Just be who you are. Remember, respect will take you a whole lot farther than disrespect."

"Yeah, but you got up in that loud-mouths face. What did you say to him?"

"Oh, he was a punk just trying to show off, trying to show his boys how hard he was. He wasn't going to do anything, and I knew it. You have to be able to recognize who the talkers are and who are the doers. I had to let him know that respect goes both ways. But I also gave him a way out, a way to keep his own respect."

* * *

Police radio dispatcher: "Sarah 1, 415, 2529 Good Hope Road SE, Disorderly conduct, verbal altercation, two black women in the McDonald's parking lot."

Sarah 1: "Ten-four"

Officer Shanita Brown, who was riding alone, accepted the call from the dispatcher. When she got to the scene, she saw two hefty-sized women arguing. She got on the radio to call for backup just in case things got out of hand. She also called her friend Melody on her cell phone, just in case her backup didn't arrive. She was taught in the academy not to engage a situation until backup arrives because there is safety in numbers. There were times, however, when action had to be taken to prevent someone from getting hurt. But it was her dad's training that she remembered and relied on the most. When confronting someone, he would always say, "Watch their hands! Hands will hurt you. If you watch the person's hands, you will know what they are going to do. I have never seen anyone hit you with their stomach or with their eyes. Always watch their hands. And never allow people into your space. That way, you will have reaction time if something goes down."

As Officer Brown approached the arguing the ladies, she sensed that the situation was about to turn violent. She looked to see who was the more aggressive one, because usually in situations like this, one wants to fight while the other is either trying to save face or is scared to death.

"Ladies, what seems to be the problem here?"

"That bitch has plucked my last nerve. If she says one more thing, I'm gonna fuck her up."

"You don't know me like that! Call me a bitch one more time, and I'm gonna show you how much of a bitch I am!"

"Now, ladies, I don't want to have to arrest anyone today. So I suggest you both calm down and let's talk about this."

Out of the corner of her eye, Shanita saw Melody coming to provide backup, so she turned to the lady who had her fist balled up and had a stance that indicated she was about to throw a punch.

"Girlfriend, you don't want to do that. You need to chill, or this is going to get ugly real quick."

Before Shanita could say another word, the girl she was facing swung at the other girl and almost hit Shanita. Shanita saw the punch coming and was able to move out of the way and returned a punch that caught the girl on the side of the jaw. Melody had subdued the other girl, so Shanita didn't have to worry about her. The girl Shanita cold-cocked got even more upset and started to throw windmill punches at Shanita. Shanita hadn't seen anyone do the windmill since junior high school. A few punches caught her before she was able to knock the girl to the ground. She and Melody were able to wrestle her arms behind her, handcuff her, and then throw her in the back of Shanita's cruiser. Shanita wiped away a trickle of blood that dripped from the corner of her mouth.

"You OK?" Melody asked after they got the enraged girl into the back of the cruiser.

"Yeah, just a few bruises and scratches. I'm good. But I know what my daughter is gonna say when I get home. She's gonna say, 'Ma, you been fighting again today, haven't you?' And then I'm gonna say, 'Yeah, I'm gonna be a little sore for the next couple of days.' I hate it when she sees me like this. I don't want her to think that fighting is the way to solve your problems."

"She's a smart girl. I think she knows why you have to do what you do."

* * *

Police radio dispatcher: "Victor 4, 415, 904 Southern Avenue SE, near the corner of Chesapeake and Southern, Domestic disturbance."

Victor 4: "Ten-four"

Officer Hoye and Steven Sullivan were engaged in a conversation about surviving on the streets of DC when the call came over the radio. Officer Hoye was explaining how life in the 7D was so much different than what was happening in the 2D.

"Life over here is a little different than what you saw over in 2D," Officer Hoye said. "The section we are riding through now we call Oz, because you are going to see some shit that will curl your hair and make you wonder how people can live like this. Most of the people you will encounter here are brainless, will kill you in a second because they have no heart, and don't have the courage to stand up and help themselves.

"Now we refer to the area in Anacostia as Beirut because there is so much violence over there it always looks like a war zone. Sometimes we just sit under a bridge or on the street and wait for the next homicide to occur, which happens almost every day. Business is good for the undertaker over there.

"The area over by Barry Farms we refer to as the Jungle because they got a lot of jungle bunnies running around like they ain't got no sense. But you stick with me, and I'll school you. Bailey told me that you was good people, and he wanted me to look after you and so that's what I am gonna do. Just stick with me, kid, and I'll get you through all of this."

Steven sat quietly as he listened to Officer Hoye ramble on, wondering what happened to him in his life to make him think and feel this way. It seemed that he hated everybody, or maybe it was that he hated himself. It wasn't that he just despised and loathed black people, but it seemed that he felt that way about everybody who didn't look like him. As the cruiser sped to Southern Avenue in response to the dispatcher's call, Officer Hoye spotted a black man driving a new BMW and inexplicably turned on his lights and siren.

"What are you doing?" Steven asked. "Aren't we supposed to be responding to the domestic disturbance?"

"Keep your britches on, rookie. Let those jigs kill themselves. We'll get there in time to clean up the mess and write up the report. Don't you see that drug dealer over there? We need to stop him, get the drugs, and impound that car."

"What makes you think he's a drug dealer?"

"Dude, come on. How could a jig get a car like that if he wasn't selling drugs?"

"That's the second time I heard that word jig. What's a jig?"

"Jigaboo! Jungle bunny, pick-a-ninny, spook, spade, nigger_ don't you know anything?"

"Oh."

Officer Hoye cautiously approached the car on the driver's side while Officer Sullivan approached on the passenger side.

"What seems to be the problem, Officer?" the driver inquired.

"Sir, would you please step out of the car," Officer Hoye stated.

"Did I do something wrong?"

"I asked you nicely to get out of the car. I'm not going to ask again."

"I'm not getting out of this car until you tell me what I did wrong."

"You ran a stop sign back there."

"What! I didn't run any stop sign."

"Well, I said you did."

"OK, then give me a ticket and let me be on my way."

"Sir, do you have any weapons in the car?"

"No."

"Well, we got a report about a liquor store robbery in the area, and your car fits the description. So we are going to search this car whether you like it or not."

"But I thought you said you were stopping me because I ran a stop sign."

Officer Hoye got on his shoulder radio and called for backup stating "We got one." Steven seemed confused by this whole scenario. He knew that the driver didn't run a stop sign, and there was no report of a liquor store robbery. Suddenly four police cars approached the scene with sirens wailing and lights flashing. The approaching officers had their guns drawn. At this point, the driver decided to get out of the car with his hands raised high. Officer Hoye ordered Steven to search the driver while he searched the car.

Steven patted the driver down and determined that he didn't have any weapons. He asked the driver what he did for a living. The driver responded that he was a principal of a charter high school. The driver was furious as he watched Officer Hoye search through his car. He complains that "this is bullshit." Steven tried to calm him down and stated that this would be over soon. The driver leaned against Steven's police car and put his hands in his pockets.

Suddenly one of the other police officers screamed, "He's got a gun!" Instantly, all the officers trained their weapons on the driver, who was in shock. Steven, who had just searched the driver, jumped in front of the driver and told the other officers to put their weapons down, stating that he just searched the driver and he was clean. Steven then turned his back on the other officers, faced the driver, and told him to slowly pull his hands out of his pockets and place them behind his head.

Officer Hoye started chuckling and announced that the car was clean, and the driver was free to go on his way. The other officers gave Officer Hoye a quizzical look and reluctantly put their guns back in their holsters. They returned to their cruisers and took off. Officer Hoye and Steven got back in their cruiser and started racing to the location of the domestic violence scene.

"Man, you've got a lot to learn about the way we do things around here if you plan to survive. Don't you ever jump in front of an officer with a drawn gun again. That's just plain suicide."

"But that guy hadn't done anything wrong. What if someone had shot him? How were you going to explain that?"

"There's a phrase we use that will get you out of anything: 'I feared for my life.' Let me hear you say it. 'I feared for my life.' Come on, rookie, say it: 'I feared for my life.'"

"I feared for my life."

"Now, if you ever get into a situation where you've got to shoot somebody, you just repeat those words and you will be fine. Got it, rookie?"

"Yes, sir."

They sat in silence as they raced to Southern Avenue to respond to the domestic violence call. When they got there, a crowd of people had gathered outside, encircling two men who were on the ground pummeling each other. It turned out to be a son and his stepfather who were fighting. Apparently, the son was defending his mother, who had been beaten by the stepfather. Before entering the fray, Officer Hoye called for backup. He and Steven then proceeded to intervene, pushing and shoving, trying to get the combatants to stop. Other family members were present and arguing with each other. Somebody punched somebody else, and before long, it turned into a full-fledged brawl. The crowd seemed to turn their frustration on the two white officers. Suddenly, Steven got caught with a punch that sent him sprawling to the ground. He was unable to get up because he could feel several people stomping and punching him simultaneously. He could also feel someone very close to him trying to unhook the snap on his gun. Before the person could get to his gun, Officer Hoye burst through the bodies, swinging his baton widely, forcing the people who were stomping Steven to disperse. Steven was able to get to his feet, and he and Office Hoye stood toe-to-toe swinging and battling the crowd.

What seemed like hours were only a few seconds before backup arrived sending the crowd scurrying and fleeing from the scene. The father and the stepson were arrested along with anyone the officers were able to catch and anyone who Officer Hoye and Steven could identify as participants in the brawl. Steven's shirt pocket was torn, and his nose was bleeding; but other than that, sore ribs and a few facial bruises, he was OK. He seemed proud when Officer Hoye patted him on the back and said, "Son, you've been baptized today.

Now you are one of us." Steven learned an important lesson that day. He learned that any situation can turn deadly at the drop of a hat and that backup was so important. He also learned that he could depend on Officer Hoye if he ever got into a jam.

*　　*　　*

Police radio dispatcher: "Charlie 2, 10-71, Shots fired, 2500 block of Alabama Avenue SE. Proceed with caution."

Charlie 2: "Ten-four."

The cruiser carrying Officer Harris, White, and Canty sped to the location. A large crowd was standing around the body of an elderly lady on the ground next to a bag of groceries. Blood was pouring out of her chest area, soaking the black-and-white polka-dot dress she was wearing. Everyone in the crowd seemed stunned. Some were crying, and even some of the hardened young boys seemed to get emotional. It turned out that the old lady was a popular figure in the community, often referred to as the Candy Lady. Every neighborhood in the black community had one. She would sit on her porch and talk to everybody who passed by. She would often give candy to the kids in the neighborhood and always had a bit of advice for the young girls and boys on their way to or from school. She would say things like, "Keep your legs closed. If you can keep a quarter between your legs you can't get pregnant." Or, "Boy, pull your pants up so you don't fall on your ass."

After calling the homicide detectives and securing the scene, Officers Harris, Canty, and White began canvassing the onlookers and people in the neighborhood to try to get witnesses to tell what they saw. No one, however, was willing to talk to the police officers. Officer Harris, who was familiar with the neighborhood, approached Boogie, a well-known neighborhood drug dealer.

"Hey, Boogie, let me holla at cha."

"What up Officer Harris?"

"Who did this shit?"

"Come on, Officer Harris, you know I ain't no snitch!"

"Man, there is a difference between snitching and citizenship. If we want to keep the neighborhood safe, we need to help each other. You know that old lady didn't deserve this. We need to get the guy who did this."

"Officer Harris, you cool and everything, and I have mad respect for you, but don't tell me about snitching. Cops don't snitch on other cops when they do wrong! I believe you call that the blue wall. Cops be killing folks for no reason, and who snitches on them? Y'all let that shit go and then expect us not to do the same thing. I watch the same TV shows just like you do. Cops who do wrong are taught to keep their mouths shut until they talk to their union reps, and then they get away with murder. Politicians don't snitch on each other, and you know it. They be doing more dirt than anybody. Plus, snitching to the police will get you killed. You know that."

"Yeah, you right about that, but I really want to get this guy."

"Oh, you don't have to worry about that. We'll take care of him."

"So you know who did this?"

Boogie smiled and walked away. Two weeks later, the guy who killed the old lady was found in the Anacostia River with two bullets in his head and candy in his pockets.

*　　*　　*

Officer Leon Anderson was thankful that he was working the evening shift patrolling the Fort Totten subway station by himself. He needed a little peace and quiet after what had transpired that day. When he first came on duty, he saw a large group of high school students heading toward the station. He got a call from a school resource officer that the students were heading that way because there was going to be a fight. The large group of kids was in a frenzy as they formed a circle so the combatants could have room to do battle. He and other Metro Transit officers, along with the school resource officers descended on the scene to put a stop to the fight before it could get started. The kids seemed determined to fight, so one officer discharged his pepper-ball gun in the air, causing the kids to scatter like roaches when the lights were turned on. It was kind of disheartening to see kids acting that way. To make matters worse, Big Lee knew that it wasn't over. He knew that they were just going to move somewhere else so they could fight. *What are these kids coming to,* he thought. *They won't stop until someone is dead.*

Earlier that day, he and Roya had gotten into an ugly argument, and he had to get away to unwind. Their relationship had become strained lately, in part because of their lack of intimacy, as well as because of the fact that he was always working. She told him that it seemed that he spent more time on his job and no longer had time for her. Working on different shifts only added to the strain on the relationship. His shift would change every two weeks, and because he was a rookie, he couldn't get off on the weekends. In addition, he was becoming more introverted, argumentative, and he rarely smiled anymore.

All these things were floating around in his head as he patrolled the platform. His private thoughts probably kept him from being aware of his surroundings because he was startled when he looked up and saw a lone figure standing on the platform with a gun pointed at his head. The sight of the gun caused Big Lee to immediately retreat and hide behind one of the stanchions so that he could get his own gun out. From behind the stanchion, he ordered the man to drop his weapon and get on the ground. When the man did not move, Big Lee tightened the tension on the trigger. For some reason, he did not shoot. He suddenly had a flashback transporting him back to Fallujah, remembering the strange look on the face of that kid he killed. He realized that the man in the subway had the drop on him and could have shot him, but he didn't. A million things started running through his head. He started to wonder why the man didn't shoot him. Maybe it was because the man really didn't want to shoot anybody, or maybe it was because the gun was not real. Or just maybe it was because the man wanted Big Lee to kill him_ suicide by cop. Big Lee called for backup before trying, again, to talk the man into putting down his gun.

When other cops arrived on the scene, the man seemed to have come to his senses and decided to put the gun down. Officers rushed him and violently threw him to the ground before handcuffing him. When it was over, Big Lee had what seemed like a rush of adrenaline, causing him to shake uncontrollably. The reality of what almost happened to him suddenly sank in and was hard to process. The only thing he could think about was getting home to Roya and lying in her arms.

It turned out that the gun was indeed a toy gun. The man was a Vietnam veteran who was homeless and suffering from PTSD. He was taken to the hospital and placed on a suicide watch. When Big Lee got home that morning, Roya was gone, along with all of her clothes.

*   *   *

Police radio dispatcher: "All cars in the vicinity of East Capitol Street and Southern Avenue, 11-54, Car with suspected juvenile kidnappers spotted at the Shell gas station. Approach with extreme caution."

Sarah 1: "Ten-four."

Victor 4: "Ten-four."

Charlie 2: "Ten-four."

"That call is right down the street," Officer Hoye exclaimed. "Steven, you up for it?"

Even though his clothes were torn and the side of his face throbbed like he had been kicked by a mule, he responded, "I'm good. Let's do it."

A black Suburban had pulled up to one of the gas pumps at the Shell gas station and a fourteen-year-old youth named Butchie got out and entered the store. The gas station attendant kept a close eye on Butchie as he wandered around picking up snacks. When Butchie got to the counter, he put down his snacks, pulled out a 9mm handgun, and ordered the attendant to give him the money in the register and from the safe under the counter. Butchie didn't have a mask on

209

and unknowingly looked directly into the security camera that was mounted above the counter. This whole scenario was a part of his initiation into the gang. In addition to the gas station robbery, he was supposed to have stolen a car and shot somebody and left the body in an abandoned building. He also had to bring the other members of the gang three orange sodas, a bag of Doritos, and some Skittles.

When Butchie walked out of the store, several police cars swarmed in from every direction. He started to run, but when he saw the guns trained on him and the cops screaming, he dropped the bags, threw his hands up, and dropped to his knees.

"Get down and hug the fucking ground," a voice called out from one of the police cars. "You move an inch and you're a dead, motherfucker!"

"Occupants in the car," another voice called out, "reach your hands out of the window and open the door from the outside with your left hand. Slowly get out of the car with your hands up and put your face on the pavement. Do it now!"

Three doors of the Suburban opened simultaneously, and three suspects slowly got out with their hands up. They immediately lay down on the ground as instructed. Shanita Brown cautiously approached one of the prone suspects and handcuffed his hands behind his back. She got him to his feet and escorted him to her cruiser. Steven Sullivan handcuffed another suspect and took him back to his cruiser. When they got there, Officer Hoye grabbed the suspect, slammed his head on the cruiser's trunk, and started searching him.

"You don't have anything in your pockets that would stick me, do you, punk?" he sarcastically asked.

Officers White and Canty grabbed the last suspect, while other officers searched the vehicle and interviewed the gas station attendant. As Shanita walked her suspect back to her cruiser, she sensed that she knew him from somewhere.

"Where do I know you from?"

"I'm Freddy. I went to school with your brother Albert at H.D. Woodson back in the day."

"Oh, I do remember you from the old neighborhood. I sincerely hope you're not hooked in this shit."

"What shit are you talking about? We just stopped to get some gas and a soda. I didn't do anything. I was sitting in the back seat. I don't know what that young boy did. In fact, I hardly know him."

"I hope not, Freddy."

As Shanita began to put Freddy in the back seat of her cruiser, she noticed the gold chain with a single gold dog-tag dangling from his neck. She had given her boyfriend Curtis one just like that. The one she gave Curtis had the words "Love, Nita" engraved on the back. She shoved Freddy against the cruiser and turned the tag over. All of the air seemed to rush out of her. She felt as though she had been stabbed in the heart when she read the inscription on the back: "Love, Nita." Freddy's eyes opened wide when he saw the expression on Shanita's face. Her eyes got real narrow, her lips pressed close together, and she reached for her gun.

"What the fuck," Freddy screamed as Shanita placed the gun on his forehead right between his eyes.

"So it was you! You're the bastard that killed Curtis," she whispered in a voice that was barely audible.

"No, it wasn't me, but I know who did it. Please don't shoot me!"

"Who did it?"

"It was your brother Alfred who gave the order to do it! He said Curtis was stealing from him."

"Hey, Officer Brown," Officer Harris quietly said as he gingerly walked over to Shanita's cruiser. "You good? Look, I need a ride back to the station. The other suspects are in the cruiser I came over in. Can you help a brother out?"

"Sure," Shanita responded as she lowered her weapon and returned it to her holster, never once taking her eyes off Freddy.

CHAPTER 14

THE CROSSROADS

"What was that all about?" Officer Harris asked Shanita after they processed Freddy.

"What you talking about?"

"You know exactly what I'm talking about. You was about to blow that guy away. What did he do to you? It must have been something awful for you to risk throwing your whole career away and possibly going to jail."

"Just leave it alone. I don't know what you saw, but I was just having a conversation with an old acquaintance from the neighborhood."

"Yeah, OK. The only problem is that your 'conversation' was quickly going in the wrong direction and would have inadvertently made me an accessory. Sweetheart, I ain't going out like that. We police and everything, and I got your back, but when it comes down to keeping my job or going to jail, I'm keeping my job. Now, you really want to tell me what that was all about?"

"Just leave it alone!"

"OK, cool. By the way, I understand you've been riding alone for a minute. I need a partner, so would you mind if we rode together?"

Shanita looked at Officer Harris for a brief second and responded, "Sure," before turning and walking away. She was deep in thought and hadn't given much thought to what Officer Harris was talking about. Freddy's words kept rolling around in her head. *It was your brother Alfred who gave the order to do it.*

Could this be true? Would Alfred do such a thing, especially when he knew how much she loved Curtis? Or was Freddy just trying to save his own worthless life? More importantly, was Alfred the leader of this kidnapping ring? She knew that he was involved in selling drugs. As far as drug dealing was concerned, she hated the idea that guys in the neighborhood were involved in that; but as someone who truly understood who the real drug dealers were and how young black kids in the ghetto were able to get access to it in the first place, she had to think twice before selling out her loved one. How could she snitch on her own brother? Her initial hesitation about doing the right thing was not only out of love or loyalty for her brother, but also out of understanding that in this world, it is always the little people who are brought to justice and those who are truly evil get to walk free. So why put another brown face behind bars for the same crime a white one walks free for?

Freddy's admission not only shocked Shanita, but it put her in an awkward position. If Freddy was right, that would make Alfred complicit in the murder of numerous people, including Curtis. Premeditated murder was a lot different from just selling drugs. Since Freddy had confessed this to her, it meant that she was now required to do or say something about his admission to her superiors. If she did nothing and Freddy told someone else, which he was bound to do to save his own ass, then she was now committing an obstruction of justice by keeping quiet. This would get her in as much trouble as her brother. What should she do to get out of this dilemma?

*   *   *

Big Lee walked into the Fraternal Order of Police building on Sixth and G Streets NW, which was a social club for police officers, and went up to the bar to get a drink. He had only been in that club a few times after work when he was with a few of his partners. He never enjoyed going there because when he did, he always got the feeling that he wasn't wanted. People would stop their conversations and follow him around with their eyes, which reminded him of the road trips around the Mid-west when he was on the football team at Prairie Village.

Tonight was different. He needed to be around people regardless of how they felt about him. He also needed to be around other police officers who could understand what he was going through. The encounter with the gunman had unnerved him a bit. More importantly, it rekindled memories from his time in Iraq where his life was constantly in danger. These bad feelings were usually squashed when he fell into the arms of Roya, who was very talented in finding ways to make him feel good and made him forget about his troubles. When he got home this time, however, she was not there to greet him or to make him feel alive.

A white guy walked up to him and asked him if he knew where he was and if he belonged there.

"Dude, you really don't want to have this conversation with me right now," was Big Lee's response. "Do you really think I would walk into a building that has a big-ass sign saying POLICE and a big-ass badge hanging over the door and not know where I am? For real, dude! You just need to walk away and leave me the fuck alone!"

Before the guy could say another word, Big Lee got off the stool and stood facing the guy, hovering over him with his six-foot-four frame. Suddenly, Big Lee heard a familiar voice from the back of the room.

"Hey, Big Lee, what's cooking, man?"

Big Lee kept his eyes on the guy in front of him, but when Steven walked up to them and sat on the stool next to where Big Lee had been sitting, the guy returned to his seat. With a huge grin on his face, Big Lee sat down as if nothing had transpired.

"What up, Stevie Wonder? Good to see you. How have things been going?"

"Man, I'm good. After the academy, I was assigned over at 2D, but now I'm working over at 7D. By the way, you ain't gonna believe this. You remember that girl Michelle from school?"

"Michelle?"

"Yeah, you know, the cute black chick. Well, we are together now. I'm actually staying at her crib."

"Oh yeah, I remember you hanging out with her at the reunion. How did you pull that off?"

"She's a teacher here in DC. I called her one day, and she invited me out to a club. We hit it off, and so now we are together. I liked her when we were in school, but I just didn't know how to approach her. She was different from all the other girls I was with."

"I know I don't have to ask this, but did you get the draws?"

"Man, it ain't like that. She's a nice girl, and I really like her … but yeah, I got the draws, and that shit was good too!"

"My man Stevie Wonder, you haven't changed a bit."

"Well, believe it or not, I think I have changed. In fact, I've been thinking about taking this relationship to the next level. She makes me want to settle down and be in a committed relationship, like you and Roya. By the way, how is Roya?"

"Ah man, not too good. She rolled out on me. She said our schedules were too conflicting, which made it difficult for us to be together. We were never able to see each other. She would really get pissed off when I hung out with my police buddies after work and on some of my days off. She said I was married to the job, and she just couldn't compete with that. She also said that all I talked about was what happened on the job. She just couldn't understand. You know how it is. I was just trying to fit in and become one of the boys."

"Yeah, I know about trying to fit in. But I do remember when we were in the academy and they talked to us about establishing a balance between our personal lives and our business lives. They talked about falling into the trap of divorce, alcoholism, and suicide that tripped up too many police officers. I try hard not to fall into that trap. When I get off work, I try not to take work home with me. I try to do different things with her and hang out as much as possible. Just like last week_ I took her on a camping trip up in the Blue Ridge Mountains off of Skyline Drive. She didn't want to go at first, saying that she was a city girl. But we stayed in one of those log cabins with a fireplace, and she loved it. The other night, she took me to this boring-ass play at the Arena Stage. I went along and pretended that I enjoyed myself. Sometimes you've got to 'go along to get along.'"

"You right! I know I messed up. I needed to spend more quality time with her. I'm gonna call her and try to make things right. Speaking of balance and quality time, shouldn't you be at home with your old lady right now?"

"She's at one of those PTA meetings and won't get home until late. Plus, my FTO wanted me to meet some of his friends. He's one of those good-old-boys with some messed-up attitudes, but he's good police and knows his stuff. I'm tryin' to learn as much as I can before I get cut loose."

"I hear you, but don't hang out too long. Don't make the same mistake I made."

"Got you. In fact, I was just getting ready to roll out when you walked through the door. When she gets home, I'm gonna take her to the movies, eat some popcorn, and neck in the balcony. OK, I'm out. Stay strong and be careful out there."

"Give Michelle a hug and kiss for me. Holla."

*   *   *

Shanita Brown and Gregory Harris rode together for a couple of weeks before Shanita began to feel totally comfortable with her new partner. She had gotten used to being by herself, but having a partner around who could give her not only direction and guidance but immediate backup was a blessing. Officer Harris was not only tough, responsible, and a good cop, he also lived up to the image of what a police officer should be in her eyes. He knew just about everybody in the community_ his neighborhood, as he called it_ and the people seemed to like him. He didn't like riding through the neighborhood, so he would often park the cruiser in a visible spot and walk the beat. He was always telling the young kids to stay in school, or giving information to those adults who would listen about job openings or job fairs. More than that, he had the respect of the people. Even the drug boys appreciated the way he handled himself and how he showed everyone respect.

Respect was a big thing in the community. He would walk into a crowd of boys and tell them that he would be back in five minutes and the area needed to be clear when he got back. He was giving them a chance to do the right thing before he had to do his thing, which was to keep the peace. He shared his knowledge and skills with Shanita, showing her where the 'hot spots' were, who she could depend on for information and who she would probably have a problem with. He had no problems, however, locking someone up when it was necessary. The word on the street was, if you got locked up by Officer Harris, then your ass needed to be locked up because Officer Harris gave everybody a chance.

The more they rode together, the more they began to trust each other. The only thing Shanita found wrong with him was that he talked all the time. He would talk a hole in her head to the point where she longed for the silence that riding alone provided. He talked about his failed marriage, his many jobs in the department and the experiences he had gotten from them, racism in the department, what he would change if he was in charge, what he was going to do when he retired, and on and on. But he was also very funny. Not a day went by where she wasn't doubled over from laughing at his jokes or antics. She could always depend on him to put a smile on her face, even when things weren't going so well.

"Hey, Greg, have you ever thought about getting married again?"

"Oh, hell no! If I did, she would have to be sixty-five years old, with no breasts and so crossed-eyed I couldn't tell if she was talking to me or the guy standing next to me. That way, I wouldn't have to do much to keep her happy."

"Boy, you crazy."

"Hey, Greg, I think that young girl over there likes you. She keeps looking at you and smiling."

"Oh yeah, well she can just keep on looking. I'm not messing with those fast, young girls. Her breath probably still smells like Similac. Plus her butt is so big that we couldn't sit on the same couch at the same time!"

"Hey, Greg, have you ever hit a woman?"

"Now, why would you ask me a question like that? The answer is no. My parents taught me better than that. But, I have been hit by one, though. Her name was Hattie Overbee. Hattie was a young girl who went to W. B. Powell Elementary School with me and who taught me a valuable lesson in life. She was a big girl for her elementary days, and as children have a tendency to be cruel, she was the victim of countless taunts about her size and looks. She was given the nickname Bear. Kids would walk up on her and shout, 'Hum mm Bear!'

During recess one day, one of my 'friends' dared me to go up and call her Bear. So like an idiot, I walked behind her and shouted, 'Hum mm Bear!' Suddenly, like a lion pouncing on an unsuspecting dinner meal, Hattie swung around and slapped the shit out of me! That girl hit me so hard that not only did I see stars and quasars, but it knocked out one of my teeth. The whole playground erupted in laughter with my so-called friend as the ring-leader. What did I learn from that episode? One, teasing people because of their looks is cruel and hurtful. Two, your friends aren't always your friends. Three, doing things without thinking and simply because someone else wants you to do them has consequences. And four, if you hit a woman, she will probably get you back when you least expect it. Lessons learned."

Shanita couldn't help but begin to admire Greg. During one conversation, he began asking questions about her private life, and she got that "Here we go again" feeling. However, he did not make any romantic or sexual advances on her. In fact, it seemed like just a part of his regular conversation, and when she didn't respond, he just moved on to another topic. Soon she began to wonder why he never made any advances on her; after all, he was kind of cute. One day, after they had broken up a fight between two close friends, she asked him why he became a cop.

"When I was twenty-one years old, I visited Atlanta with some friends. I was super excited to be in the birthplace of the civil rights movement, but I left after seeing and hearing that racism was still alive and well. That experience was present in my mind a few years later when I was at a crossroads, pondering my next career move. I was being pulled toward the military, but I just couldn't shake the way I felt that day in Atlanta. I thought, *How could I fight for other nations, to help liberate, and ensure that basic rights, freedom, and equality were being given there, when we still struggled for the same here?* That day, I decided that my services would be better utilized serving my own community directly. So I became a cop."

As Greg was completing his explanation of why he joined the force, they received a call from the radio dispatcher to proceed to a traffic accident on I-295 near the Malcolm X Avenue exit. When they got there, they saw a car facing southbound in the northbound lane. There had been a head-on collision between the car and a fifteen-passenger van, and the car had been crushed. They got out of their cruiser, and Greg immediately started directing traffic around the crash site. Shanita grabbed her flashlight and went to see if there were any survivors in the car. As soon as she reached the car, she could see that the van's engine block was in the back seat of the car. As she got closer, she saw a baby, still in the car seat, but it had been severed in half. There was a grotesque look on the baby's face like she knew what was about to happen. Next to her was another child who had been decapitated. There were severed hands and feet lying around the car and blood everywhere. Shanita quickly stepped back with her hands covering her mouth. She had seen dead bodies before, but the sight of dead babies unnerved her.

When Greg saw her reaction, he came over to the car and told her to get on the cruiser radio and call for several ambulances. He also told her that after she called it in, she needed to help out with traffic control. Having something to do enabled Shanita to get herself together and refocus on the job at hand. When the accident site was finally cleaned up and traffic flow had returned to normal, Shanita and Greg returned to their cruiser and continued their patrol. There was no humorous quips, and no conversation at all. As they drove around in silence for a couple of minutes, Shanita began to sob quietly. Greg pulled the cruiser over to the curb.

"Just let it all out," he said. "Try not to dwell on it too long. You'll get over it soon. This is who we are and what we do."

Shanita's tears turned into a raging river as Greg pulled her close, softly caressing her in his arms. She nestled her head on his chest and wept.

* * *

Big Lee gingerly walked out of the police social club, fumbling to get his cell phone out of his pocket. He wasn't a heavy drinker, but two years in Iraq caused him to overextend himself from time to time. He was eager to talk to Roya and plead with her to take him back. He dialed her number, praying she would pick up. When her sweet voice answered, he apologized profusely for taking her for granted and not giving her the type of commitment she needed in the relationship. He promised he would do better and asked if he could drop by so they could talk about it face-to-face. She was hesitant at first, but then decided that she at least owed him a sit-down even though she knew it was over.

Roya lived in a luxury apartment building located on Connecticut Avenue in the Cleveland Park section northwest Washington DC. He decided to take the subway because he could get off at the Cleveland Park station and walk to her place. He also decided to take the train because he had had a few drinks and didn't want to risk getting pulled over for a DUI. As he exited the train station, he saw a kid dash out of a store in the small shopping complex across the street and sprint as fast as he could, disappearing down a side street. A police cruiser immediately took off after the youth. Big Lee saw one officer get out of the cruiser and pursue the suspect down an alley, while the cruiser sped farther down the street. He knew that being in plain clothes while involving oneself in an active police situation was a no-no, but when he heard gunshots coming from the alley, Big Lee pulled out his service weapon and quickly entered the alley.

Big Lee could barely see in the dark alley, but as he got a little farther in, he could see that the officer was on the ground and the kid was standing directly over him holding a gun pointed at the officer's head. Big Lee shouted at the kid, telling him to drop his gun. The startled kid took off running, but before he did, he turned slightly, enabling Big Lee to see his face in the moonlight. Big Lee tightened the grip on the trigger of his weapon, but before he could squeeze it all the way, he saw the face of the kid he shot when he was in Iraq. This caused him to hesitate, allowing the kid to flee unharmed.

Big Lee started to chase the kid, but stopped to check on the condition of the police officer on the ground. He checked for a pulse but could not detect one. Suddenly, a searing pain erupted in Big Lee's shoulder. Something had struck him, causing his body to spin around before knocking him to the ground. His gun was knocked out of his hand and landed several feet away. Big Lee could see another officer approaching him, so he mustered all the strength he could to pull his badge out of his pocket. When the officer approached, Big Lee announced that he was a police officer and showed the officer his badge. The officer looked at Big Lee, let out a sinister grin, and then shot him four times in the chest and once in the head. The officer then picked up Big Lee's badge, and slipped it in the back of his own pants pocket.

*   *   *

Steven and Michelle had been standing in the line at the Uptown Theater when the shots rang out. Michelle was tired after attending her PTA meeting, but Steven had other plans for the evening. He knew she loved Denzel Washington movies, so he convinced her to go with him that night. His plan was to get her to go to the movies; then when they got home, he would fix her a surprise dinner and then propose to her. When he saw the police chasing a suspect and then heard the gunshots, he told her to wait there because he couldn't stand by and do nothing while a crime was going down, even when he was off-duty.

As Steven cautiously entered the alley where he heard the gunshots, he saw two bodies on the ground and one officer standing next to them. He announced that he was a police officer as he slowly approached the scene. Steven was in shock when he saw that one of the bodies lying on the ground was his good friend Big Lee, and the officer standing over him was his first FTO, Officer Bailey. Officer

221

Bailey was standing there sorrowfully looking at his partner, who was a rookie officer that he was training. When Officer Bailey turned to go back to his cruiser, something fell out of his back pocket. Steven went over to pick it up and realized it was Big Lee's police badge.

CHAPTER 15

BATTLE SCARS

Shanita Brown arrived at the office of Cheryl Santos, who was the chief psychologist hired by MPD to counsel officers who are involved in police shootings_ officers who have been identified as suffering from the stress that accompanies the job, or just officers who need somebody to talk with in order to process what they have been going through. The past month had been particularly brutal for Shanita. As the weather started getting warm, the violence followed a similar warming trend. The other night, she went on a call where she saw a young kid_ who had been chased into an apartment complex by a group of guys_ shot in the head. When she arrived on the scene, the body was still lying on the floor with blood running everywhere.

The week before, she went into a house where a body was discovered. It was warm in the house, so the body was a stinker. The odor was so repugnant that she initially wanted to throw up. Older officers had taught her to put Vicks Vapor-Rub under her nose so she could tolerate the stench, but there was no cute trick to avoid the sight. Maggots were all over the body, and the skin started to pop when fresh air rushed into the room. There was another situation where a baby had been shot. Shanita was trying to save the baby's life by performing CPR, to no avail. The death of children, especially babies, seemed to affect her the most.

From day one on the job, she had seen enough death, smelled it, and sometimes even tasted it in the air that she should have been used to it. But some things were hard to adjust to. These experiences gave her a different view of the world. She often couldn't go home and talk with her daughter about her day because she didn't want to expose her daughter to the depths of the evils of society. So she would come home, take a shower, and go to bed, hoping that sleep would erase the images of her day. But, sometimes those images would often follow her into her dreams. Usually, the dream would start with the very first homicide scene she observed. She would close her eyes, recall the time of day the call came in, what she was doing before she got there, and what she did once she got on the scene. For the most part, however, she learned to disassociate herself from what she saw, to become numb to the carnage. Today was different. There was one death that she could not shake, promoting an urgent need to speak with a therapist.

"Hi, Shanita. My name is Cheryl. I will be working with you for the next hour. We can schedule as many sessions as needed to find out how to resolve whatever is bothering you. So what brings you here today?"

"Hi, Ms. Santos."

"Please, call me Cheryl."

"OK Cheryl, to tell you the truth, I didn't think I needed to be here at all, but a good friend told me that I needed to take advantage of the resources available to police officers, so here I am. I mean, I thought I was doing a good job handling the stress that comes with being police, but the suicide of my close friend and fellow officer, Melody Cash, caught me totally off guard. I can't seem to shake it off.

"I took a class, offered by the department, where they talked about officer suicide, but they didn't even use the word *suicide*. They said accidental death. They said that for every 'in-the-line-of-duty death,' there are two reported or unreported accidental deaths in the nation. Imagine that!

"Melody's death, however, was no accident. She put a gun to her head and pulled the trigger. I thought, after taking that class, that I would be able to process her death, but ... I mean, she could have come to me and talked about her problems. We were tight. I had her back, and she had mine. I can't help feeling that I could have done something to stop her from doing that. I don't get it! Why did she do that? And what about her baby?"

"Shanita, I know how you feel and what you are going through, but before we talk about Melody, I think it would be a good idea to talk a little bit about you. Then we can come back to Melody. It might help explain what she was going through and why she did what she did. You said you were able to handle the stress of the job. What are some of the things that cause you stress, and how do you handle them?"

"As a police officer, you see a lot of broken homes, broken people, broken dreams, a lot of hopelessness, and for the most part, there's nothing you can do about it. No one wants to be a failure, and yet we fail almost every day. I got into this job to help people, but sometimes I feel like the only thing I am doing is picking up the pieces.

"And working with the people you are supposed to be helping can be very challenging. They don't sugarcoat anything. They give it to you raw! Like I've had people say things like, 'He stole my drugs,' like drugs were legal. Or, 'He was trying to fuck me in the butt, and I didn't want him to!' Really! It's wild. You see and hear things the average person doesn't see or hear, and it can be very disheartening.

"Then there is the violence and the people's reaction to us. For example, let's say there is a body lying in the street. You pull up and handle the scene. You secure the scene, secure the evidence, push the people back because when you've got a body on the ground, everybody in the family wants to be there, fighting, crying, and screaming, 'Oh my God.' They pretty much know who shot the person, but they are mad at the police. They say, 'Y'all ain't doing nothin'!' I'm not quite sure what they want us to do at that point. We've already called for the ambulance or the helicopter. We've tried to get witnesses to come forward and talk, but usually to no avail. It gets to be frustrating at times."

"How do you deal with all of that?"

"You have to turn all of your emotions off. It's not that you stop caring_ you just become desensitized to it all. You have to, or you will go crazy. You don't want to take that stuff home with you, but you also don't want to take it to the next assignment either. You might be fighting on one assignment in a domestic situation, and when you get your next call, you might be dealing with an unruly child who just needs some guidance. So if you take that rage you needed to survive the first incident to the next incident, you then come off as the mean officer. You have to be professional.

"The stuff that you do becomes instinctive because you've done it so many times. When I respond to a scene, I go through my checklist of responsibilities in my head. I can't undo the violence that has been done. All I can do is check my boxes, do what I am supposed to do, and make sure it gets documented for the next guys who do the investigation. When I canvass the neighborhood, I try to be as compassionate as possible. When people curse me out, I don't take it personal. When someone curses, it is rude, but it is not against the law. I've come to realize that they are not cursing at me, but they are cursing at the uniform. They don't even know me. So you train yourself to leave the drama at work. You train yourself to survive so that when something bad happens, your mind goes into that protective mode which protects you. It shields you.

"Sometimes, you might see a group of police officers standing near a scene laughing, smiling, or just talking, and people would be like 'Why are they laughing?' But I think that when we have just encountered a violent scene, we are decompressing. We are actually not trying to focus on what we just saw. We separate from it. It is our way of dumping whatever it was we just dealt with before we have to go to the next call. Our interaction with each other helps us ease the stress just a little bit. It's funny, though. I can see something at work, and it doesn't break me because I have to remain professional and handle the situation. But I can be at home and see something on the news, and it will make me cry. I don't know, you just build up … maybe our uniform is our Superman cape. You build up this defense because you know you've got to get the job done.

"Dealing with supervisors and the top brass is another issue. What really stresses me out is trying to be a great mother and a great police officer. The department doesn't care if you have a family at home.

They will tell you quick, 'That's your problem!' There are times when I have to stay on the job longer than I am supposed to in order to finish writing a report, or my leave will be cancelled, which makes raising a child by yourself very difficult. Once, I had to pick up my daughter from school, but I couldn't get away from the job. When I got to the school, she was sitting on the steps crying. It broke my heart!

"The struggle of trying to raise her and be a good cop is wearing me down. I've thought about quitting and trying to find another job, but I don't have a college degree, and most good jobs require that you have one. We have to have a roof over our heads, and health care, so it is not easy to just say, 'I'm gone.'"

"Even though it's been tough, you've been able to manage it. Why do you think so many other officers haven't been able to manage the stress? Why do you think Melody was not able to handle it?"

"This job is not for everybody. I think a lot of times people don't know what they are getting themselves into, and once they find themselves in it, they don't know how to handle it. They don't have anybody they can talk to who understands what they are going through. They don't use the resources that are out there. A lot of people think that talking to a therapist is taboo. Some people are not good at dumping what they just saw, so they take it home. They don't know how to decompress, and they don't really have anybody they can talk to other than other police officers."

"How do you decompress once you get home?"

"My daughter is everything to me! I try to do as much with her as I can. We go shopping a lot, and I try to attend as many of her school activities as I possibly can. We will sit in the living room and read together for about thirty minutes each day and talk about what we read. Afterward, I will sit in the bathtub for about forty minutes, or go running and then come home and take a long, hot shower."

"Do you talk to her about your day?"

"Sometimes, but I never talk to her about the violence. She doesn't need to hear the gory details."

"Do you have anybody other than other police officers that you can sit down with and share those horrors with? Are you dating anybody?"

"No. Not at this time."

"You should think about finding someone you can sit down with a share your thoughts. I find that sharing your innermost thoughts with a loved one or a close friend is very therapeutic. Well, our hour is up. I'd like to see you a couple more times before we end our sessions. How about next week at the same time."

"Sounds good to me, Doc. See you next week."

As Shanita walked out of the therapist's office, she began thinking about the last thing the therapist said. Probably she did need to start dating again, but who. She started thinking about her new partner, Gregory Harris. *He's a little old, but he's kind of cute.*

*   *   *

Steven stretched out across Michelle's bed with his eyes plastered to the ceiling as she stroked his forehead.

"Babe, did you hear me?" she asked.

He didn't respond because he was so deep in thought that he hadn't even heard a word she said. His thoughts were on the lifeless body of his good friend Big Lee lying on the ground face-up. For the first time since he had been on the job, Steven began to appreciate the gravity of not coming home. He used to be able to say there was a chance of not coming home the same way he could say there was a 20 percent chance of rain. They were just words. The academy tried to prepare him for this day. It didn't sink in until now. Now it was real, very real.

Steven kept going over the image of Big Lee in his head. His upper body had been riddled with bullets, but there was something seriously wrong with the image. There was an exit wound on his shoulder, which meant that he had to have been shot from behind. But how could that be? If he was chasing the subject, then how could he have been shot from behind, unless there was somebody else in that alley?

Then there were four wounds in his chest and one to his head, which meant that if the subject shot him in the back, he must have stood over Big Lee and executed him. That would seem unlikely with police sirens blaring, which meant the subject, or subjects, would be trying to flce the scene as fast as possible. These young thugs have been notoriously known for their inability to shoot straight. When they are in a shootout, they usually miss more than they hit. That's one of the reasons they end up spraying an entire neighborhood when they are trying to hit one person. That is also why there are so many innocent bystanders hit by stray bullets. Police, however, are trained to shoot center mass and then to the head. The shot in the back could have spun Big Lee around, which could explain why the remaining shots hit him in the front. Or just maybe ….

The largest piece of the puzzle, however, was what was Big Lee's badge doing in Bailey's back pocket? Bailey was a veteran cop with an impeccable record. Officers are trained not to disturb a crime scene until investigators arrive. Big Lee's badge should have either been on his body or somewhere near his body. It made no sense for it to be in Bailey's pocket.

"What's on your mind, babe? You seem to be a thousand miles away. You still thinking about Lee?

"I'm sorry, hon. Did you say something?"

"I said what were you thinking about? Where is your head right now?

"I'm sorry, honey. I was thinking about Big Lee. I was just with him earlier that evening. We were at the FOP Club talking about women, and life. He and Roya were having some problems, and he was going to try and patch things up. It really burns me up that he goes a thousand miles away to fight in Iraq, comes back without a scratch, and ends up lying on the ground in some funky alley. It just ain't right! Whoever did this has got to pay!"

"I know. It's tough, but just think: it could have been you lying in that funky alley. Babe, you've got to be more careful. Running into a dark alley is dangerous enough, but doing that while not in uniform is just crazy! You've got to promise me that you won't do no crazy shit like that again. You better not leave me. Have you ever thought about doing something else other than police work?"

Stevens mind begins to trail off again. *What was Big Lee's badge doing in Bailey's pocket? Why was he walking away with it?*

Michelle saw that she was not getting through to Steven, so she attempted to change the subject.

"By the way, when I got home last night, I saw something on the dresser. I didn't want to look at it, but I couldn't help myself. Is there something you want to ask me?"

"Huh?"

"The box you left on the dresser! Was there something you wanted to ask me last night?"

"Uh, oh yeah. Now is not a good time, though. I tell you what, after I get off work, why don't you and I go over to the National Harbor and hang out for a little bit. I really like it over there. We can go to the MGM casinos, see a show, play little slots, and then get something to eat."

"OK, but why you tryin' to make me wait that long?"

What was Big Lee's badge doing in Bailey's pocket? Why was he walking away with it?

When Steven got back to work, it seemed as though all hell was about to break loose. The shooting of Big Lee was the topic of conversation. When fellow officers get killed, it always heightens the sensitivities and emotions of other officers. It is like a family member has been lost, which usually brings the ranks closer together. More so, it makes officers think about their own mortality. This was different, however. Most of the officers didn't even know Big Lee, but the fact that a white officer shot and killed a black officer seemed to split the department in two along racial lines.

The black officers were very upset. They brought up the issue of black people being killed by white officers all over the country and how nothing was being done about it. They also talked about the fact that white cops were too quick to pull their weapons and shoot people because they were afraid of black people or didn't understand the culture in DC because they were from somewhere else. White officers were asking what a transit cop was doing in that alley anyway, why was he out of uniform, and why didn't he identify himself as a police officer. Most of them said that if their partner was lying on the ground dying, they probably would have killed anyone in the vicinity too.

Steven was torn whether or not to reveal what he knew about Officer Bailey and Big Lee's badge. He liked Officer Bailey a lot, and thought he was a very good cop. Bailey taught him a lot about community policing, but one lesson that Bailey made clear was that cops didn't tell on other cops. Bailey had admitted that he was the shooter, but didn't know Lee was an officer because he never identified himself as one.

Steven was devastated by Big Lee's death. He couldn't get the image of Big Lee lying on the ground with his eyes wide open. Those eyes seemed to implore Steven to do something, to bring the killer to justice. The circumstances that Steven kept rolling around in his head caused him to think that Bailey's explanation of what happened was suspect. Was this an accidental shooting, or did Bailey murder Big Lee? Should he bring this to the attention of the watch commander, or should he keep his mouth shut until he could get more evidence? This dilemma was eating Steven up inside, but he owed it to Big Lee to find the truth.

Steven wrestled with these questions for a few days, until he finally decided to share what he was thinking with someone in the department. Instead of going to the watch commander, he decided to tell his FTO, Officer Hoye. Officer Hoye sat in their cruiser intently listening to Steven's concerns.

"Did you ask Bailey why he picked up the badge?" Hoye asked.

"No, I was kind of in shock when the badge fell out of his pocket. I didn't know what to do."

"Have you told anybody else what you saw?"

"No, not yet. I was thinking about telling the watch commander, but I wanted to run it by you first."

"Good. I'm glad you kept your damn mouth shut. We don't need to be stirring up any more trouble around here the way things are going. All we need is for those damn 'Black Lives Matter' idiots to get a hold of this information. That shit will be on CNN for days, and we may never get to the truth. You did the right thing bringing this to me. Let me check around with some people. You just keep quiet."

Steven felt relieved that he was able to get that off his chest. For the next couple of days, he and Hoye continued patrolling their beat without mentioning Bailey, Lee, or any of that mess. The heavy burden had been lifted from his shoulders, but soon he began to wonder if there was going to be an investigation, and what steps Hoye was taking to resolve the matter.

As Steven approached his car in the parking lot, a warm feeling began flushing through his body as his thoughts focused on the evening he was going to spend with Michelle. Tonight was the night. He was finally going to pop the question. He knew the surprise was already gone because she had seen the ring box and had probably looked inside, given how inquisitive she was. His pleasant thoughts were interrupted, however, when five police officers approached him as he opened his car door. He didn't recognize any of them, but the looks on their faces indicated this wasn't a social call, and there was something amiss.

"You Steven Sullivan?" one of them barked.

"That's the name on my driver's license. Who's asking?"

"Listen, smartass, you've got to learn how to keep your fucking mouth shut."

"Snitches get stitches," another one chimed in.

"What the fuck are y'all talking about?" Steven exclaimed with a startled look on his face.

"You know what the fuck we are talking about! That shit you been spreading around about Tim Bailey with that nigger's badge," the first one barked. "We better not hear that you been spreading those lies with anyone else, if you know what is good for you!"

"It's real dangerous out here on these streets," the third officer interjected. "We wouldn't want to have to attend another police officer's funeral, if you get my meaning."

"Have a nice day, Officer Sullivan," the fourth officer stated.

With that last statement, the five police officers returned to their cruisers and drove off into the night. Steven got in his car and started the engine. He could hear the sound of his heart beating over the roar of the engine.

What the fuck just happened?

*   *   *

Another hectic day in 7D had come to an end. Earlier that day, there was a call about a naked man walking down the middle of the street on Martin Luther King Avenue. When Shanita and Greg pulled up, there were four other police cars already on the scene. It turned out that the man was high on the drug PCP. People on PCP have a way of exhibiting superhuman strength, so it took all ten officers to wrestle him to the ground and get him in handcuffs. At the end of their shift, Shanita and Greg pulled their cruiser into the police parking lot.

"Hey, Greg, what cha doin' later on this evening?"

"The same thing I do every evening after I get off. I go home, pop a frozen dinner in the microwave, open a cold one, and watch Sports Center. Why, what's up?"

"Just wondering if you'd like to come by my place and hang out for a little bit."

"What! You serious?"

"I've got some things I want to get off my chest, and I didn't want to do it while we were on the job."

"You sure that's all you want to do?"

"Stop playin'! You so nasty. No, even though a girl has got needs, all I want to do is talk."

"Sure! You ain't gotta ask me twice. What time you want me to come by?"

"Let's say around 9:00 p.m. I gotta put my daughter to bed first."

"Cool. See you at nine."

When Shanita opened the door to her apartment, the smile on Greg's face immediately disappeared. He was hoping that her invitation would end up with some wild, butt-naked sex; but when he saw her dressed in sweat pants and a shirt, he figured that wasn't going to happen. As he walked in, his initial disappointment began to change. The lights were low, there was smooth jazz music softly playing in the background, and the smell of cherry incense permeated the room. His smile quickly returned. *I'm gonna tear that ass up,* he thought.

She sat down on the couch and beckoned him to sit next to her.

"Man, today was one crazy day!" she said. "Did you see the johnson on that crazy guy we had to take down on MLK? He was hung like a horse!"

"Yeah, and I wasn't too happy that I had to get that close to that whack-o. That was disgusting. Some people just don't need to be doin' drugs. Didn't he realize he was supposed to just say no?"

"That shit was funny, though."

"So what's up, girl? You seemed really serious when you asked me to come up here tonight. What did you want to talk about?"

"I don't know if you know this or not, but I've been seeing a therapist."

"That's a good thing! I wish more officers would take advantage of therapy, especially with all the shit we have to deal with. Did you see Ms. Santos?"

"Yep, she was the one I spoke with. She was pretty good too. She got me thinking about a lot of stuff."

"And she's cute too, with that big old booty!"

"Man, what makes you think I was looking at that girl's booty? Anyway, she was asking me how I dealt with all of the violence and death I was seeing. She also asked me if I had anyone to talk to about my day. I told her that there wasn't anybody I could really talk to. I talk to my daughter about some things, but I don't talk about the gory details. I can't talk to my family members because they just don't understand, and I don't have many friends. Santos said I needed to find somebody I can bounce things off of, and the only person I could think of, off hand, was you. I feel comfortable talking around you, so I was hoping that maybe we could just sit down and talk from time to time."

"Why, sure. I would be honored, but if you think I'm gonna sugarcoat anything or hold your hand while you go through a pity party, I'm not that guy. I'm gonna give it to you straight and tell you what I really think. I will hold you in my arms and let you cry on my shoulder, though."

"That's why I came to you."

"So where do we start. I've seen you in action. You're a good cop, so something must be bugging you. What's up?"

"My best friend, Melody, killed herself, and that shit got me fucked up right now. I can't seem to let it go. She was a rookie cop just like me."

"Do I know her?"

"You met her before. Remember when you taught my class at the academy? She was the one you said had daddy issues and the reason she became a cop was because she and her daddy used to watch police shows together."

"Oh yeah, I do remember her. This job is not for everybody. It can really stress you out if you let it."

"Let me ask you this: do you ever feel bad when you have to shoot or kill someone?"

"You may think I'm weird, but none of the shootings I've been in bother me. As long as I know I am right, I can deal with it, and to date, I have never been wrong. If I was in a situation where I could have done something differently, then maybe it would bother me, but when I have to pull my weapon, I have no qualms about using it.

"If a dude is shooting at me, I don't have a problem with shooting him_ none at all. I hope I get him! That's how I think. I'm not one of those guys who second-guess what I have done because I know at that point, if I hesitate, it might cause the death of my partner, someone else on the street, or worse yet, my death. Once we get to that point, whoever it is, is getting it. And when I shoot somebody, I shoot to kill. I'm not trying to wound him. If I have to shoot, he's getting the full clip.

"I have been in too many close calls where, if things were different, I wouldn't have gone home that night. There was one incident when I was coming from court. My partner and I were riding back to the station when we saw some guys in a stolen car. We followed them into an alley and they jumped out of the car and split up. I was on the passenger side. The driver jumped out and started shooting at my partner, and the other guy started shooting at me while I was still in the car. The shots didn't hit me. I guess it wasn't my time because the shots came really close. One bullet hit my door and went through the mirror. So we jumped out and returned fire. I killed the one who was shooting at me, and the other one got wounded. In that situation, it was him or me, and I didn't want it to be me.

"There was another situation where we got a call for sounds of gunshots in the neighborhood. Some kids had shot out all of the lights at the rec center. When we pulled up, they didn't see us, but we heard the gunfire. We got out of our cruiser and approached them. We heard one guy scream, "POLICE" and they started shooting at us. We could see silhouettes of them running along a tree line, but we could also see flashes of gunfire coming at us. We started firing back at the muzzle flashes. We didn't hit any of them, unfortunately. We ended up finding out who they were later and arrested them.

"Would I have been bothered if I had shot any of them? Absolutely not. I went home and slept like a baby."

"You mean, with all of the shootings you've been involved in, you've never felt bad about any of them?"

"Well, I must admit, the first person I had to shoot was a woman. I killed her, and that stayed with me for a while. That's probably because she was the first person I ever killed. It was also probably because it was a woman. I did a lot of praying and a lot of thinking through things to see if there was something else I could have done to avoid doing that. I couldn't think of anything else I could have done in that situation. Again, it was either she was going to go home, or I was going to go home that night. I decided that I wanted to go home."

Shanita thought for a long time before asking her next question.

"Greg, let me ask you this. What would you do if a loved one, like a wife, son, or daughter, or a close relative like your mom, dad, sister, or brother committed a serious crime that could get them a life sentence, or even the death penalty, and you found out about it? Would you turn them in?"

"Well, if it was my former wife, I'd turn her ass in, in a heartbeat! In fact, I'd probably arrest her my damn self. No, I'm just joking. That's a really hard question to answer. Let me try to answer it this way: If it was rape, or a crime against a child or the elderly, the answer would be yes, absolutely! That is a no-brainer. It would pain me to do so, but in my opinion, there is no excuse for that. If the crime happened while I was present and on duty, then I would have a legal obligation to make the arrest. However, I don't think I would go out of my way to turn in a family member for a crime that didn't occur in my presence. If one of them committed a crime and was able to beat the system, then that is the nature of the cat-and-mouse game.

People get away with crimes all the time. Usually, they are the ones with the resources to pay for a good lawyer, or influence the system in some way so they can go free. Each individual has to answer to their Maker and be guided by their own morality. The universe will self-correct at some point."

"That's a good answer."

"Why did you ask that question? Somebody in trouble?"

"No particular reason. I have been asked that question before, and it made me think real hard about what I would do. My daughter is my world. I'm not sure what I would do if she ever got into trouble. I know I would whip her butt, but to send her to jail … I don't know if I could do that."

Shanita tactfully tried to change the subject, hoping that he wouldn't press her to the point where she had to talk about her brother.

"Hey Greg, you ever thought about getting married again?"

"Oh, hell no! I already told you that women are too much trouble. Why would I ever subject myself to that foolishness again? Not happenin,' Captain."

"All women ain't like that. Why you always ranking on women?"

"Women have been giving me a hard time as long as I can remember. I remember the first girl I kind of fell in love with. Man, I really liked that girl. I saved my little money and bought her a friendship ring, and we were cool. Then I find out she has another boyfriend. The way I found out was because I was over her house and he came by. At first, she didn't want to open the door when she saw who it was. I was wondering what was up. Then he started yelling that he knew she had somebody in there. That is when she finally opened the door so she could keep him quiet. When he saw me, he stole me in the face and we started fighting. I whipped his ass, but the next day, he brought some of his boys around the way, and they jumped me. I don't remember the ass whipping as much as I remember the feeling of being dogged out by her, the little skank.

"Then there was the time when I was engaged to this girl who cheated on me with my best man! That one really hurt. I wanted to beat both of their asses, but I just walked away. I didn't want to catch a charge. Of course, we didn't get married. Finally, my wife decides to leave me for whatever reason. You just can't win.

"So no, I'm done with those kinds of relationships. If I get lonely, I'll get a dog."

Shanita and Greg continued their conversation which got louder and louder when suddenly the bedroom door opened, and Princess came out, rubbing her eyes. Shanita rushed over, turned her daughter around and lead her back into the bedroom before she could see Greg sitting on the couch. She was very protective of her daughter and didn't want her daughter to see a strange man in their apartment without introducing him first. She put Princess back in the bed and pulled the covers up to her neck before giving her a warm kiss on the forehead.

"Mommy, who was that man sitting on the couch?" Princess asked.

"Oh, baby, he's just a friend from work. He came by to drop off some papers. He was just getting ready to leave, so let me tell him goodbye, and I will be right back. OK baby?"

"OK, Mommy."

When Shanita returned to the living room, she apologized to Greg for the interruption and thanked him for coming by. That was a polite way of saying that it was time for him to leave, so he got up and reluctantly started heading toward the door. She told him that she hadn't had such a refreshing conversation with a man in a long while and hoped they could do it again soon. She walked him to the door, but before he left, she touched his arm and planted a quick, innocent kiss on his cheek. They had been riding together for weeks, but they had never had any close contact. Getting that close to her and smelling her enticing fragrance aroused a warm feeling inside his chest.

*   *   *

Steven and Michelle sat in the cabin of the huge Ferris wheel at the National Harbor overlooking the Potomac River, Washington, DC and northern Virginia. The wheel momentarily came to a halt when they reached the top, giving them a breathtaking, panoramic view of the arca. It was at this moment that Steven turned to her and softly asked for her hand in marriage. He knew that this wasn't a surprise because she had already seen the ring, but he was still a little nervous, praying that she would say yes. He was also wondering how she would react if he asked her to move back to Prairie Village, Kansas, with him so they could start their lives together there.

Of course, she said yes_ she would marry him.

CHAPTER 16

WHO'S WATCHING OUR CHILDREN

A silver Chevrolet Equinox had been parked across the street from West Elementary School, in northwest Washington, DC, every day for the past two weeks. The shadowy figure in the car keenly observed the daily routines of the school officials, the children, and everything that went on in and around the school. When school let out at three fifteen in the afternoon, the large crowd of screaming children gleefully exited the building and started their trek home. Some rushed to the parked cars that contained waiting parents, while others walked either to the bus stop on Fourteenth Street or directly home. Some stopped at the adjacent basketball court for a friendly game of afterschool basketball. The shadowy figure sat patiently, taking it all in before he would stealthily follow groups of children who walked, singling out the ones who would peel off by themselves.

Princess Brown and her best friends, Sharron Mason and Debbie Tyler, would get a ride from Sharron's mom, take the short bus trip, or walk together to and from school_ along with a group of kids who lived in their apartment complex, every day. Sharron was the daughter of Princess's new babysitter, Tonya Shepherd. Finding a good babysitter was an arduous task, but Shanita got lucky this time. Tonya was a stay-at-home mom with several kids who lived in the Concord Apartment complex located on Fourteenth Street in upper Northwest. Shanita and Princess had just moved into this neighborhood because it was relatively crime free and was in close proximity to a very good elementary school. Princess and Sharron were the same age and participated in some of the same activities like gymnastics and jump rope, sponsored by the DC Department of Recreation. When Shanita couldn't attend some of the activities the girls were involved in because she was on shift work, Tonya was always there to make sure the girls were represented.

Debbie was the quiet girl who lived next door to Sharron. Debbie was a cute, light-skinned girl with hazel eyes, long flowing hair, and a deep Southern accent. The older adults in the neighborhood would always say she had good hair. When Debbie first entered West Elementary and saw that most of the girls had short nappy hair, she told her mother that she felt she was going to have problems with some of the girls. Debbie and her mother had moved from North Carolina. Her mother had gotten a job working at the Library of Congress.

All the kids knew that Princess' mom was a police officer. In most cases, this elevated Princess's celebrity status among her friends. When she could, Shanita would pick up Princess and some of her friends from school in her police car. The kids always got a charge out of that. During Career Day, Shanita was always one of the most popular presenters. She would let the kids try on her bulletproof vest and touch her handcuffs, badge, and baton. She would tell them interesting stories about things that happened on her job and answer a bevy of questions the kids would throw at her. At the end of the sessions, Shanita would give Princess a big hug and a kiss in front of everybody. Princess could tell that some of her friends were envious. The kids were always asking Princess about how her mom was doing and asking her to tell her mom that they said hello. Because Shanita was very attractive, many of the boys had crushes on her. They would often say to Princess, "Don't forget to tell Ms. Shanita I said hey!"

Being the daughter of a police officer wasn't always peaches and cream, however. Shanita had a very strict set of guidelines for Princess to follow, and she enforced them with an iron hand. She had seen too many children who were victims of abuse, violence, or human trafficking, or who were growing up like weeds with no parental guidance. Even though she couldn't spend the amount of time she would have liked raising Princess, she was determined to do everything in her power to steer Princess from those pitfalls.

Shanita would block certain channels on the television, preventing Princess from watching popular movies or shows. When the kids at school talked about a movie or something that came on cable, Princess didn't have a clue what they were talking about and was thus often left out of the conversation. There were other rules that if broken, would merit punishment. Some of those rules included: don't open the door for strangers, go to bed at a specific time, don't bring any grades home lower than a B, no electronics when on punishment, stay in your room or in the living room with a book and read for a half an hour every day, and absolutely no lying. Lying brought the harshest punishment, which was a spanking. That only happened once or twice because Princess found that it wasn't worth it going through the type of spankings that Shanita administered. Princess found out early in life that trying to pull the wool over her mom's eyes was fruitless. Once, Princess thought she was being slick by watching television when she was on punishment and then making sure she left it on the last channel that her mom left it on, but that didn't work. Shanita would come home from work and feel the back of the television set to see if it was hot.

One of the strict rules that Princess had to follow was that as soon as she got back to the apartment from school, she had to call her mom and let her know she was safe and sound. One day, however, Princess and her friends got sidetracked, and she forgot to call her mom. The Pokémon game was the rave around town, and everybody was mesmerized by it. Sharron had a friend named Lauretta who lived right beneath her apartment. Lauretta invited Sharron and Princess to stop by to play the game. Princess knew she was supposed to call her mom, but she got caught up in the excitement of the game. Before she knew it, an hour and a half had gone by. Princess frantically told Sharron that she had to go home and call her mom. Before she could get out the door, however, Princess heard the whaling sounds of a police car getting closer and saw the flashing lights of her mom's police car speeding toward the apartment.

Princess went outside to meet her mom, who was livid. Princess didn't think that being a little late calling her mom was such a big deal, but the look on her mom's face told her otherwise. Later that evening, Shanita had a long conversation with Princess. It was virtually a one-way conversation that lasted for over an hour about the importance of following rules. Princess discovered that when she didn't call, her mom had some of her police friends out combing the area searching for her, thinking that something sinister had happened. Her mom shared some of the things she had seen happened to little girls out there on the street. After listening, Princess began to understand why her mom was so upset and promised to never let it happen again. On the inside, however, she felt that her mom was being overprotective because nothing like that was going to happen to her. The next day, Shanita got her daughter a cell phone with a tracking app placed on it so she would know where Princess was at all times.

School let out at noon because it was the beginning of spring break, and the school would be closed for a whole week. Tonya was not able to pick the girls up that early, and instead of taking the bus, Princess, Sharron, and Debbie decided to walk home.

"I really like your mom, but what is it like having a mom as a police officer?" Sharron asked.

"Being the daughter of a police officer has its ups and downs," Princess responded. "It is really scary because a lot of people don't like the police, so the job itself gets more dangerous every day. There are a lot of people who don't know my mom, so when they see her, they think she is bad. What if they kill her or something? That is kind of scary."

"Wow, I would be scared all the time if that was my mom," Debbie interjected.

"Sometimes, I wish my mom did something else other than being a police officer. I don't want my mom hurt. I don't want her to be hurt physically or emotionally from what she has seen or what she has done. I have been afraid that she will get hurt or won't come home at all. Every time she leaves for work, I will say, 'Have a good day,' or 'Be safe.' She always says, 'OK, I'll be fine.' When I was younger, I would play around and then sit by the window and wait for her to come home. Sometimes, it would be past my bedtime, and I would be tired, but I would wait anyway. When I would see her in the morning, I would be all happy and say, 'Mom how was your day? How are you?'

"It is kind of lonely, though. There would be times when she would not be there for my birthday. She would have to go to work. She would leave me a card and give me a call, but I always wanted her to be there. Or it would be Christmas and she would say, 'Oh, I have to do the Christmas shift.' That would make me sad."

"Wow, that would make me sad too," Sharron said. "Even though my mom gets on my nerves sometimes, we do everything together. If your mom is gone most of the time, what do you do together when she is there?"

"Not much," Princess responded. "When she would come home late or early in the morning, she would be too tired to do much. She would read to me at night, and we would talk about a lot of stuff whenever she wasn't too tired. Sometimes she would take me to the mall and we would get our fingernails done together. When I was at another school, sometimes she would come to pick me up after school. But two times she was really late, and that would make me cry. One time, she was so late that it started getting dark. That was really scary and I cried all the way home. She cried too. After that, she told me to walk with the other kids to the library and I would sit and wait for her there.

"So to sum it all up, I would say to be the child of a police officer is fun, scary, sad, and happy. Fun when you are with her in her car and you are zooming around the street; scary when she is gone and you don't know when she is coming back; sad when you see her crying because some of her friends have died and you realize you can't get them back; and happy when you see her coming through the door and she says, 'I'm home.'"

As Princess, Sharron, and Debbie nonchalantly walked home, they saw a large group of their classmates quickly approaching. The group singled out Debbie; and before she could do anything, the group encircled her, preventing her from escaping. Debbie was horrified when a girl who was known as the class bully, approached her and said, "You must think you are cute." Debbie knew what was going to happen and searched the eyes of the screaming kids in the circle, who seemed anxious to see a fight, for an ally to help her get out of this situation. Fear gripped her, preventing her from moving or speaking. She briefly saw Princess and Sharron, hoping they would offer some assistance to get her out of this mess, but they seemed to be as horrified as she was and did not move to intervene.

Suddenly, the bully threw a punch that caught Debbie on the side of her face. The punch made a noise so loud that it sounded like an atomic bomb had just exploded, causing the raucous crowd to scream in unison, "DAMN!" A searing pain erupted in her jaw, traveled down her neck, down her arms, and all the way down to the bottom of her feet. Debbie fell backward, and before the next blow arrived, she felt a small trickle of pee flow down her leg, which quickly turned into a raging river. The urine flow was accompanied by a flow of tears. Debbie lowered her head and tried to shield her face from the next blow she knew was coming. Before the next blow arrived, she heard the crowd erupt in laughter. Over the laughter, she heard someone shout, "Damn, she knocked the piss out of that bitch!" Princess and Sharron began to cry when they saw this happening to their friend.

Suddenly, a man came from somewhere in the crowd and barged into the makeshift ring in an attempt to stop the fight. He got in between the bully and Debbie, pushing the bully backward. "Stop this right now," he shouted. "You girls should be ashamed of yourselves fighting like cats and dogs." Debbie didn't know this man but thought, *He must have been sent from God!* She could have hugged him right then and there. He put his hand on her face, turning her chin back and forth as if he was inspecting the damage.

"Debbie, are you OK?" the man asked.

He turned to the crowd and barked, "You children break this up and go home before I tell your parents!" When nobody moved, he turned back to Debbie and said, "Come on, Debbie. I'll take you home. You live at the Concord Apartments, right? Your mom couldn't pick you up today because she had to take your sister to the hospital." He started leading her to his silver Chevrolet Equinox that was parked across the street. Debbie was more than happy to go with him. After all, he knew where she lived, knew her mom, and, more importantly, he saved her from that beat down she was getting.

"Debbie, don't get in that car with that man," the bully shouted. "You don't know him. He's a stranger!"

Debbie would have gotten into the car with anyone at that point. Her face was throbbing, her pants were soaked from her urine, and she saw no other way out of this dilemma. She gingerly got into the front seat with her savior. The car sped away, heading in the direction of her home. She was never seen or heard from again.

*　　*　　*

Much to her amazement, Shanita got a call from Greg asking her out on a date_ a real date. She really enjoyed talking with him and having someone to share her innermost thoughts and feelings. But going on a date was a different animal, something she had to give a little more thought to. She had terrible luck with men. Maybe it was her fault because of the types of men she chose to date.

Curtis was her first, but he became a drug dealer and ended up dying as a result. Then there was Michael Holiday, whom she met when she was working at the fire department. He was a nice guy who had a smile that could light up a room. He was a good lover too. He became her best friend, but she soon found out he was a dog. He became very manipulative and was a terrible liar. He ran with a group of about ten guys who were wild and carefree. He was the only one in the group who was in a serious relationship.

Soon, his behavior began to change, which was a red flag to her police instincts. Her job required her to recognize patterns of behavior, so when somebody came home every day and did one thing, and then one day did something totally different, those things stood out. When she brought up the subject of whether or not he was happy at home with her, he denied that anything was wrong. Later, she read a steamy text message from another woman on his phone and saw pictures of naked women's body parts and questioned him about it. He was furious about the fact that she was questioning him, as well as the fact that she was "snooping" around, invading his privacy. He let her know, in no uncertain terms, that she had better not do that again. However, later, when a woman called their home, Shanita began questioning the woman, and she found out that the woman was a side chick. Shanita was crushed. Before things escalated to the point where she felt the need to whip his ass, or worse, she decided to leave the relationship and move on.

Then there was Oliver Hunter, who was a young corporate lawyer she met at a funeral she was attending with her sister. He thought Shanita was stunningly beautiful and asked her out. He took her to some of the finest restaurants in the city, introducing her to other lawyers, politicians, and important people. But he expected her to dress up in high heels and low-cut dresses all the time. It was like he wanted her around so he could show her off to all his friends like she was a Barbie Doll or something. She was a little more low-key than that. She was more comfortable in jeans, sweat pants, or shorts, and thought it was silly to wear shoes that hurt her feet. So that relationship fizzled.

Her sisters and girlfriends told her that she needed to start dating older men because they were more mature. She had a policy, however, of not dating anyone more than four years older than her. She didn't know how she got to the number four or why it even mattered. But there was something about Gregory Harris that attracted her. Maybe it was his quick wit. He had the ability to make her laugh at the drop of a hat. Not many men, or anybody for that matter, could do that. Laughter, in the world she lived in, was so important. He was also a very strong man who seemed to have a good character. He genuinely seemed to care about people and how they felt.

Maybe I'll give him a try, she thought. *What have I got to lose?*

The next day, after roll call, Greg dropped a bomb on Shanita. He told her that he had been asked to consider becoming a homicide detective and decided to do it. That meant that they would no longer be partners. He said that one of the reasons he asked her out on a date was because he wanted to continue seeing her. He also felt that it was time to take their casual relationship to the next level. Shanita was initially saddened by the fact that they would no longer be partners, which meant they wouldn't see each other every day. She did, however, begin to think that dating him wasn't such a bad idea after all.

Then he threw one more curve at her. He told her that he had talked to some of his buddies about getting her on the Vice Squad. If they accepted her, she would be going undercover investigating prostitution rings and human trafficking. He knew that she had been devastated by the abduction of Princess's little friend, Debbie Tyler. He felt that giving her the opportunity to at least try to do something about it would be good for her. The reason he gave his vice buddies was that even though she was a rookie, she was young, fearless, good-looking, and had a big ass! When the lieutenant saw a picture of Shanita, he immediately offered her a position in his squad.

It didn't take Shanita long to warm up to the idea. Everyone was crushed by the disappearance of Debbie. It took Princess a long time to get over it. *Why didn't I do something to help my friend?* was the question that kept rolling around in her head. *Why didn't I stop her from getting in that car?* Princess now understood why her mom was so strict with her. For Shanita, the loss of Debbie hit too close to home. The same thing could have easily happened to Princess. Accepting this position would get her out of 7D and put her closer to home. This meant she would be able to drive Princess to and from school more often. Before this opportunity came up, Shanita had put in several requests to her supervisors for a transfer, but her request had fallen on deaf ears. Family issues weren't a concern for the department, especially for a rookie. Shanita also felt that by accepting this new assignment, she would be in a better position to improve her pay, as well as build up a resume that could help her get a promotion down the line.

Working vice was a real eye-opener for Shanita in so many ways, filled with many surprises and enormous frustration. She was shocked to see so many girls willing to live the lifestyle of a prostitute and so unwilling to help the police bring to justice those individuals responsible for trapping them in the system_ the pimps. Some local politicians had introduced a bill to decriminalize prostitution, but until that bill became law, it is still a crime to buy, sell, or facilitate the sale of sex in the District of Columbia. According to the statute, people commit the crime of prostitution by engaging in, inviting, offering, or agreeing to engage in sexual contact in exchange for a fee. This applies to both the prostitute and the john. It is still a crime even if money is not passed between the john and the prostitute, as long as there is some type of agreement between the two regarding the terms of payment and the sex act to be performed.

Shanita's work on the vice squad began with gathering intelligence. She would go into places like clubs, bars, and hotels to perform surveillance of what was actually going on. If she saw girls at a club giving lap dances with blankets around their waists, she concluded that they were not just giving lap dances. Something nefarious was going on. She would include this information in her report. She went to one club that sponsored a "clapper" party. Women would get on the stage and shake their behinds so their butts would make a clapping sound, to the elation of men and women throwing money at them. Shaking your ass onstage was not illegal, but if the women were fully naked, which they often were, the owner would be fined and the police department would begin the long process to hold or revoke the owner's license. Usually, those clubs had back rooms where the girls could be seen leading men in and exiting a short time after. She started using her cell phone to record what she saw for documentation purposes. She also would hang out at certain hotels, especially in the downtown area, and watch the flow of young, unattached women coming in and leaving out after a certain amount of time. Usually they were being transported in the same vehicles, which could indicate a pimp was involved.

Shanita was diligent and thorough with her surveillance and was soon elevated to the position of sting operative. Her job now was to pretend she was a prostitute and offer her services to a john. She was a little naïve when it came to prostitution in the twenty-first century. The idea of a prostitute wearing short skirts and high heels and walking the streets had drastically changed from the movies she had seen when she was younger. Many of the prostitutes have incorporated technology into the game. Instead of walking the streets, they would advertise electronically, posting a picture on a website, letting people know when and where they could be located for a hook-up. If you went on Craigslist and searched for dates or massage services, you could find tons of ads that were subliminal advertisements for prostitution. Manicures and nail services were often used as code words for sexual services as well. As far as the modern-day hooker walking the streets was concerned, those who did that were often considered the feds, the police, or a transgender.

The way Shanita set up her sting operation was to post on a website that she was looking for a date for the prom. She would post where she could be picked up, like at the Marriott, room 810. When she got a bite, she would be dressed in a pair of black stretch pants and a tank top, which were easy to get out of. When she and the john got in the room and he said the magic words, usually when he mentioned money and what he wanted, she would give a signal, and her team, who had been waiting in the next room, would burst in and arrest the john for sexual solicitation. The maximum penalty for sexual solicitation in D C is 90 days in jail and/or a $300 fine for the first offense; 135 days and/or a $750 fine for the second offense; and 180 days and/or a $1,000 fine for the third and each subsequent offense. First offenders, if they have a good lawyer, are able to get off with doing community service for a period of four months.

The frustrating part of this assignment for Shanita was that because the conversations about money were not recorded, it became a "he said, she said," situation and since it was a misdemeanor, the case was decided by a judge. The well-connected johns who had highly paid lawyers would either get community service or discretely get off altogether. It did, however, make them think twice about doing it again.

Male members of her team posed as johns so they could arrest the prostitutes. Shanita's responsibility in that case was to arrest and transport the female prostitute to jail. After locking the young ladies up, members of the vice squad would interrogate them and ask if someone was forcing them to be a prostitute. If that was the cases, then the squad would offer support, helping them get away from the pimp or whoever was forcing them, as well as providing a list of programs that would help them find jobs, and counselors to help them with any emotional issues that might have developed from their experiences. It was sad that very few accepted the help.

Shanita was astounded to find out the type of women, especially the older ones, who worked as prostitutes. Just like the images she had about how prostitutes dressed, she assumed that most prostitutes were either poor, down-on-their-luck women who couldn't find employment or young girls who were victims of human trafficking. But that was not always the case. She arrested one lady who was the president of the PTA of the school her kids attended and lived in a big house in California with two expensive cars paid for in cash. Every three months, she would tell her kids that she was going on a business trip that would last for a week. She would come to the District, service her regular high-paying customers and then return home. During interrogation, when she was offered support, her response was,

"Listen, I mean no disrespect, but I made over two hundred thousand dollars tax free last year! What trade are you going to teach me in your little program that is going to help me make that kind of money?"

Shanita jokingly responded, "You know what, you're absolutely right! I am clearly in the wrong business. I need to find out those little tricks you do so I can make that kind of money."

Those types of cases, however, were few and far between. Most of the cases Shanita was involved in were of young girls who were either being coerced or manipulated by a pimp. Trying to help the girls in this situation was not only disheartening and sad, but frustrating as well. As the vice squad began focusing on human trafficking, a field Shanita had particular interest in, she realized that it was extremely difficult to prosecute the pimps. The main problem was that even when the pimps were arrested, when it came time for a trial, the girls would refuse to testify, forcing the judge to dismiss the case.

There was one case that helped gain Shanita notoriety and respect among her fellow officers. In this case, Shanita arrested a girl named Chocolate Thunder. Chocolate looked every bit of forty years old, but when asked, she said she was only twenty-three. She said that she had "tricked" so much that she had the vagina of a seventy-year-old woman and she was tired of it. More than being tired, she was fed up with her pimp and wanted to "get his ass back." At one time, she was considered a bottom bitch, which was the girl closest to the pimp. She would either be the pimp's girlfriend, baby's momma, or confidante. She would often tell the other girls where to go for a job and would often be the one to pick up the money for the pimp from the other girls.

Chocolate worked for a pimp named Reggie. Chocolate said that someone else had taken her spot_ a young girl who couldn't have been more than sixteen years old. When Chocolate confronted Reggie about it, he beat her. He had slapped her around a few times before, but this time he beat her so bad, she had to spend a few days in the hospital. Chocolate had had enough of the beatings, the disrespect, and the lifestyle itself. More than that, she wanted to get him back!

Chocolate told Shanita that Reggie and his brother Earl had just brought in a batch of new girls. A convention was coming to town, and conventions were always good for business. The only problem was that most of these new girls were really young, like thirteen and fourteen years old. There was even one girl who couldn't have been more than twelve years old. Chocolate didn't think that was right. It was one thing to be a whore if that is what you wanted or needed to do, but these were babies.

Shanita convinced Chocolate to tell her how the operation worked, when and where the convention was being held, and when Reggie and Earl would be bringing the girls. She even convinced Chocolate to wear a wire which was a tiny transmitter hidden in one of her earrings. On the night of the convention, Reggie drove one van and Earl drove the other. They had received a request for a number of young girls_ the younger the better_ to service the patrons of the convention. Chocolate was in the van with Reggie, and the vice squad overheard him instructing the girls which room to go to, how much to charge, and how long to stay. Squad members got pictures of the girls exiting both vans, and even got a picture of Reggie slapping one of the girls who seemed reluctant to participate.

The vice squad had enough officers to follow each girl to each room, surround both vans, and arrest everyone involved.

When Reggie and Earl were brought to trial, Chocolate was the main witness. It turned out that some of the young girls had been kidnapped, so not only were Reggie and Earl convicted of sexual solicitation, but for kidnapping as well, and transporting minors across state lines. The judge threw the book at them. Chocolate had gotten her revenge after all.

CHAPTER 17

CLOSURE

Detective Gregory Harris loved the different aspects of working in law enforcement. Walking the beat, working with the community, and even working undercover were the things that stimulated him. Working as a homicide detective was a little different, but he found it intriguing. Doing in-depth homicide investigations required getting background information on a suspect, the family history, and talking to everybody related to a suspect, once a suspect had been identified. In terms of normal days off, Greg found out that nothing was *normal* when working as a detective. The shift concept didn't apply to a homicide case. You worked the case until it was done or until it was determined to be "cold." You could get a call at two in the morning, and you had to get up and go handle the case. You were not going to get the work done in eight hours. You may not even get it done for two or three days, so you were always on the go, grinding and checking out leads. But like everything else, he was good at it.

It had been barely a week when Detective Harris got a phone call that the body of a little girl had been discovered in a shallow grave right below the Nature Center in Rock Creek Park. He had been attending a live performance of *The Lion King* with Shanita and Princess at the Kennedy Center when he got the call. The hastily dug grave was found by some hikers who were following the Nature Center trail. Their dog found a pair of dirty panties under some leaves near the grave. The dog started digging and exposed the leg of the little girl. As the detectives canvassed the scene, Detective Harris found a small Chevrolet insignia, which could be found on one of those remote car door openers, lying on the ground near where the body was found. It could have been nothing, but Greg bagged it anyway in an evidence container. The coroner on the scene said that based on the limited decomposition, the body couldn't have been there more than a week.

There was something about that Chevrolet insignia that made Greg think of another case. When he got back to the station, he looked in the cold case files and found the report of the abduction of little Debbie Tyler. Greg noticed in the report that a witness reported that Debbie got into a gray Chevrolet with a middle-aged black man who had on a bowtie. DNA testing proved beyond the shadow of a doubt that the body found in the park was indeed Debbie Tyler. Greg was more determined than ever to solve this case and bring Mr. Bowtie to justice.

That case was of interest to him because Debbie was a friend of Shanita's daughter, Princess, and the abduction hit both Princess and Shanita very hard. As a result, Shanita decided to move out of that neighborhood and withdrew Princess from the school. They moved to an apartment complex in Northeast that seemed a little more secure. It had a security guard posted, a community room, a swimming pool, and was a very short walking distance to LaSalle Elementary School.

While Greg was working on the Tyler case, another report came in about another little girl who was reported missing. This little girl was walking home from Shepherd Elementary School. A crossing guard said she saw the little girl get into a silver car_ a Chevy, she thought. She didn't think much of it because the girl seemed to know the driver and got in the car willingly, so the guard thought the person was coming to pick her up. Greg started looking at the similarities in both cases: (1) the abductees were little black girls coming home from school; (2) they were both in elementary school; (3) the abductions occurred at the end of the school day; and (4) both girls willingly got into a silver or gray Chevrolet. When the call came in that a third girl turned up missing leaving Barnard Elementary School, Greg began to think there was a serial killer on the loose, and the case needed to be solved before panic gripped the city.

Greg realized that all the afterschool abductions so far had occurred only in elementary schools in Ward 4. On a hunch, he began driving to all the elementary schools in Ward 4 and looking at the cars parked in and near the school's parking lots. When he got to Lafayette Elementary, he spotted a silver Chevrolet parked on the school lot. He wrote down the license plate number, and then parked his car across the street from the school and waited to see who got into the car. At 3:30 p.m. a middle-aged black man with a bowtie exited the building and got into the Chevy.

Well, hello Mr. Bowtie, Greg said to himself.

Greg followed Mr. Bowtie to a house on Quebec Place in Northwest and sat watching the house for about an hour before returning to the school. He went into the school to speak to the principal about Mr. Bowtie. When Greg described the man with the bowtie, the principal stated that the man's name was Sylvester Crooms and was a popular, reliable substitute teacher. The principal said that he had offered Mr. Crooms a permanent teaching position, but Crooms turned it down stating that he preferred the freedom that being a substitute offered. He enjoyed going from school to school and working with a variety of kids.

This seemed more than a little suspicious to Greg but wasn't enough to get a search warrant. The next morning, Greg returned to Lafayette and parked his car, waiting for Bowtie to show up. When Bowtie did not report for work, Greg decided to set up surveillance at his home. Bowtie's car was in the same space it was parked the day before, so Greg parked his car down the street and waited for him to move. There was no movement the rest of the evening. The next morning, Bowtie got into his car and drove to Powell Elementary school_ another school in Ward 4_ where he parked his car in the school's parking lot and entered the school. There was no suspicious activity for two days.

On the third day, Bowtie exited the building at the end of the school day, but this time, he sat in his car and waited until most of the adults who came to pick up their children had left the area. Two

Hispanic girls, one much older than the other, exited the building and started walking on Upshur Street heading towards Sixteenth Street. Bowtie turned on his car and slowly followed the kids until they reached their home. The older girl pulled out a key from around her neck and opened the door. Greg, who was following Bowtie from a distance, saw him writing something down in a notebook before he drove away. Greg figured that these kids were probably Bowtie's next victims. The fact that they let themselves into the house with their own key meant that, probably, no parents or adults were home, a perfect setup for a killer. Greg figured that the next abduction attempt was going to go down soon.

The next day, Bowtie did not report for work at Powell, but around 3:00 p.m., he parked his car on Upshur Street, along the same path the kids followed the day before. Greg assumed that it was about to go down, so he called for backup. Just as Greg expected, the Hispanic girls left the school after most of the other kids were gone and started walking home. When the kids were two blocks away from the school, they stopped and started talking with Bowtie, who had pulled up next to them in his car. Greg couldn't hear what Bowtie said to the kids, but they started laughing and got into his car.

Before Bowtie could take off, Greg pulled his car in front of Bowtie's car and a police cruiser pulled up behind his car, preventing him from leaving the scene. Greg and the other police officers got out with their guns, drawn screaming at Bowtie to turn off his car and get out with his hands up. Bowtie got out of the car without resistance, and lay face-down on the pavement. Upon searching the car, Greg found a gym bag with several ropes, a hatchet with dried blood stains still on it, a butcher's knife, and a ten-inch barber's straight razor with a black Micarta handle. Bowtie never said a word as the officers placed him in the back of the cruiser.

*   *   *

Steven Sullivan sat alone in his police cruiser eating a chicken salad sandwich as a bevy of images and emotions raced through his head. It had been a very eventful week, filled with a range of emotions from fear and self-doubt, to passion and exhilaration. The news that a female rookie officer got killed on her first day on the job was heart breaking. It reminded him of the ominous predictions of teachers at the academy when they said that you would probably have to pull your gun on your first day, or probably would be involved in a shooting on your first day.

Just the other day, he had attended a ceremony at the District Building where his fiancée, Michelle, received a certificate and cash award for being selected Teacher of the Year for DC public schools. He couldn't have been prouder, especially when she jumped into his arms after the ceremony and planted a big kiss on his lips in front of everybody.

Earlier in the week, Steven had attended the funeral of his good friend Big Lee. That was extremely sad. Not only was it sad, but it finally hit home how dangerous this job really was and the fact that any day could be his last day on this earth. There were tons of officers there paying their respects to their fallen brother, but Steven wondered how many of them really gave a shit about Big Lee. Roya was there, and she was beside herself with grief. Michelle, who also attended the funeral, tried to console her, but to no avail. It seemed that Roya was so wracked with guilt because she had left Big Lee that she just couldn't get herself together.

Later, that day, as they were riding home, Michelle became furious with Steven when he shared his suspicions about Big Lee's death. He confessed that he didn't think it was an accidental shooting and that Big Lee was murdered by Officer Bailey. She was adamant about him telling the investigators what he knew before the investigation was over. She said he owed it to Big Lee to do the right thing. He did not share with her, however, the threats that he received from Officer Hoye's friends. He knew it was Officer Hoye who told them about what he knew because Officer Hoye was the only one he had shared that information with until he told Michelle. Steven knew that cops snitching on other cops was taboo, but he also knew that Michelle was right.

The next day, Steven happened to see Gregory Harris in the hallway at the police station. He remembered Officer Harris from the academy. For some reason, Steven felt Officer Harris was real and got the sense that he was fair and honest.

"Officer Harris, can I holler at you for a moment?"

"It's Detective Harris now, but sure. What's up?"

"I don't know if you remember me, but you taught one of my classes at the academy, and a lot of the things you said stayed with me. I have a dilemma and need some serious advice. It involves another officer."

"Wait a minute. Let's go into this room so we can talk."

"Well, I know officers are not supposed to tell on other officers, and I don't want to violate the code, but I have some information that kind of contradicts the statements of the officer who was involved in the shooting of Officer Leon Anderson. The officer who did the shooting claims that he didn't know Officer Anderson was a police officer, but when the officer turned to leave, Officer Anderson's badge fell out of the other officer's pocket. That didn't make any sense to me."

"Son, I see where you are going with this. Let me say it this way. We have an obligation to weed out bad cops whenever we can. Bad cops give the whole department a black eye, and ultimately, we all suffer if they can continue doing bad things. You have an obligation, both morally and professionally, to tell what you know and let the people who make decisions decide what to do about the evidence. Our job is to protect and serve. Officer Anderson's name and memory deserves protection as well. And think about this: it could have been you. Wouldn't you want somebody to come to your defense? Let me ask you this: was the other officer, the shooter, white?"

"Yes sir."

"Well, that adds a different dynamic to this situation now, doesn't it?"

"I didn't even think about that."

"How could you not think about that with all this mess that is going on in the country about cops shooting unarmed black people?"

"There's something else. I've received death threats warning me not to say anything about it."

"What do you mean? Somebody said they were going to kill you if you told?"

"Not quite like that. They implied that I wouldn't receive backup if I was in trouble and the streets were dangerous, so anything could happen."

"Well, son, look at it this way: you've already told someone, me. So you might as well go up the food chain and tell someone who is a little more important. You're a police officer. We knowingly face danger every single day. Do your job! And as far as not receiving backup, I wouldn't worry too much about that. Backup will always be there, and if it isn't, just call me. I'll be there."

"Thanks, Detective Harris."

"No problem."

Steven did not feel any more relieved about his situation after he spoke with Detective Harris, but he decided to go to his sergeant and tell what he knew. The sergeant thanked Steven for coming forward and telling him what he knew. He told Steven that he would report this information directly to internal affairs and the district attorney and let them handle it. A week later, the district attorney announced that no charges were going to be brought up against Officer Bailey, stating that it was an unfortunate, accidental shooting. The justification for that conclusion was based on the fact that Officer Anderson should not have been in the dark alley out of uniform, brandishing a gun, and failing to identify himself as a police officer. Furthermore, the DA stated, a uniformed officer had been gunned down, causing Officer Bailey to fear for his life. As a result, the shooting was deemed accidental and not criminal.

The DA's announcement caused a stir in the community but received a mixed reaction in the police station. Many officers agreed that Lee shouldn't have been in the alley in the first place. After all, he was a transit cop, and a rookie to boot. What was a transit cop doing chasing a robbery suspect? Some officers, especially black officers, felt that the case should have at least gone to the grand jury and been investigated further, and that this was just another case of a black man being shot by a white cop, and then being swept under the rug. As far as Steven's role in this situation, the word somehow got around that he was a snitch and was not to be trusted. Steven was quite sure who was spreading that rumor around but was helpless to do anything about it. As a result, after being cut loose, other officers seemed reluctant to want to ride with him, so he rode alone.

As Steven sat in his cruiser eating his sandwich and thinking about his dilemma, a call came over the radio about a man with a knife. Steven was the first officer to arrive on the scene and saw a Hispanic man with a machete arguing with a black man in the parking lot. Before Steven got out of his car, he called for backup. Then he got out of his cruiser, shouted for the Hispanic man to put down the machete, and get on the ground. The Hispanic man started walking toward Steven, not saying a word. He had a strange look in his eye. Before he could get too close, Steven pulled his gun, aimed at the man, and commanded him again to put the machete down and get on the ground. The man ignored the command and continued walking toward Steven. Steven realized that he was going to have to shoot this man if he came one step closer. Out of the corner of his eye, Steven saw another police car arrive, but when he saw who the police officers were, his heart sank. The two officers were the same officers who had threatened him if he told what he knew about Officer Bailey. Now Steven began wondering if he was going to have to shoot the Hispanic man and the officers too.

Before he knew it, another police car arrived on the scene and two more officers got out of their car_ Officer White and Officer Canty_ with their guns trained on the Hispanic man. When the Hispanic man realized he was surrounded by armed policemen, he stopped in his tracks and slowly put the machete down on the ground. Officer Canty walked over to the man and cold-cocked him, knocking him to the ground. Canty then proceeded to handcuff the man and placed him in the back of his cruiser. Officer White walked over to Steven and told him that Detective Harris had informed them of his dilemma and wanted him to know that they had his back.

Steven was extremely relieved, but his internal alarm went off when he observed the black man who had been arguing with the Hispanic man doing something in the bushes. Steven raised his gun again, this time aiming at the black man. Not knowing what was happening, Steven ordered the black man to turn around and show his hands. When the black man turned around with his hands up, his penis was dangling out of his pants and the pee was still coming out. It turned out that the whole incident had scared the man so bad that he was over in the bushes urinating. After it was over and the man put his "thang" back in his pants, he wanted to shake Steven's hand for stopping the Hispanic man. Steven was appreciative of the gesture, but there was no way he was going to shake that man's hands.

A few weeks later, Steven got a call from Detective Harris.

"Hey, Officer Sullivan, I got some interesting news for you. I'm sending you some photos of some guys I got off the Internet. Look at the photos and let me know if you recognize any of them."

"Yeah, Detective Harris," Steven responded after looking at the photos on his computer. The first one is of Officer Craig Hoye, my FTO. The others are of the guys who approached and threatened me. Where did you get these photos?"

"I got them off an obscure website called MySpace. They are all members of an organization called the Order. That is a Neo-Nazi, white supremacist hate group. Each of them wrote about how they perpetrated violence against Hispanics, Jews, Muslims, African Americans, and immigrants. They posted information about killing young black children, setting fires to schools and churches, providing weapons to rival black gangs so they could continue shooting each other and raping Muslim women. These dummies even posted photos of themselves participating in some of those acts. We have already started an investigation. I plan to not only have them fired from the force, but put them in prison as well. Maybe some of them will be put in a cell with Bubba and receive the true punishment they deserve. At any rate, I don't think you will ever have to worry about them again."

CHAPTER 18

THE MOVEMENT

As the massive crowd continued growing in size and demonstrative behavior, a wall of police wearing with riot helmets and protective body-length polycarbonate shields, and carrying long batons, stood shoulder to shoulder, with instructions not to interfere unless they had to arrest anyone who got out of hand. Police officers from all different units were pressed into service in order to handle the massive crowd. Officers Shanita Brown and Steven Sullivan stood next to each other in the police line, each deep in thought as they watched the crowd get more agitated with every second. Down the line stood Detective Gregory Harris and Officer Tim Bailey, both veteran officers who had seen their share of protest rallies.

The demonstrators consisted of people from many different races and ethnicities, and stretched across the Mall as far as the eye could see. The crowd was very peaceful and respectful for the most part. There were always some people who would try to take advantage of a situation. Some of the individuals would get in an officer's face and scream, "Fuck the police," seemingly trying very hard to get a reaction. When the police officers remained stoic, the vocal protesters would move on.

MPD police officers were very familiar with demonstrations and protests on the National Mall. Washington DC was the place where people came to voice their opinions and displeasures so that not only could Congress and the president hear them, but also so that issues could be brought to the attention of the rest of the nation and the world. Officers from different units were all pressed into service when these rallies occurred, be it a presidential inauguration, opposing factions on the abortion rights issue, the Million Man March, or the Women against Fascism march. This protest rally, however, was somehow different. This demonstration was aimed directly at the police, and it made many officers uncomfortable.

A large stage had been erected close to the Capitol, surrounded by huge speakers and two enormous video screens that enabled the massive crowd to hear and see the organizers and celebrities who were on the stage. Abdul Cramer, a leader from the Black Lives Matter movement, stood at the microphone and asked the crowd for a moment of silence as he read off the names of the black men and women who had been killed by the police. Suddenly, all of the chatter came to a halt, creating an eerie silence. Cramer started reading the list of names, pausing a brief moment in between each name so it could sink in.

"Eric Garner … Tamir Rice … Freddy Gray … Travon Martin …."

As Cramer continued reading the names, someone way in the back of the crowd broke the silence with a chant that was barely audible.

"Stephon Clark …"

"Fuck the police!"

"Alton Sterling …"

"Fuck the Police!"

"Philando Castille …"

"F u c k   t h e   P o l i c e ! "

With each subsequent name called off, the chants of "Fuck the police" got louder and louder. Soon the people standing closest to the wall of police officers turned and faced the officers and started screaming at the top of their lungs, "Fuck the police!"

Why are these people all up in my face? Officer Shanita Brown thought. *They don't even know me.*

Say what you want, but the first one that puts his hands on me is a dead nigger, Officer Jack Cavanaugh thought.

What about all these black people killing other black people?
Officer Tim Baylor thought. *Why aren't you protesting about that?*

My job is as a police officer, Detective Gregory Harris thought.
*But when I take off this uniform, I am a black man just like you. Shit,
even when I am in my uniform, I am still a black man.*

*　　*　　*

Earlier that week

Twice a year, DC police officers have to return to the police
academy, once for sharpening their skills at the shooting range and
once for professional development. According to the buzz around the
station, this year's PD session was going to be a hot one. The word
had gotten out that the leaders of the Black Lives Matter organization
were going to sponsor a rally on the National Mall and rumor had
it that it was going to be large and volatile. The highly publicized
killings of unarmed black citizens across the country had become a
national, and now international, issue, as a result of the discussions,
demonstrations, and interactions of politicians, entertainment
celebrities, and sports figures.

The debate had made an already-tenuous relationship between
the community and the police force even shakier, and police officials
were groping for solutions to the problem. A widening gap between
black and white officers was also developing over this issue, which
was more alarming to police officials. Usually, the professional
development sessions took the form of a lecture followed by a
question-and-answer segment. This year's session, however, was
going to include a panel discussion, followed by an open debate
where officers would be encouraged to give their honest opinions
with no fear of reprisals.

Steven was happy to see so many of his academy classmates. The
isolation he had been experiencing recently made the trip to familiar
grounds and smiling faces that much more enjoyable. When he ran
into Shanita Brown, she gave him a hug and thanked him for having
her back when she was out there by herself. They talked briefly about

her new assignment, which made him think about finding ways to get out of 7D. The street work didn't bother him, but it was the internal drama that soured his feelings. He ran into his academy buddy Victor Thompson and inquired about some of his other classmates.

"Hey, Vic," Steven said. "How's it been hanging? You staying safe out there?"

"What up, Stevie?" Vic replied. "Man, it has been hanging pretty good. You heard the old joke about the two men standing on the bridge peeing in the water. One pulled out his thang and said, 'Man, that water sure is cold!' And the other one said, 'Yeah, and it deep too!'"

Victor and Steven both broke out laughing.

"Vic, you haven't changed one bit!"

"Man, I'm good. They got me over at 6D, and it's a real trip, but they can't keep a good man down. You heard what happened to Jonathan?"

"You mean Johnny Blake, from Durbin, West Virginia, population 293, or something like that?"

"Yep, that's the one. He was involved in a shooting the other day and is on administrative leave."

"No shit! What happened?"

"Well, the word I got was that he and his partner got a call about a robbery in progress at a small corner store. When they got to the scene, the owner and his daughter had been shot in the head _ execution-style. They heard a sound, and when they turned around, a young black kid bolted out of the back door. Johnny and his partner started chasing the suspect, who hid behind a tree and started shooting. Of course, Johnny and his partner returned fire. When the suspect ran out of bullets, he threw his gun under a car and took off running again. Johnny saw the kid take off and got off a couple more rounds, hitting the kid in the back, killed him dead.

"It turned out that the suspect was a popular kid from the neighborhood. He was an honor roll student and sang in the church choir. When the neighbors came out and saw that the kid was shot in the back, all hell broke loose. It took a while to get the crowd under control. I guess we'll be talking about that mess today."

"What you think about that? Oh, oh, looks like they are getting ready to get started. We'd better take our seats. Talk to you later."

"Atten-hut! Ladies and gentlemen, please take your seats and come to order. Today's professional development will cover a topic that will impact everyone in this room. When you attended the academy, you all took a class called 'Shoot, Don't Shoot,' where you were introduced to when it was acceptable to use deadly force, as well as what force is deemed to be excessive. You all went through the 'Shooting Village' and were introduced to numerous scenarios where you had to use the proper judgment when deciding to use force. Due to the national uproar on the use of deadly force on unarmed suspects, we wanted our new recruits to hear from those of you who are out there every day making those decisions. But we also want to get some sense of how you interpret and apply the training you received here at the academy, and what your reactions are to the national uproar, so that we can begin to address the problems.

"Today's PD will be a little different. First of all, we really need to hear from you, so give us your honest opinions without fear of reprisals. Our new recruits need to hear this. We have a panel of representatives from different organizations who would like to partner with the police department in an effort to find common ground and develop effective strategies for reducing the number of 'bad' shootings. Our panel includes Raymond Simms from the Peace-o-holics, a local organization that works with inner-city youth to stop gang violence and bullying; Abdul Cramer, from the Baltimore Branch of the Black Lives Matter organization; and, of course, you know James Harrington, from the DCMPD Police Officer's Union. We will start with Mr. Cramer. Please give him your undivided attention."

"Good afternoon, officers. I would like to start by doing something a little different, if you would indulge me. I would like you to rearrange your chairs into what we call the power circle. Your chairs should be arranged in a series of concentric circles. We are going to start with a discussion on police violence and the use of deadly force. Those of you who are willing to give your opinions and participate in the discussion should sit in the chairs closest to the center. Those who might want to chime in from time to time should sit in the chairs on the inner circle. Those who just want to listen, have no opinion, or would care not to participate should sit on the outer circle with the students from the academy. OK, let's move, and don't everybody sit in the outer circle. I would really like your candid opinions and participation.

"I would like to guide the discussion with these five questions: (1) When is it justifiable to use lethal force? (2) If a suspect is running away, do you have the right to use lethal force? (3) What do you consider a 'bad shooting?' (4) Why do you think there are so many cases of white police officers killing unarmed black men today? (5) What is your opinion of the *Black Lives Matter* movement? Now, before you speak, I would like you to tell us who you are, and how long you've been on the force. OK, who would like to start?"

"I'll start. My name is David Grady and I have been on the force for twenty-eight years. I work in 7D. In terms of using lethal force, if a person is not using lethal force, then I am not supposed to respond with lethal force. It is not uncommon to have to fight somebody. It's a part of the job. For example, let's say you run into a guy who is committing a crime and he is six foot three and three hundred pounds of muscle. It's your job to stop him and lock him up. You are five foot seven, and your female partner is five foot three. You can't shoot him because he doesn't have a gun. So what are you going to do?

"You can't ignore the situation, so you roll up your sleeves and take action. We are authorized to go up one level in terms of the type of force we can use. If they have fists, we are allowed to use our batons, pepper spray, or a Taser. But in order to use those tools, you have to get close, and you may get hit a couple of times. That's why we always call for backup. There is strength in numbers. Usually, suspects don't have much fight in them when there are five or six officers present. Back in the day, the drug boys would say, 'I don't have any weapons on me, so if you want to lock me up, you're going to have to fight me first.' They often wanted to see if you were a punk or not. Those kinds of fights wouldn't last long, but those first thirty seconds to a minute can seem like an eternity.

"The problem is that some officers can't fight, have never been in a fight, and six months of training at the academy did not sufficiently prepare them for that kind of fight. Therefore, their threat level is high, and the first thing they do is to pull out their gun, thinking that the gun will de-escalate the situation. Unfortunately, the sight of a gun in some cases only escalates the situation."

"Well, if that is the case, then why are we experiencing so many incidents of white officers shooting and killing unarmed black men?" Cramer asked.

"My name is Charles Cobb, and I have been on the force for five years. Personally, I believe this has always been the case. It's just that now everyone has a cell phone with a built-in camera, and they are posting this stuff on social media."

"My name is Jasmine Taylor. I have been an officer for four years. Personally, I don't think a lot of white officers understand us. I think a lot of them fear us, and that fear escalates the situation. If you don't understand black people and you have this perception that all black people are criminals, or all black people are dangerous, then you come off a little more aggressive than you have to be because you are scared. That fear pumps up your adrenaline, and too much adrenaline clouds your judgment."

"Wait a minute? Are you saying that white guys are afraid of black people? Get the fuck out of here! Oh, my name is Jim Erlacher, and I have been on the force for nine years. I'm not afraid of black people, and I don't think that all black people are criminals. Being white has nothing to do with it. I served in Iraq with a lot of black guys. It's just that when you are in a situation where you think your life might be in danger and people don't comply with you and they start getting all haughty, it makes you anxious. That makes you think that something is about to happen. I was taught that it is better to act rather than react because being in a situation where you have to react can get you killed."

"You might have had extensive interaction with blacks," Jasmine responded, "but there are too many white officers in this city who haven't. They come from rural areas of Pennsylvania, West Virginia, and even Virginia and were not raised around black people. I work with them. They are scared of us. They see this black man with his pants hanging down, his dreadlocks, and him acting like a fool and not knowing how to handle him without jumping to the extreme."

"Earl Baker, twelve years on the force. A lot of white officers don't know what we are going to do. They don't know if we are talking shit or if we are for real. I can pick up in a minute if a guy is bullshitting or not. I can tell if a guy ain't gonna do nothing and just talking smack, or if he is serious and a real danger. When a black guy says, 'I'm gonna fuck you up,' the first thing some of the white officers do is put their hand on their gun. When a guy steps to me, the first thing I do is put my hands up and say, 'Bring it!' That's when you find out if the guy is bluffing or not. But those guys don't get the chance to bluff with the white officers."

"But what happens when a black officer shoots a black suspect," Officer Erlacher retorted. "Why don't we hear anything about that? You guys are doing the same thing society does to cops every day. People assume that just because I wear this uniform, I am a bad person. Now you are assuming that just because I am white and I shoot a suspect, I am a bad cop!"

"That's not what we are saying at all," Officer Baker responded. It's an issue because you have all these white cops coming into the ghetto and shooting black people. If the dynamic was different; if you had black cops policing white neighborhoods and shooting white people, you can best believe it would be a huge issue. It would be on CNN, MSNBC, and Fox News every day, all day."

"In terms of these national shootings of black men by white officers," Grady interjected, "let me put it to you like this. All of these high-profile cases that we have heard about are just a fraction of what is going on in our society. When something like this happens, the system works. The people have trust in the system when law enforcement and the courts function together to resolve the issue. The problems arise when people stop believing in the system and begin to take matters in their own hands. People get frustrated when the district attorney makes a decision to not even prosecute a case when a white officer is involved in a 'bad shooting.' Movements usually develop when there is a problem that is not being addressed.

"We have always had a part of society that dislikes the police for a variety of reasons. Police officers have been getting killed since the beginning of time, and that is not a Black Lives Matter issue. When a black person kills another black person, the killer is usually arrested, eventually goes to court, and has to face a jury. So when we do wrong, we should be held accountable regardless of the color of our skin. The line that goes, 'We feared for our safety,' is just a line. We always fear for our safety, but fearing for your safety is not a justification for taking someone's life. Our job is inherently dangerous, and we sign up for that. But our job is to protect and serve as well. Because you are afraid doesn't authorize you to kill someone. Every situation where you can shoot doesn't mean you have to shoot. We encounter people with guns, and knives every day. We give them an opportunity to respond to our instructions. We don't just shoot them."

"I hear that," Officer Erlacher responded, "but I don't feel comfortable Monday morning quarterbacking a situation when I was not there. When people ask me about a shooting, I usually tell them I wasn't there so I don't know all of the facts. Even before the facts get to the right people, you have the media passing judgment on the officer, and the media never has all the information."

"Yeah, but what about that officer who shot the man on the bridge that was only having car trouble?" Officer Baker interjected. That was a bad shooting as far as I am concerned. I'm sorry. The officer who did that should go to jail. I wasn't there and don't know what was said, but you can't tell me that from all of the video evidence that I saw from the helicopter that the black man was being aggressive in any way. Should he have complied with the officer, of course. It is always smart to comply. But it didn't look like he did anything to warrant being shot and killed, except being black of course."

"Accurate information is out there," Grady added on. When you gather the information, you then present it to the grand jury. You let the grand jury decide if they are going to charge or not charge. You have a lot of cases that aren't even brought to the grand jury. The DA says, 'I know you saw what you saw, but I am not going to take it to the grand jury.' As I said before, if the people don't believe in the system, that is when they start turning against us because we represent the system. You had that situation in Chicago, or maybe it was Cincinnati, where police arrived in the park, and two seconds later, they shot down two unarmed kids. And then you decide not to charge the officers. The video alone is enough to charge. That doesn't mean the officers were guilty_ it only means they have to go through the system. It then becomes attorney against attorney to present the evidence to determine who was right and who was wrong. That is our legal system."

"We go to work every day and to court every day, and we watch the system fail," Erlacher lamented. So you want me, as an officer, to put myself willingly into a system that I know doesn't work? How many times have you watched a criminal get off scot-free because of a technicality, or because the state's attorney is green and the defense attorney does this in his sleep? And you want me to subject myself to that. Police officers have to live up to a different standard and shouldn't be scrutinized by the same standard as everybody else."

"So what you are saying is let's forget about the system altogether, or let's have one system for the people and another system for the police," Grady interjected. "If that is what you are saying, we can't expect citizens to respect the system if we don't respect the system. That is why they are out there protesting."

*   *   *

The day seemed to have the makings of a great day. Michelle Johnson lay across the bed and was wakened by a ray of sunlight slashing through her blinds and the melodic sounds of birds chirping outside of her bedroom window. She wanted to just lie there and savor the moment. She was truly happy. She had received the Teacher of the Year award which was a testament to all of the hard work she had put in. More-so, it was an indication of the love she received from her colleagues and students alike, and she couldn't have been prouder. In addition, she finally had a man who loved her. She knew that marrying a white man could bring some problems, but she loved him so much and knew that everything was going to be all right.

As she rubbed the sleep out of her eyes, she began thinking about the million and one things she had to do before the day ended. She was supposed to meet up with a few of her girlfriends for an early lunch. Then she had to make a list of guests for the wedding, and then go shopping for a wedding dress and shoes. Finally, she had to go to Manassas, Virginia, to visit a former college classmate who was in town for the weekend. She wanted to turn over and go back to sleep, but it seemed like those damn birds got louder and louder as if they were trying to wake her up.

Manassas wasn't that far away, but she decided to wait until the rush-hour traffic died down before trying to drive. Her classmate was staying in a house that was located in a new housing development that she was unfamiliar with so she keyed the address into her GPS and took off. She came to a red light at the street where she was supposed to make a right turn, so she got in the right lane, which was a turn-only lane. When the light turned green, she made the right turn and started searching for the address. Suddenly, she heard a police siren. When she looked in her rearview mirror, she saw a policeman with his lights flashing. She immediately pulled over to the right so that he could pass by, but he pulled up directly behind her and got out of his car.

"Ma'am, I need to see your license and registration."

"Of course, Officer. Is there something wrong?"

"Just give me your license and registration!"

The officer went back to his cruiser for a couple of seconds before returning.

"I need you to turn off your engine and get out of the car."

"Excuse me?"

"You seem to be hard of hearing. I usually don't like repeating myself. Now turn off your engine and get out of the car."

"Sir, you don't have to talk to me like that. I need to know why you are stopping me. Have I done something wrong?"

"Ma'am, you made a turn without putting on your turn signal, which is a traffic violation in this area."

"Wait a minute, sir. I was in a turn-only lane, and there was no other direction for me to go, so why did I need to use my turn signal.

Plus, there were three cars in front of me and two cars behind me and none of them used a turn signal! Why did you stop me?"

"Ma'am, what are you doing in this area? We don't usually have your kind out here."

"What! What do you mean by my kind? Look, man, just give me a damn ticket and let me get the fuck outta here before I say something I shouldn't."

"I told you to turn off your engine and get out of the car, and I'm not going to tell you again."

"You must be crazy if you think I'm getting out of this car. My fiancée is a police officer, and I know the law. I'm getting my cell phone so I can take your picture and record the rest of this conversation. You need to call your supervisor_"

BAM...Bam, Bam, Bam, Bam!

*   *   *

"Michael Brown ...."
"Fuck the police!"
"Sandra Bland ...."
"Fuck the police!"
"Eric Clark ..."
"Fuck the police!"
"Michelle Johnson ...."

One of the protesters got a little too frisky and got nose to nose in Steven Sullivan's face screaming, "Fuck the police, you punk-ass white boy," as if he was daring Steven to do something. Steven stood stoically and didn't flinch or move a muscle. He stared straight ahead, not hearing or seeing anything. A small tear tenderly trickled down the left side of his face before stopping at his chin. He didn't care about what was going on around him. All he could think about was Michelle.

EPILOGUE

THE DILEMMA

Asa Thorn

When the blue is put on
The whole world becomes the enemy
When it is taken off
The enemy becomes me

To be dutiful means to obey the law
Even when the law doesn't mean justice
Even if to be just doesn't mean to be right

We are born with one shade and die with two
The shade of skin that tells our story
And the shade of uniform that decides our end
And every day I wake,
There is another wake I must attend
One of my birth shade
Caused by the other of my work shade

Two colors clashing
Refusing to become one
Both causing me pain in the worst way

I pledge allegiance to prosperity
Not the disparity
Between who I am and who I've become

The choices I'll make
And the choices I come from
Empty hands waiting to fill
My soul or my pockets
Betraying myself or my future

They say once the blue goes on
It never comes off
The same as your past being a power
That never turns off

So if you want out
You gotta pick a side
Be it the jury or the judge
Or the person being tried
Guilty is the verdict
Betrayal is the crime
The past being the victim
And the victim being mine

Cuffed to this fate
I am a prisoner in my own jail
Cursed to be a savior of the people
While being sentenced to my own hell

DÉJÀ VU

The investigation into the kidnapping and murder of drug dealers ramped up after yet another murder. Some in the department were happy that dealers were killing each other off and didn't seem in a hurry to do anything to prevent the killings from happening.

Department officials, however, feared a gang war was imminent and wars have collateral damage, usually innocent citizens. Department officials were going to extreme lengths to gather any information they could in order to solve the problem before things got out of hand.

The walls seemed as though they were closing in around Shanita Brown. She had information that might help the investigation, but that information could harm her brother, if indeed he was involved. Alfred was currently locked up for possession with intent to sell crack and marijuana. He had a good lawyer and was probably going to get out on a technicality, like he always did. Was he really responsible for the death of her lover, Curtis, or was Freddy just blowing smoke trying to save his own ass? If Alfred was the leader of the kidnapping ring, how would her family, especially her mother, feel if she was the one responsible for turning him in? What should she do? All these questions kept rolling around in Shanita's head. Suddenly, the phone rang, interrupting her thoughts.

"You have a collect call from Jessup State Prison. Alfred Brown is calling. Will you accept the charges?"

Shanita Brown hesitated for a brief moment then stated, "Yes. I'll accept the charges."

"Shanita, what's up, girl? Haven't heard from you in a minute. You good?"

"Yeah, I'm good, Alfred. What do you want?"

"Damn, girl, you sound like you mad or something. I was just calling to see how you're doing. You haven't visited me in a while. I was wondering what's up with that. How's Ma and Dad?"

"You know something Alfred, the other day, Princess was asking me about her father. She's at that age where she is starting to ask a lot of questions. She wanted to know what he did for a living and how he died. I was reluctant to tell her the truth, but then decided that I wasn't going to lie to her. How did he die, Alfred?"

"Hey, he just got caught up in the game. You know how the game is played, being a cop and all."

"Yeah, I know how the game is played. What I want to know is, who gave the order to kill him? Did you have anything to do with it?"

"Hell, nah! Why would I do something like that? He was one of my best workers."

"But Freddy told me a different story!"

"Freddy has got a big fucking mouth. Hey sis, why don't you come up here for a visit so we can talk about this face-to-face? You know how people be listening on these phones."

"I'll think about it."

"Why don't you bring Princess with you? I would love to see her. I bet she is growing like a weed."

"Not a chance in hell. I'll try to get up there next week. Goodbye, Alfred."

Shanita decided that she was going to tell officials what she suspected about her brother. Too many young kids were being killed by stray bullets, and a gang war would only exacerbate that situation. She wouldn't be able to live with herself if another kid was killed, knowing she could have done something to prevent it from happening. Two weeks later, she drove up to Jessup State Prison to see her brother. She needed to meet him face-to-face and look in his eyes to determine if he was lying.

When she got there, however, she was informed that he was dead. They said he committed suicide. She automatically knew that was a lie. There was no way her brother would have done anything like that. He had a good lawyer, who probably would have gotten him out, or at least gotten his sentenced reduced. Plus, he had asked her to come up and visit him and was irate when she refused to bring Princess with her. That didn't sound like a man ready to commit suicide. Somebody killed him! It could have been that street justice was administered after Freddy revealed that Alfred was responsible for the deaths of so many others, or he could have gotten into a beef with anybody in that place. But if he was murdered, someone was involved in letting the murderer get into his cell.

Through the grief Shanita was feeling, an eerie feeling came over her. It was a feeling of déjà vu. She remembered the day Curtis wanted to buy a car and was coming over to her house to get his money. She remembered the fear she felt when she found out the money was missing. She also remembered the conflicting devastation and relief she felt when Curtis ended up dead. His death ended her dilemma. Ironically, Alfred was responsible for solving her dilemma by killing Curtis, and in return, he was killed in retaliation for killing Curtis. Alfred's death ended her current dilemma. Life can be a real trip sometime.

WHEN ENOUGH IS ENOUGH

Steven Sullivan was a mess. Even though he had become accustomed to death, almost desensitized to it, he took the death of his fiancée Michelle very hard. For the second time, death became real and personal. He had developed an emotional shield protecting himself from all the death and carnage he witnessed every day, as most police officers do. The death of Michelle somehow stripped him of that mental protection, and all that he had seen came crashing back to torment him. He became listless, distant, and appeared to be in deep thought all the time. His sergeant thought Steven was on the verge of depression and ordered him to see the staff therapist. After a couple of sessions, the therapist suggested that Steven take some time off and go on vacation. She felt that a change of scenery would do him some good and help speed up his recovery. He told her that he really didn't feel like going anywhere but agreed that he needed some time off.

Unfortunately, Steven did not take her advice, and instead of traveling to some exotic place, he retreated to the sanctity of his bedroom. For two weeks, he sat around the house and did nothing, with the exception of playing video games. He didn't eat, didn't bathe, didn't change his clothes, didn't shave, and didn't even brush his teeth. It seemed that he retreated into a fantasy world where he could control everything that went on. When things didn't go his way in the game, he would simply start the game over, or switch to a different game.

It was Steven's therapist, Cheryl Santos, who stopped by to check on him. She was concerned that he would disengage with reality. She didn't think he was suicidal or anything like that, but when he didn't call her to check in as she requested, she decided the prudent thing to do would be to stop by. She didn't usually make house calls, but there was something different about him. When she got to his house, she took one look at him and realized that her fears were correct. She decided to take a different approach to getting him out of the funk he was in.

"Steven, look at you, man. You're funky, your breath stinks, your hair is all over your head, you look like you are homeless, and this place looks a mess. Wake up, man! You're better than this. This is what I want you to do. Go take a shower, wash your ass, put on some fresh clothes, and when you finish all of that, I'm going to shave you myself. Then we are going to go out and get something to eat. I don't have all day, so step on it!"

The approach seemed to work because after he cleaned himself up, she got his razor and shaved him. While she was shaving him, she asked him about what it was like where he grew up and why he decided to come to DC. He started fondly reminiscing about Prairie Village. He talked about the house he grew up in, with its little screened-in porch with a front and backyard, the old metal swing set in the back and the trench dug around the house to waterproof the basement. He talked about the lack of crime and how you could leave your keys in your car, or your bike in the front yard, and nobody would bother them. He talked about his job being a manager at McDonalds and the girls he used to date. The trip down memory lane brought a smile to his face and planted a seed in his brain that maybe he needed to get back there sooner rather than later. He had thought about it before but wasn't sure if Michelle would want to live there. That wasn't a concern anymore.

He and Ms. Santos went out to get something to eat. After eating, they got back in his car and started the journey back to his apartment. While driving she started asking him questions about Michelle, like how they met, what he liked about her, and what made him decide to marry her. This opened a floodgate of pleasant emotions, and he talked and talked. Then she asked him if he had cried for her. His demeanor suddenly changed, and he his voice became very soft, almost inaudible. He said that he hadn't been able to get a good cry out even though he shed a tear or two here and there. She told him that he needed to grieve and have a good cry if he wanted to become whole again. As she talked, she could see the tears welling up in his eyes. Suddenly, he pulled the car over to the curb, put it in park, and the river of tears that he had been holding back came uncontrollably gushing out. He buried his head in Ms. Santos's shoulder as she gently stroked the top of his head.

After a month off, Steven went back to work patrolling the streets of DC. Things seemed different to him, however. His enthusiasm for what he was supposed to be doing had dissipated. He began to realize that it was becoming more difficult to control his temper and that little things seemed to bother him. There was a rage inside of him that seemed harder and harder to control. He got a call that a child had been left in a car outside a grocery store, and the child appeared to be unresponsive.

When he got to the scene, he saw a group of people standing near the car knocking on the car window. After moving the people away from the car and knocking on the window several times, he decided to go to the side opposite where the little girl was seated and smashed in the car window. The sound of the crashing window woke the little girl up. She had been sleeping, and the sound of the crashing window scared her to death. A woman came rushing out of the store screaming, "What the hell are you doing?" Steven felt the rage beginning to swell up inside.

"Ma'am, is this your car?"

"Yes, Officer, that's my car."

"Don't you know that it is against the law to leave a child in a car unattended? Plus, it is just plain stupid!"

"Officer, I had to pee really bad, and she was sleeping so soundly. I just ran in the store for a couple of seconds to go to the bathroom. I wasn't gone that long."

"Well, you should have taken her to the bathroom with you, or peed on yourself until you got home. Turn your dumb ass around and put your hands behind your back. You're going to jail."

"Wait a minute_ you don't have to talk to me like that. What's your badge number?"

"Shut the fuck up and get in the car."

While waiting for Child Protective Services to come get the child, Steven began to reflect on the situation, and especially his behavior. He had never been that type of person before. He had always been respectful to people, and things didn't use to bother him as much. He began to think that maybe it was time to do something else, or go someplace else. His decision to leave became final when he attended the ceremony where Officer Tim Bailey was promoted to captain and praised for his work in the community. That was a little too much for Steven to take_ the straw that broke the camel's back, so to speak. He started searching the Internet for job openings in law enforcement around the country. He became ecstatic when he saw there was a job opening in Prairie Village, Kansas. He applied online and was asked to come in for an interview. Before he even got the job in Prairie Village, he turned in his resignation, packed his bags, and was gone.

When he got back to Prairie Village, he was shocked by how much it had changed. The opioid crisis had hit the city hard. Crime was on the rise, the young kids seemed out of control and very disrespectful, and a group of vicious drug dealers had begun taking control of city streets. The police department started an effort to recruit police officers from cities across the nation who had experience fighting these new problems. Steven was hired immediately. Within two years, he was asked to head the narcotics investigation unit. He spearheaded an effort to clean up the town.

After getting off work one day, he was sitting on the couch when the phone rang.

"Steven, this is Cheryl Santos. I was just calling to check up on you. How you holding up?"

"Wow, Cheryl, this is a pleasant surprise."

ALL GOOD THINGS

Gregory Harris couldn't believe how stunningly beautiful she was. Her soft, Nubian skin with its deep chocolate hue was like velvet to his touch. The way she looked at him with those dark brown eyes caused his heart to pound a mile a minute. Her wide nose, thick hips, large luscious lips, ample bottom, and enticingly large breasts made his manhood stand at attention. All he wanted to do was grab her, throw her on the bed, and ravage her over and over again. The fact that she actually wanted him blew his mind and made him want her even more.

She waved her long slender finger at him, beckoning him to come closer, which he did without hesitation. When he got close enough to feel the heat of her body, she started nibbling on his earlobe. She whispered something in his ear that he couldn't quite make out. As she rubbed her body against his, her whispers became louder and louder, until she started screaming in his ear.

"Get out ....Get out ....GET OUT!"

Suddenly, she pulled out a huge knife whose sharp blade extended from one end of his neck to the other. Without warning, she began slashing his throat from ear to ear. Blood splattered everywhere, staining his clothes, the bed-sheet, and the walls. As she drew the blade across his throat, she let out this eerie scream as if she was laughing at him.

Gregory woke up drenched in sweat and sat straight up in his empty bed. He hadn't had one of those nightmares in quite some time, especially since he started seeing Shanita. He wondered why they had returned and what this one meant. What was the woman in the dream trying to tell him? And more importantly, why didn't she let him hit it before she started slashing? Was the woman warning him to stop seeing Shanita, or was it time to get out of the department.

Being a detective was beginning to hamper his relationship with Shanita and her daughter, Princess. The more he was with them, the more he enjoyed being around them. He started accompanying Shanita when she attended Princess's basketball games and gymnastic competitions. Princess was a little jealous of him at first. For the longest time, it had just been her and her mother, but now he was taking a lot of her mother's attention and affection. But when she got to know him and found out how funny he was, her attitude began to change. She began referring to him as a member of her family, and that gave him a warm feeling inside. He began thinking that maybe he could give this family thing one more try. But being a detective meant he had a very crazy schedule, and taking time off was unpredictable. When he was on a case that was all he had time for.

He liked being a detective, though, and he was good at it. He was able to solve the child abduction case before it started a citywide panic. Solving that case brought him a lot of accolades from the top brass. He was able to solve the case of the lynching of a ten-year-old black youth in Anacostia that had received national attention. It received national attention when it was discovered that five police officers, Officer Craig Hoye and four of his fellow officers, were arrested in connection with this murder. The officers were convicted and sentenced to twenty-five years in prison. Detective Harris was quickly becoming the superstar in the department, and when there was a high profile case that needed to be solved, his sergeant would assign him the case.

In addition to his rising stature in the office, Detective Harris had developed a reputation for being invincible on the streets. He had escaped death so many times that the guys in the office started calling him the Black Panther because like a cat, he had nine lives. They said he had ducked so many bullets he needed to find something else to do before his luck ran out. And they were almost right.

While investigating a double homicide, he was rummaging through some debris in the alley behind the house where the murders took place. He came across what he thought was the murder weapon that had been dropped or conveniently placed in the well of an old discarded tire. The gun had palm smudges all over it that could possibly reveal the true identity of the last person to use it. His euphoria over finding this potential piece of evidence probably prevented him from hearing or seeing the dark figure that snuck up behind him, pointing a gun six inches from the back of his head. In that brief instance, Greg's life flashed before him. He realized that he had messed up and that his life was about to come to an end.

The gunman pulled the trigger, but the gun jammed and didn't go off. The gunman seemed stunned that the gun didn't fire. In that moment of uncertainty, Greg swung into action. Like a lethal panther, he quickly pounced on his attacker and threw the hardest punch he had in his arsenal of punches, sending the man sprawling to the ground, unconscious.

Greg had thwarted death one more time. After coming down off of the adrenaline rush, he began to think that maybe the woman in his nightmare was right. Maybe it was time for him to get out. Maybe if he challenged fate one more time, fate wouldn't be as kind and would punch his ticket.

After successfully closing the double homicide case, Gregory decided it was time to call it quits. He had given the department thirty years of his life and had done all he could do for his community. Now it was time to ride off into the sunset. He put in his retirement papers, to the chagrin of his commanders. They tried hard to get him to reconsider, but when they saw he was adamant about leaving, they offered him a position as an instructor in the police academy. He told them that after he came back from a long-needed vacation, he would let them know. Without consulting anyone, he made reservations at a five-star, all-inclusive resort on the island of Grenada and purchased three airplane tickets_ one for himself, one for Shanita, and one for Princess.

SPICE ISLAND

Dear Diary,

He finally asked me to marry him. He said he wanted to give marriage one last try, and he couldn't think of anyone better to do it with but me and Princess. When he asked me, I was stunned and didn't know what to say or do. I love him, and he and Princess have a great relationship, but something inside of me held me back from saying yes immediately. I don't know why I hesitated. I must be crazy. Even though he is older than I am, I have never met anyone like him. He is mature, makes me laugh, and is dedicated. Maybe it was because my relationships with men have all ended badly, or maybe it was because I have devoted all my love and attention to Princess for so long that a permanent relationship with someone else is scary.

The good thing about it was that he didn't trip when I asked him if I could take some time to think about it. He just smiled and said, "Sure, but don't take too long because I'm not getting any younger." He also said that while I was thinking about it, I should pack my thongs, my bathing suit, and some sunglasses because he was taking me and Princess to a place called Spice Island.

I had never been anywhere outside of the United States, so when we got to Grenada, I was in awe. It is absolutely beautiful. I had never seen clear blue water before except on television or in the movies, but seeing it for real is so much better. The people were very friendly, and the resort was spectacular. We watched the sun go down every evening, had dinner on the beach or in a restaurant on the pier, where we could listen to the waves crash against the shore. The food was fabulous. It was seasoned with so many spices, I could understand why they called the island Spice Island. It was like we were in heaven.

One day, we went snorkeling off a reef. There was an explosion of color because there were so many colorful fish and coral. The only thing I didn't like about that was I didn't like being exposed to so many live animals. In the back of my mind, I kept thinking about *Jaws*. I didn't want to be a blue-plate special for any sharks lurking about. I had fun, though.

One night, when we were at the hotel restaurant, I saw a girl that I thought I recognized. She was gorgeous, with pretty eyes, pretty brown skin, and long flowing black hair. Greg and I went over to her, introduced ourselves, and asked her, had she ever been to D C. She said her name was Roya Korrapatti, and that she used to live in DC. She said she left DC after her boyfriend was shot and killed. She said he had brought her to the island, and she fell in love with it. She decided to move here, and she was now the manager of this resort. I asked her if her boyfriend was a Metro Transit police officer and she looked at me with a surprised look on her face before saying yes. I told her that I was a police officer and that I remembered her from the funeral. We sat down and talked for a long while. We talked about death, recovery, emotional survival, but more importantly we talked about living life to the fullest. I wonder what Greg would think when he finds out about the life growing inside of me at this very moment.

That same evening, Greg got down on one knee in front of Princess, Roya, and everybody in the restaurant and asked me again if I would marry him. I looked into his eyes and could see that he was both nervous and serious at the same time. I let him squirm for a few seconds before I said YES!

OTHER BOOKS BY MAURICE A. BUTLER

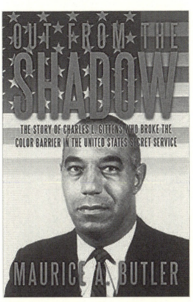

Published by Xlibris Corporation (Orders@Xlibris.com)

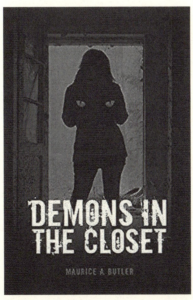

Published by Green Ivy Publishing (www.greenivybooks.com)
Both books can be found on Amazon.com & Barnes&Noble.com

ABOUT THE AUTHOR

Maurice A. Butler was born and raised in northwest Washington DC. He is a proud product of DC Public Schools, having graduated from Cardozo High School (1970), and an alumnus of Bowdoin College (1974, B.A. in history), Cambridge College (2001, master's degree in education), and the International Graduate Center (2005, Ph.D. in educational leadership and policy).

He served as a DC Public Schools teacher, coach and administrator for thirty-six years, most of which was at Theodore Roosevelt High School. His desire to write and publish resulted from his affiliation with the DC Area Writing Project, which is the local site for the National Writing Project. He is the author of the authorized biography entitled, *Out From The Shadow: The Story of Charles L. Gittens Who Broke the Color Barrier in the United States Secret Service* and the novel *Demons in the Closet.*